WHEELIN' ACROSS THE LAND: SPRING 1967

Also by Jeri Hilderley

Mari

Time Traveling with Sappho

Fire Dragon Street Theater: 1962-1967

Sequel to *Fire Dragon Street Theater: 1962-1967*

Fire Dragon Street Theater: 1962-1967 is a complex inter-weaving of the lives of the counterculture voices that dared to defy socially prescriptive roles, the Vietnam War, and oppressions of sex, race, and class....[It] is a shepherding guide for artists, dreamers, and political activists alike who wish to work together in creative, activist collaboration.... [and a] rare example of the artistic struggle of politics filled with lessons and insight. A gift given to us as an embrace.

—Excerpted from a review by Roberta Arnold, *Sinister Wisdom,* a multicultural lesbian literary & art journal, 132

Pre-publication Praise for *Wheelin' Across the Land: Spring 1967*

This is a very unique book centered on characters that are multi-dimensional, with human flaws and contradictions shaped by a historic period of revolutionary upheaval with mass opposition against an unjust U.S. war in Vietnam abroad and the struggle against racism and sexism at home. It is another example of how global and domestic events are a process of shaping one's awareness as individuals and amongst others. How these characters interact with each other on a daily basis within a theatrical setting is beautifully explored by the author with excellent dialogue steeped in sensitivity towards oppression and realism. This combination of politics and mass culture is well worth the read.

—Monica Moorehead, former presidential candidate, political writer & editor

As an artist, I am always thrilled by the unfolding of the creative process. *Wheelin' Across the Land* is particularly engrossing because it involves the *collective* creative process of young thespians striving to make a difference in the tumultuous era of the 60's in the United States. Now, during these equally difficult times, the book also speaks to me as an older activist because it poignantly brings back our struggles for a more humane world that are all too relevant today. What a tour de force! Thank you, Jeri, for reminding us in your beautifully crafted novel that our struggle continues.

—Rain Bengis, award winning photographer

For all of us who rose up against racism and the Vietnam War in the 60's; for all of us who struggled to find and express our sexuality and sexual identity during an era when being out to ourselves and others was far from easy; for all of us who dared to challenge misogyny, Hilderley's historical novel brings back such powerful memories. She also reminds us of how we young people collectively pooled our talents using various theatrical modalities and venues to speak truth to power—and of the painful lessons we learned along the way. As she chronicles, we learned to resist obstacles the college administrators and other people in power threw in our way; to know our audiences with all their contradictions; to gently (or not so gently) raise aware- ness; to encourage burgeoning activists and to join movements already under way. Her memoire-driven prose is not only for us older folks, but for the new generations who are once again forced to bravely rise up. *Wheelin' Across the Land* is a relevant addition to our collective consciousness.

—Janet R. Mayes, author and psychologist

WHEELIN' ACROSS THE LAND: SPRING 1967

Jeri Hilderley

WHEELIN' ACROSS THE LAND: SPRING 1967

Cover Design by Jodi Miller; cover illustration by Jeri Hilderley.
Book Design & Typesetting by D. Bass

Print ISBN: 979-8-218-57854-1

Published by Seawave Recordings

DEDICATION

I dedicate my book to everyone who understands that only through struggle, steadfast hope and tender revolutionary solidarity can we create the humane, just, compassionate, and non-violent world required to sustain our planet and all its living creatures—and particularly to all oppressed people who are rising up to meet this challenge.

Finally, my book is dedicated to collective-supportive-activism, in which each person's precious and unique abilities are crucial in the struggle for change. Twenty-four years of teaching my curriculum, "Learning the Language Arts through Music," to students with special needs validated my conviction that individual and group development thrives in a caring, creative supportive environment. We are all connected!

"One cannot live with sighted eyes and feeling heart and not know or react to the miseries of the world."

— Lorraine Hansberry

CONTENTS

Prologue
Lucina Holzer's Journal
March 25, 1967

Lucina's Journal Entry. March 25, 1967. This is it— what we've been working on, dreaming of—I don't know how long. Take our sweat-and-guts, earnest but rough-hewn plays and tributes cross country. Wake up! Wake up! "The times they are a-changin'," Dylan told you. And Kerouac would cheer us on, but we ain't doing it his way. You can't be high and keep track of a schedule like ours: big-deal college drama festivals, radical community groups, campus protests. We've got to be ready for all kinds of reactions and keep on an even keel, find common ground. I mean, fourteen of us—all shapes and sizes! Well, we gotta do it—no turning back, Jack. I just wish I could call up Mom and Dad—"You won't believe what your darling daughter is about to do! You'll read about me in the New York Times." That's a joke—maybe if we're all thrown in jail we'll get a mention somewhere. Oh, forget it. I'm my own Ma and Pa now. I can't go back home, and I don't want to. I know that Louis' and my connection will keep changing. Let's just say we're both growing into our full I-dentities. I can't be afraid.

What I have to do right now is make sure the prop committee has lists of all our stuff. Each mask is so goddamn precious. It's goodbye to Hell's Hundred Acres and hello, my big fucked-up country that is in no way united. Who made that one up? We're Fire Dragon Street Theater and we're going on tour April 1. No foolin' here. Headed for upstate New York. New Point College, first stop, is about to experience an uprising, we hope. So here we come, ready or not.

PART I
THE FIRST GIGS

1
Packing Up

She squatted to the red drum and hugged it to her; then rising with it, she surveyed her brood. But she couldn't think like that. They weren't her anything! A new type of funky family, maybe. From where she stood on the top step of the loft building entrance, Lucina saw striped shirts, rough jeans, and an abundance of growth splaying from heads and chins. Figures bent to their loads: satchels, backpacks, suitcases, guitars, and wire boxes crammed with props. Back and forth they went in the silver morning light, from the mound on the sidewalk to three vehicles parked nearby.

"Such hairy beasts," she murmured affectionately, trying to sight Louis in the crowd. Where was he? Making some last-minute arrangements with the New Point people about their performance schedule, maybe? She wanted to share this exact moment with him, this pride swelling inside her for the band of troubadours now gathered around the two of them. Would she always feel these twinges of possessiveness?

Hugh and Courtney's long hair especially touched her that morning. Hugh's was woven into one long braid down his back and Courtney's hung loose, like a girl's. But that's exactly how she didn't want to think anymore. Why shouldn't men have long hair? It was simply Courtney's hair.

"I think we have everything, Lucina." Marlene, thin and athletic, was huffing beside her with a large carton.

Her sentimental bubble burst. "That's good. I'm hot to trot."

Marlene giggled with pleasure. "Aren't we adorable?"

"One way to describe us, Marlene." *Does Marlene's pert efficiency bug me because Louis digs it?* she wondered. To soften her prickly reply, she turned to the excited woman with a smile. But Marlene was already preoccupied with her next task, issuing car assignments. The two women quickly descended the steps to join the other members of Fire Dragon Street Theater, clutching backpacks as they griped and joked around their three jalopies sporting dented fenders, patched windows, missing hubcaps, one bent aerial, and a patchwork of rust and scrapes.

When they stopped at the large gray station wagon, Lucina let the drum slide carefully down her body to the cement. She wondered if Jim and Donna ever did their puppet shows from the back of the station wagon. Their mobile home for four years was now carrying the props: dragon puppet, tree pole for *Ghost Dance*, Dreamer's hammock, and masks (Triple Goddess, Politicians, Gangsters, Stool Pigeons, to name a few). After Marlene placed her carton of costumes on the trunk door, Lucina watched her hop over suitcases, guitars, backpacks, and miscellaneous paraphernalia that had to go in Jenny's '62 Dodge Dart (a solid red car with the slant-six engine that Hans wouldn't stop talking about although he couldn't drive or change a spark plug), and the group's green, gas-guzzling Chevy van, named Isadora by Marin.

Jim, official prop packer, shoved the costume box into the trunk of the station wagon, then addressed Lucina. "Can I have the drum now?" She heard him mutter: *Damn! Nobody listens to me about cutting down on props.*

"Wrap a blanket around our baby, Jim!" she directed. That red drum was precious to her, the heartbeat of the troupe. Its deep pulse accompanied each of their dramas. With them since that disastrous police attack on Louis during a Central Park performance, the drum, too, was under constant assault by pro-war agitators. Its nicks and bruises attested to the extent of animosity the troupe faced at every performance. She'd warned Louis, "Only a matter of time before some enraged maniac goes after our dragon puppet as well. We're inviting disaster, the way we make her snort and shimmy. God, I pray our new members can handle a sudden attack."

With the drum carefully swaddled and tucked behind the other props, she turned away to scout out Louis. Had he padlocked the loft door?

*****

Marin handed out hot cups of coffee and buttered rolls from Kasts, while Al stood next to her studying a map spread out on Isadora's hood. "Do we have maps for all the states we're going to, honey?" she called out to him.

"We'll get 'em on the road," he answered abruptly.

"I can't believe it—New York, Michigan, Illinois, Indiana, all in five weeks! And I've never been in Iowa before. This is a big deal, Al. I sure hope the students dig us."

Al grunted and finished tracing their route for the day with red ink. When Marin's body pressed against his, he put the pen behind his ear and held her. "You're right, I probably should have gotten some maps from Triple A. Oh well, we can always stop at a gas station." During these last-minute tasks, there was a reluctance to finally set off. Five weeks was a lifetime for the actors. And clamped together every day in cars and makeshift sleeping quarters? A totally new experience. You learned on the go. No such thing as a degree in street theater. Didn't exist.

And better stay alert! Sure, hecklers helped shape their style, but still… Had to dodge hostile remarks and missiles, retrieve equipment—especially that red drum—then run for it.

While the young kids swarmed to the West Coast and the psychedelic rock stars, these young actors huddling with coffee cups and backpacks were warriors in the turbulent realms of Peace, Freedom, and Justice. However they could, at campuses and community meeting places across the land, they would challenge their government's hawkish stance. Why was the U.S. policing the world, anyway?

*****

Courtney and Dawn, munching on rolls near the Dart, were giddy with disbelief: they were going to be paid for five weeks of publicized gigs in auditoriums with real stages! Courtney was touched by Dawn and how her long black hair relaxed comfortably on her shoulders like a shawl. His mop was always "ratty looking"—his mom's words. "Yeah, Dawn, it's going to be cool." He began swaying his hips and arms, tufts of brown chest hair peeking out from a V-neck T-shirt. "We'll have real beds and people actually buying tickets to see us, baby."

Dawn ignored his gyrations. "It's not a piece of cake, you know. I've heard that touring is hard work." This was a huge event for her, a new member. She'd only acted in high school plays before. She couldn't tell her folks about it, even if it was a success—they were so down on her for dropping out of college. But she sure wasn't going to tell Courtney how scared she was. Cheryl was the only one she'd tell. She could trust Cheryl, who supported her the most around her shyness. She'd never forget that chair exercise with the women's group and what Cheryl said to her. And look how she helped her sister take care of that kid, Marcel. Didn't just think of herself. Where was Cheryl, anyway? Maybe they could ride in the same car.

*****

After calling Marcel one last time to say goodbye, Cheryl sat in Kasts finishing her hot chocolate and English muffin. Luckily she'd had enough change for her nephew's anxious questions: "Will you call me lots, Auntie Cheryl? Will you bring me back some toys?" She'd had to reassure him one more time how much both she and his mother loved him. He'd decided his mom's depressions were his fault. *Spending time with me is helping him understand that isn't true. And Sadie is happier now she's working part-time at the bookstore. Who can be Mom full-time anyway?*

"Be strong for your Mama and me, Marcel!" "Okay, I try, Aunt Cheryl." He made her tear up.

Well, time to start my new adventure. This gang really needs me. And they'll have to change or I quit. Their blindness about Choice—*I had to shake them: "Did you leave what happens to Black men in the military out on purpose?" Not a clue about all the humiliations young Black men face when called to serve. They better keep their commitment. Start working on it on tour. Incorporate two Sams in the play, one white and one Black. Compare their so-called choices.*

Can I take one more time of being seen as the group's token Black person? One more time of choosing the high road? "We're trying to expose racism, ignorance…look past skin color and help each other grow." Each time I say it, I mean it. Time will tell…

But I'm learning from them. Lucina knows how to take up space. Louis? He knows about being treated like shit. He signals an alert, they all listen. Al, a quiet guy—really smart with dialogue, from writing his short stories. His gal pal, Marin, a drama major. Solid and really clever with movements. She knows subtle—and flash. The court jesters, Courtney and Hugh—good musicians, but so stiff in the hips. Poor babies. Jenny is fun; nice costumes she makes. Her blond Hans, obsessed with jarring people, can be oblivious to the group's safety. Lucina says he's changed. What about Dawn? That sweetie hides in herself like a turtle, shy but one eye always open. "I'll have to find a way to pull that girl out of her shell," she heard herself saying aloud.

Maybe she was kind of in love with all of these clever artists. She blinked Marcel out of her thoughts one more time, grabbed her backpack and small suitcase, and shot out of the restaurant door to join her gang.

*****

Hugh, anxious to be off, strutted around Isadora shouting, "We got a play to do tonight! What are we waiting for? Let's go!" Soon he had several of them shouting, "Let's go, let's go, let's really go!" But it wasn't clear yet—who was riding where? Hadn't the travel committee worked that out?

He really loved this roving theater. So much more spontaneous than the traditional theater venues he'd studied in college, with scripts to memorize and the ruthless competitions for a role. Fire Dragon was always trying out new techniques: energy circles, sound-and-motion transference, mirroring, passing faces, emotion-to-motion, agreement exercises, all the new-age street theater jargon that could make you dizzy. Ideas came from everywhere: Broadway, Brecht, Punch and Judy, Bread and Puppet, San Francisco Mime. If it was out there, man, they used it. Look how Jim and Donna, who'd only worked with puppets before, were getting into these exercises. That Jim sure knew how to work the steel-string guitar; he could jam with him and Courtney, knock some tunes around. Donna seemed nice, kind of a take-charge mother type, not high-strung like Marlene.

He caught a glimpse of Jim and Donna by their station wagon, getting it on with Cheryl—like they were trying to impress her or something. Why was he a bit afraid of her? Same age, but compared to her, he'd had it soft. Supported by his parents through college: she called it "privilege." She was

10

something else. She'd grown up in Harlem, worked for CORE in Atlanta, taken part in King's marches, my god! And helping to raise her sister's kid, what was that like? The kid must be mixed up—two mothers. "Yeah, obvious. Jim and Donna are courting her."

*****

Louis, still catching his breath from two last-minute treks up to the loft and back, was also eyeing Jim and Donna. *Why are they pawing Cheryl now? Trying to recruit her for their puppet theater if the tour bombs? Well, it's time to get going!*

He yelled toward the station wagon, "Lucina needs to get your advice on something, Cheryl. She and I are riding together in Isadora!" He saw Lucina and Marlene talking near Isadora and he shouted again. "Hey, Lucina! We have to work out some of the final arrangements for tonight."

His calling out like that both touched and embarrassed Lucina. She ignored his urgent swipes at the air and turned to address Marlene, who was fussing with some papers. "Don't you have the list we worked out last night for who rides where, Marlene? You gotta tell them now. You're the travel director."

Marlene dug again into her denim jacket pocket, under her comb and gum: "Oh god, where did I put it? How'd I get stuck with all this work? Yes, here it is. Jesus! Is everyone waiting for me?" She cupped her hands to her mouth and shouted, "Let's get going then! Listen up. Here are the car assignments. Jim and Donna, you're taking Courtney and Hugh in your station wagon. It's up to you who drives. Louis, Lucina, Al, Marin, and Cheryl, you're in Isadora. Myself, Hans, Jenny, Jack, and Dawn in Jenny's car, the Dart, with me driving. Jenny, Hans, and Dawn sit in the back, okay?" Despite moans coming at her, Lucina's encouraging nod nudged her on. "Okay, everybody, get in. We're about to roll. Don't worry—this order is just for today, so don't fuss it. We're going to have a great trip."

Lucina kept nodding, glad that Marlene was actually handling the who-goes-where (*better it comes from Marlene and not from me or Louis!*). She put her arm through Louis' and headed for Isadora. "Thank God that woman knows how to take charge, Louis. I have to appreciate her more." *At last! I can just rest near him for a while. If anyone grumbles that couples should be split up, well, that'll be another arrangement for the next lap of our trip. Let the travel committee work it out.*

As they squeezed into Isadora's backseat, Louis remarked, "The Rockefeller masks would not have been left behind at the *Guardian* benefit under Marlene's watch."

"Are you saying it was my fault that happened?"

"No. I was just saying she has a knack for keeping track of things."

"Masks aren't things, Louis."

"Forget it, Lucina. We're on tour now."

2
On the Road

As trees flew by on the Palisades Parkway, their shiny new leaves flickering in the April wind, Donna felt her city tensions fly out the window. Driving the station wagon made her feel stronger, in charge. She grasped the steering wheel more firmly; she was responsible for her passengers' safety! A giddy joy rose in her: *Maybe as troubadours they really could rejuvenate hope in young people. They weren't hippies, whatever that meant. More like responsible cultural workers. And if they could keep that West Coast spirit alive here, without drugs and depression...*

Courtney and Hugh were wailing an off-key rendition of "Like a Rolling Stone" behind her. "Let's do one of our songs," she shouted above their din. When she started a Kiowa chant they'd adapted for the *Ghost Dance Tribute*, "The spirit will descend, the earth will tremble," Courtney and Hugh in back, and Jim beside her soon joined in, improvising. "The sun is on fire, the trees are on fire, my eyes are on fire with the fire of desire," they warbled. Courtney's melodic tenor soared above the others: "All things are on fire—on fire—on fire."

Hugh and Jim rooted the chant with bass voices: "Follow the Fire Dragon! Follow the Fire Dragon!" as Donna's alto voice wove in harmonies: "To the fire of hope…to the fire of love… to the fire of justice…" Sunlight, flashing through the leaves, entered the car windows and splashed on their eager faces.

"Okay, that's enough for me, guys," Donna called out. "I've got to keep focused on driving." *Life can be really good,* she decided.

*****

Cheryl, confident that Al was driving the van safely, was fretting over her nephew again. Louis' voice brought her back to the moment.

"Lucina, is this correct? I'm keeping notes on how our first gig goes. Okay. Lucina, you're in charge of staging and props. Al, vehicle maintenance and travel routes. Marin, you work with Dawn and Hugh on housing and meals. Marlene does the packing, travel arrangements, and prop assisting. Jack, meditation and deep-breathing sessions. Let's see now—Hans and Courtney, media connections and outreach to student groups. Cheryl, you and Jenny, costume care. Jim and Donna, performance programs. I think we're covered. Oh yes, I'm in charge of performance scheduling and payments."

"You and Marlene will keep us organized, honey. Now can we relax for a while, please?" Lucina snuggled against his chest, glad they were in the back seat with Cheryl.

Cheryl spoke up. "When do we get paid? I need to buy my nephew some clothes when we get back." Louis reminded her that colleges paid by checks. "That's why we all had to bring cash for our immediate needs. But not to worry, I'll keep informing every one of their earnings to date. And we'll cash our paychecks as soon as we're back."

Cheryl looked at Louis pointedly. "Who's in charge of rehearsal times and places? The women are working on scenes and we need to rework *Choice* like we discussed. That's a must!"

"You're right, Cheryl. Sorry. Can I put you down for that job?"

"I'll do that, Louis." Cheryl, satisfied, asked if anyone was keeping a scrapbook and exactly what the sleeping arrangements were for the night.

"There are gobs of beds for our first gig," Marin said. "Bunk beds, two double beds, some fold-out cots, mattresses— lots of places to sleep, attics, sunporches... "

"Some of us alone," Cheryl sighed wistfully. There was an empty feeling between her arms and heart. *But Sadie and Marcel would get on fine without her. "Not to worry," like Louis said.*

"Janice is quite well known," Marin spoke out. "Makes a good income from her books."

"Who's Janice?" Al asked.

"John Milan's wife. They're our hosts at New Point. You spoke to her on the phone, Al." Marin patted his knee as if he were a forgetful child. "They seem to have a huge house. He's a drama professor, contemporary theater; she writes gardening books. Very friendly."

Lucina turned to Cheryl. "You just brought up something important. A scrapbook. We don't keep a record of anything we do. Well, I do a little bit in my journal."

"I'll work on that. Maybe Dawn will help me." Cheryl, excited, reached past Louis to squeeze Lucina's arm. "We can all collect vital memorabilia, reviews, newspaper articles, photos, people's comments." She was relieved to forget about Marcel and be there with the others.

"Marlene wants to lead warm-ups," Louis droned on. "Hans and Jenny volunteered to get the props on stage with Lucina—"

"Please, Louis, relax now," Lucina cut in. "We'll go over everything before the performance."

"Don't worry, Louis—we're responsible," Cheryl spoke gently. "I need to be here now, too. Don't the tiny green leaves look like butterflies?" And there was Marcel back in her mind again. He'd refused to pin dead butterflies on corkboard for the science teacher just the week before.

"What will I be like in five weeks?" Marin wondered aloud to Al.

He smiled but kept his eyes on the road, then impulsively switched on the radio.

"Oh, that's the Beatles song 'Yellow Submarine.' 'Sky of blue, sea of green,'" Cheryl burst out. "Let's listen!"

*****

Dawn, needing to muffle annoying voices, crouched in the back seat of the Dart, hidden under a bright red poncho borrowed from Jenny. Why were Hans and Jenny in some kind of snit again about the so-called "Big Four"? She knew the couple had been in on the street theater's formation with Louis, Lucina, Marin, and Al, when they'd stayed at a cabin in Vermont together. So why did Hans and Jenny align themselves with the newcomers and drop snide remarks about the Big Four—Hans especially, as if he weren't part of the group's founders? He and Jenny must have coined that pejorative term; she never heard anyone else use it. She'd once heard Cheryl flat out tell them to stop disempowering themselves. If only Cheryl were in the Dart, they wouldn't be talking like that!

Dawn tried to ignore them and went into her own worries. After tonight she'd better have some money in her pocket! No more handouts from Mom and Dad, not after quitting college on them. She'd warned them that it wasn't working for her. She couldn't keep her focus on what the professors were telling her she had to learn. When she read about young people joining together to make their voices heard, she felt pulled to escape the classroom, and her roommates. Be where the action was!

What were those chattering birds contesting now? Something about graphic photos of napalmed Vietnamese in a performance piece at Washington Square Church.

"I'm so sick of seeing those horrors!" Jenny was sure upset.

"Those photos make for revolt!" Hans declared, in his annoying Danish accent. "I don't care what the Big Four think."

Dawn dug more deeply into her cave. *Why couldn't those two just shut up!*

She would say something if Hans and Jenny kept up with their bickering. *That Hans! He'd already messed up bad, from what she'd heard. Probably on the CIA's list.*

Dawn peered out from her red tent. She saw Jenny paw Hans' arm, trying to get him to put it around her. Heard her whisper, "Do you want Mommy to be mean to you, honey?" Dawn cringed. *What had she gotten herself into?*

*****

Marlene kept her eyes smack on the road. She was determined to enjoy driving, getting away from all the city irritation. She tightened her grip on the steering wheel. Traffic had escalated; cars were exiting the parkway to get to the turnpike. She followed them, her whole body veering to the right with the long curve. When the highway straightened out, she sought Hans' scowling face in the rear view mirror.

"You know what, Hans? I don't want to make our audiences anxious. I want to invite people to watch us. That's participatory democracy."

"Yes, participatory democracy," Jenny echoed. "I agree with you, Marlene."

17

Dawn muttered from under her poncho: "Geez, could you just drive, Marlene? You slow down when you listen and speed up when you talk. I'm getting car sick." She should say something to Hans and Jenny as well: "*Be quiet, I need to sleep.*" *Just like that. If only Cheryl were riding with them.*

Hans' shoulders jerked nervously as if he'd heard Dawn's thought. He eyed the lump beside him. If they got harassed at a tollbooth, it wouldn't be because of him or their dragging muffler. *Nothing about Dawn's story smelled good. Was she a California runaway? Then state troopers could be on her tail.* He rested his hand on the covered body beside him.

"Some of us are sitting dogs for the bastard U.S. hawks," he grumbled pointedly.

"Ducks," Jenny corrected.

Dawn groaned through a crack in her red tent. "What are you complaining about now, Hans?" Her head emerged slowly. "Everyone in our troupe is from this country except you. Does it make you feel lonely?"

Hans' back tensed. "You don't want to see those hawks for what they are, that's what I think." He nudged the lump beside him.

Jack, who'd been nodding off in the front seat beside Marlene, suddenly piped up, "Hey, guys, give it a rest. Dig the chlorophyll energy."

Marlene eyed Hans' handsome yet haggard face in her mirror; it seemed almost maniacally lit up by the bursts of blond hair framing it.

"You should join the Living Theater, honey," Jenny piped up. "They get orgasms dumping on white, middle-class sitting ducks."

"Well, there's no Sitting Bull here, for sure," Hans jeered.

"Come on, sweeties—Jack is right!" Marlene pleaded to the two faces blocking her back window view. "Enough put-downs." She pretended to scowl, then realized she really was angry with them; the way they forced others to witness their haggling was disgusting. She'd been able to ignore their bantering for the first hour of the trip, but no longer.

Jack swung around to the back. "Did you guys hear that they're suppressing speak-outs on Vietnam? What's that university in Utah that won't let students speak out?"

"And look what's happening in L.A.," Marlene added. "UCLA is scared the Black Panthers are going to out their racist hiring practices." She could talk to Jack; just ignore the back seat trio. "God, I'm impressed with them."

Jack turned to her. "I dig 'em, too. They do really smart things, like their breakfast program."

"It'll take all of us to change things," Marlene reflected. "Not only Hayden, Lynd, and Aphtheker. I'm tired of hearing their names."

Jack nodded and stayed silent.

"Peace is all I want now," came up from the red poncho.

Hans groaned. "Is that why you sleep so much, Dawn?"

"You always want the last word," Dawn snickered.

"Yeah." Hans grinned and muttered something inaudible.

"Boring," came from Jack as he retrieved his bamboo flute from the dashboard and started up a blues run.

"That's nice," Marlene sighed. "Please don't stop."

Jenny's hand went to Hans' shoulders; she worked her fingers into the taut muscles. Sometimes the poor boy just didn't know how to talk to people. Well, she knew how to calm him. As he relaxed with Jenny's massage, Hans looked out at the light green trees flying past and thought of his grandfather's farm in Denmark.

3
The First Gig

They reached New Point by mid-afternoon, a small bustling college town in the Shawangunk Mountains. Lucina and Louis unloaded their suitcases from Isadora in front of a sprawling wooden house with giant pointed windows and long, frail porches. She bent toward him. "That house is a gothic monster."

"I thought you liked big houses."

"Not this big. And look how it hangs over the hillside. With all of us inside, it could fall off." She imagined gray-haired women with hair buns, staring at them from the multitude of second story windows hung with lace curtains.

"Don't get nuts, Lucina. Everything's going to be okay," he soothed.

After the troupe rested and reviewed assignments for the night's performance, Janice, their hostess, sat them down to a meal of soup and salad, with ingredients from her spring garden. The tall, lanky woman, whose black dress and gold earrings set her apart from the Navy Store attired actors, couldn't stop talking about the group's size.

"I'm used to six at my table, but fourteen! Sorry if I don't call you by name." She went on in a perky voice, explaining her light fare. "Actors can't do their best on empty or full stomachs."

John accompanied them to the small, comfortable student auditorium. He was short, chunky, ponderous—his wife's opposite. He watched from a front row seat with some middle-aged envy mixed with fatherly support, as youthful bodies stretched, then executed a Canadian mounted police exercise routine with ease, and finished with yoga exercises, deep breathing, and vocalizations. He knew their pre-performance workout was extensive, having seen an early version of *Choice*. Their plays, more ritual enactment than realistic scenes, contained a lot of movement, singing, chanting, and expressive recitation that demanded vigorous use of the body, voice, and breath.

*****

John wished Janice had joined him for Fire Dragon's performance that night, part of a new series he had organized, "Theaters Speak Out." But the faculty wives were meeting again. While the players finished their stage preparations, he studied the program notes for their first presentation, *Ghost Dance Tribute: Massacre at Wounded Knee Revisited*. He'd always meant to read Mooney's report on the controversial happenings there. He needn't stay for *Choice*, the anti-war play about a young man called to serve, which he'd already seen in the city. The troupe's gutsy and ritualized style had moved him to invite them. However, he had office business to attend to.

Program Notes for *Ghost Dance Tribute*

Our ritualized testimonial to events surrounding the Massacre at Wounded Knee, South Dakota, Dec. 29, 1890, where the Sioux tribes gathered to do their Ghost Dance, is meant to inform our audiences of the genocidal treatment of these Indigenous people by

the U.S. government. We are not Native people or pretend to be. In portraying their sacred chants, rituals, Ghost Dance and their spiritual leader, Wovoka, we want to give tribute to the true and genuine spiritual ancestors of our country, the Indigenous people of this land we call the United States. With this testimonial we affirm the right and necessity of resistance to all forms of Colonial genocide as was enacted, for example, at Wounded Knee.

Indigenous tribes, confined to reservations, while their sacred buffalo were rapidly being exterminated, sought salvation in Wovoka, the self-appointed savior preaching survival through the return to ancestral roots via the Ghost Dance, which induced trance states. Evoking the Great Spirit, participants intertwined fingers and began a circling dance, clockwise, slowly increasing in speed. With the dust lifting under their drumming feet, many fell into trance-like states, aided by a shaman's hypnotic movements. The hypnotist, stationed near the sacred cedar tree planted in the circle's center, waved feathers and scarves leading those already stiffening and trembling within the mesmerizing dance to break away and collapse into visionary states. These visions became the power stories and songs of the Ghost Dance Movement.

Before the Massacre at Wounded Knee, the U.S. Government, fearing the rising power of the Ghost Dance, machinated the murder of Sitting Bull, Arapaho medicine man and Ghost

Dance leader who had led many into the spirit world. Sitting Bull's murder was followed by increased presence of hundreds of U.S. militiamen ordered to squash all rebellion in the Sioux tribes of South Dakota, arrest leader Big Foot, and disarm his warriors.

As the armed white soldiers closed in, Big Foot led his tribe to the Pine Hill Reservation for safety. But they were intercepted and forced to camp in the open at Wounded Knee.

Who fired the first shot is contested, but the facts remain: the U.S. Army's Hotchkiss guns raked the Indian teepees with gunfire at Wounded Knee, causing the people to run for their lives. When the smoke cleared three hundred Sioux were dead, including Big Foot, while only twenty-five U.S. soldiers lost their lives.

This massacre stomped out the Ghost Dance Movement and brought an end to Native peoples' resistance to Government occupation.

Scene 1: The Ghost Dance

The Ghost Dance usually began at dusk and took place around a cedar tree. No beads or ornaments made by white men were attached to their shirts and no metal was worn.

*****

At seven-thirty, the auditorium was buzzing with excitement and many students, eager to see a street troupe that was touted in the underground press for having endured police attacks, while sporting torn jeans, Stop the War T-shirts, and no-nonsense attitudes. Fire Dragon had the stature of a rock band for some. John, now behind a microphone at center stage, introduced the street theater and explained to the audience their inclusion in the "Theaters Speak Out" festival.

"Fire Dragon, first in our series, invites change at the roots of our society—city streets, where all classes, all colors, mingle and meet. They bring rituals to everyone, exposing the sad, violent realities upon which our country has been formed. The program notes to *Ghost Dance Tribute*, which you all have in your hands, spell out the brutal treatment of our Indigenous. If change is going to come about in our country, it's because of what is being exposed at our roots. Please welcome our players from the trenches—" His final words were lost in a sudden roar. Shouts, foot stomping, and whistles filled the auditorium.

*****

Back in his front row seat, John, impressed by the program notes, looked up to watch two of the actors, in a strange mix of solemnity and cockiness, carry the sacred cedar tree to center stage. With its foliage of green felt, crow and eagle feathers, strips of cloth, the object seemed to tremble with each of their steps. When it was firmly secured within a stand, the stage lights dimmed slightly, while the auditorium remained lit.

He watched keenly as the actors, dressed in their Ghost Dance shirts, moved slowly out from the wings onto the stage. *Quite interesting,* he thought. *By leaving the house lights up, it's as if we, the audience, just happened upon this ritual. Whether we were here or not, it would be carried out.*

The loose-fitting shirts of white cotton, with wide flowing sleeves, painted with moons, stars, animals, and birds, had real feathers added so the actors seemed to fly as they stepped rhythmically in silence, grasping the shoulders of the one ahead. With forward flowing movements halted by spasmodic gesturing, the dancers rocked and writhed as if in pain and mourning, before moving on again in rhythmic precision. Five minutes passed before they formed a circle around the Sacred Tree.

In continued synced motion they dropped hands to their sides and bending downward, mimed scooping up earth, rubbing it in their hands before tossing the soil over their shoulders. Then standing upright, still in their circle, the dancers paid homage to the four directions, and in the name of the Sioux tribes called out to their dead ancestors.

This honoring finished, they turned to the Sacred Tree, raising their arms to the Great Spirit before clasping hands. Fingers interlaced, they began to circle clockwise, gradually moving faster and faster until they were swinging their arms and running.

*****

Even as Lucina felt her moccasins slide fluidly along the floor, her leg muscles tightening slightly as arms and shoulders began swinging, she struggled to stay within the spirit of the dance. *Feel what the Sioux felt*, she commanded herself. *Identify.* This was the first performance of the revised *Ghost Dance Tribute* since that disastrous enactment in February at the Academy of Art in Providence, Rhode Island. Watching half the audience tiptoe ever so politely out of the auditorium at that so-called "Radical Theater Symposium," when they were just halfway through the last scene, the blood scene—a nightmare! Those disappearing, disappointed spectators still haunted her. And she had cried out to them, "Please. Don't leave! We need to hear your comments." Only one matronly woman in a gray business suit shouted back to the stage before exiting, "Sorry! I didn't come to see actors wallowing in blood. I came to get some history."

Lucina tightened her fingers within Dawn's and Cheryl's, and lifted her head defiantly as the troop revolved lithely around the Sacred Tree. To increase their speed together, each had to fixate on the momentum of the whole. Her glance wandered to the sea of faces watching them: *No one in the auditorium was moving. No one turning away. Not yet, anyway! Can't control a crowd. Well, the "Blood on Their Hands" scene depicting the U.S. militiamen exalting in their wanton massacre of the Sioux by miming the thrusting of their hands into the bowels of those massacred was absolutely necessary. At least they had shortened it.*

Lucina closed her eyes again. Soft, circling footsteps seemed like distant drums beating to the Arapaho chant now begun by Marin: "We circle around, we circle around the boundaries of the earth, the boundaries of the earth. Wearing our long wing feathers as we fly, wearing our long-wing feathers as we fly." Velvety contralto tones moved about her like a gentle zephyr. Here with her Fire Dragon tribe, her circle of people, she was flying, lifted upward by the chant and the feathers on her shirt.

*****

As Hugh glided to the Sacred Tree, waving a red feather and white cloth, and focusing on the one dancer whose body jerked and swayed, he sang, "In this circle, in this circle, all will be as I now reveal it." John recalled the solemn, silent kid, sitting at his dining room table earlier, lost in a private meditation. *Ah yes,* he mused. *Now Hugh, probably WASP, is emulating Wovoka, a shaman initiating the hypnotic state to invite visions inspired by the ancestral beings. Why does this bother me?*

Hugh swirled his feathers and handkerchief in front of Jenny, the Trance Dancer. When she suddenly collapsed to the stage floor, fully hypnotized, all motion stopped and the auditorium and stage went pitch black.

In the darkness, John rubbed tension out of his hands. *A professional dance troupe might have done the ritual with more developed choreography,* he thought. But the Fire Dragon actors had touched his guts with their earnestness. *And that Hugh! Both a riveting and disquieting presence in such a young man.*

John watched as scene 2 began: The Sacred Buffalo. Only the stage lights were up. Jenny, still in trance state, remained prone where she had fallen, stage left. Center stage, the actors, simulating a Sioux tribe, sat intoning softly around a standing figure wearing a beautifully rendered buffalo-head mask.

Nice transition, John thought. *The buffalo becomes the ancestral power figure in the Trance Dancer's vision. Where is my own power figure,* he wondered as the droning chant continued. He turned awkwardly in his seat and saw row after row occupied, as far back as he could see. *Well, if Dr. Rollins, prodigious head of the Theater Department, decided to skip Fire Dragon's performance, he'll regret it. Thank heavens attaining tenure allows some risk-taking!* He could stand proud before his boss and any scoffing colleagues. He wasn't the only professor who believed the university should be a forum for debate on urgent, timely issues.

*****

Al, the Buffalo Spirit, strutted and gyrated awkwardly, endearing himself to the audience, whose oohs and aahs seemed like gentle stroking of the beloved animal. Dawn offered a prayer: "Oh, beloved Tatonka, Buffalo Spirit, you are the greatest gift of the higher being to the tribe. Your meat feeds, your hide clothes and shelters. Your bones and sinews are the arrow points and bow strings that protect. As your tribe knelt down to you, so do we." One by one the actors began chanting again, in harmonious homage to Tatonka. "The spirit will descend, your buffalo will feed you. The earth trembles as the tribe bows down." As they sang and bowed, the Buffalo Spirit tamped down a place on the earth, where he lay prone before his worshippers

In silence, one by one, the actors, as tribe members, mimed scooping food from the bowels of the buffalo with rhythmical gestures and began to eat. When stage lights dimmed, the actors now seated declared: "Oh, kindred Buffalo Spirit, who feeds and clothes and protects, your tribe will not let the white man take you. They will not let the white man shoot you."

*****

Scene 3: The Massacre. When the lights came up, both on stage and in the auditorium, the actors, first seen in frozen standing positions, begin desperately running for their lives in exaggerated slow motion as the silence was shattered by the sound of gunfire.

Simultaneously, large shadowy figures appeared marching down the aisles from the back of the auditorium. Four actors dressed as U.S. Government militiamen mimed aiming rifles at the fleeing Ghost Dancers whose desperate, slow-motion running ended in abrupt, spastic collapse as each Ghost Dancer was shot and murdered.

When Lucina faced the audience, playing a slow funereal beat on the red drum. she was overwhelmed by the multitude of eyes staring dumbly back at her. *Would someone scream out, "Lies, all lies!" at any second? Would this audience, like the Rhode Island one, reject their portrayal of brutality done to the Lakota Sioux tribe? What were they trying to do with people's emotions and perceptions?*

The militiamen departed with only motionless bodies visible; stage and auditorium were submerged once again in darkness and silence.

*****

Scene 4: Blood on Their Hands. With lights coming up on stage and auditorium, Lucina began a marching beat as she chanted: "The Native peoples' lives, land, and resources were plundered. This was genocide." All of the other actors, now gloating militiamen-murderers wearing white gloves coated with blood (red paint), sat on the floor miming laughter and digging into the bodies of slaughtered Sioux. Whereas in Scene 2, The Sacred Buffalo, Sioux hands in the bowels of a dead buffalo depicted a holy, loving communion, in this scene, the bloodied militiamen's hands evidenced inhuman, violent hatred. As the drumming and chanting faded, the actors/militiamen rose drunkenly and uprooted the Sacred Tree. Their wanton degradation ended with a frieze.

Hans finalized the drama with a statement spoken out to the audience. "We, Fire Dragon Street Theater, demand that the U.S. Government confess to the genocide of the Indigenous peoples of this so-called democratic United States. We demand an immediate release of all Indigenous political prisoners. We demand the government return all land stolen from the Indigenous, land that must be cleaned of nuclear waste. We demand that a Department of Justice for Native Peoples be created and made responsible for providing federal assistance in education, health, and welfare programs. Finally, we demand that these reparations to the Sacred Nations be declared as law in an Amendment to our Constitution."

*****

John, scurrying out of the auditorium during the troupe's final statement, was taken aback by the boldness of their condemnation of the treatment of the Indigenous. *No pussyfooting around with them!* he mused, imagining a time when they would be calling him up for bail money.

During a brief intermission, the audience, too moved to leave their seats, turned to those nearby to exchange reactions to what they had just witnessed. Only the announcement of the street theater's second drama stopped this intense dialogue.

"*Choice* will be performed next…though the experience of young people of color in the military…we regret to announce… has not yet been incorporated into our play. Tonight's performance has some comments from one of our actors, who will bring the experience of her cousin, a Black GI, into the play."

John, still standing by the auditorium doors, curious as to what the gutsy troupe was now announcing, sighed deeply. *Was such an apology for* Choice *really necessary? How much could you cover in a thirty-minute anti-war play, anyway?*

4

After the Performance

Choice received wild applause and boot stomping. After the evening's performance, a small crowd of students gathered at John's house. Janice ushered everyone to one of the large porches. "You can enjoy your talk, your beer, your grass, and the almost-full moon out here," she chirped. Students bubbled over with admiration and questions: How did the players create collectively without fights? Did they all live together? Were the couples monogamous?

The actors, giddy with relief that their performance had been well received, enjoyed giving their various responses to the eager listeners. Only Marin stayed quiet. She was still annoyed with Courtney and Hugh. Instead of the slow, dignified walk-dance she had taught them to perform while carrying the Sacred Tree to center stage, a ritual within the Ghost Dance Tribute, she had watched them jerk the tree this way and that, turning a sacred procedure into a comic tug of war. *They probably smoked a joint before the show,* she fussed. *At least no one in the audience laughed.*

On John and Janice's moonlit porch, Courtney and Hugh definitely were higher than kites. Courtney flung himself off the

33

railing trying to catch the handle of the big dipper and Hugh felt himself to be in the Hayden Planetarium.

Al told a macabre hitchhiking story about a trucker who'd picked him up on a road in the Rockies on a full-moon night. The driver announced he was "lunatic" and started howling like a wolf, edging his car closer and closer to a cliff with no guardrail. As Al carried on, Marin stopped fuming over the tree bearers and relaxed back in an Adirondack chair to enjoy a glass of wine. Giving herself up to the starry night above, she resolved to confront "the oafs" some other time.

After the students left, the actors helped their hosts clean up, and John asked them to join him in the living room for a few minutes. Dawn felt some kind of relief—at last she would get paid for her work!—not aware that Louis had gotten their check before the performance, and they wouldn't get paid until they were back home.

John was talking. "You guys were great—you could tell it was a real turn-on for our students. You saw how many of them came dressed as street kids? I even decided it was smart that you owned up to what was missing in *Choice*. So, you're going to become a touring research task force on the military, huh? You can talk about your process tomorrow at the panel and no doubt you'll get some tough questions. There's one problem though. Your epilogue, 'Blood on Their Hands,' might be too challenging for most audiences. Who exactly is guilty of trying to wipe out the Indigenous? Also, folks in general can't easily relate to people digging into an animal's guts to pluck out raw food, unless it's in a grade-B horror movie. Know what I mean? And then you want us to witness bad white guys digging into peoples' guts? We don't see ourselves as cannibals. You want to win over people's compassion for the Sioux, but to the average Joe it's going to look like you're getting off on being macabre."

John's comments made Lucina wince. *Our gutsy blood scene is getting dissed again!* Someone handed her a joint. Instead of passing it on as she'd promised herself to do after a bad experience where she felt a treacherous force was trying to kill her, she held it firmly in her mouth and sucked in eagerly, hoping the ingested smoke could somehow snuff out the anxiety churning inside her. *Fuck it!* John's attack on their carefully reworked scene brought up the Rhode Island disaster again—audience members fleeing their performance just months before. She wanted to shout at John. *The students here loved our show. I saw their faces in the auditorium. They knew what we were saying. They could take our blood scene; they could take the truth. Tell us what moved you about what we did tonight. Or didn't you really watch us?* She would definitely ask for feedback from the students coming to their workshop the next day. Especially which scenes really meant something to them. She watched Louis question John; was he asking him the same thing?

Voices became muffled. One of the students, a thin blond boy, had remained behind and was strumming a guitar on the porch. Lucina, relaxing with his rhythms, entered a more comfortable space. As she sank back into her chair, she felt her exhaustion. The grass was strong but thank heavens not crazy-making. She could think clearly about what they'd done and why. Forget John and his judgments. *We have to show what the U.S. government did to the Indigenous people, rob their land and their dignity, and then murder them. It's just like talking about what our government is doing to the Vietnamese, massacring them so they can have an outpost in Asia to build U.S. imperialism. Our plays and tributes speak to people who can face the truth and make it better. They speak to students who can hear. They spoke to that guitar player over there, sharing his musical gifts with us. Maybe John is too caught up in his role as theater professor; he has to one-up us with criticism—show his right to his institutional position. Or maybe he's just plain envious—worse, maybe he's an apologist for his country, right or wrong. Well, at least the guy invited us to perform here! That's a good thing.*

Sweet sounds wrapped around her thoughts again. *I bet that musician believes you can't trust people over thirty. Maybe he's right.*

She watched as if from a far distance as Louis and Hans gestured animatedly while John, arms folded in front of him, carried forth. *Was John saying that theater should present several viewpoints, so that people would know that truth was complex?* Then her mind changed gears: once again she was obsessing on that Rhode Island fiasco.

She, Louis, Al, and Marin had gone to the directors' symposium the day after their disastrous performance. The presenters, directors of well received, Off-Broadway plays, not street theater groups, were touting their various styles. The symposium's main focus? The play, *Our Heroes*: "Three astronauts die instantly in fiery capsule just 218 feet above the ground, locked behind sealed hatches. The space craft was still on the launch pad and the three men were hooked into a breathing system of pure oxygen that fed the fire." The actors depicting this recent tragedy were devastated by the violent deaths of these U.S. citizens.

That was understandable. Besides, that play was backed by high-voltage media. But when the deaths were of Vietnamese, violent deaths deliberately caused by their own government— did they want to hear about this violence! It felt like that "radical festival" didn't see the subject matter of street plays—Stop the War in Vietnam; Fight for Justice and Equal Rights; End Racism Now—as "serious, real theater." And the presenters, all male directors, were obviously dedicated to their top-down structures.

Fire Dragon had to protest that patriarchal bullshit. So Louis shouted at one of the pompous directors, "It's obscene for one man to take the position of 'the Director' of any group. Especially in these times. Fire Dragon Street Theater rotates male and female 'guides.' We use that term so that everyone feels free to add suggestions."

Her Louis was no outlaw! Rather, he was a fighter, a Ché. No one else had the guts to support him. But she did. She stood up and calmly added, "Don't any of you know we are in the Age of Women and Teamwork? We desperately need street theater to incite real change in our country."

The last straw? The festival promoters upped their own take from 10 percent to 15 percent, after an agreement had been signed. The greedy bastards. Who needed that arrogant theater festival anyway!

She shouldn't do grass anymore. Too many up-and-down emotions. Just have a cold beer. There was John droning on and on: "So the question I ask you is: Who are you trying to reach?" His pedantic tone bore into her like a drill. "Whose minds need changing? Where are the people coming from who most need to see your plays and understand your message?"

She watched Marin sidle up to him. "I don't know if we need to change the blood scene, John. But we do need to make sure our Sacred Tree is carried with dignity and respect!" With these words she shot a stern look toward Hugh and Courtney.

Then Louis piped up quickly: "We'll deal with this, John. I mean, of course we want to communicate with our audience. But now some of us are high and all of us are exhausted."

Mumbling thanks to their host, the actors dragged themselves up the stairs and stumbled from room to room looking for their suitcases and bed space. Dawn hoped two Bufferin would knock her out. *Wasn't John going to pay them? Or was he too upset with their blood scene? Oh, shit! Where was Cheryl sleeping tonight? She really, really needed to talk to her.*

5
Guerrilla Action or Performance Theater

The first panel for "Theaters Speak Out" featured the Fire Dragon group and focused on the topic, "Guerrilla Theater versus Performance Street Theater." Only three of the actors, Louis, Lucina, and Hans, had volunteered to talk. They sat with John Milan at a conference table in front of a classroom filled with students and a few professors sitting in chairs, desks pushed to the back. Louis spotted many Stop the War T-shirts peeking out of jackets, while a few older folk, probably professors, wore sport coats or blouses. John's introductions were barely out of his mouth when Hans launched into his hard sell on guerrilla tactics. Phrases like "take the enemy by surprise" and "shoot from the hip" shot through the small lecture room like spitballs. Lucina saw the "wild-eyed radical" the conservative press so loved to caricature. She wondered: *His willful actions got Louis bludgeoned by the cops, but we all forgave him when he showed true remorse. But he hasn't learned. Here he is showing off again!*

As Hans provoked further, "You students have never lived in a war zone," a student in the front row, looking especially troubled, shot back, "How do you know what we've been through?" Lucina eyed Hans sharply. *Don't put others on the defensive! This event is a discussion, not a competition.* She had to talk to him!

Louis, next to her at the cold metal table, looked as concerned as she felt. Before Hans could respond she broke in, "Let me explain something. We express tribal togetherness in our plays, as in the *Ghost Dance Tribute* performance last night. Our plays are not guerrilla actions. But at the same time, we have different approaches to inspire activism and some of us have done guerrilla theater. The fourteen of us are as different say as any fourteen people picked off a New York City street might be." Before she could add, *except of course we all want to end the war*, John intercepted and skillfully interjected an academic approach to the discussion. "Hans has some good ideas on the topic. Let's remember it was Ronnie Davis of the San Francisco Mime Troop who first coined the term 'guerrilla theater' a year ago in the *Tulane Drama Review*. He saw that war-zone guerrilla tactics, e.g., unexpected actions, could be incorporated in political street theater to attract attention." John then outlined a working definition of guerrilla theater: "Small, mobile bands of actors carry out unpredictable actions in unlikely situations in order to create confrontation and make a political point. But be careful," he added quickly. "These actions should not incite or invite violence."

Lucina, relieved for once by John's professorial control of the discussion, and his obvious awareness of the dangers of mindless antics, gave Louis' knee a nudge. She still wanted to shout out, "We don't all approach change in the same way." *Maybe this shrewd professor could temper their alpha-male Hans.* She unclenched her fists and tried to make eye contact with John, now describing a flower power action some guys in a group from San Francisco called the Diggers had either already performed or were about to perform in New York.

"You Fire Dragon people must know about it. Something about plans to dump bags of soot on Con Ed executives?"

Louis bent to Lucina with annoyance: "He shouldn't be talking about something he doesn't really know about," he whispered. "Besides, there could be an informant in this room."

A serious-looking woman, despite her tufts of green hair, sat upright with a raised hand. "Certainly, the primitive aspect of the action has appeal," she commented. "But wouldn't passersby see the soot dumpers as the polluters, not Con Ed?"

Another student from the back row broke in: "However, a surprise action like that could expose the truth in minutes—if it were followed by a clear explanation of what Con Ed does to our air."

John responded almost apologetically. "Those are two good comments, students. I don't support aggressive actions that confuse who the bad guys, the exploiters, are. I brought this up as an example of spectacle theatrics, a kind of guerilla theater event that can get free media attention."

Lucina tried again to send a please-keep-the-peace look in Hans' direction, but he had disappeared into his shell.

"You do have to be careful with actions like these," John was saying. "We already feel too manipulated. Too brainwashed. As Evelyn has suggested, wary passersby could easily mistake the actor-activists as culprits."

College professors like John aren't public activists, Lucina thought. *They could be fired.* Her gaze went to the dirty green walls of the room they were in. *They sure could use a radical paint action here! Real color, like bright yellow or violet.* Then John's professorial tone caught her ear again.

"I'm in a dialogue with the Fire Dragon folks about this very topic. How do you win over your audience rather than alienate them with scenes that might seem unbelievable to people brought up to honor our founding fathers? I'm not going to say any more now except this: I encourage you to go to Fire Dragon's acting workshop on Wednesday and tell this group directly how you experienced last night's plays."

Lucina reconsidered. *Maybe a diplomatic professor does have a place in the movement. John has helped us "save face" by not criticizing our blood scene at this panel. He can use his clout to inform and educate without proselytizing.* Well, she would follow up on his suggestions and ask for feedback at the workshop.

*****

The students in front of her were laughing. Jim, stationed in the second row, had pulled a puppet out of his knapsack—a gorilla with a large grin. He was making it growl and scratch at itself. "Here's a gorilla action for you!" he called out.

John chuckled. "Right! Good point, Jim. A guerrilla action can have humor." He waited until Jim had finished with his improvisation before launching into the other half of his panel topic, "Performance Theater."

"First off," he said, "Performance street theater takes place in an area designated as stage, whether it's in a park or on a sidewalk. The audience is composed of people who have gathered to watch a play. That play may be political or entertainment or both."

"Like Brecht's work," a student shouted, waving a book in the air.

"Good point, José!" John shouted back. "He was a master in raising dramatic tension and consciousness. You guys have been doing your homework." He looked out at the room of students with obvious pride and affection. "Brecht, a great political artist, if you will, rose to the needs of his times. We too are in a decade super-bent on politicizing culture and meshing it with entertainment. The boundaries between art and politics are breaking down. We're being constantly challenged to react, think, and make choices."

"We've been talking about Guerrilla Theater," José called out again, standing this time. He took his cap off and seemed to grow taller as he spoke. "I'd call it Activists' Theater, not for armchair types. But what about Ghost Dance? In your program notes you say its's a testimonial to the Indigenous people and call it Ghost Dance Tribute. Is that a kind of theater or isn't it theater at all? Is Hugh trying to be Wovoka, the guy who started the Ghost Dance? Wouldn't that be insulting to an Indigenous person—I think he was a Paiute. Imagine a white actor portraying Martin Luther King by putting on black face. I think it's ethically, even morally questionable—I mean the audience is supposed to see this spiritual leader on stage. At least have a Native person play Wovoka!"

"Okay, I better speak to that!" Hugh, seated with the other actors not on the panel, but near them, also stood. "Of course I'm not trying to be Wovoka..." He paused, his head dropping apologetically. "Look, I'm just trying to represent what he stood for to his people—a powerful spiritual leader." With a deep breath, he sat down and continued. "I try to identify with him, what he was trying to do for his people. So, I can't be some mousey guy strutting around on stage."

Marin, seated behind him, called out, "And we appreciate all your efforts, Hugh. Your presence, your strong articulate movements. As we've said in our program and as Hans clarified at the end of our tribute—we believe it's our responsibility to relay to others as seriously, truthfully as we can, the facts about Wounded Knee. We're activist actors! Someone else might write an essay about it, another give a lecture. But our mode of communication is making images through scenes, chant, dance."

Louis, nodding his head as Marin spoke continued: "I hear you, José. Your concern that we don't pretend we're something we're not. But, look at it this way... In a sense, we bring history to life again so the viewer experiences it too, with all their senses. We don't put make-up on, or wear masks to make us look Indigenous. We've worked very hard in this tribute to show that we aren't trying to be Sioux, or Paiute, Native people... We're just us, a mixture of ethnicities, giving live testament to the massacre of the original inhabitants of our country. Do you dig me, José?"

Several students stomped their feet and whistled in appreciation of all the comments made by Hugh, Marin and Louis.

"Can I say something, please?" A Black woman, seated with a small group of professors, raised her hand, then started talking. "I personally think it's great what you're doing with Ghost Dance Tribute. You've educated me, and I definitely know about the endemic racist injustice that runs this country. For all I know, some of you Fire Dragon actors could be part Indigenous. I have a friend whose blood quantum proves she's 'half-blood' Cherokee. Yet, because her mother was Swedish, she has blond hair and blue eyes and not believed to be Indigenous. What I really want to say is this. How else can we understand, embrace, identify with, honor others not like us, but to stand in their shoes, relive their chants and dances, connect to them spiritually and tell the truth about the injustices done to them? So I applaud your work. But I do have a suggestion that could clear this whole concern up so that everyone seeing your tribute would clearly, immediately understand what you're doing. You need actual photos of Indigenous people projected on the stage during your Ghost Dance Tribute. I don't know how you'll do it. You'll figure that out. Do you have a slide projector? A colleague in the history department here has a great collection of portraits of Native people on slides, men, women, children from several tribes—I know he would love to give Sioux and Paiute portraits to you. I'll speak to him and get slides to you.

Appreciative nods and comments followed Professor Harmen's support of the troupe's work. Her solution to end any possible criticism of their intent, portraits of actual members of the Sioux and Paiute tribes projected on their stages, felt like the missing ingredient to their Tribute. Indigenous people must be present. John felt the need to offer his own acknowledgment within this collective affirmation. "Professor Harmon, thank you for your support of this serious street theater troupe. Your profound suggestion certainly clears up my own concerns. And thanks to my other colleagues for coming today and making this discussion so rich. Students, José, Aisha, Betsy, Sammy your comments were great! Anyone else need to say something before I carry forth again?"

Jim signaled to John that he had a comment. "I want to follow up on Professor Harmen's suggestion that some of us could be part Indigenous. I believe I am part Lakota Sioux. My mother's investigating this. So far no proof. I haven't talked about it to the troupe. I know what you're saying, José...but to do our job as an activist theater troupe—expose injustice done to people, as Hugh, Marin and Louis expressed—we need to experience what the Sioux were up against. The U.S. government, through its hired violent, colonialist killers were out to wipe out these people, their ancestors, their beliefs off the face—"

Her voice breaking, Lucina interrupted: "We say prayers—to the Sioux, the Paiute. We ask for permission to do our Ghost Dance Tribute—in their name. We expose the atrocities."

Hugh joined in: "I also pray to God to show me how to best honor Wovoka, this great man's spirit. I try to go into a kind of trance state so I'm not pretending. It's exhausting. I'll do anything to help get the reparations due them. One group of people should never be allowed to commit genocide of another."

By now, most of the students were moving restlessly in their seats. John cleared his throat, "Amen, Hugh," and changed the topic.

*****

Dawn, seated in the front row, yawned and stretched as John highlighted Sam's dilemma in *Choice*. *Thank god she wasn't stuck in his classroom! Gets off on the sound of his own voice,* she thought. She moved her arms as carefully as she could in the cramped desk chair, but her half eaten apple went spinning to the floor. Cheryl, in the next seat, immediately scooped it up and tossed it back to her. A spasm of laughter flew between them. Taking a bite from the apple, Dawn smiled broadly. *Cheryl's bored too with his blabbing:* "…all those good things, characters, plot, images, songs—of course, we don't have a brilliant display of wit and character development here—street theater isn't Shakespeare." Some students laughed. *What's funny about that? Uh-oh, Lucina's making growly faces. She must not like us being compared to Shakespeare.*

"Lucina, let's hear from you." John was looking directly at her. "What do you think about this?"

Lucina shot up from her chair, causing Dawn and Cheryl to be suddenly attentive. "Your professor knows we work very hard in constructing our dramas," she began, consciously moving her glance to take in all the students. "These are not tossed-off skits. In fact, street theater is the purest place where art and activism really work together for humanity. John spoke to that when he introduced us last night." Her voice rose with conviction. "*Choice* took months to develop. We tried to show Sam's mental and emotional states during his crisis of consciousness. And it's going to take weeks more to incorporate the reality of people of color in the military — how much choice do they have? Did Shakespeare address that issue? I don't think so. And our collage of scenes, rituals, and chants making up the *Ghost Dance Tribute: Massacre at Wounded Knee Revisited* were carefully and artfully constructed to inform and engage. We need to address the fact that an ancient, integrated, developed, and Indigenous people—we don't use the word 'Indians' any more—have been denigrated, almost obliterated because of greed, and always with the assumption of white privilege in the name of progress."

Dawn looked at Cheryl: was she impressed with Lucina too? She'd never been able to talk back to a professor like that. *Lucina has a Master's degree, that's why. She's like a professor herself—but not so confident that she doesn't listen to our ideas.*

Dawn watched John sink to his seat at the panel table, his eyes blinking nervously. *Oh my God, he looks mad! What if he decides not to pay us?*

"Let's forget about Shakespeare for now. Why not use the Living Theater as a comparison?"

Dawn smiled to herself. *Lucina's still telling him off?*

"You've all heard of this internationally known repertory theater, directed by Julian Beck and Judith Malina? Well, within their grand productions, they often invite us rough and tumble vagabonds to perform. They know we represent theater of the street, the people's theater, activists' theater. We performed *Choice* in one of their productions, in fact, and welcomed the opportunity. But understand this: even though they are seen as a huge cultural, political force of our times, I sometimes think they confront their audiences too strongly. Make people uncomfortable on purpose, to make a point. As if that were the quickest way to arouse people to wake up and act. Sometimes, we might offend people with our subject matter. Yet, since our group wants the audience to consider our viewpoints, we don't put them down."

Holy Cow! Dawn wanted to clap. *These students are turned on by her—they're really listening.*

"Wow!" John exhaled. "I have to say, that's all true!" The irritation was gone from his face. "Fire Dragon doesn't punish the audience with insults. They inspire the audience to feel and think deeply."

Dawn relaxed. *He sounds like a professor again. And he actually praised us. Louis and Lucina are smiling at each other—she sure defends us! So, maybe we'll get paid after all.*

*****

Jenny, seated near Dawn and Cheryl, was in a funk. All this smart talk around her. *Her poor Hans had his dejected, "nobody understands" look. She would have to console him later.*

Now Louis was carrying forth. "Guerrilla theater makes good guys and bad guys, but no human beings."

Jenny checked out the students around her; their eyes were glued on him. He had the same assuredness of Professor John. "It uses people and events, and people use it." She had felt too shy to be on the panel, and she was very glad she'd said no. Who could handle all this fancy talk to students almost her age? *Now what was Lucina saying? Something about abusive theater?* "That's right. The people don't want to pay to get hit over the head." *Always advocating for "the people." What people? She could hardly listen—Hans' ranting was enough. And why wasn't Cheryl up there, giving her viewpoint? There she was whispering with Dawn, so worried about getting paid. Well, she and Hans brought extra...if Dawn needed. Damn! This panel better end soon. She really had to pee! Oh, no. Louis was still on a roll!*

"With performance theater in general, illusion is offered and accepted as reality. Actors and audience agree to pretend together. But Fire Dragon Street Theater is yet another type of theater, ritual theater and okay, José, sometimes a tribute theater. We ritualize real events to stress their essential meanings. The Ghost Dance Tribute we perform is based on actual accounts of Sioux rituals and of the events at Wounded Knee. As a testimonial to the Indigenous people, we experience, relive, go into that ritual as deeply as we can."

Just as Jenny started to appreciate Louis' take on their work—*he did make it seem special!*—John interrupted him. "'Theatrical Style' is a yearlong course in my department, Louis. Not something we can cover in one hour." *Maybe John resents Louis, and Lucina too, for sort of one-upping him in front of his students.* He was almost shouting now: "My concern in my forum is how a dramatic event rouses an audience to mindful action. With that focus in mind, have any of you students seen or done a guerrilla theater event?"

A diligent note-taker responded from the back row. "How can you tell if you're seeing such theater, since it is a kind of trompe l'oeil?" Jenny sent Hans a thumbs-up. This was his chance to shine.

"Can't use the words *guerrilla* and *theater* together anymore," Hans pronounced. "The correct term is guerrilla action—ja? I did a guerrilla action once in a liquor store with just three of us."

Jenny's eyes widened. *Well, I've never heard about a liquor store. Last time it was a bodega! But I'll just keep nodding my head to support him.*

"The first one steals a bottle of gin, hides it in his jacket pocket. The second guy starts yelling, 'That guy stole a bottle of gin!' Then me, dressed like a cop, goes up to the first guy and grabs him by the collar. But now the Accuser puts on a black facemask, and the Thief puts on a white mask. By now people in the store, not an audience but real customers, have gathered to watch us, the action-initiators, not actors, you understand.

Suddenly me, the Cop, pounces on the innocent Black Guy and handcuffs him, while the White Guy, the real thief, sneaks out of the store with the stolen gin. See? That's how you rub racism into people's faces. People of color are guilty before proven innocent!" Hans ended his account by checking for Cheryl's reaction. But Lucina and Louis' questioning looks butted in. *Don't they get me?* Hans wondered, annoyed. *The students are digging what I'm saying.*

A young Black man seated at the back of the lecture hall shouted out, "Hey, man—I get you! You've got guts. Most performance theater is no better than TV soaps. Entertainment for the mesmerized masses. Doesn't shake anybody up that much. Guerrilla action is where it's at! But putting masks on? Doesn't that make it like theater? If three people plan a certain action for an appropriate setting, that's like a play. You don't charge money to see it and it's done in a public space. But what I want to know—did any of the spectators in the liquor store defend the Black guy?"

"With all due respect to you, Hans, and your intelligent example," John interjected with a slight but earnest bow of the head, "my student, Lionel, has brought out a final important link between our two forms of acting out, guerrilla theater and performance street theater. Guerrilla street actions, conscious manipulations of reality led by a political agenda, can be put under the heading 'Art,' just as performance street theater can be. Maybe we could call it action art for lack of a better term. Keep in mind, students: all types of theater have complexities and interconnections. Easy labels can hide that fact. But for a general distinction between guerrilla art and performance art: the first indirectly confronts the passersby, the second directly confronts an audience.

"But our time is running out. I hope you students keep up the dialogue and bring it to class this week. And please go to

Fire Dragon's workshop on Wednesday. I'm sure you'll enjoy and learn." With this summing up, Professor John turned to his panel, thanking them. As the students finished writing down their professor's summation, Hans jotted down some thoughts for the next time he had a chance to talk about his liquor store guerrilla action.

****

Lucina left the conference room with ambivalent feelings about all the labels tossed around. In one way she felt energized; in another, bent out of shape as if thrown into a clothes dryer and spun about. *Hopefully at our workshop we can engage students in a less heady way,* she thought. *After all, theater is about using the mind and the body. John is both clear and evasive. He seems to be saying one thing, then suddenly he switches to another point of view. Maybe this is the secret of keeping a respectable teaching job even while introducing controversial topics. All points become food for thought, not really actions to be taken.* Suddenly it came to her: she didn't really know if John and Janice were definitely against the war. *Should she ask them directly which side they were on?*

****

Lucina's Journal Entry. Tour: Wednesday, April 5, 1967. How lucky for us that John and Janice let us hang with them for a few days. I think they like having us around—it's a big house just for the two of them. We help out with the chores and some of us are helping Janice with her vegetable garden. We want to leave them on Friday with good feelings. I've decided not to ask them if they've ever joined a protest of the Vietnam War on campus. They have been supportive of us and they know where we stand.

If New Point College students are an example of what we can hope for on our tour, what a gas. They're so real and hungry for what we gave them; and we needed what they gave us. They especially loved the exercises we did at the workshop today that encouraged their improvisation skills. All about picking up cues and clues from what others do and going with it. And knowing when to pass the motion and the emotion on so the story is collectively developed. A scene is built together. It's like we did in grade school: sit in a circle; one person starts a story and the next person adds to it and on and on around the circle. It's a wonderful way to learn how to think with others. I'm so glad Donna asked for feedback from them about what they really liked and didn't like about both our plays and our comments at the Sunday panel. Jenny made a list of their comments. One comment that got to me—it was from Lionel, who was at the panel. "The cops use any excuse to arrest Black people. You can do all the guerrilla actions you want to teach people about racism, but when are we going to stop the cops from beating up on us? We have to change the whole stinking system." And the woman, Mei, who said, "I see you as chosen brothers and sisters. You allow your differences and you quarrel, but you're struggling to understand each other; you don't have ancestral rules you have to follow; you're creating your own ethical rules. I wish my whole blood family could see you perform."

I've been thinking about Hans' liquor store action and Lionel's comment that what we really need is to change the whole damn system, create one that doesn't beat up on Black people. But if we can do a dramatic action in a liquor store or a bank or a library, that will wake people up to injustice— racism, sexism, war—in some way, isn't that a beginning to create a more humane and just system? I would have loved it if students had come into my classroom at college and done some action—maybe showing how the subject being taught did or didn't help us live life better. The fact is, while we debate whether performance theater or so-called guerrilla actions are better at inspiring change, another Vietnamese and another U.S. soldier are dying. I can guess what John's response to any direct question about the war will be. "I hate war," he'll say. "But ask me again next year, Lucina. You guys are going to be around with your plays for a while, I hope. Maybe I'll have more answers next time."

6
Lucina's Reflections on Fire Dragon's Process

Lucina's Journal Entry. Tour: Thursday, April 6, 1967. I think of us sometimes as one big complex creature with all kinds of different parts. Timid parts, flamboyant parts, confused, clear parts. Each part needs its turn to break out and shine; no part invisible. One complicated being in different shades of tans. But we need an experience, a real out-of-body, ecstatic, no-more-boundaries-between-us experience, where our parts blend naturally, freely. Who needs the tension all fourteen of us bring?

Get real, Lucina. Our group is too self-conscious to surrender to each other in such a generous way. People think we're so together, so in sync. We know how to act like a team. People dig teamwork in sports and in theater; it's like, wow! We do play off one another, sometimes improvise. When someone miffs a line, we work with that. I don't think anyone but Marin was upset with the way Hugh and Courtney carried our Sacred Tree. She can be a perfectionist—I understand that, but we can't get hung up on our fuck-ups. Have to be flexible. I guess that's why I'm imagining us as one big awesome, sometimes awkward, many-faceted creature. Maybe I can come up with some exercises that would build on that idea. We already do mirroring exercises that build on each other's movements.

How can we inspire our audiences to fall in love with us? Inspire a feeling in the heart? We're asking people to think. When we articulate complex and controversial issues of the day, are we building a following? Look at rock and roll, rhythm and blues, even anti-war songs—they all have a beat that gets the emotions going. I mean when you see a rainbow or a cherry tree in bloom, do you analyze your emotions, or just feel them? We need to get people's emotions going with rhythm, beats, images. Inviting the audience to chant with us is good. We have to find more ways to connect with people's spirits. It's good to break the fourth wall, like when we do asides and invite the audience into our deep feelings, as if we were talking to a friend. I like it when Al says to the audience in the ecology play, "Too bad Joe sold his soul to an abusive system; he was my home boy," in a real sad voice.

We're trying to present a leftist, humanist, pacifist, and environmentalist sensibility to expose endless injustices. But it's like we're babies when it comes to deeply identifying with the rights of Black people, women, gays and lesbians. I can't even say that word "lesbian" without feeling I'm saying something so taboo. We all have emotions that we're not addressing yet about our work.

More and more we each have to find an experience inside ourself that can inform our emotions in the scene. Our current Choice really tries to portray a passionate pacifist, not a privileged draft dodger. And now we have to show the real life dilemma of young Black people, caught in the web of racist conscription. I pray we can do what Cheryl says is absolutely necessary if we're going to be a voice for everyone. We should have used some of our time here at Point College to start working with her on that. We're not organized enough yet—just groping with how to tour and improve Ghost Dance.

Something's going on with Hugh. He keeps himself separate in some way—I think it's his angst about how to portray Wovoka. The panel discussion with the New Point students and Professor Harmen's solution that we project portraits of Sioux and Paiute on the stage gave us great relief. She's given us the slides already from her history professor buddy. In our next performances of the Ghost Dance, we'll hold up a large white canvas sheet at the front of our playing area, both at the beginning and ending of the tribute, projecting the faces of actual Sioux and Paiute peoples on it, saying something like, "We wish to convey the tragic events of Wounded Knee in the name of Native people," and then say the names of those projected. We've rehearsed it already so hopefully Ghost Dance Tribute will now be better understood as our genuine effort to identify with and convey facts about Wounded Knee. Not us being disrespectful white kids, getting off play-acting wild Indians, or something. Still, it's a very complex balance. It should be the Sioux and Paiute themselves, rising up in resistance to the government's genocide, not us interpretating their tragic struggle. We're trying to evoke real emotions through a ritual enactment. And it's new for us, trying to honor (what's the best word to use?), an actual historical human being, Wovoka. He was a larger-than-life man determined to prevent the genocide of his tribes. I mean, isn't that what Martin Luther King is doing? Protect, dignify, lift up his people. How can a twenty-two-year-old privileged WASP be expected to portray the spiritual charisma of such a profound, middle-aged Paiute messiah and leader of the Ghost Dance Movement in a twenty-five minute scene? Are we expecting too much from Hugh? Maybe that student, José, was right. We need an Indigenous actor to portray Wovoka!

Hugh is really determined to give it a shot. He says he's been reading numerous accounts of the spiritual leader. And he's meditating on what qualities such a man must have. He told us that Martin Luther King came to his mind, so he felt he's found a living model to guide him. What more can he do but try to emulate Wovoka in some sort of believable way? He's so creative about it. Working with his musician's skills, expanding upon the fluid rhythm of his own fingers on the guitar—trying to extend that dexterity and alertness into all his limbs—so he can lead the Ghost Dance with the full fiber of his being and body.

Yes, Hugh! Dance Wovoka as an engaging presence. Pray that the spirit, hope, strength, courage of this great man will come into you as you move. Be a life force, a current, a magnet, attracting and directing energy. We're all trying to do that in our meditation exercises before we perform **Ghost Dance Tribute**.

We're all telling him what a good actor he is. But he's not just acting; he's empathizing, identifying with. Still, it's hard to know what's really going on with him. I hope it doesn't drive him crazy—evoking a superman part of the time; being a regular human being the rest of the time. I guess as long as he can take it, he'll be our Shaman. Though pretty soon we have to consider how else to present this dynamic force. That's our philosophy: be inventive as we try to inform our audiences.

If only we can electrify others with our stylized rituals and improvised scenes like exciting football plays do? That's a possible goal. We don't have the money the Beatles, the Rolling Stones, the Bee Gees have for their staging. We aren't the Broadway cast of **Cabaret** *or* **The Killing of Sister George**. *We aren't professional actors belonging to a union. (I wonder, do they have medical coverage?) We're not weekly wage earners. But we are cultural workers who report to our jobs each day.*

Fourteen troubadour-activists who share a common purpose, a small income and sometimes living quarters. We have no assurance of popular appeal, no monetary or public proof of our value, no job security, no backing from institutions, and certainly not government support. We've come together with hope that we can be a part of making a difference. I for one know, however, that the forces that brought us together can just as easily split us apart. No wonder we aren't that giant, together, complex creature that I imagine!

Louis reminds me that we already have one gig, one panel discussion, and one workshop that were incredible, under our belt. I think of us entering an exhilarating landscape, wheelin' across the land, unleashing new longings and possibilities. It's like the stage is our nomadic home. And though roles, actions, gestures, and dialogue are repeated, we're always finding new meanings and deeper understanding of our collective responsibilities.

7
Walking the Moon Together

The next tour stop, Friday, April 7, was on the Middleton campus in a suburban area near Albany, the state capitol. Was this why the buildings were larger and more modern than New Point's, Lucina wondered, and why it was an academic community in political upheaval? Faculty and students were contesting ROTC recruitment of freshmen and sophomores. Though Fire Dragon had contracted to perform *Choice* (the version still lacking portrayal of the Black experience in the military), the performance organizers swarmed the troupe upon arrival and requested they exclude it from the next night's program. College officials were in the process of eliminating academic credit for ROTC courses that very week, concluding that such a curriculum "didn't allow open discussion of the US role in Vietnam." A performance of *Choice* at that time might prevent a peaceful resolution to this new policy, given the various factions against it.

The troupe gladly conceded to the reasoning of their Arts and Ethics Coalition sponsors—"You don't fan unwanted flames"—and were thrilled to have the entire performance time freed up for their *Eco-Drama*. Addressing the health of the environment was an issue everyone could relate to.

The actors were quite aware that the campuses in their tour were in various stages of political unrest; they had to be responsive to the students' immediate needs in each situation. Fluidity was a main component of their street theater process! And since it appeared that the majority of Middleton students, like the faculty, were anti-war and anti-ROTC recruitment, maybe Fire Dragon could honor this campus' brave stand by creating an uplifting mood with their Saturday night performance. Thanks to Cheryl's immediate communication with the Drama Department they tightened up rough places in *Eco* and tossed out ideas for engaging the audience on the same stage they performed that night,

*****

When Marin and Lucina sounded the final beats on the red drum, marking the end of *Eco-Drama* that night, another spectacle burst forth, just as the troupe had envisioned.

Hans, Courtney, and Jenny flung their shirts and sweaters, shoes and socks toward the impassioned youths now encircling them onstage, all still chanting, "The earth needs our help! The Vietnamese need our help! Make peace not war! Build hope with love!" Yes, their audience definitely craved a celebration.

Lucina became a woman possessed. She felt raw, ancient sounds nudging her vocal chords, wanting freedom. Wolf howls crawled up her backbone, expanding her lungs, and exploded from her mouth. Then words, recognizable and disturbing, shot out. She blasphemed repressive systems, harsh rules, racist killers and the whole U.S. imperialist regime. With each "fuck you" her voice rose in pitch and intensity, struggling upward; like the mythical rope climber, she was reaching for the hole in the sky. A chorus of students to her left, then to her right, echoed each one of her oaths.

Hans took up the outcry. "Fuck the United States' killers in Vietnam! Fuck the pig cops who beat demonstrators! Fuck Madison Avenue mind-fuckers!" The chorus hollered on: "Fuck Johnson! Fuck McNamara!" Then another group from the audience stood and hollered out, "Bravo! Bravo to Middleton! Bravo for taking an anti-war stand!"

Jenny, as if hearing a divine signal, flung her tie-dyed shirt (a gift from Trish who'd stayed with the actors at the Yellow Farm) to the four winds. In a tan-colored leotard, she seemed naked. Moving to center stage with large sweeping arcs, she enticed those around her to arc and carve the space as well. Dawn spun near her, rapping a tambourine in intricate rhythms on her elbows, hips, knees. Jack slithered snake-like around their pulsing bodies toward the red drum. He would be its guardian tonight. Yet even as he lurched toward it, it moved, slipping from his sight. *Was someone trying to steal their sacred drum? There it was torpedoing toward the lobby; thieves must be passing it overhead as fast as they could.*

Jack followed the precious instrument like a laser beam. He spotted it again, surfacing near the swinging doors at the back of the auditorium. He sprang forward and plucked it from the arms of its kidnapper. No longer snake but panther, he welded the drum to his chest, reversed direction and plunged through the throbbing crowd back to the stage.

Rooted onstage next to Jenny and Dawn, he began to drum. Never had he punctuated Jenny's dance with such intricate rhythms. Her fluttering fingers, pulsating arms, and rapping feet, enhanced his sounds as Dawn's tambourine laced dancer and drummer together. Jack riffed back, embellishing with ever-new patterns. The three of them merged their rhythmic expression into one deepening pulse, harnessing the staccato claps of the crowd.

"We're doing natural crowd control," Jack shouted to Jenny, who in her ecstatic state heard but had no words to return. *This is drum power,* he said to himself.

Hans, an awkward creature in jock shorts and undershirt, emerged beside Jenny. He circled about her with small, jutting motions. The often confident young man looked terribly fragile. In contrast, Jenny crystallized into a svelte vamp. Lucina, still shouting an extravagance of "Fuck you!" ended with "Fuck clothes!" She tore off her pants and T-shirt, as if one more second of enduring them would mean suffocation. She danced bare-breasted as more and more bodies were freed of cloth.

Courtney, performing un-Courtney-like movements, swayed hesitantly and bare-chested beside Jack, his body apologizing for its existence. Harmonica glued to his mouth, Courtney pierced Jack's beats with high-pitched birdcalls. He was finding himself in this wild, delicious pandemonium.

More students joined those already on the stage, deliriously happy to rid themselves of shirts, jackets, pants, skirts, shoes, and socks. With the stage packed, there was no longer room for sweeping arms, creative leaps and jumps. But to be separate was unbearable. Limbs reached for limbs until all arms of the vibrating monster intertwined. Trembling bodies clung and breathed in life, jelling slowly into one enormous, rocking organism.

A last rush of students claimed the creaky stage, abandoning cramped aisles and worn seats. They climbed out of the crevices of their bodies, shattered their restraints and walked on air. It seemed that this shaking, awkward monster, desperate to abandon its weight, would slip up the walls, lift the rooftop, take flight.

Then a sound entered the space, as if an invisible conductor had decided, "Enough from the chorus—bring in the soloist!" Enter now a lone creature, crooning forth in alto voice.

The sea of bodies bent outward as the young Black woman, a fury of hair haloing her hypnotic voice, sang herself across the stage. The resonating Oms from her throat inspired chanting responses spiraling around her. Time, blood pressures, thoughts, and heartbeats slowed as her voice deepened with the humming crowd. Would the celebration spend itself with her exit?

No! New drumbeats surged. Heartbeats quickened. Suddenly, motion again! Holding hands, dancers circled Jenny, who'd first freed them from restraint, as long strands of her hair stroked the air around them. Drum and bamboo flute joined in, all weaving a blanket of love.

*****

A sudden rip in this humming cocoon! At the back of the auditorium, desperation bruised the air. A young man dressed in army fatigues locked his eyes like menacing binoculars on Jenny and the rosette of naked bodies on the stage around her.

"What is this fuckin' bullshit?" he sputtered. "Why is she dancing up there, naked, like a slut?" As if pulled by a force outside his control, he whipped his taut body to the aisle. Ramming himself through bone and flesh, he made his way to the stage, to the naked woman searing his brain. *He must save her! She didn't know what she was doing.* "Don't do this!" he managed, imagining his voice a net surrounding her. *Could she hear him?* He raised his hand, imagining a gun there; he would blast this evil display apart. *She heard!* She came toward him.

"What's the matter with you, brother?"

Had she said that?

"It's all right. Come. Join us. We're the soul—the soul of our country. This is only the beginning, my friend."

Then she was gone, swallowed up by the others. The crowd was pushing on him, crushing him. He couldn't breathe. *No! This wasn't right! He would fight. Stand tall. Like the man in the photograph, saluting, proud. His dad, forever his soldier dad. His dad in the photograph had served his country like a man, and he would too. He would never betray his dad.*

His binocular eyes tore away from the stage; his metallic body marched back down the aisle. A bullet aimed for an exit. He would do that, die for his dad. He would kill for his country. Already a dead soldier, he broke through the auditorium doors into the night.

*****

***Lucina's Journal Entry. Tour: Sunday, April 9, 1967. Eco-Drama** was thrilling last night at Middleton. I just reread my last entry—it's like my vision of us as a mythical monster, joining differences, came true. We moved an entire audience to action! Everything clicked. Our scenes of payoff between corporate CEOs, government agencies, and the inspectors of hazardous waste were hopped up by ominous, funereal drumbeats. Louis and Al were really creepy as Tarnished Politicians. Just four of us playing the Impassioned Environmentalists were enough. We showed how people that are lied to over and over again can turn anger into action. The students dug it. I couldn't believe the foot stomping and catcalls.*

Our slides of people, fish, animals, and vegetation dying from polluted water, chemically saturated foods, ozone-depleted air, acid rain, and the devastation caused by tornadoes, floods, hurricanes, wild fires (with comments about what causes them) are terrifying. Since we can't decry pollution and at the same time blast our audience with that theatrical smoke-screen stuff, using dry ice for the "smoke" of chemical waste is a much better idea.

We put the audience into an incredible silence before our global explosion and blackout. I don't think of us as control freaks, but we really held their attention. I heard a lot of gasps when we moved in slow motion to the front of the stage, then down the steps into the audience, chanting, "The earth needs our help. The earth needs our help." They took up that chant like starved people.

In the after performance fervor—God, did I holler! Did the stage and auditorium shake! We were all exalting in a great spiritual reunion, I thought. I'll never forget that unearthly humming when that enchanting, incanting woman escorted us all to heaven. And Jenny? She danced us to the stars. We rocketed to the moon for sure. And I wasn't even stoned. And Louis, I can't believe he missed this great reunion, this great rocking toward Freedom. My man was taking care of us, while we danced around naked, showing off and acting out. He was in the student union having coffee with our sponsors, the Arts and Ethics Coalition, getting our paycheck for the performance. I wonder if he wishes now that he hadn't offered to do this work. He said it's his responsibility to make sure our contract is honored. But if something gets fucked up with that, Louis will get blamed. Well, God almighty! Maybe revolutions are run by people like Louis, people who do the nitty-gritty work of making sure our labor is fairly paid for. Probably not by those of us who need to walk on the moon and dance to the stars.

8
Reviews

In the back seat of Isadora, Lucina and Louis scoured the *Middleton Daily* for a review of the evening's performance. This would be a first, seeing themselves in print outside of New York City. In the corner of the Daily Living section they found a small article signed by Daniel Crisp with no further identification.

"Not So Radical Theater" by Daniel Crisp

Nothing unusual happened at the performance of Fire Dragon Street Theater last night. There was no inciting to riot, no call to arms or shedding of blood ("pouring in whirlpools fierce," Blake's The Four Zoas). But the students were receptive to an agitprop display on environmental concerns by a roving political theater band.

"What bullshit!" Lucina's eyes flared with disbelief. "It's like the guy never came to our show. Or he did, and he couldn't accept our great reception."

"Or he did come and that pro-war, pro-ROTC paper paid him extra to pan us," Louis clipped.

69

"World's shortest review. Panned in three sentences, " Al snarled and clenched the steering wheel.

"What a jerk!" Marin grumbled beside him. "It was an incredible response by the audience! Why are there always repressive reactions to a show of solidarity?"

"You're right, Marin. Deniers of truth," Louis chimed in. "And the Dow Chemical Company doesn't make napalm and Johnson didn't escalate the bombing. Assholes keep a blind eye so they don't have to change their smug lives. We need to write our own reviews!"

Courtney in the back beside Lucina hung his head out the window. "How far is this Wellingfield place? I don't feel so good," he whined into the wind.

Lucina patted his back. "You did good last night, babe," she said softly.

"Weren't Jenny and Dawn incredible?" Marin piped up. "Dawn was a Jezebel with that tambourine."

"Maybe Dawn was a Jezebel, but Jenny was a showoff!" Courtney, head back in the van, was ranting now. "And some jerk stepped on Hugh's toe; it's black and blue. That's why he wasn't dancing."

"Come on, Courtney," Marin shot back. "Let's give ourselves credit—we were catalysts for those students!"

Louis, oblivious to the comments flying around him, imagined Daniel Crisp morph into a cartoon bully with button eyes. "We put our guts out there and all we get back is this schmuck's turd!" he muttered.

Lucina was back on the whirling stage. *Why hadn't anyone in the group mentioned her "fuck this, fuck that" bit? Had she embarrassed them?*

Louis, back to his newspaper, spotted a report on the Ia Drang Valley bombing. "My god! We bombed our own men!" He read the news brief out loud, silencing the others.

"Killers! What do they expect?" Marin groaned in the same tone she'd used for Daniel Crisp. Suddenly she barked out, "Al, turn to the right! That's our road!" The passengers tensed up as the van swerved onto the Wellingfield exit.

"Louis, that's so awful." Lucina recalled a terrifying photo in the *New York Times*: a soldier watching his flesh fall away from his arm bone, *like rotten papier maché,* she had thought. She snuggled against Louis' chest, wanting to hide.

*****

Behind them in Jenny's Dodge Dart, Jack spotted another review printed that morning in the college newspaper. "Listen to this, guys: 'Street Theater Wows Student Audience. Last night's performance of New York City's Fire Dragon Street Theater used a calculated yet artful buildup of hypnotic images to give an investigative exposé of the consequences our everyday choices have on the environment.'"

"Hold it, Jack," Jenny clipped. "I'm looking for our road sign. Can't see the van anymore."

"There! To the right!" Hans' fist hit the side window. "The van's way up there."

Jenny maneuvered the car with ease. "Thanks, sweet. We're on our way. Though I hate going right to get there."

Hans was out of sorts. His Jenny had stripped and strutted after their performance, almost bare naked! He felt like crying or scolding her.

"I'll read aloud to myself," Jack mumbled audibly. "'There are three aspects to becoming humane: having awareness of the impact of our actions; developing compassion for all life forms; and then acting with conscious consideration to increase quality of life for all. The message I came home with last night: those of us who decry being political as if we might be soiling our soul must realize that our silence in fact supports destruction.

Their anti-war drama, *Choice*, which they did not perform last night, but which I was lucky enough to see in New York City, carries this underlying theme: the horror of silence. I quote the protagonist, Sam: "Silence is the sound of pellets exploding bone, of napalm charring flesh, the murder of a Vietnamese mother and child, the slaughter of young men in a senseless war." The battleground focused on in last night's performance was not Vietnam, but our Earth-home, in their mixed media revelation *Eco-Drama*.' Wow!" Jack enthused loudly. "She really dug us."

"Jack, please read louder," Jenny requested. "I want to hear it, but I'm trying to keep my eye on the van."

"'I bow down to this group and others like them,'" Jack spoke out. "'They are helping to clear away the smog of misinformation our government and our institutions would rain down upon us. We are all inhabitants of the same planet and we have to live and work here in solidarity. *Choice* addresses individual ethical choices, while *Eco-Drama* is a call to arms of all Earth's citizens to save our planet and our children. This message, reinforced scene by scene, was finalized in the last scene, a brilliant transformation. No wonder the students of Middleton erupted for an hour afterward in passionate solidarity with the actors' brilliant appeal to tune into our Earth-home with more responsible caretaking. The work now is to harness all that energy into education and action. Though our students and faculty are already at the forefront of making our university a place of open, healthy dialogue, Fire Dragon Street Theater showed the dire need for global action in building a healthy, safe world for all.'"

"That's a reference to their ROTC issue, I bet," Jenny enthused. "Who wrote it?"

"I'm not done." Jack read on, "'As a circle of actors chanted, 'The Earth needs our help! The Earth needs our help!' a series of transforming images were projected. A cloud of radioactive nuclear waste turns into a sky filled with tears. The tears change into large, clear raindrops, which water the earth and nourish seeds. Suddenly the entire stage is covered with tiny, twinkling flowers—or are they stars?—also created by a series of projections. This scene was one I will never forget. Our colleges ought to be places where we lose sight of neither outrage nor wonder, feelings so beautifully expressed by this group.'"

"My god!" Marlene who'd been listening with eyes shut, sat upright and pulled the paper from Jack. "She's brilliant. It's signed by Laurie Becker, graduate student, Theater Arts Department at SUNY, Middleton. Of course, who else but a woman!"

"What an angel!" Jenny tried to imagine a face for Laurie Becker.

"She's an activist, like us," Marlene added.

"Goddamn!" Jack jerked the paper back to his chest. "I love you, Laurie Becker!"

9

Drama in the College Cafeteria

At Wellingfield, a small, innovative, and moneyed liberal arts college in the outskirts of Syracuse, the troupe did a Sunday night performance of *Choice,* focused on Sam's story of draft resistance. It had been requested by the Drama Department and was meant for theater majors interested in contemporary theater forms.

Cheryl's anger was increasing with the play's flaw: there was still no reference to the military's racist treatment of Black soldiers. *When were they going to incorporate her cousin Nelson's story! The changes he went through. Proud to have signed up as a GI, then a few months later, an anti-war soldier. That's the story that had to be told!*

Reluctantly, she agreed to introduce *Choice,* explaining that their plays were always works-in-progress. "What we're performing tonight depicts only a young white man's moral struggle with signing up to kill for his country. A young Black man's experience as a soldier in 'Nam is in rehearsal...our next performance will deal with his resistance." Her statement was received first by silence and then by a burst of applause. Her comments made the students question: how many of the plays in their drama department curriculum left out their own experiences?

After the performance, a handful of Black students gathered around Cheryl, begging her for suggestions on how to include their personal experiences in a street play, or guerrilla action.

"Be direct," she told them "Tell your real-life stories and act them out, like we're doing in our women's plays. Get an Activists' Theater Club going here with drama majors involved," she asserted. "I'll give you some notes on guerrilla theater tactics." She had no clue that her theater comrade, Dawn, would enact her feelings in a gutsy guerrilla action the next day.

*****

After a leisurely Monday lunch in the student cafeteria, most of the theater troupe had headed to their dorm rooms to rest and pack up for their scheduled early evening departure for Richdale College, where they would next perform. Originally a private Christian school, it was now a small liberal arts college near Ithaca. Only Dawn, Hans, and Jenny lingered behind to talk with two Wellingfield students.

Active in student politics and the drama club, Don, a sophomore, and Becky, a freshman, were very impressed how Fire Dragon used drama to express political complexities. The Sunday evening performance of *Choice* had challenged their assumption that a political science major was more practical than a drama major for obtaining work, though neither held a guarantee.

Don, husky like a football player, spoke with kid-like wonder. "You guys are making a living, right—doing this political stuff?"

"Sometimes!" Dawn snickered.

Becky, brushing at her bangs of fine blond hair, had a wide-eyed kind of shyness: "You must be so close to each other—it's like you're a family—not a regular one. Oh, I can't say what I mean."

"That's okay," Jenny said good-naturedly, smiling warmly at them both. "People have trouble understanding me because I have to dance my feelings."

Hans swung his arm around her, glad there had been no freak-out like at Wellington. "Well, I sure understand her," he quipped proudly.

Becky, glad to be understood, replied eagerly, "Dancing is like painting the air with beautiful pictures."

"Yeah, I can see that," Don added.

"I used to paint pictures and teach art," Jenny continued. "Now I like to dance." She looked at Hans, waiting for him to comment. *Why did he seem antsy? And Dawn too.*

"We do an exercise in drama club where we speak our parts as we dance," Becky enthused.

Hans opened a pack of cigarettes slowly, trying to stop the trembling in his hands. *It'd be just like Jenny to tell them about Middleton!*

"Hans is from Denmark!" Jenny announced suddenly. "Left college after two years. Dawn is a college dropout. I forgot, Dawn, what college did you go to?"

Dawn jerked her slouched body forward. "University of California at Davis," she mumbled, her mind already groping for how she might carry it off, an action to blow people's minds.

Hans, cigarette now lit, was ready to talk. "I learned more from my studies in two years than the students do here in five." He drew in slowly, and then blew a shaft of smoke over Becky and Don.

Don puzzled, "They cram in more subjects?"

Jenny cringed. *Why can't he just talk with people, not at*

them? He'll never get over his humiliation—being kicked out of college. Here Becky and Don are so eager to talk with us. She turned away from their group to scan the tables of students near-by. Heated banter punctuated the air a few feet away.

"We only have three universities in Denmark," Hans continued. "It's an honor and responsibility to attend one."

Jenny kicked at his feet under the table. *Be nice, Hans—*

"College is hard for me," Becky offered, seemingly oblivious of Jenny's discomfort, Hans' defensiveness, and Dawn's distancing.

"It's just different there, Hans," Jenny smiled apologetically. "So tell us, what play is your drama club working on?"

Suddenly a shout from the table nearby: "Hey! The hippies are in town." A thin man with a butch haircut and black-rimmed glasses pointed directly at Hans. His face, pitted from acne, twisted with anger. "The big revolutionaries are going to change the world." He turned to two others, obviously sidekicks, who echoed his taunts. The three spat out animal sounds and beat their fists on the table.

Don and Becky exchanged shrugs and knowing looks. Don said, "The assholes are at it again."

With no response coming from his objects of ridicule, the bully started up again. "You think you're going to change anybody with that artsy-fartsy crap?" By now he had captured the attention of people from other tables. Voiced objections to the bully's taunts rose up. Several students began crowding around the hecklers' table. Fired up by the attention, the antag-onists shouted above the ruckus. "No pseudo-commie bastard's gonna preach at us," they bleated.

"You talking about us, man?" Hans shouted out. "Why you don't have the guts to come over here. You're jerkin off in front of everybody and that's not nice." He stood abruptly to face his challengers, cigarette clamped between his tight lips.

Ashes dropped onto Jenny's arm. As she stretched to pull him back down, the ashes fell away.

Hans moved out of her grasp, crossed his arms in front of his chest, and glared at his challengers, the cigarette still burning in his mouth.

"Please, Hans, ignore them. He's some weirdo." She pawed at his belt; again he pulled away, holding his aggressive stance.

"That's Richard Berman," Don whispered, his mouth and brow now tightening with concern. "Our campus dis-or-ganizer. He keeps trouble stirred up, that's for sure. He thinks SDS has gone soft. Hates art and artists—'opiate of the people' kind of thing—so he says he's starting a Marxist group. A fascist group, really." Torn between standing up with Hans or staying put, Don's hands stayed pressed down on the table. "Don't even try to talk to him, Hans."

"Don's right," Becky added. "He doesn't talk. He puts down. One-upmanship."

"Who are his lackeys?" Jenny asked. "I don't like this at all."

"Maybe we should all leave together," Becky whispered.

In an abrupt change of mind, Hans took his seat and ground his cigarette butt in the ashtray. "So, the creep doesn't think street theater is where it's at," he snarled.

Jenny shrugged with impatience. *Now Hans was defending street theater! But Becky was right; they should all get up and just leave. But what was Dawn doing, for god's sake? Why was she making slash marks with a red pen on several napkins? She's gone bonkers!*

Jenny put her hand on Dawn's shoulder. "We can leave, Dawn."

Dawn didn't hear her. She was waving one of her large napkins like a flag and shouting at Berman, ten feet away. "What are they doing to my villages?" she shrieked. She stood up, waving her napkin flag.

Jenny saw a smile creep over Hans' face. *Were these two oddball pals of hers in cahoots?*

Hans squawked, "What is Dawn doing?"

So, he didn't know either?

Dawn went into a slow motion mime. She stepped up on her chair, mounted the table and unfurled one white napkin after another filled with marks in red ink. Were they words? A sudden rattle of pans from the kitchen seemed to accompany her.

Jenny was embarrassed; the people around them seemed frightened. Even the bullies looked nervous. Served them right.

"The houses…in my village…bombed." Dawn's high-pitched words singed the air. Nervous laughter spilled from one table and spread to the next, and the next. Kitchen doors opened. A young man, red bandanna around his forehead, slapped a tray of dishes down on the counter in front of him. "What the hell?" he gasped. His eyes targeted Dawn.

Dawn's face was now a mask of compressed horror, anguish, and disbelief. "My home is on fire! Smart bombs kill my babies! Napalm bombs. Hate bombs. U.S. military bombs." Her voice, unreal, scorching, branded the silence. "You bastards burnt up my babies."

A row of kitchen workers in white aprons stood frozen in front of the steel coffee urns. "Is she for real?" mouthed one.

Dawn pulled a lighter from her pocket. In seconds, its tiny flame licked at the word scratchings on the napkin-flags clutched in her hand.

"Why's she doing this?" a voice cried out. "What's she doing?" another voice whined. "She's a nut," yelled a third. Nobody moved.

Flames from the napkin tongued the air. Dawn shrieked out again: "They are burning my babies alive with napalm!" When it was fully ablaze, she dropped it to her feet. Then she lit another napkin, and another.

Hans supported her, holding her ankles; he would not let her fall. Now Jenny had Hans by the shoulders. Don and Becky stood with them, mouths agape. Berman and his cronies hunched in their chairs, ashen-faced. Dawn had upstaged them!

"She's doing 'Nam," came a voice from somewhere. "She's from the street theater group that performed in Dalton Hall last night. She's doing 'Nam." A deep, somber, thick sound came from the back, near the carts filled with dirty dishes. One of the workers, an older Puerto Rican woman, moaned in empathy. Another woman mounted her table, and held a lighter to her napkin. "They're burning babies with napalm," she echoed in a deep, penetrating voice.

By the exit doors, an older man, perhaps a professor, mounted his table. "The U.S. military is burning children," he declared. He too lit a napkin.

Another and yet another lit their napkins, crying out, "Shame. The U.S. army is burning children!"

From the kitchen came others carrying bowls and small buckets of water to the tables. They quickly scooped the still flaming napkins into water. Still others poured water on the table tops to smother falling pieces of flaming paper. Chants and smoke created an eerie atmosphere of mourning.

The table near Dawn was empty. Berman and his cronies had vanished.

Through the wails, a new sound. Higher pitched, more penetrating, mechanical. The smoke alarm.

A voice screamed out, "Let's go to the president's house!" A shrill response: "Let's build fires on the lawn!"

A quieter voice moaned, "We must do something! Do something!"

"This we can do," another intoned.

*****

Students flowed out of the cafeteria, past black lampposts, bushes of forsythia and lilac. Gray arabesques of smoke swirled among yellow and purple clusters, around the marchers, then disappeared into the deep blue dusk. Words rose up in the distance, a chant, a hymn. "Light a fire for peace" filled the evening air.

Jenny and Hans, with Dawn sandwiched between them, scooted away from the crowd. "Dawn!" Hans gasped. "Incredible!" Chanting was heard in the distance. With his free hand, he zipped up his army jacket. "Let's cut out of here fast!"

Grasping her elbows, they ran along the row of parked cars in the cafeteria parking lot, looking for the Dart.

Jenny hugged in closer to Dawn. "Should we have tried to stop them from going to the president's house, Hans?" They were at Jenny's car.

"Get in," Hans snapped.

Seconds later they were speeding to the dorms, Jenny clamping the wheel. "There's going to be talk about who started it," she said. "Could be bad trouble. What should we do?"

"We never sent them to the president's house. Jenny, we can't tell anyone what happened in the cafeteria. It could be the end for me." His lips were again clamped on a cigarette.

"It's a promise now," Dawn said. "A prayer." Her voice, distant and breathy. "They won't hurt anyone."

Hans patted her knee. "Are you okay, Dawn? It's our secret, that's all."

Jenny felt the seat tremble underneath her. Her hands gripped the wheel more tightly. She saw Dawn's head flying back, her body shaking.

"Oh, my god, my god," Dawn cried, between short gasping sounds. "I can't believe I did that! The red slashes, the flames. It meant my rage, our rage has to be reckoned with." She didn't comprehend yet that by taking center stage on that modest cafeteria table and doing what she did, she'd turned Hans into a back-seat radical, in awe of her while she single-handedly start-ed a riot.

"You were so beautiful!" Hans beamed.

"Fantastic!" Jenny pronounced, screeching the car to a halt in front of a box-like building.

"I had to do something in my way. I can't talk like you guys." Dawn pulled herself up, out of the car, her face beaming.

Jenny slowly retrieved the key from the ignition, ex-hausted. "I wish I could do something that gutsy." Her glazed eyes searched Hans' awestruck face.

10
The Women Work Together

They had a few days at Richdale College for free time and rehearsals before the Friday night performance. The women would perform their play, *Moments of Pain/Moments of Gain*, composed of a series of short dramas, each focusing on an extraordinary event in one of the women's lives. They planned to do three or four of the dramas at each performance of the play on tour. They hoped that the Richdale women students, no longer bound by the strict Christian teachings the college was once known for, would welcome their exploratory styles. This would be followed by *Ghost Dance* now beginning and ending with the projections of Sioux and Paiute faces on a large canvas screen held by two actors, accompanied by stating the names of those projected and an explanation of Fire Dragon's intent in presenting this Testimonial. The epilogue, Blood on Their Hands remained unchanged, in spite of Professor John Marin's advice not to offend the audience.

As Donna readied herself for a rehearsal with the women on Tuesday morning, Jim called out to her, "What's with Dawn? I don't know, but something's different about her. Is she working okay with you girls?"

He said "girls" instead of "women" to rib me, Donna decided. *He's just jealous that I and the other women are so excited about our new play.*

She mumbled back, "What are you saying about Dawn?" She flashed back to their puppet tours—*just the two of us setting up shows and performing from the back of our station wagon. He never talked to me about other women, just had eyes for me, he said. But he's right—Dawn is changing, "coming out of her shell" is how Cheryl puts it. The group thing must be energizing her or maybe she's soaking up Hans' bravado. Well, Jimmy and I both need to adjust as well.*

When he brought Dawn up again—"She's quite a looker when she isn't sullen"—Donna rushed off without a goodbye.

By Tuesday evening she'd had enough of hearing about Dawn's "inner wisdom and glowing eyes."

"What's this thing you have for Dawn, for god's sake, Jim? You're acting like a lovesick puppy."

He sank down on their bed in the dorm room and hugged himself protectively. "Why are you women working alone so much?" he whined. "Segregation's illegal, you know." He'd been wondering, *Maybe he wasn't meant for this Fire Dragon business, anyway. A group within a group? What is that? Too many needs being thrown about!*

Donna felt tension growing inside her. *I was right! It's not just about Dawn. He's obsessed with all of the women, including me. I have to talk to him.*

"Listen, honey. We're more honest when we're away from you guys. If we're more honest, then you can be, too. Just be open to our needs. That's what this tour's about—opening up to other people's needs. I want to be happy working with the women."

That afternoon Jim and Donna sat on the grass in front of the administration building with Jack, who had been meditating, and had a long talk about energy circles and psychic expansion. In the middle of Jack's explanation of "raising one's chi," Jim blurted out, "I feel like a wimp, getting bent out of shape just because the women are working without us."

Donna nodded at him, glad he was finally opening up to one of the guys.

"You know, man, why don't us guys do our thing too." Jack gave Jim a playful slap on the back. "We can go running and then do meditation exercises. That'll make us not care what the gals are up to. It's all about feeling good about ourselves!"

"I'm game for anything you can recommend that calms me down, Jack. I heard about that far-out moon ritual you led at that incredible-sounding place, Yellow Farm Commune, or whatever it was called. I should call you Guru Jack. Why do you think I'm hung up on Dawn? It's like I want some of her inner light or something."

"I'm no guru, man—though I'm a damn good yoga teacher—but I can advise you. What's wrong with wanting to be like Dawn? We can all inspire each other to be better people, you know."

Donna was a bit miffed. *Jack's supporting Jim's obsession with Dawn? Well, if he can help him, I sure can't.* "I thought you two were getting together with Hugh and Courtney to work on some songs. You guys do great music together."

Jim stayed silent as she patted Jack's arm. "I really like you, Jack. You don't play games."

Jim was back. "So, Jack's a better man than me, honey?"

"Oh, sweetie, you're impossible! Definitely, on the red drum. Who can forget Jack's drumming at Middleton?" There was a victory lilt in Donna's voice.

"Middleton? Come on," Jim whined. "We were out of our minds!"

"What's going on with you two?" Jack gave them each a thoughtful look, then tossed his cap at Jim. "Let's get together for some meditation tomorrow, man. Okay?"

After checking for Donna's response, Jim nodded hesitantly. "Have you spoken to your girlfriend, Joan, while we've been on tour, Jack? Is she good about you going off by yourself?"

"Sure. She's at the Ashram near Hunter Mountain. It's north of Woodstock. Got her own thing going there."

"She's incredibly disciplined," Donna said. "What's her trick?"

"Practice," Jack said.

Jim threw himself back on the grass and looked through the leaves of the giant oak, spreading over them. "Jeez, it's beautiful today. April is usually rainy—I wonder if our earth is warming up."

Jack, laying back as well, turned to Jim: "Tonight, for twenty minutes before you go to sleep, light a candle," he instructed. "Sit in front of it and let your mind go wherever it wants, then start concentrating on your breathing."

"I guess I should do that every time Donna's off with her girlfriends," Jim muttered.

Comforted by the men's soft voices, Donna's mind relaxed.

"Try it—tell me what happens, Jim."

"Okay, Doc Jack."

"I specialize in con-ray, consciousness raising without LSD."

"So, doesn't the women's club get to you too, doc?"

Their voices had blurred into one drone. Then suddenly an electric flash sped past Donna's eyes. She imagined a spark flying from Jim to Jack. It was a wink! They were in cahoots, disrespecting her with a wink.

*****

That wink lingered on. Had it really happened? Coincidentally, the women's rehearsals that week were focusing on Jenny's scene which featured winks; in fact, *Wink* was the name of her play. They had to analyze the meaning of that strange, tiny gesture.

Donna remembered Jenny recapping her play to the new women, Dawn, Cheryl, and herself, as it'd been performed at the Yellow Farm the summer before: "I played myself being interviewed for art teacher in a small private school by the headmaster and the chairperson of the Art Department. When they asked me to discuss projects I'd like to do with the youngsters, I told them I wanted to revamp the intimidating master-apprentice approach to teaching, work alongside my students. And that's when this weird wink flies back and forth between them, along with sarcastic comments like, 'What d'ya know—a veritable Renaissance lady.' It felt like something creepy, hostile, was brushing against my face!"

Winks had never been a big deal for Donna before she heard about Jenny's play. But now she understood how those subtle, or not so subtle gestures could show the bonding of two at the expense or exclusion of a third. Jenny's interviewers hated her open enthusiasm and passionate approach to teaching; their winking was nasty, hateful. But why would Jim and Jack, her partner and her acting buddy, use that vapid gesture? Jenny's Winking Men were mean, macho bastards. But her comrades, Jim and Jack? Spooky!

Lucina had another take on winking at the rehearsals. Her mother would wink at her during some prickly altercations with her dad. She'd felt that her mother's wink was meant as an unstated understanding between them, a gentle reminder: her father just didn't know how to deal with emotions. So Lucina should stay cool!

But to Donna, a wink was weird. She'd never thought of Jack, the New Age mediator, as a winking type. Maybe she'd only imagined them winking; she hadn't actually seen some kind of subtle male bonding between them. Still, it was obvious: all the men were thrown by how much the women were getting off on working together. They were jealous, threatened maybe? If the women had gone off to knit or shop, that would be okay. No winks for that! Maybe she should meditate as well. Not let the guys' jealousy bend her out of shape, too.

11

Jenny's Play

By Wednesday the women have Jenny's play ready to perform. After a short welcome to the students, Jenny is to discuss how the women's play, *Moments of Pain/Moments of Gain*, is their form of consciousness raising, an organizing tool started recently by the feminist group New York Radical Women.

"Women need to wake up and articulate what upsets us in this male-centered society," Jenny will say. "We're doing it through drama. Here's how: We take turns remembering painful experiences that demean us, hold us back. While we tell our stories as honestly, as clearly as we can, our sister actors improvise dramatic scenes to illustrate. When we put our specific oppressions out there, we see better how we can change the situation, stop blaming ourselves, and gain self-respect. Let me tell you—making it clear to the men in our troupe that we need to work alone as well as with them, is a major CR action. They're still trying to get what we're about. So, here's my story. It's called *Wink*. A wink means more than you might think. I sure learned that when I was interviewing for a job I thought I wanted."

No props are needed for this scene. Cheryl and Lucina, as male Headmaster and Art Director of an upscale children's school, are dressed in men's shirts and ties over their leotards.

91

They approach Jenny with stiff handshakes. A realistic mood quickly turns into a surreal farce.

Jenny, portraying herself, undergoes a humiliating interview. Her genuine responses to their questions are ignored, as exaggerated winking between the two men exposes increasing disdain for her.

Cheryl and Lucina preen and parade grotesquely, all the while winking and blinking nonstop to mock the interviewee. (Marin, director of the scene, explained: "These exaggerated facial expressions clearly expose how Jenny is being duped and humiliated. All those subtle winks coming our way can actually foretell more demeaning act, like spitting on us. We're showing hatred of women in action. Especially hatred of experienced, articulate women."

Even though Marin acknowledged there might be a supportive type of wink, as Lucina described experiencing with her mother, Jenny's *Wink* would focus on the inherent and often hidden disdain in the gesture. Marin's keen focus on seemingly innocuous words and actions was becoming part of the Fire Dragon women's revelatory style: use of exaggerated gestures to expose blatant sexism and misogyny, often hidden in men's words and body language.

When the scene switches abruptly back to realistic mode, showing Jenny as still the innocent, unaware woman openly sharing her observations and successes as a professional artist, blindly hoping to win the two men's approval, the Art Department chairman no longer even feigns interest in hiring her. He becomes overtly antagonistic: "Madam, our students would make mincemeat out of you in seconds. They need to be disciplined, not coddled!" His statement rings out as pompous and a threat.

As Jenny suffers through more vicious eye-batting and blatant disregard of her resumé and credentials, Dawn and Mar-

lene, protective Wonder Women in capes, swoop down to res-
cue her. As the scene ends, the Winking Men rush her off stage,
shouting, "Don't call us and we'll never call you!"

Jenny then returns center stage to make a final comment
to the audience. "As you young people know, job interviews
can be intimidating. How do we deal with that? We have to
prepare ourselves ahead of time. Do the research. Who will
be interviewing you? Who have they hired in the past? How
are the other employees treated? In other words, interview the
interviewer. Do role-play exercises, and a mock interview with a
friend when you have the information. Be prepared and avoid the
abusive situation I went through. My gain here? I finally found
a student-oriented school to teach at. But if I'd done research
from the get-go, I wouldn't have put myself in that humiliating
experience."

The women agreed: Marin's directing had brilliantly
used macabre humor to dissect and illuminate blatant male
power plays. Every woman had to be sensitized to the misogyny
inherent in a patriarchal system and then do something to
change it.

*****

Donna, especially moved by Marin's grasp on the whole
thing, admitted in rehearsal, "If I'd been directing, I probably
would have fastened on what Jenny could have done to ingra-
tiate herself to the male interviewers. I still have to learn how
to speak up immediately when guys put me down." With this
realization, she fantasized caricaturing Jim and Jack's faces in
masks; each would have a slit mouth and one tightly closed eye,
caught in a frozen, grotesque wink. But had they really winked
at one another as she imagined? The women needed to talk more
about how the guys' envy toward their work was affecting them.
One thing she knew for sure—she would never ever wink at
anyone again.

12
Lucina's Play, *Markings*

Now that *Wink* was set, they worked on Lucina's story. They had started working on *Markings* the previous winter. Her revelatory moment was actually an anguished period of several hours during which she unwittingly exposed her mother's fear of wrinkles (and anger with Lucina) through the act of drawing her. Her mother marked up the drawings after Lucina had carefully placed them in her suitcase. Before the Richdale rehearsals, four scenes for *Markings* had been developed with Lucina playing herself and Marin playing her mother.

Scene 1: Lucina, daughter, sketches Mother in what appears to be a very needed warm moment between them. To her parents' alarm, Lucina has been living unmarried with Louis; she hasn't told them that she has stopped sculpting and is doing anti-war protests.

Scene 2: After storing the drawings in her suitcase, Lucina, home for a weekend visit, takes a walk. Then, sensing something amiss, she races back to her parents' house.

Scene 3: Lucina goes to the suitcase where her drawings were stored and is shocked to find check marks in red ink carefully placed on several face lines. "Wrong, wrong!" the check marks imply. Daughter runs to find Mother. Mother is obviously terribly angry not only about her depiction, but with Lucina.

Scene 4: Mother has locked herself in her bedroom and doesn't respond when Daughter knocks and whimpers at the door: "Come on, Ma. Everybody has wrinkles. If you want a wrinkle-free portrait, you can get Norman Rockwell to paint you." Her imploring tone shows more guilt than rage. *It's her own fault that her mother marred the drawings; she has disappointed her!* The scene ends with an image of impotent frustration, as Daughter clasps her hand over her mouth to still her rage. Silence stops communication.

This fourth scene always left Lucina depressed. Instead of letting truth set her free, she hadn't been able to tell the women her whole story. If she had, she would have needed a Scene 5.

What actually happened was this. In response to her mother's silence and locked door, Lucina crawled out a second-story window onto the roof and slowly edged up to her mother's bedroom windows. Pressing against the glass, she saw her mother in a dressing gown, curled up like a young girl, doing the crossword puzzle. When Lucina rapped on the pane, her mother did not respond. The memory of her mother's non-response and her own desperate crying was so painful and shameful that she couldn't tell the others about it. Did she even understand the extent of her trauma?

Whenever she tried to recall the feeling of being perched precariously on that roof while peering at her non-responsive mother, she blanked. Distressed behavior was one thing; but didn't this interaction verge on madness? What went wrong? At one moment they were sharing a special communication: she drawing her mother, who was reading to her. *But wait a minute! Remember, Lucina, remember. What was Mother reading? Dag Hammarskjöld's diary,* Markings.

Markings? Had her mother been inspired by that title to make her own kind of markings? Lucina felt nauseated as emotions churned inside her. What terrible resentments festered inside her mother to cause this marring of her daughter's drawings? The first four scenes would have to do for now. A fifth scene would unravel her.

Cheryl, director of the play, fastened on Lucina's frustration with the enactment so far. "You say she didn't respond to your knocking. You imagined her curled up with the crossword puzzle, which suggests she works with words to calm herself in a traumatic situation. On the other hand, she doesn't know how to use words to express herself. She can't talk feelings; she stays mute. Is she punishing you? I wonder what you could have done to get her to talk to you? You wanted to confront your mother. Instead, you confronted a locked door. Did you at least yell at her for defacing your drawings?"

"You're right!" Lucina's face contorted. "I should have done something more to show my real feelings." *Why the hell couldn't she just say what happened? What was so terrible about it?*

Cheryl was clearly frustrated. "Where is the gain in the scene for you? The transformation? That's the point of these stories—to show change. Do you want us to fantasize an ending, Lucina? How about Mom opens her door, apologizes. You hug each other and cry… No—that won't do! The scene needs more grit, more depth, and more truth."

They would try something different in rehearsal that day. Mother would stand behind the imagined door, glaring with anger, as Daughter whimpered and knocked.

Cheryl said, "The real issue here is the mother's need to control, punish, and not communicate. Her silence will scream out cruelty and impotence. Maybe this staging will be more truthful than the actual event. It will show Mother's passive-aggressive stance. You, Lucina, have to step out of your guilt, be more active. We're trying to learn something about ourselves here, aren't we? Break down walls? Our dramas need to uncover what represses us, what hides us."

"I know what you're saying, Cheryl." *Was she not telling the whole story for fear of humiliating herself somehow, or criticizing her mother?* She wished she'd never exposed their painful relationship to the group.

Finally, it was decided: Marin, playing Mother, would not stand frozen behind the imagined locked door, but would dance out her sad aloneness. So how would the audience see this locked door? Lucina would have to create it through mime, by pounding and struggling to open the door, while all the time, mother and daughter are within inches of each other.

As Cheryl detailed stage directions to Marin and Lucina, Donna, pacing in the back of the small classroom serving as rehearsal space, was thinking, "Lucina's poor mother didn't have a women's theater group to help her!" The two winking eyes she'd embedded in her mind opened, spilling out tears.

*****

Lucina's Journal Entry. Tour: Wednesday night, April 12, 1967. Marin is incredible at portraying strange behaviors through dance in my play. She sees the Mother as using her daughter's emotions to purge herself. She doesn't stay frozen, as Cheryl had first wanted. Now each time I call out to her and beat on the door, she makes a reflex action, showing a symbiotic connection in a despairing, call-and-response dialogue. Marin says she wants to express the turmoil of someone obviously terrified of aging as well as unable to accept her daughter as she is. Mother acts out through marking her daughter's (my) drawings of her. But she's unable to talk about it. This interpretation exposes an angry, envious woman, who acts out

feelings in destructive ways. Cheryl says we need to exagger-
ate our age differences in body language. Daughter, youthful,
reaches out; Mother, afraid, recoils. The play is already an
invention of what actually happened. In a way, Marin's char-
acter seems to be trying to communicate. Those contorted body
motions are saying something. Why can't I tell them I wit-
nessed my mom from the roof curled up in her bed like a fetus,
a mum mom?

I see now how my mother was assuming and creating a
battle between us; she treated my drawings as a deliberate put-
down of her. Someday, I'll have the guts to ask her if she knew
what she was doing. She was acting out years of disappoint-
ment in me. When I didn't become the daughter she wanted,
it felt I was thwarting her own repressed ambitions. One thing
for sure, she has trouble seeing me as a separate being. And
she didn't take responsibility for her actions or her feelings at
that time. She was almost autistic in behavior. If she'd talked
about it, I wouldn't be making a play about her today. So, is art
our hope for connection?

*****

At Thursday's rehearsal Cheryl was still not happy with
Lucina's scene. "Something is missing in your acting, Lucina.
Like you're hanging back."

Lucina barked back defensively, "Isn't that the point of
my scene: a mother and daughter with hang-ups?"

"Somehow you, Lucina, aren't into your story. Yes,
you're portraying someone who's conflicted in how to connect
to Mom. But your acting can't be conflicted. This is tricky stuff."

Marlene jumped in. "This can get confusing. Frankly,
something is missing in all our scenes. We're confused about
how to act; we're holding back. That's our problem. Maybe
we're showing pain more than gain."

"Keep going, girl. What are you saying?" Cheryl put her hand excitedly on Marlene's arm.

"You should be madder than hell, Lucina," Marlene said. "For god's sake! Your mother defaces your drawings, and then locks the door on you so you can't even reach her to tell her off. And you're still whimpering about her wrinkle obsession! There's no moment of gain here."

"I'm with you on that, sister," Cheryl enthused.

"But that's how I was then," Lucina minced. "Our relationship is much better now."

"We've got a scene to put across, baby," Marlene said. "The truth of the scene."

"What truth, Marlene?" Lucina felt like kicking the wall. They should drop her play! It was all too confusing.

"Your truth," Marlene emphasized. "How did you feel when she mutilated your drawings? Underneath the guilty whimpering?"

"My mother was very lonely. By not talking to me, she was really calling out for help."

"Forget your mother!" Marlene shouted, her face tightening into a fist. "What did *you* feel?"

"I'm getting angry, Marlene." *Neither her mother nor her feelings for her mother deserved this kind of grilling! Marlene was definitely using this situation to vent at her.*

"Cheryl, isn't that what's missing?" Marlene pursued. "Some evidence that Lucina was very angry behind that placating pose? Neither of them can accept who the other is, or accept their own feelings."

Cheryl's head bobbed up and down in agreement.

Lucina was ready to spar. "When did you become so expert on the topic of repressed anger, Marlene?" *The woman was out to get her. Maybe she wanted to fuck her Louis! No, Louis wasn't her type. She needed someone she could control.*

"How's ten years of therapy for a starter!" Marlene, who stood a couple inches taller than Lucina, faced her head-on. "My mother didn't hug or show real affection to me, and she was a school psychiatrist. I'm probably seeing myself in your shoes, okay? I want your play to break open the locked doors between mothers and daughters in general." She paused a moment to say, "I'm sorry, Cheryl—don't mean to upstage you!" Then she went on. "Letting go of illusions about closeness can't take away what is good, Lucina. You were in a guilt and punishment complex with her. Like the mother's hell should revisit the daughter. What can I say? Your mother's little red check marks are a schoolteacher's slap on the hand. I should know, I feel like I'm chiding a kid with every check mark I give out when I teach. I learned to check the right answers instead of the wrong ones. My contribution to education."

Lucina felt pinned on a wrestler's mat. She needed a break, or aspirin. Marlene pelted her with words, like Louis did, before she taught him about his body, about being more than a talking head. Marlene and Louis—there was something similar about them. Something connected them. Maybe there was an attraction between them? She must tell Marlene that those check marks made by her mother showed distress as much as aggression. They were little flags of distress.

Cheryl was antsy. She wanted them back on the floor, working the scene. They would take a new tack, she declared. No one would play herself. It was too hard to be truthful about your own experiences. There were always self-imposed restraints. Having each one's story acted by another would give their dramas a fresh perspective. They could get out of the mire of therapy.

"Cheryl's right!" Lucina let out a pained sigh. "Let's get all the skeletons out. I'm twenty-six years old, guess it's about time."

"I think this is a breakthrough." Marlene spoke out thoughtfully. "It's fine to say no one else can feel what we feel. But what is more extraordinary is to try to feel what someone else does feels."

"Okay, Marlene. You've convinced me. You're the new Lucina." Cheryl's pronouncement left no room for discussion. "Make her outrageous!"

*****

Soft, almost inaudible sounds came from the floor where Dawn sprawled like a Raggedy Ann doll. As she stretched upward, she spoke more clearly: "So many theories about what we're doing."

Cheryl went up to her and gave her playful kicks with her bare feet. "You're definitely outrageous, sleeping through a rehearsal. Have you decided to be with us at last, Princess?"

"Empress, not Princess," Dawn grinned.

Cheryl, solidly built and confident on her feet, looked like a karate champ standing over a limp opponent. Her short hair, a thick black cap about her head, allowed her features to stand out in their full beauty. Though Cheryl, in her late twenties, was only a few years older than Dawn, both were deeply thoughtful women. And both could flash into action spontaneously. An unspoken respect joined them, though Cheryl still didn't know that Dawn had inspired a cafeteria full of strangers to act.

Dawn, now fully alert, steadied herself against Cheryl's legs as she sat up. "I haven't been sleeping, just thinking. I think best when I'm sleeping, I mean when other people think I'm sleeping. But with me, one of my eyes is always open."

"Thank God for that," Marlene sneered. "It really isn't fair of you, Dawn—spacing out during rehearsals. We're wasting time."

Dawn threw Marlene a "who-asked-you" look.

Cheryl said, "Give us your ideas, Dawn."

"Besides performing our scenes, why don't we do our women's play as improvisations? Like we do *Catching the Dreamer*—that is, when we do it. We can invite women from the audience to tell their stories, and we'll act them out. Go with the flow."

"Sure, and then we'll improvise on *Ulysses*!" Lucina shot out. "Well, I really need my story acted out!" Right then she knew she could no longer hold back. Once again, she saw herself perched precariously on the hot-shingled roof of her parents' house, grasping the window ledge with one hand and smashing at the window frame with the other, crying uncontrollably—and yet unable to let out one word at the frozen, curled-up figure of her mother staring at her crossword puzzle behind the window-panes. Overwhelmed with the memory, she sank to the floor and began pounding it with both fists. The women hovered over her in silence, obviously shaken by her actions.

*****

Lucina's Journal Entry. Tour: Thursday night, April 13, 1967. It's all right what I feel. It's all right! I can have my feelings, all of them. To think I almost didn't tell them about climbing out on the roof. Shame and pride were going to silence me once again. Now I know how brave I was to defy that locked door and crawl on my hands and knees on that hot, rough, slanted roof, afraid I was going to fall off any second and break my neck. I was in a rage. I'd meant well. Here, I'd tried to communicate with Mom; drawing her was my way of trying to improve our connection. I was trying to break down that wall of silence, of judgments, of hurts that had built up over years.

The real culprits: envy, jealousy, and rage. I, her daughter, was making my own choices, being an artist, not married but living with a Jew, a political poet, a radical. I'd said No to her tyranny over me and she'd found revenge: marring my drawings of her. Maybe an impotent and pathetic revenge, but very destructive and hurtful to me. But how dare she go after my sacred drawings, denigrate my tender attempts to communicate with her, to recognize her.

The women's theater group has saved me; I must have cried and sputtered for ten minutes before I could spill the beans. They've allowed me to own all of my feelings for the first time. We decided we didn't need to show the daughter on the roof, putting herself in danger and crying unheard. We took a leap. We'll show the daughter breaking down the mother's locked door, exposing the suffocating, unspoken, real shit that was going on between them. This is how we're doing the scene now:

Scene 5: Marlene plays me with vengeance! She mimes picking up an axe and testing its sharpness. After some warm-up swings, she smashes down the imaginary door with one well-placed blow. (Dawn shakes a large, thin, aluminum sheet offstage for the crash.) Now Mother and Daughter face each other, more like opponents in a wrestling match. No more controlling Mother and passive Daughter. Daughter says, "I'm very angry with you, Mother, for marking my drawings. I truly meant well and you overstepped your boundary. When you can say you're sorry and admit you did wrong, we'll talk. I want that to happen." Does this feel good! The character of Lucina is past the screaming stage. She speaks her truth loud and clear.

I love how the scene ends with the two women staring at each other during the Daughter's speech. There's no incredible breakthrough in communication between them, but at least my character speaks up and the Mother stays, listening. The Fire Dragon women have set me free. Sometime soon, I'm going to talk directly with Mom about that time in a calm voice, I hope. It's amazing how hung up I was about telling them how I really acted; and they were so supportive. "Gutsy, brave," they called me. I felt I cast off some really fearful shell I've been carrying around ever since that happened. If I can own myself, maybe Mom can own herself too. Own our separateness and connect in a healthy way.

Marlene keeps making me face my feelings about this. She says if Mom had really respected me as an artist, she wouldn't have dared touch my drawings, no matter what. The time Mom and my brother came to the loft and saw **Rune,** *she didn't know what to say, except, "Can it be dusted?" I think it frightened her. She wanted me to be clever and artistic enough to hook a rich husband, but not actually to be an artist. If she'd blessed my choices, allowed me my life, I might have had a firmer belief in myself, who knows? I might not have given up my sculpture work, not even to work with Louis. Not even for the Movement. I know I was trying to draw what I saw, my mother, not hurt her in any way with those lines.*

When we finished rehearsing **Markings,** *Jenny announced, "Whoever is going to play me in* **Wink** *better do it with the same force as Marlene plays Lucina." Then Dawn offered to play her. Her idea is to tickle the Headmaster and the Art Director to death.*

On Thursday we finally got to Cheryl's scene, **Birthing**—*the witnessing of her sister Sadie's birth of Marcel. Jenny plays Sadie, giving birth to Marcel. I will be Cheryl, Dawn will be the doctor, and Donna will direct. We're showing the horror of giving birth in a hospital. I wish we knew how gravity and muscle contractions work in the squatting position. And also the history of its replacement by the passive, prone*

105

position. We show the doctor struggling to pull out the infant and the mother's experience of excruciating pain. It feels like imposed pain, rather than natural pain. It's funny, the way Jenny watches the doctor slap her newborn on the rear end —I don't think the doll works here, but that's what we'll work with—and how she suddenly sits up and slaps Doctor Dawn's face. It's Abbott and Costello-ish and will get laughs. But Donna says it should be more macabre, not slapstick, and she's the boss for this one.

Jenny slapped Dawn too hard on the second run-through today. We have to learn how to do a theater slap. Was that accidentally or on purpose? I don't really know what they feel about each other. There are some peculiar vibes between them. One minute I think they like each other, the next, I see sparks. Not nice ones. Jenny doesn't like Dawn's glib remarks about men, she says. Maybe what she really doesn't like is the way Hans is shadowing Dawn lately, as if they shared a secret. We'd better do that old trick of slapping two wide slats together offstage, or they're going to wreck each other. A slat for a slap. We need laughs in these rather lugubrious tales of ours. The tone is in keeping with the exaggerated physicality of both **Wink** *and* **Markings**.

Cheryl's idea that we shouldn't play ourselves is a breakthrough. We're actually developing our own style. A style of different styles. And Dawn's idea about improvising on stories from women in the audience is a real challenge. We can be like jazz musicians who work with both set melodies, chords, and changes, but have places to invent. That can help free up our acting.

13

Lucina Makes a Phone Call

Louis found Lucina quite distraught in their dorm room on Thursday night. "What's up, babe? You don't look good. Getting tired of being with the girls all day?"

"I'm tired from working hard, dodo! We women are doing amazing work."

"Like what?"

"You'll see tomorrow night—when we perform our play. We're doing my scene for the first time."

"Here we are on a tour together and I'm missing you, our closeness. You're so focused on your women's stuff, we haven't made love once. Plus, you're all so secretive about it."

"We're not secretive, Louis. We're just doing our work and trying to make scenes out of really heavy things that have happened to us, that we're still trying to understand. I can tell you—it's incredible how freeing it is, telling personal and painful things about yourself to others, really opening up like that, and then having them interpret it and put it in a form that others can see. Like a big weight gets lifted and a light goes on. "Oh, that's why my mother did that…" Or "that's why I felt rotten in that situation." You'll see when we perform tomorrow night. It's

107

not about my being secretive with you. In fact, honey—I need to talk to you right now! Something just happened."

"So talk to me!"

"I just called Shauna in New York to check if everything's okay. I started worrying if *Rune* was okay, stored in that corner of her loft."

"How's Shauna? I'm sure your sculpture's fine, honey."

"She wasn't there. Her phone recorder was hooked up, the one she uses for her business. I don't know why, but I started wondering about *Rune*—if she's okay. Maybe it's because my scene in the women's play is about my mother—how she put red check marks on a drawing I made of her because it showed her wrinkles. Mother didn't want me to be a serious artist. It's so weird, Louis—to make my best sculpture, my woman-whole, and then just wrap it up and leave it at somebody else's studio. Am I covering up part of me, too? Maybe I'm not taking good enough care of *Rune*—because of my mother, or something."

"Luci, I know it's been hard for you. When we get back to the city, you should do some of your art again. You can make drawings of me. You used to draw me a lot."

"You sure you won't put check marks on them? Oh, don't mind me, Louis; I'm really nervous about my scene—and now I'm upset about *Rune*. The weirdest thing happened. Before Shauna's phone recorder came on, I swear I heard a woman's voice saying, 'Hello?' It wasn't Shauna. It sounded like Sally talking! Isn't that weird? And then I heard the machine."

"You mean Sally—of Sally and Karen?"

"She heard my voice and put on the tape machine!"

"It doesn't happen like that, Lucina. Either the person answers, or the recording machine does."

"I can't explain. It was spooky. I'm sure I heard Sally's voice! Gave me chills. We really hurt them and they really hurt us. Just when we needed supportive friends, outside of the group. We should have tried to talk to them more. There was a good feeling between the four of us once. Remember?"

"I know…" Louis' voice trailed off.

"So I called Karen's number. I just wanted to see if she or Sally would answer. Well, guess what? It's disconnected. Could they be staying in Shauna's studio? When Shauna goes away, she lets friends stay at her loft. She's generous like that. And I remember—they knew her from some group. Did Karen ever mention Shauna to you?"

"I'm trying to get them out of my mind. But babe, listen to me. I'm sure your sculpture is fine. You left her safe in the corner of the loft, you told me."

"Shauna and I have known each other since grad school—she's also an old friend of Marin's. And she was fine about storing *Rune* while we're on tour. We saw her on the street, remember? She told us *Rune* would be safe, right?"

"Stop worrying, honey. Try to call Shauna another time—you'll feel better."

"You know what's even weirder? I called Shauna's number right back again. And this time it just rang and rang. Nobody answered. No Sally and no machine." She paused, her face pulled into disturbed thought. "But there's no need to worry. Karen and Sally were angry with us, not *Rune*, right? She's safe in the corner by the bookcases, all swaddled up like a mummy."

14

The Women Discuss Donna's Scene
with the Men Present

Friday morning the women were still hoping to get at least one image from Donna's story presentable for the night's performance, after they had coffee with the men in the college cafeteria. So why did the fellows plunk themselves down at a separate table? Obviously they weren't happy campers.

"C'mon, guys. Cheer up. We can use your support." Lucina tried for a calm, lilting tone, as they seemed like moping children. "If you need something to do, how about repairing our props? The wire stems of the *Eco* flowers need straightening. The *Ghost Dance* tree has broken branches. Several masks need touch up work." She suddenly sounded like her mother dishing out chores.

No response from the men's table. Each had an injury or a gripe. Jack had twisted his ankle and Jim had wrenched his back playing basketball at the college rec center the day before. Al had cut his hand trying to fix a sagging tailpipe on Isadora. Courtney's funk was apparently due to the coeds of Richdale College.

"The chicks here have bugs up their asses," he griped.

"Well, it's still a tight-assed Christian school," Hugh grumbled. "So let's just get the show over with and scram."

Louis was just plain impatient. "Haven't you women rehearsed enough? Every day so far this week. The whole group needs to rehearse the ending of *Ghost Dance*. Our friezes during the massacre are getting sloppy. And we haven't even started to rework *Choice* with Cheryl!"

Inspired by Lucina's courage to face the grumps, Donna spoke up. "Listen, you guys. This is my day and I'm not giving it up. If you need our company, I would consider working on my scene with you nearby, though I can't say I feel comfortable about it."

"This sucks," Courtney said. "I'm going!"

Donna stuck her tongue out at the departing Courtney. "What's wrong with them?" Dawn beside her snickered, "They're babies."

Lucina broke off in a coughing fit, needing several gulps of water. *The props really should be repaired,* she thought.

"I'm with Donna!" Cheryl barked out. "Let's get to work on her play. The fellows can stay or leave."

Hugh smirked, "Gee, thanks, Cheryl."

"Don't you care about what we're doing, Hugh?" Cheryl snapped back. *She sure was in no mood to make nice: the women's work was vital—she'd run around getting them a classroom to work in, except for today, Fridays were booked for student committees—but when were they going to work on the new version of* Choice! *It was getting painful—their constant apologies about not portraying her people's reality.*

To zap the dour mood, Jenny started singing and snapping her fingers: "*Zip-a-dee-doo-dah, zip-a-dee-ay,*" but no one was moved. Hugh scuttled after Courtney, who was mumbling about something he had to get at the drug store. And Jack, trying to be nice, wished the women well, saying he was going to use the morning to meditate. Louis, Al, Hans, and Jim stayed seated and silent.

Donna whispered to the women. "Okay, time to get going. Let's move to that other table, further away from them, so we can concentrate." When they were resettled, Donna addressed them again. "How can we perform my story, even as work-in-progress, if we don't work on it? We spent so much time on Lucina's…"

Lucina couldn't read Donna's mood. Was she pissed off or stating a fact? "I'm sorry, Donna. I didn't know it was going to take so long. We don't have to perform mine, either."

Donna softened. "It's okay. I'm just nervous about my scene. It can't be dashed off in one rehearsal. We can start work on it. I just have to ignore our guys over there. At least they can't hear us, I hope."

"And while we're talking about rehearsals—we shouldn't be performing *Choice* again." Cheryl's voice rose with agitation. "Not without the Black perspective!"

The women agreed: No *Choice*. There wasn't even time to prepare four of their dramas for the evening's performance. But at least get started on Donna's scene. They could always ask the guys to leave if they bothered them.

"I feel like a guinea pig," Donna whispered to the women. "But you know what? If one of them even dares to come over here and wink at us, I'll kill him." The other women burst into laughter, without knowing Donna's personal paranoia about winks.

*****

After Dawn came back with more cups of coffee, Donna began reading from her notes.

"In high school, I was called 'butch-boy' because I preferred study dates with my girlfriends," she read. "I didn't even

113

know what butch meant until Jolie, my girlfriend, told me. In my school, girls' gangs were common. But even if a girl fought with belts and fists, she still was expected to wear some guy's ring. I lived in a better neighborhood, supposedly, because two doctors moved there. My father was one of them. But I didn't fight. Middle-class girls weren't violent. They just hung themselves or took Dad's hunting rifle and killed somebody, nice stuff like that."

Lucina sought Marin's face, remembering her anguish at one of their rehearsals when she revealed her brother's suicide. The tender smile coming back told her Marin could take it. Lucina's thoughts went to Cheryl—*she must be chomping at the bit. When were they going to revamp* Choice*!* Then something about Donna's story caught her interest. *Maybe she could direct it?*

Donna continued reading. "I wasn't all that class-conscious when I was a teen. I mean, I didn't have a clear analysis of what was going on." Donna put her notes aside and looked shyly at her sisters. If she talked softly, the guys wouldn't hear her. "All the blocks in my neighborhood in Flint were the same to me: filled with small wooden houses with front steps, a small yard, a driveway and side garage. The dads mainly worked at the Ford plant and made more money than mine did. He made house calls and emergency trips at all times of night. My mom, like all the moms, did her own housework and washing and ironing. And I didn't care if my girlfriend was one of the toughs or shy like me. I just wanted to hang out with the girls."

Lucina, nodding and smiling at Donna, broke in. "I've got a funny title for your scene. How about *I Love Lezzie*? I mean, that's what you want to focus on, right? You liked being with girls more than boys because—"

"No, Lucina!" Marlene's interruption was like a teacher's reprimand.

Donna's grimace silenced her as well. "Shh, Luie. Now you know why I really didn't want the guys around."

"For once, I'm glad they aren't listening to us," Lucina offered apologetically. "Look, I'm sorry if I said the wrong thing."

"Just inappropriate," Marlene responded.

Cheryl was impatient. "Can we let Donna go on with her story?"

"So, back to your comment, Lucina, if you were serious. Your play on *I Love Lucy* is funny but not pertinent to me. It also seems insulting to lesbians. Sure, back then I was butch-boy Kennedy. But I was exploring myself in high school. I think I want to call my scene *All Love is Normal*."

"Besides, the word 'lezzie' is derogatory toward women," Marlene chimed in.

"Why can't we play around with words—butch, lezzie? They're both derogatory words for girls," Lucina countered. "And that's a point we'd be making: In a sexist society girls are supposed to be sweet, pretty, and wear pink. Look—maybe we can talk to our audiences, ask them what names are used to put us all down. Donna, maybe we can use some of your puppets for the bully name-callers, so it's not us insulting each other with ugly words. The puppets can surround Cheryl—she just volunteered to play Donna's character—as she talks about her harassment to the audience. The puppets can call out all the slang, put-down names used to denigrate women, especially women who love women."

Dawn broke out of a reverie. "That's gutsy, what Lucina's saying."

Donna spoke up. "Do we really want to put words that denigrate women out there, in our sacred performance space?"

Suddenly Marlene, her schoolmarm's tone gone, spoke in rhyming falsetto: "There's something wrong with you, my dear. You're not like other girls, I fear." Dawn improvised with her: "Yes, yes, we think it's clear, so very clear. You're different, dear. Perhaps you're queer."

Lucina's mind was churning. *The terrible onus on even mouthing dangerous, destructive put-down words was lifted for a moment.* "We're trying to make a point by exposing cruel words," she affirmed. "So, let's camp up the scene. While the puppets are busy putting our heroine down, she's busy finding her self-respect."

Dawn was ecstatic. "It's our style! A funny, even a slightly satirical play. Maybe we're getting sophisticated? I thought we were going to drown ourselves in tragedy. But how do you find your self-respect on stage in five minutes?"

Cheryl, momentarily inspired, stood up and began stroking her cheeks as if applying cream in a mirror. "I'll be looking in a mirror, putting cream on my face and body. And exploring myself."

Donna's mouth hung open. "You guys, I mean gals, are going so fast; slow down a bit. It's my life we're talking about, right?"

Cheryl sat down quickly, apologizing. "Sorry, Donna. It's so rich, it has such potential for—oh, never mind."

"No, no, Cheryl. I'm sorry. I got scared. Go on like you were doing, in front of the mirror. Please—"

"Oh, Cheryl, yes!" Dawn sang out. "You move so beautifully."

As Cheryl took up posturing again in a seductive way, Louis, Al, Hans, and Jim, still seated nearby, were staring at her.

Donna glowered back at them. "Those fuckers can't leave us alone!"

Cheryl addressed the women. "Let's just keep focused on us. As I get more and more into myself, the bully pulpit, I mean, bully puppets, slowly back away." She continued moving and thinking aloud: "I'm not going to give the puppets, or the guys over there. my energy by responding in anger. I'll give it to myself, love myself."

Marlene lit up: "I think this could be very effective. We've never done anything so…so risqué!"

Lucina beamed. "What do you think, Donna?"

"I love it. I wish it were ready to do tonight!" Her eyes lit up as she imagined her fantasy winking puppets squashed by the bully puppets. *They deserved each other.* "Everything's coming together," she exclaimed.

Marin, chuckling throughout the brainstorming, was all ears. "What's coming together, Donna?"

"Oh, using puppets instead of real people for the nasty roles. That's all I meant." Donna bit at her lips to stop breaking out in laughter. *Yes, the perfect revenge for those two winker-stinkers,* she told herself.

All this time, Jim and Louis stayed gazing at Cheryl with some kind of awe. Her lack of restraint in front of them and in a public setting was gutsy! This was a Cheryl they didn't know, sexy and playful. Louis rubbed his hands on the table. *What had Donna been telling them? And why was Cheryl posturing like that?*

Al and Hans weren't fazed by any of it. Al had his notebook out and was making a sketch; he'd just figured out how to fix the tailpipe. Hans was in his own mind, still trying to decide what he was going to say in a letter to the Chicago activists. Should he agree to do some action with them? Maybe he shouldn't let Jenny or even Dawn in on his plans. They'd spill it to their girlfriends. He glanced toward Jenny; she was staring open-mouthed at Cheryl, who was miming something; he couldn't tell what.

*****

A man's voice shattered the women's concentration. "I really like what you're doing, Cheryl."

"Oh, you scared me!" Cheryl, taken off guard, stretched her arms out, as much a warding-off gesture as a welcoming one, toward Louis now approaching her.

"I don't know if that's going to be in one of your scenes. But you have such a presence when you move." Standing un-apologetically next to Cheryl, Louis placed an unpeeled orange on the table. "Lucina," he started up again, "you're directing, right? I just want to—" Then looking from woman to woman his voice quieted as he realized his presence was not welcomed.

Lucina, now in a frozen grimace, stumbled a response. "We're working on—on Donna's scene now, Louis." *How could he have broken into their work space like that! And how did he know she was thinking of directing Donna's play?*

Taking mincing backward steps, Louis managed to say, "Forget about that title, Lucina. It takes away from the serious-ness of the piece."

Lucina's mouth dropped, her shoulders shot up. "Louis! This is our business." Her cheeks flushed with embarrassment. Had all the guys heard them talking? Or was it only Louis with ears and eyes in the back of his head! "Please, Louis. We'll be done working soon."

He returned to his seat, embarrassed. *Why had he done that? And now Lucina was really mad at him.*

Hans grabbed at his pack of cigarettes. Within seconds, the four men were swathed in smoke.

Lucina shook her head in dismay. "I'm sorry about that."

Cheryl reached past Dawn to squeeze Lucina's arm. "Hey, friend. Not to worry. Louis is Louis. It's not your fault. He meant well. Just clueless."

"Still…" Lucina groaned, grabbing at Cheryl's hand. "He didn't allow our space." To herself she murmured, *Jeez, he's so uptight about us saying "lezzie." He probably can't even say "lesbian."*

*****

The women finished outlining Donna's play, occasionally eyeing their cohorts across the aisle, now back into their books and newspapers.

Marlene got up to stretch. "Do you realize what we've done? In four days, we've developed four scenes. Three are performable and Donna's is ready for rehearsal."

Lucina gave Donna a big smile. "I'm so happy with us, queer dears," she said. "I'm going to enjoy directing your scene, that is if it's okay by you."

"How many times do I have to say 'yes, Lucina!'" Donna turned to the others. "I just want to say, this is cathartic work. But is the women's play real theater? It's not like *Ghost Dance*. It feels more like therapy. I think that's what you were feeling about your scene, too. Right, Lucina?"

Lucina turned serious. "Maybe we just don't think the stuff from our lives is worthy of being on the stage. It should stay in the kitchen or the bedroom."

"Or the therapist's office," Jenny piped up.

"Oh, look. What we're doing is really courageous!" Donna rejoined. "At least we won't die horrible deaths, like the women in opera do. I was just voicing an observation, not a judgment." *Why did Lucina have to be so serious about everything?*

"Listen, my sisters," Jenny put her hands on Lucina's and Donna's backs. "We're doing great. If we have half the vitality in tonight's show as we've had in our rehearsals this week, we're going to blow their minds. People will be peeing in their pants. Don't get me wrong, Donna—*Ghost Dance*? I love it. In some ways it is more awesome, but that's because of the way we do it. We call it a tribute, a testimonial, an exposé. It's not intimate like our women's play. By the time we're through, our play will be many different styles: docudrama, surrealism, impressionism, satire, irony, exposé, pop…I mean, it's happening! We tell it like it is. Look! We can't be labeled and neither can our dramas. Personally, I think having different styles is great."

"We can never be accused of 'stylistic entrapment,' whatever that means," Marlene called out, moving toward Louis and Jim, who stood waiting for the women, still gathering their notes and bags. Al and Hans had already left to retrieve Isadora from the far end of the parking lot.

As the actors exited the nearly empty cafeteria, Marlene maneuvered between Jim and Louis, taking their arms with a little curtsy. "Isn't that right, guys?" She gave Louis a big smile and squeezed Jim's arm.

Lucina felt a sudden exhaustion. That little episode with Louis had made her weepy. *It wasn't like they'd actually ordered the fellows to stay away from their table, but maybe they should have.* She wished she could take a nap before the afternoon rehearsal with the whole group.

"Oh great, we're being picked up." Cheryl wiggled her hips at Dawn before hopping into the back seat of Isadora. "You lezzie, you," she teased in a soft voice, as Dawn slipped in beside her.

In the station wagon, Donna laid her head on Jim's shoulder in the front seat. *Why couldn't they all just be friends without the tension.*

15
Al and Louis in the Wings

Louis and Al watched the scenes from *Moments of Pain/ Moments of Gain* from stage-wing right of the Richdale Performance Theater. For them, sitting out front in the audience would make it all too obvious: the women were performing their own stuff without them. The other guys sat scattered throughout the theater, eager to observe reactions. As Marlene announced their first drama, *Wink*, Louis shuddered to Al, "I feel nervous for them and anxious for myself."

"I know, man." Al pulled his seat, one of the metal boxes used for props, closer to Louis. "Next thing we know they'll be off on their own tour. We should have gone for a beer."

Louis hadn't seen Lucina so happy in months. Every time she returned from a rehearsal with the women her eyes twinkled, like she had a light inside her. Even when she turned her attention to him, she seemed preoccupied, a constant smile playing on her face. He better deal with his jealousy! She had played second fiddle to his journal project, *PAN*. Now it was his turn to support her baby.

Cheryl and Lucina were on stage clawing at the air, their distorted faces winking wildly.

"They're begging for laughs," Al grumbled. "Jeez, where's the dialogue?"

"Aren't they playing two jerks putting something over on Dawn, like they did at the Yellow Farm—only it used to be Jenny playing herself?" Louis puzzled. "Lucina doesn't talk that much about their work with me."

When Dawn pulled out a feather hidden in her sleeve and began tickling the rear ends of her patronizing interviewers, waves of laughter flooded the stage.

Clutching his head in his hands, Al wrenched his elbows into his legs. "Damn it, man. This seems like high school slapstick."

Louis folded his arms woodenly in front of him, as if for protection. "Who are we kidding, Al? They've got the audience wrapped around their fingers."

Al went limp. "You're right. It's going to be tough to follow."

Louis slapped a thigh. "We gotta make use of their energy! Expand on it."

Al furrowed his brow, then sat upright. "What if we start our Ghost Dance from the back of the auditorium, chanting all the way to the stage, while Courtney and Hans hold the screen for the Lakota Sioux and Paiute portrait-projections? We can frieze when they say the names. "

"Brilliant, Al. The Living Theater won't mind us borrowing their ideas. In fact, we could do the entire play in the aisles, around the audience."

"Come on, Lou. That sounds like Lucina's circle shit. We need the stage."

"Okay. But coming through the audience chanting is great."

"We'll do it. Listen, man, if I don't watch this, Marin won't speak to me."

"Lucina will kill me."

"Damn—look at that! The audience is eating this stuff up."

*****

During Lucina's story, Louis' mind was churning. *This is what she was talking about yesterday. Drawing her mother was her way to connect, like she does with me…But her Mom takes offense for some reason and messes up her drawings? I knew that woman was angry with me, but ruining her daughter's portrait of her? That's sick!*

Just before *Birthing* began he remembered some details he'd not worked out about their payment. And Al had to fix some props for *Ghost Dance*. The two snuck away from their viewing spots like burglars.

*****

Lucina's Journal Entry. Tour: Saturday, April 15, 1967. We did it! We wowed 'em with our women's scenes. Cheryl said it was like a revival meeting. Constant "Right on, Sisters" from our audience, perhaps three hundred. A woman came up to me at half time and began to cry. She said she didn't know what her feelings were most of the time, let alone be able to express them to someone else. She said we could wake up women all over this country if we wanted to.

The Ghost Dance with the powerful, haunting faces introducing and closing our Tribute was so profound. I feel these real Indigenous people are blessing us, thanking us for keeping the truth of their carnage burning into the minds of our audience witnesses in 1967.

16
Crazy Vibes to Weymouth

On route to Weymouth College outside of Rochester, the riders in the station wagon were bit by a lovebug. Hans flirted openly with Dawn, inspiring Jim to gaze at Cheryl from the back seat with a shit-eating grin on his face. Donna, driving, eyed him in the rearview mirror. *Well, she was taken by Cheryl as well! She was so touched that this gorgeous woman had wanted to play her. She wanted to talk to her...* But Cheryl, in the passenger seat, was looking intently out the window. Donna wouldn't intrude on her space. Why was her discomfort with Jim and Jack coming back to her again, how they'd disrespected her in some oblique way? *Keep your eyes on the road. And stop worrying so much how others see you!*

Oblivious to anyone's focus on her, Cheryl was distraught: once again, they would be performing *Choice* without the Black soldier's perspective! The drama department had specifically requested their anti-war play. And they wanted her to explain their omission and express how they were going to change that, asap! She'd heard that Weymouth had many Black students from Rochester, who were pushing the administration to have a Black Studies curriculum. She felt her body tense. How could she explain one more time that they were in the process of reworking the play! These students would be really upset to hear their reality in 'Nam was missing. She thought about her nephew, Marcel. How she would do everything she could to keep him out of the army.

"Is Marcel doing okay without you, Cheryl?" came a voice from the back seat. *Oh, that Dawn is so empathic.*

Cheryl turned to answer. "Thanks for asking, Dawny. I was just thinking about Marcel. His mom is spending extra time with him."

"I was just wondering how he'd feel hanging with our group."

"He sure wouldn't go for you people telling him what to do!" Cheryl stared again out the window. *Was Marcel doing his homework?*

*****

Jim turned his attention to Hans and Dawn. *"Ghost Dance* was the best ever last night. Right, guys? Hugh was an incredible force. I think he really hypnotized you, Donna."

Her thoughts still on Cheryl, Donna managed a response. "Jenny did it better. She can really go into a trance state."

Jim went on. "Well, he really got to me. The guy's a mystic. And Jack's candle meditation is helping me dig the slow-shuffle dance. Honest to god, last night I saw my crazy uncle Joe waving his cane at me and he's been dead for ten years. Maybe I'm finally getting what we're trying to do. Really go back in time…"

Cheryl, snapping out of her worries, turned to face Jim. "What about the candle meditation, Jim?"

Jim bent forward toward her. "You should try it. Stare at a candle and then follow your own breathing. It's a cheap high."

Cheryl laughed. "Sounds good. I could use a little high. That couch I slept on last night was lumpy. By the way, where did you end up?" She turned to address Dawn.

"Secret."

"Tell me your secrets and I'll tell you mine."

Dawn giggled and stayed smiling.

Cheryl wondered: *She couldn't have slept with Hans? He sure is taken with her. And is she aware of the signals she sends to me? Maybe the kid is confused!* She'd have a private talk with her soon.

Hans pulled a pack of cigarettes from his front pocket and offered it to Dawn. "The dorm rooms at Wellingfield were nice—didn't you think so, Dawn?"

Donna glared at Hans through the rearview mirror. "You two aren't going to smoke?"

"We'll open the window," Dawn said testily, adding, "Okay, okay, we'll wait 'til the rest stop."

Jim nudged Dawn. "What do you like about smoking, Dawn?"

"The smoke. I like to watch smoke curl."

"There's something fascinating about smoke and flames," Jim said. "Since I started meditating on a candle flame all of three days now, everybody looks different." He squinted at Dawn. "For example, you have a halo, Dawn."

With an audible groan, Donna stayed fixed on the highway.

"Did you say something, Donna?" Cheryl said.

"I said, 'fuck,'" Donna growled.

Cheryl swiveled around to Jim again. "Are you really into fire meditation, Jim?"

"Yeah, fire. Almost burnt the garage down when I was a little kid. Started smoking when I was seven."

"Fires and riots," Dawn muttered with a quick smile at Hans.

"Fire and haloes," Jim added.

"Sure, Jim," Donna sighed.

Cheryl suppressed a laugh. *Everyone was jiving. They didn't know what they were talking about.*

"Fires and riots," Dawn repeated. She sucked hard on her unlit Gauloise. Each time she remembered her outrageous action at Wellingfield, a delicious chill flooded her. If only she could tell Cheryl.

Jim tapped Donna's shoulder gently. "Hey—baby! You goin' to stop at the first food and fuel place so we can get some coffee and cigarettes? I need some fire."

Donna's hands tightened on the wheel. A sign ahead said, "Road Construction: Keep Right." *What would it feel like to hit one of those cones?* she wondered. "Jim, you should stop making your little smoke fires," she said.

"Right, Mister Fireman," Cheryl added with a chuckle. "Stick to your candlelight and Jack's very own meditation."

"Didn't know you girls cared." Jim gave them each a quick pat on the shoulder.

"Stop saying girls, Jim!" Donna snarled.

"Smoking and meditating cancel each other out," Cheryl piped up.

"I disagree." Jim pushed forward again toward Cheryl. "Donna, stop at the next turnoff."

"Say *pleeze*. There's one in about ten miles. Oh god, why do I fuel your addiction?"

"I fuel yours, Donna."

"Not so. You haven't said one thing about the women's play, sweetie."

"Didn't ask me—that's how come."

"We got so much applause," Dawn said to a nodding Hans.

"Why aren't the guys mentioning our plays?" Donna huffed.

"You know what I need—" Cheryl burst into the silence.

"A coffee?" Jim piped up.

"Some groovy Black guys at Weymouth. You guys are okay, but—"

"We're no fun?" Donna eyed Cheryl carefully.

"White people don't know how to have fun," Cheryl teased. She wanted to turn around again to see Dawn's reaction.

"I never heard you talk like that, Cheryl," Jim said.

Cheryl, eyes straight ahead on the road, snapped, "Honey, the truth is, you haven't heard me talk at all!" She could just imagine what the guys would feel if she did a striptease in Donna's scene. "Have you read Eldridge Cleaver's book, Jim?"

"Started it." Jim sat back and stared out the window. He had an uncomfortable feeling that Dawn and Hans were holding hands under his army jacket draped between them. He forced himself to talk to Cheryl. "How do you figure his rap—that the system made him rape. Doesn't a person have to take responsibility?"

"Are you sure he said that?" Cheryl returned sharply. "Black people are trying to talk real."

"Women are trying to talk real, too," Dawn said. She ignored Jim's restless glances in her direction and reached out to touch Cheryl's shoulder. But Cheryl had hunched forward to open her no-draft window.

"I dig his armed guards," Jim said. "I think we should—"

Cheryl broke in. "So, last night after *Ghost Dance*—you were cool, Jim. Getting the audience to chant 'I Circle Around.' You play a smooth guitar, like you went into your own trance state."

"I'm just mimicking Hugh. But yeah! We were in a groove. Hope Marin feels better about the tree-planting ritual now. Remember how upset she was about it after our first gig?"

"Nobody messed up this time," Donna said. "Anybody see the sign for food?"

"Not yet, sweetie," Jim said. He couldn't figure Cheryl out. Prickly one minute and real nice the next.

"And Hugh, once again, was an incredible trance-maker," Cheryl enthused. "I love following him in the dance. The guy really has focused energy."

Donna spotted a strange look on Hans' face in the rearview mirror. "Hans, are you okay?"

"A Buddhist monk set himself on fire last week to protest the war." Hans' voice was uncharacteristically soft.

"That's terrible," Donna moaned.

"How someone can have the guts to do that," Dawn said. "Remember Norman Morrison? Such a gentle man. I heard him talk once. To sacrifice yourself for a cause—that's holy. And right outside McNamara's office at the Pentagon. That bastard McNamara."

"It was for the Vietnamese," Jim said

"I'm sorry, but I can't hear any more of this now. I get too depressed." Donna hunched up her shoulders and the others turned silent.

There was little traffic on the road and soon Donna was mesmerized by the humming sound of tires on pavement. Her thoughts went to Jim. *Something sweet about his willingness to meditate. I shouldn't tease him. That was nice of Cheryl, to praise his guitar playing like that. She's one gutsy lady. Going on tour with us—us no fun whities…*

Cheryl had swiveled around to the back seat again. "You talk real good, Dawny." She spoke gently. "Morrison's death by fire was a bold, inspired death."

"I know," Dawn echoed. "Fire lights up our unconscious."

Jim tried to spot the Dart and the van behind them. "I know we passed them, but I thought we were going to stick together," he complained. "Where are they? Doesn't Jenny know how to stay in a convoy?" He looked pointedly at Hans and Dawn with discomfort. *Jenny must be disgusted with these two!*

"There's the food sign, Donna," Cheryl shouted out. "Good, I need a strong coffee—with lots of sugar."

Donna slowed the station wagon onto the exit road and rotated her shoulders up and down to release tension. *Jeez! There was so much horror in the world. And Jim burning his lungs up with smoking. The goddamn coffin nails!*

Then the other cars were there. It seemed people were waving at her in slow motion. She must be sleepy. Why was everybody off-kilter? Better ask Jim to drive. "Hope they wanted to stop," she said.

As the five loped to the rest stop restaurant, Cheryl pulled Dawn aside. "I need to talk to you, sister. It's hard to get private time around here."

17
Words Between Cheryl and Dawn

It felt strange but really exciting, sitting alone with Cheryl; just the two of them in the hall-like space echoing the sounds of travelers needing a break from the highway. Then something nudged her foot under the table. Had she imagined it? The questioning smile on Cheryl's face—what did it mean?

At a distance, Dawn could see the others in their group looking befuddled, everyone trying to squeeze their trays onto the small metallic tables. They didn't fit in this functional but impersonal place, she thought. *How could eating bad food with other travelers, mostly families and couples and mainly white, be good for anybody? Moreover, nobody else looked even faintly like her and her comrades, with their berets and bandannas, beards and loose hair, blue jeans and jackets covered with patches, pins, and designs. Well, they were shape-changers (she loved that word), and warriors for justice (Hans liked that phrase), and they were on a mission.*

She and this nifty woman sitting across from her and all the rest of her buddies were out to shake things up, get people to talk about important issues. And she, Dawn Jamieson, was part of this. Did any of these people surrounding her even vaguely consider all the things she and her comrades talked about day and night? She should take a quick poll right now and see who wanted the Vietnam War to end and who didn't. And who thought about acid rain, or about the silencing of women? Or the way young Black men can't expect to be promoted in the military like white men are? The Fire Dragon actors believed that all communities of people needed to be woken up—not just college students.

"How's the hamburger, Dawn? I wanted to get a blueberry muffin with my coffee, but did you see them? Really stale."

The woman looking directly into her eyes was peering into her soul. She would not be able to hide a thing from her. But she'd promised Jenny and Hans: she would not tell until they were out of New York State. It should be safe then. "You need to talk to me? Is it about Marcel? He must miss you so much, Cheryl." The hamburger meat was tasteless and dry—or was she just feeling nervous?

"I called my sister, Sadie—they're doing good. But I do miss him—he's so sensitive. And if it weren't for you, I'd miss him even more. He loves mustard on his hamburgers, too. But look, Dawn, we don't have a lot of time together; the others are going to get antsy soon to leave. Damn! Why do I feel guilty just wanting time with you now?" Cheryl, suddenly bursting out in nervous laughter, pulled her cap off and was twirling strands of her jet black hair, slowly, as if finding some comfort in the act. *Why did she feel pressure to tell Dawn now? Must be the incredible support she was getting by playing Donna rising above the taunts of bullies: butch-boy, lezzie, diesel dyke. Ironic how Donna denied it all, while she...*

"I don't understand, Cheryl," Dawn managed awkwardly. She felt both embarrassed and excited as the woman did that thing again—looked straight and deep inside her. But what did that laughter mean? Was she laughing at her?

Cheryl sent her an apologetic look. "In this very public, not very comfortable place, I feel the need to say something very private, fragile, and potentially dangerous, to you, my stranger-comrade. And I'm nervous, okay?"

Dawn could find no response; it was enough to hold her gaze on the woman she'd been impressed with for weeks: someone who could speak up for herself and knew her mind. Ever since that women's workshop when each of them had been asked to act out a deep fear, and she, Dawn, had stood on a chair in the rehearsal, so nervous she almost fell off it, singing out, then shouting at an imagined audience, trying to break through her fear that she'd always be shy. That's when Cheryl had talked really personal to her, like a friend. "You know, Dawn, we're not that different. I bet when something moves you terribly, you won't be shy, you'll speak out in your own way." And that's exactly what she'd done in that Wellingfield cafeteria. Stood up on a table and acted out her sadness about the killing of Vietnamese people. After that time, how often she'd sought Cheryl's glance, then looked away, embarrassed to even hope they might be able to share some understanding together. And yet this same woman was the one she felt most herself with, most seen by, most empathic with of all of them.

"Don't you want to know what's on my mind, Dawn?" It was Cheryl addressing her—in this huge, impersonal place. "You are inquisitive and sensitive. And all the time, even when you seem to be sleeping, I know what's going on, sister. The wheels are turning and your mind never stops. Right? Am I right?"

"You're a mind reader, or something, Cheryl." She felt again that giddy, bubbly sensation this city woman gave her. Incredible—how much Cheryl seemed to understand about her. But she couldn't tell her about her action, not yet. "If I don't keep my mind going, talking to myself, I kind of go nuts." The words came so easily, even before she knew what she was going to say. "I'm a small town kid, not as articulate as you, Cheryl. So, I work on my thoughts around a topic that grabs me. I put words in shapes on a page in my mind. Then when I have a chance, I write it all down."

"Sounds like poems to me, honey."

Had she heard right? Had Cheryl said, "honey," as in "sweetheart"? Some tightness in her chest gave way and somewhere else inside her she suddenly knew the truth. Cheryl's belief in her—"you will forget your fears"—had been an invisible force behind her action that Sunday in the Wellingfield cafeteria, with those arrogant guys taunting her and Jenny and Hans so confused. She needed to do something extraordinary, beyond words—act out her emotions, forget the bullies at the next table and speak out her horror of the war. She must startle people, make an impact! It was this very woman who had just called her "honey" who had said, "Yes, you can do it."

Maybe she should tell her—the thing she'd been able to do. Not Jenny, not Hans—she, Dawn, had done something very brave. "Cheryl, there's been something I've also wanted to tell you too. It feels like forever. Remember that exercise we did with just the women? When we had to exorcise one of our fears. Actually, it's all because of you—I see that so strongly now—that I forgot my fear and stood up and showed my outrage."

With a lot of pauses and hand gestures, Dawn described her fire action: the fear of falling off the table, setting her hair and clothes on fire, having campus police barge into the cafeteria and arrest her, people calling her crazy. Finally, she would tell Cheryl everything. They would be out of New York State soon—Cheryl would not tell her secret. She was too into justice for people, wanting her people to be treated right!

As she talked, feeling Cheryl was taking in every word, it all came back again. And once again she was standing on that slippery cafeteria table, holding up napkins inked with blood words, and setting them on fire, incanting: "My babies are being burnt alive. My babies are being burnt alive."

"I knew you could stand up like that, Dawn. Speak out about the horrors the U.S. is doing there. I see it as racist genocide!"

"Boy, would Dad flip out if he saw me in that cafeteria!" She heard herself almost bragging and felt embarrassed. Cheryl must be anxious to get back to the others.

"You mean your parents didn't know how to give you support?"

"Are you kidding? Money, well kind of—but emotional? Not at all. The day I left for college...?" There she was again, talking so easily about herself. "Mom and Dad still arguing about where I should be going. Dad didn't want me to go to a big university and flunk out. 'Let her go to community college first,' he kept saying, 'then we'll see.' But Mom wanted me to have the opportunity she'd never had, and that's why I was heading to the University of California at Davis. Suddenly Dad stops arguing, we're sitting in a Howard Johnson's, it looked something like this place...He stands up in front of Mom and me and blurts out, 'Someday I'm going to be somebody,' like he's the kid going off to college, not me, his daughter. Bizarre. Well, now that I quit college cold turkey they're both down on me. So I'll have to be somebody on my own!"

"You definitely are—" Cheryl paused. "Listen, I meant to tell you—I know you've been concerned about our getting paid. If you need cash, anytime, I brought extra just in case. Please, borrow money from me. Okay?"

"Wow! Yes. I didn't know who to ask. I should have talked to Louis about that. I might need to borrow from you. If that's okay, Cheryl?"

"What are friends for, Dawn?"

Cheryl's kindness touched her deeply. Maybe she shouldn't have talked so much? Yet her anxiety about betraying Hans and Jenny had already lifted. She could trust this woman!

"So, Dawn?" Cheryl's chestnut brown eyes bore into hers again, questioning, impatient. "Do you remember how I exorcized my fear at our women's workshop, that same day?"

Dawn felt heat in her cheeks; she was embarrassed, not because she didn't remember, but because she did. Like it had happened yesterday. But she was afraid to talk about it because Cheryl herself hadn't wanted to talk that much about it back then.

"I didn't forget any of it. What you did—what you said."

"Tell me. Tell me what you remember, Dawn."

"You mimed a sexy dance."

"That's how you describe what I did?"

Cheryl was laughing at her; she was sure of that. "Well, okay. It was more like an exorcism. Like you were stripping away feelings, but not like a striptease."

"I'm enjoying this, go on."

"This is embarrassing—but okay. Your movements were so, so natural and real—I mean, you blew our minds. You know that. And you said you had Nina Simone's song blasting in your head."

"Which song was that, Dawn?"

"'Tomorrow Is My Turn.' You said her passion drove your dance. That was so cool."

"That's right, Dawn, and afterward you said to me, 'You're so in your movements. You're not shy about being your whole self in front of any of us.'"

"Sure, I remember what I said. And you said, 'I'm reluctant to be spontaneous in front of white people because of the stereotyped way they see us Black women. They think we've got something up our sleeve or we're on the make or something.'

I thought you meant me, when you said that, Cheryl. After that I was afraid to look at you."

"Is that why you've been playing hide and seek with me, honey? You look at me like you've got the hottest secret to tell me and then you run away."

There was that word "honey" again! Sitting here with Cheryl was becoming unbearable. She wanted to run away or throw herself on the table. Bang her head, grab Cheryl's hands. Do something!

"Don't you see, Dawn? I'm actually shy about being open and emotional in front of women because it means too much to me, how I'm seen."

What did she mean! Wouldn't it be easier to be one's self in front of your own sex?

"Let me say that again."

Cheryl was in her face, not letting her hide at all.

"I'm afraid of being sensual in front of you, because it means so much to me. Now do you understand?"

Dawn felt something warm on her hand, causing her to tremble: *it was burning her!* Cheryl had placed her hand over hers and was cupping it in a protective manner.

"Thank you for what you did at Wellingfield. Brave Dawn, brave woman! Thank you for telling me all this. You've given me, what shall I say, a gift? A shove? You've fired me up, that's for sure. Now I have to speak out too—and it's scary. I'm very upset that we haven't started to expand *Choice*. I've lost my patience. It's wrong! When are we going to show how young Black guys are treated by the military? My cousin Nelson is in 'Nam and no one has heard from him in months!" Her guarded calmness disappeared as she pulled away from Dawn abruptly. Then she was signaling their comrades. "Okay! We've got to go join them now! They're leaving. But I've got four words to add to your fire journal for the day."

They had both stood up, slowly, carefully, each aware that they'd been in a kind of awkward psychic embrace, with all the wondrous and scary feelings that kind of closeness could bring.

"You have four words for me?"

"Yes, I do. Can you guess what they are?" And then Cheryl was pointing at them both. And what was she shaping with her fingers? A heart!

As they sped through the revolving doors to catch up with Donna, Jim, and Hans, Cheryl pressed her hand to Dawn's back. "So, next time when you want to cuddle with someone on a couch, baby, remember four words: I love you, Dawn. And look for me!"

18
A Call from Wellingfield

The group accepted that Al always drove the van and that Marin, Lucina, and Louis often rode with him. After the highway pee-and-snack break, Hans' Big Four fell into silence. Lucina didn't want to come down from the Richdale high of the night before, but she had and was in a funk. Her head felt screwed on wrong. If only she could understand what was going on. The women's scenes had been great! So why wasn't she celebrating? All that worry about the blood scene in *Ghost Dance Tribute*? Professor John Milan was wrong. Even Richdale College with its conservative Methodist roots dug their in-your-face style. They could pull it off in the Midwest too. And what was with Louis? Ranting on and on how great the massacre ritual was, but barely mentioning her scene, *Markings*. He usually had too much to say about what she did! Here she'd practically had a nervous breakdown over it. But ever since that ecstatic dance/chant blowout with their audience after the Middleton performance —Al had told him about her "fuck this" and "fuck that" rant—he was acting weird toward her. Maybe he thought she was putting herself in danger; he was worried for her, that was it. He would have loved her Chaplinesque dance, though. Poor guy! Not fair that he'd been doing business stuff with the Drama Department to get paid, just when the action got going!

And Marlene that morning! She wouldn't shut up. Louis thinks this, Louis wants that. Yuk! So why doesn't she just say it: "I want to fuck your Louis!" Continually complaining about travel maps in the wrong place and luggage in the wrong cars. *She's an agitated woman. Only her lists give comfort,* Lucina decided. *Always keeping track: How many days are left in the tour? How many miles before the next town? How much money has she spent so far?*

Was anybody happy? And what was going on with Jack? Plowing through a huge bag of greasy potato chips for breakfast as if he'd not eaten since they left New York. Maybe he was missing his Joan. What if he decided to quit them so he could be with her? He just kept saying over and over, "Gotta keep the faith," as though he were in a crisis.

*****

"What's the matter with everyone? Why can't we have fun?" That was Marin hollering at the top of her lungs. Suddenly a cloud cleared in Lucina's head. At least she wasn't alone with her doldrums. Everybody was messed up. Marin said Al was having trouble sleeping and was keeping her awake.

So, when Al, at the wheel of Isadora, pulled a cigarette from his pocket and lit it with the dashboard lighter, Lucina broke her silence.

"What did you guys think about the lesbian stuff?" she blurted out. "You heard us working on Donna's play in the cafeteria yesterday. Any reactions, Al?" Getting no response, she added, "Donna really loves Jim. It's about her past."

"Cheryl's seductive dance would be too much. Subtle is more powerful. That's what I think." Al's clipped words flew at her along with an exhalation of smoke.

Lucina's skin prickled. "Cheryl wasn't being seductive. She was affirming Donna! You've been spending too much time with Louis."

"She's not really planning to do it?" came out with another shaft of smoke.

Lucina snapped back, "Does everything in our plays have to be about pain?" *Maybe she should keep her mouth shut… No, she would speak up.* "Why can't women be their sensuous selves without it being about guys getting hard-ons?" Did he have a clue what she was talking about?

"But that's what I'm saying. Cheryl will inspire hard-ons!" The tension in Al's voice made Lucina realize it wasn't an easy subject for him, either. His parents probably never talked to him about sex.

Then Marin burst in, "What you're not saying, Al. Black women and lesbians confuse men sexually."

"Who said anything about les…" Al's voice trailed off.

Lucina felt her shoulders relax. Hurray for Marin. Marin was coming through for her.

Louis' attention was alerted now. "Confusing to whom, Marin?"

Oh my god! A competition, Lucina fretted. *She and Marin against Al and Louis. Not a conversation at all.*

Marin snapped back, "Confusing to white males, that's who."

"Maybe I'm a lesbian," Louis returned, causing explosive laughter from Al. "Well, shit. I dig women."

"Sure, man," Al jibed. "And maybe your balls are boobs?" The two guys broke into raucous laughter.

Lucina leaned forward, whispering to Marin, "I don't like talking about Cheryl when she isn't here. It feels disrespectful."

Marin nodded in agreement. Al's comments had really jarred her. Cheryl moved beautifully, period. Not seductively.

Lucina sat back in her seat and fixed her attention on Louis. "Just tell me! What was it like watching us from backstage, honey?"

"The curtains got in the way."

"You could have sat out front, then."

Louis mocked a guilty hound-dog look.

"We heard the cheering," Al said in an unreadable tone.

Marin sent a grimace toward Lucina. "It's sad. The boys can't give us a simple congratulation, Lucina." Lucina nodded in agreement.

Then Louis blurted out, "I have some suggestions—want to hear them?"

Lucina groaned, "We need your good will. Say something positive first."

"I listen to your suggestions, Lucina. We've always worked really well together."

"We still do, Louis. That's not the point!"

"I thought *Markings* was very good, Lucina," Louis offered. "You told me a little about your scene and, of course, I know your mother. I think it really shows how she didn't—well, doesn't—understand you. That door scene is really painful but didn't you tell me you climbed out on the roof and knocked on her bedroom window? That was gutsy! Maybe that should be in your scene…"

"We worked really hard on the ending, didn't we, Marin? Breaking the locked door between Mom and Daughter is a metaphor. We're not trying to do a memoir. You should understand that. Your poems aren't literal—"

"Okay. You want to show envy and hurt by—"

"Come on, man." Al stomped his cigarette out in the ashtray. "They don't need our check marks!" Opening and closing his hands on the wheel, he added, "It was brilliant. I just know you women are going to take over the group." No way would he let on how they'd missed the birthing scene. But the other guys had seen it all; they said the response was very enthusiastic, especially from the females.

"We don't want to be glorified, Al. And we don't want to take over the group. We just want credit and support." Lucina wanted to ruffle his hair or whack him on the back. He was so elusive. "We worked very hard on those scenes. Now we have to work out more scenes before the Chicago performance. I don't think we'll have them ready for Detroit."

"Are you really going to do that scene, Marin? The one you told me about?" Al's hands and shoulders stiffened. "Are you sure you want to?"

"I don't want to talk about it now," Marin whispered, then started rubbing her shoulders and neck.

Louis had his hangdog look back. "I didn't sleep good last night, babe."

Now what did her Louis want? Pulled by his neediness, Lucina stroked his head softly before pressing her fingers firmly into the rocklike bone of his skull. How did she always know what he needed?

He was purring. "Do it some more by my ear—yeah, that's it."

She dug harder into his scalp. "Louis? What was that phone call you got from Wellingfield about?"

"Oh, that call! I was going to tell everybody. The dean of students called. Apparently, a group ended up at the president's house last Monday, making bonfires on his lawn. Dean Johnson wasn't directly suggesting we had anything to do with it—just wanted to know if I'd heard anything. How'd you know I got a call?"

"You left a note to call him back by your billfold in our dorm room."

"You shouldn't read my private papers."

"Aw, come on, you two," Al whined. "Stop quibbling. Tell us what he said, Lou."

"He asked if we'd gotten our check—and was sorry he couldn't be at the performance. Then he wanted to know, this was weird—exactly what time we left the dorm on Monday. Why would he want to know that?"

"What did you tell him, Lou?"

"Around six. The fires were started around six just before we left." There was anxiety in his voice.

"Probably some frat boys were having fun. Right, Louis?" Lucina retrieved her hands from Louis' head and let them fall in her lap. "Well, I know for a fact," she offered quickly. "We were all gone before six. How dare he suggest we had anything to do with it!" She looked out the window at the billowy clouds looking like giant animals racing across the sky.

19
The Pact

"So, we all swear secrecy!" Marlene reiterated.

The five in the Dodge Dart had formed a pact: they would do their own anti-war action on the Weymouth campus early in the morning of their Saturday night performance. Planning a spontaneous demonstration, without the labored input of all group members, made them feel daring and nervous. Jenny considered: *If Dawn had told everyone what she wanted to do in the Wellingfield cafeteria, they would have discouraged her— too dangerous! Sometimes a strong protest action needed just a few to carry it out.*

Marlene had offered to drive, freeing Jenny up to talk tactics from the back seat. "Listen up, comrades. It's good we're doing this. A group is only as strong as its parts. We're strengthening our group's purpose, not being subversive or irresponsible. Okay?"

Courtney elbowed her. "'Comrades' sounds right-on when you say it, Jen. I'm with Hans more and more. Like he says, 'We have to shake people up.'"

"Well, we aren't just entertainers for a bunch of white middle-class students, that's for sure," Jenny added, aware how

Courtney reached out to both her and Hans when they weren't clamped together.

Then Hugh piped up from the front, "Go, Jenny! The workers gotta take charge." *Without Hans around to sniff out her every comment, she was a different person.*

Jenny threw her head back and let out, "Wow! I feel good!"

*****

Marlene loved the earnest bravado. She looked for Jenny's pretty face in the rear view mirror. "Have you ever done a guerrilla action, Jenny?" All she could see was Courtney's reddish, unshaven face turning this way and that and Jack's head drooped on his chest.

Slowly a plan was soldered. Three would play music near the center of campus, feigning a jam session. While two, circulating in the crowd, would approach simpatico students and invite them to join in their guerrilla action. Word of mouth was safer than traceable flyers. As soon as they had enough supporters, the musicians would lead them to the administration building where the deans' offices were located. Since it was Saturday, only a few deans would be there doing paperwork and talking to students—not too crowded for their first protest action.

Jack, now awake, volunteered to get the layout of those offices beforehand. Marlene noted that he didn't usually make offers like that. *He's trying to fit in more,* she decided. *Even gurus need buddies.*

"No snake in the crowd is going to mislead us," he enthused. They all agreed; his sweet look, short hair, and open manner would make him invisible to any campus police patrolling the area. Campuses, just like city parks, had their snitches sniffing out "rabble-rousing hippies."

The guerrilla action would be to march single file through the administrators' offices to a slow drumbeat. They would remain silent; their signs would do the talking: "Colleges should be centers for debate"; "Let's talk about the war in Vietnam today"; "Don't be robots for the Imperialists." Strong, challenging words.

"But we can't forget!" Jenny added abruptly. "If there're any repercussions, we, the five of us, have to take responsibility."

*****

As they neared Weymouth college, which was squeezed into the suburbs of Rochester, Jenny's nervousness surfaced again. "Could we get arrested just for walking silently through college offices?"

"I don't know." Hugh turned from his front seat to look at her. "Maybe for protesting on private property? Blocking the administration's passageways?"

Jack put his hand on her knee. "I really think that as long as we keep moving, we're untouchable," he assured them all.

But though Jenny remained silent, she wasn't reassured. She was also obsessing about Hans and Dawn. *If she went to jail, then Hans would take up with Dawn for sure.* She began murmuring, "I can't afford jail, I can't afford jail..."

Jack broke into her drone. "We don't live in a police state yet, Jenny. Come on! Keep your chi up. Look at it this way: Meditation meets action. I'm just learning about that."

Courtney joined in as well. "We just have to be courageous and carry on. Every time a Black Panther gets murdered, a thousand new warriors rise up." He tried to picture Hugh fighting for his release if he were locked up; instead he saw an aloof Hugh, oblivious that his pal, Courtney, was shouting for help, over and over from behind a locked metal gate.

20
Cheryl's Face

Cheryl had spotted a small group standing in the back of the auditorium all during *Choice*. Not until they charged down the aisle during Sam's last speech did she see that they were Black: two men and two women, sporting sunglasses and leather jackets. As Sam was declaring, "I won't be a hired killer for the military!" they belted out in unison, "No choice for Black people. No choice for Black people!" and abruptly leaped up onstage.

"This is a half-baked, color-blind, shit of a play by so-called political people," one of the men bellowed out. One of the women had seized the red drum and was now punctuating the critical comments by her companions with a sharp beat, squelching every impulse from the audience members to applaud the troupe's performance. Cheryl determined: *They must not be connected to the group of Black students sitting in front with what looked like professors, older and less casually dressed, all seeming as bewildered as she and the other actors were.* For a few seconds she had a startling thought: *If the Fire Dragon actors had added a scene like this to their currently incomplete play, she wouldn't have felt so bereft all this time. How incredible that would be, incorporating self-criticism into their own drama!*

The four intruders, now commanding center stage, were hurling more reproaches at the actors.

"Your goddamn Sam should be a Black man!"

"For the Black man, the army is at least a job with pay and maybe a little respect."

"There's no choice for Black people. We're the ones in the front lines who lose our lives."

"And we didn't hear our Black sister speak out once to the Black dilemma in 'Nam."

A student from the front row stood up to address the cadre now owning the stage. "Tell us who you are! We're trying to organize a Black curriculum here at Weymouth."

The woman who was not drumming took off her sunglasses and eyed the questioner. Nodding thoughtfully and checking with her comrades, she went to the edge of the stage, where she sat and beckoned those in the front row to come closer to her. She soon had them shaking their heads with understanding and good humor and one even began laughing until the others shushed him.

Cheryl, in a state of great agitation, had moved away from the other actors and was now standing at front stage right. She had one hand reaching out to the actors and the other to the students in the front row as if trying to be a connector.

She felt the audience looking to her for an explanation of what was happening. No words came. She hadn't been heard. And she'd declared emphatically to all the actors: "I should introduce the play again but with a much stronger explanation of why *Choice* doesn't yet include a Black man's experience!" "Do it at the end," Louis had demanded. "Then you can say whatever you need to." *They all supported him, probably afraid my comments would take attention away from their Sam!*

In that moment of anger toward her troupe, she saw them as the white people they were. Their ethnic mix of Jewish,

Italian, Scandinavian, WASP, and a vague claim of Indigenous ancestry by one of them did not matter! There was only one Black person among them: herself, Cheryl.

She stood taller, still stunned, as she faced her questioners. How could she have allowed the unfinished *Choice* to be performed one more time? These activists were her flesh and blood, speaking what she should have been speaking!

Now Louis was shouting out in her defense, "We're revising the play! Cheryl is helping us—she'll tell you!"

She couldn't look at him. *Damn—it was his fault her speech was moved from the beginning of* Choice *to the* end *of Sam's last speech. She was to shout out, "What's missing in this play?" If no response from the audience, she would answer: "The young Black man's experience of serving in the military, obviously." Then she could speak out whatever she felt was relevant.* His approach had seemed condescending. She wanted to address the audience from the beginning, with obvious, undeniable truth: "We don't portray the young Black man's experience with the racist Vietnam War because we don't know how to, yet! But, I promise—as soon as possible, we will incorporate how the military may be treating my cousin, a war resister!"

The Black politicos had done what she'd failed to do! *She'd failed her people…her cousin…Marcel.*

*****

"Our Black brothers and sisters are being used as cannon fodder as we speak!" The four activists, standing together again, ramrod tall, shouted out in unison.

Hans' desperate defense—"We have a film strip on rampant racism!"—yelped out between accusations, was not even heard. The politicos made their points in rapid succession, continuing to criticize the troupe for their omissions.

153

Cheryl stepped forward then back, forward then back, as if she would erupt, remaining silent.

No one from the audience shouted out in protest to the takeover. Instead, "The Black activists are right: *Choice* doesn't express their reality," was murmured throughout the auditorium.

Courtney, Jack, and Louis tried to cut through the rising reproaches. "Let Cheryl speak!" Louis shouted. "The point we want to make in our play is that everyone should say no to the racist military. It's racist to be killing Vietnamese! We're still a work in progress." To no avail. The condemnation had by now incited an uproar. Actors, audience, and the intruder-activists were all shouting out.

*****

The quartet of intruders marched defiantly, accusingly off the stage and down the aisle, facial expressions masked by their dark glasses. Cheryl felt herself disappear with them out the auditorium doors.

Signaling each other, the troupe packed up quickly. Several surrounded Cheryl protectively. She was hanging back, fixated on the students and professors rising from their seats in the front row, gesturing and talking in obvious agitation.

Cheryl's need to talk with her brothers and sisters was obvious to the other actors. They would leave her for a while to do what she needed to do. Should they even try to perform *Eco-Drama*? Their once attentive audience was headed for the exits. Seems they had no choice! Who could perform under that kind of fire? But what about their contract? They'd just have to accept a cut in pay.

Later Lucina wondered: *Was there some metaphysical law about achievement needing to be tempered by failure? Only the night before, the women's play had been a huge success. Now this disaster.*

*****

The actors regrouped outside the theater building, trying to make sense of what had occurred. They huddled together, consoling then reprimanding themselves. Then it hit them: almost an hour had passed since they'd left the theater; Cheryl should have joined them by now! Anxiety took over. Who had seen her last? Had she spoken to anyone? Dawn had searched for her, but stage and auditorium were empty.

Lucina, unable to grasp what was happening, kept reassuring the others, "Cheryl has to come soon, then we'll go to a quiet restaurant off campus and talk." She was still defending *Choice* in her mind: *Except for the Cummington Peace Coalition performance in Massachusetts, loaded with pro-war students, audiences have responded intensely to our play. It has brought up a lot of questions and debate; it's only a beginning...*

A shudder went through her. *Cheryl's absence is real. She can't look at us. We didn't honor her pleading to speak first, for god's sake! Why did we let Louis convince us otherwise— fuck! Those activists are right! We're color blind!*

And why hadn't she, Lucina, tried to talk to those militants? She should have said, "Fire Dragon Street Theater wants to expose racism in all our plays!" Louis and Hans tried to tell them—Courtney and Jack too. *If they'd come up to us after the play, told us their demands, Cheryl would have agreed with them completely. The way they did it was meant to be humiliating. What if I'd taken over the mike and explained that Cheryl wanted us to revise the whole goddamn play before we ever performed it again, but we didn't listen to her. We didn't honor her advice! Oh my god—She must hate us now!*

Lucina sobbed uncontrollably as Louis led her and the others to their vehicles. It was past midnight and Cheryl had not come back.

*****

The door groaned open. Two figures, Jenny and Dawn, looking withered and panicked, stared down at Lucina as Louis

155

shot up from their dorm cot. Then she too jerked herself awake and checked her watch: two a.m. "Have you seen Cheryl?"

"No, not exactly," Jenny whispered. "But a student we talked to in the student union saw her getting into a car with one of the Panthers, or whoever they were. And she told us, 'Gossip is spreading like wild fire. People are saying that Cheryl dumped Fire Dragon and is going with the Black activists.'"

"But who told that student this?" Lucina cried out. "Did you get her name? Cheryl wouldn't leave us cold."

Jenny and Dawn backed away, completely wasted. "Got to get some sleep now," Dawn whimpered. "She'll come back. She's upset, that's what it is. We'll get some information." The door shut with a soft moan.

Lucina collapsed against Louis' body; she clamped herself to him and fell into a fitful sleep. Cheryl's face loomed over her, a frightening presence and a condemnation. *Tell us what to do!* She pleaded. When Louis tried to comfort her, she pulled away and began rocking herself until her breathing evened and she relaxed. Then something changed inside her; a soft light filled her. Cheryl's face was there again, but smiling, sending warmth into her whole being.

"Jack's right," Lucina murmured at Louis, who had given up attending her and was sleeping soundly. "We do have to keep the faith—keep faith that Cheryl hasn't left us for good."

21
Cheryl Speaks

Sunday morning, Lucina and Louis had barely settled at a table in Weymouth's functional but bland student union, when they spotted Cheryl standing in the food line with a tall, thin man, one of their accusers from the night before.

Cheryl seemed to be looking in their direction, so Louis signaled awkwardly. No response. They didn't exist. She seemed at ease and engaged with the man accompanying her through the line.

Lucina shoved her chair back, readying herself for confrontation. "I'm going over there."

"No, Lucina!" Louis grabbed her arm tightly. "Let her do her thing now. She'll come back."

"I just need her to tell me—what's going on with her!"

"Look! They're her political family. But she chose to be with us—her theater family. We just didn't do right by her. We have to do better." Louis' hand shook as he sipped his coffee. "Her sister's kid loves me—Marcel and I are pals. I'd really miss him if..."

Lucina calmed down. It was true, their theater troupe was a kind of family! She flashed on Louis and Marcel playing together in the loft on several occasions with such joy. When

Louis picked the kid up and swung him around, Marcel couldn't get enough. "More, more" he'd cry until they fell in a heap together, exhausted. *Of course! This is the kid play he couldn't have with his son. That painful photo falling apart in his wallet...a sad, wide-eyed four-year-old boy, always questioning: Where's my daddy? That little one had no choice in the matter.*

She stared at Louis. *I'm part of that sadness...I'm with him...with Louis who broke his little boy's heart.* Like little Joel in the photograph, at that moment, he too seemed to be frozen in sadness.

But how bizarre was this? Cheryl, only thirty feet away from them, acting like she didn't know them from stones. Was this her choice, or had those strangers shamed her into dumping her acting pals?

"Blind love..." came out of Lucina's mouth, followed by a fit of coughing. A gritty piece of bacon had caught in her throat.

"Drink this, babe!" Louis held the water glass firmly.

"Louis, we've been blind to Cheryl. We've all been so glad she joined the troupe. But we didn't act fast enough to acknowledge, embrace her reality. We've been blind to her needs, blind to our own racism in not changing *Choice* immediately. Being blind to Cheryl—it's so upsetting—it makes me think of Joel! There, I've said it. I've always felt guilty about your son. Here I'm with you—and your little boy doesn't get to be." Tears welled up as she spoke.

"That's my guilt! Nothing to do with you. I don't want to discuss my son right now."

"Okay, Louis. Okay! But it's true. Performing *Choice* all those times without really dealing with Black people's reality—I mean, that wasn't just blind, but ignorant. And Cheryl was trying to help us grow."

"Look, we talk and talk—how our plays are works in progress. And we're always reworking them. She never said,

'Stop the play, I want to get off.' The speech she gives about her cousin is mesmerizing. She should have spoken before the play. That was my arrogant blindness."

"Why didn't she push us harder? And why couldn't we admit we weren't prepared to perform *Choice* at this campus? We knew the Black students were organizing for a curriculum that speaks to their needs. Why didn't she say, "I'm quitting unless you…"

"Maybe she's been considering how to compare a white Sam and a black Sam? We need intense rehearsals to portray her cousin's experience. Maybe she's not sure what's safe for her to say about him. I don't know. She doesn't just barge in and take over. She's respectful. She waits for the right time to say something."

Lucina shoved her half-eaten sandwich under the jukebox. "We'll never perform it again until we've completely revamped it with her. I don't need militants putting us down—and abducting our sister. I'm not going to let her just leave us, cold. Without trying to make it better. How are we going to explain all this to the Theater Department? What if they don't want to pay us at all?"

Louis reached for his French fries. He couldn't cram them down fast enough. He finally managed, "Jesus! We're always changing that play. Will Sam commit suicide? Won't he? Will Sam go underground? Will Sam go to Canada? We just weren't concentrating on race issues. Okay, we were wrong. Damn it! We'll change it again." His glance darted past her. Where had Cheryl gone?

"How come, Louis?"

"How come, what?"

"How come we didn't see?"

His fries washed down with gulps of coke, he spoke defiantly. "Fire Dragon Street Theater is not consciously racist. We need to be educated."

"People just can't deal with the Black problem."

"Lucina, you didn't say that!"

"I was purposely being retrograde. You know, how they say the 'woman problem'?"

"We're talking about Cheryl! You can't cry how much you love Cheryl at one moment, and then say 'the Black problem' the next!"

"Oh god, Louis! Words are treacherous. Why do you think I was a sculptor? Let's admit we did the wrong thing with *Choice*. Look at me! I grew up in a well-off Republican town getting my fill of whispered, patronizing, ignorant comments about Jews, Italians, and the three Black families living outside of town. There has to be a mean-spirited xenophobe in me!"

"Where'd you learn that word?"

"I got tired of saying 'X is for xylophone' when I was five. You know something, Louis Altman—I hate white people. They are so clueless and arrogant. And I'm one of them."

"Oh, stop it! Listen, don't talk to me about hate."

Realizing they were both shouting, Lucina did a quick check of the tables behind and in front of them. Was anyone listening? Behind them, a couple bent sweetly toward each other; a busboy stacked silver trays on a cart nearby. And in the distance, she spotted Cheryl and her bodyguards again, talking and gesturing.

Louis was ranting, "Hate wiped out most of my father's family. Every Jew knows hate like they know the smell of their own armpits. We have an intimate relationship with hate. Hitler didn't stop with skin color; he went right to the genes."

His comments incited her. She wanted to scream out just as she'd done after the Middleton show, "Fuck hate!" There were all kinds of words she wanted to scream out right then and there. But most of all, she wanted to run up to Cheryl and hug her, and beg her to come back to her Fire Dragon family.

"The truth is, I object to any group using us in a self-righteous way." Louis spat out his words now. "Sure! They have a political message to get across! Yet it feels like I'm being hated, demeaned, all over again! That quartet could have spoken to us in good faith after the show. Criticized us, without humiliating us. But really, they assaulted us, then started pandemonium. Ruined us. They used us instead of helping us. Plus, they didn't care what Cheryl or I or any of us had to say. There was no attempt at communicating with us." Catching his breath, his tone softened. "Don't worry, Lucina. We'll get paid for the work we did. We did perform *Choice*."

Lucina watched the couple nearby give each other funny looks, then jerk their heads toward Louis. *They were being overheard, after all!*

"Louis, I know." She gentled her voice. "We have to rework the play, that's all. We were wrong not to."

"If Cheryl wants to help us," he shrugged defiantly, "she can't ignore us. She has to take charge and tell us what needs to be done."

"If she decides to leave us, do you know what that would do to us, Louis?" Her head was exploding. *Damn this vile prejudice about skin color! When did it begin...* "What's wrong with humans anyway?" Scraping sounds were filling her ears. She wanted to cry out to Cheryl. Cheryl and her protectors were only thirty feet away, moving chairs about.

Suddenly students to their right and left were shooting up from their seats, straining to see something. What had grabbed every one's attention?

"My god. It's Cheryl. She's going to make a speech." Lucina was out of her chair. "I feel dizzy. What's going on?"

Louis shot up, bracing her to him. "Hold onto me. Let's hear what she has to say."

"I just know. She's going to say goodbye to us, Louis."

*****

161

Lucina's Journal Entry. Tour: Sunday, April 16, 1967. We saw Cheryl and the two guys with her standing on a riser to the right of the cafeteria line, near the wall. They looked charged, luminous at the edges. Sunlight was coming through small rectangle windows behind them. And they weren't moving. It was really eerie.

Each of them was frozen in an exaggerated pose. Some kind of disgust. Hard to tell from where we were exactly what they were doing. At one point they seemed to be staring at Louis and me, as if Cheryl had pointed us out to the other two. I suddenly felt both exposed and obliterated. Most of us in the room were white.

Everybody began to laugh nervously. It was painful, embarrassing to be looked at, objectified like that.

A girl near me whispered to her friend, "What are they doing to us?"

"Zapping us," the person answered.

I also felt they were mocking us. I really felt faint. My arms were tense, shaking. That wasn't the Cheryl I knew up there. But it was incredible. These guys aren't just politicos, I said to myself, they're actors too, of some kind. They're making a guerrilla action. And last night too, that was a guerrilla action.

All I could think of was deflated balloons. I felt myself shrink; there was no air to breathe. Then they were applying something to their faces, their arms, and their hands. I said to Louis, "White face." He said, "They're disappearing."

What was going on? What were they doing? Questions hung in the air.

When their skin was covered with white paste, their postures and demeanors changed. They began waving in a friendly manner. Then I thought Cheryl was signaling to someone behind me. I turned back to look. I saw confused faces that must have mirrored my own. I decided Cheryl had sent me a mock greeting.

The three of them were waving at the crowd, as if greeting friends. But what did it mean?

Then they were wiping away the white paint, but leaving designs on their faces. Lines were shooting across their cheeks—triangles of white were left above their eyes. The blackness of their skin vibrated with the sharp edges of the white shapes. They looked like warriors, like shamans and medicine men. It was incredible. There were sounds, sometimes words, coming out. They began saying harsh things: "Wretched, pitiable white creatures—when we become like you, you invite us into your rooms. When we're Black, beautiful, you despise us." They said many shocking things like this.

At first, Cheryl's voice was unrecognizable to me. Then she was like a clarion call: "This is the land of struggle and opportunity. We know the struggle, now we want the opportunity. Our Constitution says, 'We the people.' It says, 'All men are created equal.' But who is that 'we?' That 'we' has not included us, Black people. It has not included women. Freedom has not been given to us. This country has been, is being built with our enslaved bodies and minds. Equality has not been given to us, so we must take it." At that point I remembered so clearly when Cheryl spoke to the group before the tour—how she would help us see the endemic racism inside us. Her voice so clear, strong, and so kind. That is our Cheryl. She's a female Martin Luther King.

In contrast, the men's voices chopped like clubs. "We want our lives back. We want our dignity, our schools, our churches, our hymns, our music, back. We're here ... and we're Black."

One of them went for the jugular. "We'll get these fruits of freedom by any means. We'll use the gun if necessary." It was powerful how they mixed poetry with slogans. I think they were speaking with the voice of the Black Panthers. No one else uttered a sound in that room.

When the three of them leapt from the risers, they were holding machine guns. Were they real? I couldn't tell. They moved like lions stalking prey through the crowd toward the doors. When they were gone, I felt faint, like the blood had run out of me.

22
Action and Reaction

The Monday morning after *Choice* was attacked, after Cheryl vanished with her brothers and sisters, a small band of actors and students marched silently but quickly with placards through the deans' offices at Weymouth. Jack's investigation of the Administration Building on Saturday morning, revealing an almost empty building with deans' offices locked and no students present, forced this Monday action. Administration staff nodded discreetly from their tasks and desks, but with little comment and reaction. A handful of students milling around the building flashed thumbs up and watched the procession respectfully.

When the Fire Dragon marchers gathered later to reflect on their guerrilla action, standing on the only patch of campus grass without a Keep Off sign, they had the aspect of whipped dogs. Courtney threw his placard on the ground. "It was dumb of us to do it when we're so fucked up." The others let their signs drop as well and sat beside him. "Admit it," Courtney carried on. "It was like a funeral march."

"No!" Jack spoke up with uncustomary fierceness. "It was an act of defiance—a defiance march. It was a rehearsal for our next protest march. Staff and students paid us respect. Nobody tried to stop us. We did good. We can't let anyone, administrators or a political group, stop us from our work, Cheryl or no Cheryl!"

"But nobody talked to us. Nothing. Just like Saturday night. Those four activists could have come onstage after *Choice*, given us some credit, some trust that we're in solidarity with them. Then they could have made their points, you know?" Courtney fell back in exhaustion on the carpet of grass checkered with placards. "Next time, maybe we write into our contract that our sponsors have to provide us with bodyguards," he whimpered.

"They didn't hurt us, Courtney. I mean physically." Jenny sat down beside him, speaking softly. "I agree with you—we didn't need to be chastised like that! We needed them to support and teach us. They used our play to make a point—actually to shake us up and the people in our audience. Let's try to look at it from their viewpoint—and educate ourselves."

"Jenny's right! What do we need to learn from this?" Marlene had the presence of a teacher, as if she was comfortable assuming the role she was trained for. "If we couldn't even listen to our comrade, Cheryl, practically begging us to develop *Choice* before we performed it again—why should these Black activists pussyfoot around, politely asking white people to understand them and deal with our racism? Our country treats Black people like second class citizens, keeps them at the poverty level and poorly educated, which keeps them from having leadership roles in government, education, health—you name it. It's a rare Black man or woman that heads departments and committees. The Fire Dragon troupe says: 'We want justice, equality, fairness.' And what these Black activists are saying is: 'We aren't asking for our civil rights any longer—we're demanding them.' We have to deal with our egos being roughed up, accept their criticisms, and find a way to build the solidarity with our Black sisters and brothers that our country needs. Cheryl is finding her voice with them, I guess. She needs their support. Why don't we support her in every way we can?"

"You mean, Marlene, that we shouldn't try to talk to her—or to those activists?" Hugh looked at Marlene with something like disbelief. "She could go off with them? Puff… disappear! Aren't we responsible for her?"

"Hugh's right!" Courtney stood up abruptly and edged toward Hugh. "Those tough guys are allowed to put us down and steal our Cheryl."

"It's scary." Jack's bravado was gone. "We have to figure out how to handle this…We need some food." He held up a stuffed brown bag. "Here, let's eat these." He'd purchased ham and cheese sandwiches from the student union and began distributing them. "Where are the others," he implored. "Let's get Cheryl back and then get out of here!"

"Look, we have to be diplomats," Marlene affirmed. "We have some political skills. After all, we managed to get ten students to join us in our protest march. Not bad. And we proved that fifteen people can keep step through a bunch of offices without a drum beat."

"At least they didn't call the campus cops," Jenny uttered woodenly as if she'd been hit by a stun gun. "That was easy compared to convincing Cheryl to stay with us and we'll change *Choice* before we ever do it again."

"Well, it's a fuckin' bad dream," Jack insisted, tearing into his sandwich. "Does anybody know if they at least paid us for half a show?"

23

Agonizing over Cheryl's Departure

That same Monday morning Hans, flopped on his cot in the dorm housing all of them, stared at his half-smoked cigarettes atop a Pepsi can and snarled, "Do we have to perform tomorrow at that filthy-rich white school?"

Not knowing where Jenny, Marlene, Courtney, Jack, and Hugh had gone, the others had gathered to strategize their next moves, ending up in the room Hans shared with the missing five. Oddly soothed by his petulant tone, Lucina sat down beside his limp body. *How can we pack up and leave Cheryl behind? Go on to one more college and probably fuck up there? She's one of us! We don't even know who she's with.*

"I know what you mean, Hans." She felt like a mother comforting her child. "We've got to decide what to do in the next hour. Go on, or stay here and hunt for Cheryl. Do we report this to the people who hired us? Call her sister and say she's missing? Find the students and professors who were there, in the front row? They might know these activists. I've been looking for Jenny and Dawn. They thought they could get information from someone who might lead us to Cheryl. Where are they—didn't they sleep in this room last night?"

169

At that moment, Dawn burst into the room. "Thank God, you guys are here. Cheryl just came. She got her clothes." Collapsing on the floor beside Hans and Lucina, she managed to add, "I had her backpack and little night case with me last night, for safekeeping."

Lucina jumped up. "Did she talk to you? I want to see her."

"She left so fast—" Fighting back tears, Dawn pulled herself upright to address the others. "She demanded we shouldn't contact her sister or the organizers of last night's performance. She told me to tell all of you—she has to do this for herself and someday soon we'll all understand. She'll join us later—over and over she said that. She'll contact me at Hamtramck, like in a week—we're going to be there at Marlene's parents' house, right? She had so much to tell me! She has to go to Chicago to meet with a Black movement group that the activists are members of—and get more information about her cousin, Nelson. She said when she directs us in *Choice*, this information has to be accurate and handled very carefully so we don't put Nelson in any more danger than he's already in. You see? She's not leaving us! Just before she left, she said, 'Don't worry. I'm safe with these four activists.' She knows people in New York who know them. They go to colleges where Black students are already organizing, doing actions against racism. It was like a coincidence—our performance on Saturday was on the same weekend as a meeting they had with the Black Students' Collective at Weymouth... You know, they have to convince the head honchos that a Black Studies curriculum is needed at their college. I guess you can say they used us to help teach the students and professors at the college swhy that curriculum is needed today, not tomorrow—"

"Cheryl really trusts you, Dawn!" Lucina broke in. "Thank god. Tell us, what else did she say?"

"That silence keeps the disease of racism growing! Cheryl said she doesn't intend to suffer the horror of being invisible any longer. 'You have to forgive me for departing abruptly'—that's what she said. 'And I have to forgive all of you for not taking my needs seriously.' She said she has to do more than talk about her cousin, Nelson. She has to find out what happened to him and then help us portray that truth. She also said, 'Louis and Lucina can tell you all what happened in the student union.'" Tears now streamed down Dawn's face as she faced Lucina and demanded, "Tell me! What happened there!"

The small group bending toward Dawn, needing to hear every word, were astonished: was this their shy, often apologetic comrade addressing them so fiercely?

Lucina spoke first. "I can't believe this is happening. She was with those same activists, acting out what it's like surrounded by us blind, arrogant, racist white—" She stopped abruptly.

Louis had burst into the room, sweat pouring down his face. "I went to the administration office to see if they had any information about the politicos who disrupted our performance. They have some info about what happened—they're checking to see if they were ever students here so they—"

"This is fucked up, Louis!" Dawn cried out. "Cheryl doesn't want anyone going to the administration. That will make trouble for her. She needs to find out what's going on with Nelson, not have cops track her down! Don't you under-stand? Her cousin may have been imprisoned or even murdered in Vietnam!"

In the shocked silence that followed, Lucina saw Dawn's face tighten with resolve. Louis stared in confusion at Dawn. "Jeezus! I was trying to do right—by her, Dawn," he sputtered. "Cheryl saw us in the cafeteria. We tried to signal to her when she was doing a guerrilla action with her comrades."

"What do you mean she saw you?"

"Oh, my god! I'm just another clueless white guy," Louis moaned.

Lucina grabbed his arm. "Louis! You have to go back to the administration people, to whoever you talked to about it—I don't know—tell them everything's okay. Tell them—we support the group who came on stage during *Choice*. You could say we've talked to them. Don't say anything about Cheryl. Just say we're not accusing anyone of doing anything wrong. We welcome the education that this group gave us and the audience. Make it better, Louis. You know how to do that!" She watched Hans' stricken face as he saw Dawn slump to the floor again, exhausted.

"Cheryl left before I could hug her," Dawn muttered, hiding her face in her hands.

Louis lit up one of Hans' crippled cigarette butts. "What a mess!"

"It's a mess we have to clean up," Lucina asserted, now grasping her hands as if they held an answer. "We have to listen to what Dawn is telling us!"

Louis leaned toward Dawn, who was weeping openly. "Cheryl trusts Dawn," he affirmed with awe. "Thank you, God! And she's told you she's going to come back to us, and help us do right by her cousin. Is that right?" Then suddenly he began kicking at the floor. "Big change agents we are!"

Hans, jarred out of his stupor by Louis' emoting, cried out, "We have to be more sensitive. Really listen to what people say they need, when they say it!"

Then Lucina's hands were at his shoulders, working into clamped muscles. "Hans can't stand our country's endemic racism—" She paused abruptly, as if suddenly waking up to an unimaginable truth. "Oh, my god, now I really do understand our Ghost Dance Tribute! Our country is founded on brutal savagery—on slavery and genocide. How do we ever deal with that!?" Her hands clutched at her own arms now. "At least Cheryl has the courage to act! For our sake—let her inspire us!"

Louis, overwhelmed by Dawn's information and all the jarring events leading to Cheryl's departure, was still driven by his own emotions. "Damn, how can we go on! No other choice—we have to go on."

Hans jumped to his feet. "Well, one thing for sure. We aren't ever, ever performing *Choice* again. Not until Cheryl has made it speak for her!"

"And neither she nor you need the cops sniffing around," Louis added. "I'm going to talk to the administration and our sponsors right away, like Lucina says."

"Ja, man, like Lucina says," Hans echoed.

"We don't walk on a minefield. And we don't create false minefields," Louis added, calmer now.

Dawn, almost inaudible, affirmed, "She's promised to contact me in Hamtramck and work with us. She confided in me…"

As she spoke, Hans interjected in affirmation, "Ja, ja, ja," nodding with each ja.

Lucina, shaking her head up and down as well, spoke out calmly, "For now, Cheryl is gone and there's a big hole inside of us. But, let's keep the faith. That's what she would want." She looked at each of them, then shared a personal reflection. "I've been wanting to paint her portrait—but I don't think I have the ability to portray her so she would feel seen, truly seen."

*****

Lucina's Journal Entry. Tour: Tuesday, April 18, 1967. Hans and I took a walk together. It was the first time I genuinely felt him as a real person, because of his feelings for Cheryl. If only he didn't have that off-putting bravado. I know

173

he suffered his fuckup with Louis, but I never accepted his tears until now. He said Cheryl should go to his country. It's civilized compared to here. Ever since Danes from all classes worked together to smuggle most of the Jews out of Denmark to Sweden and out of Hitler's grasp in twenty-four hours, repressions of all kinds were being addressed there. And, according to Hans, more and more Black people are going there. Only time will tell if somehow Danes have escaped the racism disease.

He said women occupy prominent positions in business and politics; they even have high positions in the church. Obviously, he goes for tough women. His two best friends in the group are Jenny and Dawn. He doesn't really hang out with the guys. Now I see how much he respects Cheryl. He seemed really moved, maybe shocked by Dawn's closeness to her.

PART II
GOING ON WITHOUT CHERYL

24
Lucina Gets an Idea

Lucina's Journal Entry. Tour: Tuesday morning, April 18, 1967. Before heading for Sonya Lighthouse College, near New Rochelle.

We can't say, "Sorry—we don't feel like performing tomorrow. Our comrade actor had to leave us because we failed her. And we feel impotent, not worthy of performing anything."

We have to believe that Cheryl would want us to go on. And since she told Dawn she would come back to us, we have to be ready to rework Choice. Be a responsible street theater, responsible to Cheryl. She's teaching us, just like she said she would. I pray she'll keep believing that we can do what she's asked for all along. Under her guidance we will strongly alert our audiences about the unjust treatment of her cousin. We have vowed to do this work.

So, going forward, we'll be unloading our props from the station wagon at Sonya Lighthouse College tomorrow at two p.m. Warm-ups have to be short. We still haven't decided how to fill in for Cheryl. She could change her voice just enough to distinguish the characters, Mother Earth, Mother Eve, and the Green Woman under the Triple Goddess mask

in our Eco-Drama. Cheryl, you challenged Judaic-Christian white supremacy. You were our magnificent Black Triple Goddess. I worked with you to distinguish each character's voice, remember? Did you think of me at all in a forgiving way, in the union when you were impersonating a white woman? I'm beginning to understand why you had to break away from us. I feel shame that we didn't hear you. What a lesson you have taught us.

*****

After writing this entry, Lucina had a brainstorm. *Why not make this performance a kind of process sharing? We can be honest with the students. We actors are a work in progress—not only our plays and tributes. And I'm sure those smart, rich kids at Lighthouse need to learn what current political street theater is about.*

I've got to tell them how much we have to learn about Black history, Black experience, Black culture. We white people have all been brainwashed by our endemically racist society. As we struggle to give our audiences honest reportage like a progressive newspaper and struggle to reveal injustice wherever it takes place, we have to own our own racism first and then change it. Weed out our own ignorant stereotyping of people of color: Afro-Americans, Asians, Chicanos/as, Puerto Ricans. I don't even know if these words are unbiased!

Her thoughts gave way to churning emotions and a weepy unsureness. How could she give a talk about all their good intentions when in fact they had miserably failed their own Black sister's needs? How could she be both honest and helpful to these students? The audience weren't their therapists! She took some deep breaths and tried thinking the situation through clearly: *There are probably no courses in grassroots, people's theater at Lighthouse. I'll have to check that immediately.*

Though a professor at the college did contact the Angry Arts Coalition, who then contacted us to arrange this spring gig. That's why we're going there. I have to find out from Louis how to contact that professor and check again what we're expected to perform. Louis' schedule just says Street Plays. Why didn't we clarify this—way back in February? Damn, we were so eager to line up enough colleges to make our tour worthwhile. Well, we can't do the women's play without Cheryl. We can't do Choice. *We can do some* Eco-Drama *and* Ghost Dance Tribute *scenes and* Catching the Dreamer. *And if I can give some kind of talk about the roots of our theater work without breaking down in tears… If I can say something about what we as a group are struggling with now, without losing face with our audience and especially without disclosing anything specific about Cheryl's search for information about Nelson. If I can present this information as a reminder why we can't fail our brothers and sisters of color ever again! Well, one thing is sure: As I present street theater as a way to give people information that can mean survival, I better not look like death warmed-over.*

*****

She hunted out a quiet area behind the arts building to jot down some notes. She must work quickly; they had to leave for Lighthouse soon. A cherry tree pulled her; its branches of luscious pink corsages gave comfort and soon lifted her spirits as she wrote:

Talking Points

Point 1. Political street theater in our 1960s is not being taught in most colleges though its roots are in Brecht's work, medieval plays, even the stylized Kabuki dance-drama of Japan.

Questions to students: Why, when street theater, the people's theater, has grassroots in many cultures throughout

179

history, do mainstream newspapers like the **New York Times** *tend to portray street plays as the work of rabble-rousing activists out to make trouble? Are these kinds of newspapers acting as guards for the ruling-class establishment to prevent the changes that the majority of the people need for a better quality of life? What can you students do to incorporate street theater in your curriculum? Is there an ingrown kind of prejudice behind your administration's choice of curriculums?*

Point 2. This specialized form of theater, demanding mobility and clarity, has unique characteristics and components: a multiplicity of purpose. To entertain, inform and inspire action means subject matter has to be timely, vital and challenging for its audience. Techniques have to fit with a variety of performance spaces and situations. Characters must be boldly drawn, dialogue terse and rich, and plot has to unfold within a short time frame—twenty minutes on the average. Action needs to be dramatic, engaging, stylized, and succinct (like a striking poster) without elaborate, unwieldy stage sets or too many masks, costumes, slide projections and props. Since performances are geared for the street, parks, and demonstrations where focus is often interrupted, audience attention needs to be seized and guided.

Questions to students: What kinds of acting exercises would you consider necessary to increase improvisation skills? Since street theater groups usually rotate roles, can you conceive of yourself playing several: director-guide, actor, storyteller, mask-maker, etc.

Point 3. Its rooting in working-class communities makes it a powerful organizing tool for building a political-cultural grassroots movement by establishing core beliefs and building common ground, dialogue, and purpose.

Questions to students: How can street theater actors develop flexibility and versatility given that quick adaptations

to different playing areas and situations are needed? A cement playground or a grassy park one day, a college gym or a professional stage another. A heckler's shouts can force impromptu mime or spoken responses to sustain spectators' focus on our message. Actors have to think on their toes, be able to dodge stones and hostile remarks, run from the police, and retrieve precious equipment (like our red drum) when under attack.

*****

After reading her talking points out loud Lucina realized she had a lot more thinking to do before talking to these students.

Who's my audience? Young, well-to-do students, coddled by overly protective parents and most likely mainly white? Like their professors, probably quite informed about and comfortable with classical and traditional theater. But blood-and-sweat street theater? Don't scare them with guerrilla actions (e.g., Hans' liquor store agitprop) or talk about police brutality and how their clubs smash bones and innocence. But they do need graphic examples, not just words. So, how to inform them, but not frighten them? How to get them thinking about and not dismissing the possibilities of street theater, just because they want to keep their dreams of performing on Broadway!

I can talk about our tour as a more stable type of performance situation. Begin with situations they're familiar with—indoor stages, college auditoriums. I can say how on our tour we have comfortable beds, good meals, considerate hosts and of course, paychecks, all of which gives us some kind of entrance to the establishment. Entrance to the establishment! That sounds like we're inherently outsiders, illegal aliens, agitators, street people at the mercy of the weather, hostile passersby and cops. That kind of talk can put this audience on guard. Most members of our troupe have college degrees after all, and everyone has had some college study.

181

Maybe I should simply say, Fire Dragon needs these gigs to support ourselves, so we can also do benefits and demonstrations. Yes, I must be flexible and clever. No, I can't tell them our whole truth. I can't tell them about Cheryl. We have to protect her now.

Well, I certainly won't use the word "hippie"! We're culture workers, creative activists, shape-changers, not psychedelic druggies. I'll talk about how dedicated we are to this work, to our audiences and how our choice of collective work necessarily means each of us has many roles and responsibilities. And we often give workshops back-to-back with a performance. I can even mention some of our particular skills: Al's knack for fast-paced dialogue; Marin's skills in effective gestures and movements from her major in Movement as Language; I can say that all of us are like discus throwers catapulting a vision forward. Or is that too presumptuous and confusing?

I have to talk about our concept of work. None of us wants to be locked in the same tasks over and over. So we rotate jobs. Students should understand that. There's no one top honcho. Each of us is given an opportunity to guide our work. We try for structures that keep us alert and growing. Each person's unique abilities has to be cultivated and realized. And I must not forget my big selling point: street theater is a place where all the arts can be incorporated, even sculpture.

*****

Why was it that every time she reaffirmed an amazing fact—*street theater is a place where all the arts can be incorporated, even sculpture*—she saw *Rune* huddled and silent in Shauna's loft? It was because of making Her, that she, Lucina, was now doing exactly what she was doing. *Rune* had been shown many times in *A Sculptor's Theater* along with her other works, where she'd worked with musicians and dancers to interpret the sculptures within scenes. *Rune* wasn't only a sculpture, but a character, a doppelgänger of her own longings. Yes, *Rune* had shown her the way to Fire Dragon. And now she was carving out dramas, not from wood but from life. *And in street theater all the arts have a chance to address the needs of all... But I failed Cheryl! I failed to respond to her needs! And now she's gone. I have to rest for a while. I have to stay upbeat. The show must go on.*

25
Making Adjustments

Louis was under the tree shaking blossoms into her hair. His handsome face so expressive, it shook her! She hadn't really looked at him for days. *Hold onto this moment*, she told herself, *this precious moment*. A flashback: They were back at the stream in Sandstorm, Vermont again. Two wild beasts madly in love.

"Yes, babe. That's a great idea. Talk real about our work and add some humor. But you better hurry, we've got to get going."

She wouldn't share her thought of wearing a leather jacket and sunglasses—was it to hide her sadness and shame? He'd pooh-pooh that! "Dressing like a Black Panther would be demeaning of them," he'd say. So she'd have to find her own style to feel strong.

Then Louis was off again to hunt down the performance organizers before it was time to leave. They hadn't been paid yet! "I'll agree to some cut in our pay," he called out. "But we did do *Choice*."

*****

Courtney, Dawn, and Jenny found Lucina alone under the pink tree, writing furiously.

"I hope you're writing a new play quick, Lucina. How can we perform any of ours at Lighthouse without Cheryl?"

"I'm trying to write about our street theater process, Courtney. I can fill in the program with it."

"That could work," Courtney agreed. "But it shouldn't sound like a lecture."

"More like a reminder to us, about our struggles," Lucina replied. "We can still do parts of the ecology play and *Catching the Dreamer*. I don't think we have enough spirit or space to perform *Ghost Dance Tribute*. What do you think, Dawn?"

"Well, I don't think we can do any of our *Eco-Drama*. Cheryl made the Triple Goddess work. It won't make sense without her. Aren't we trying to show that all humans come from the same African woman—Mitochondrial Eve, they call her? That we're all connected?"

"I can make the three mask faces look more African," Jenny enthused. "I can get acrylic paint from the art building. Black shading over the green will make more distinctive features."

"That's creepy, Jenny!" Dawn snapped. "Our Cheryl replaced by an African mask!" She felt sick. The memory of their private talk in the highway restaurant seemed like a dream. Could Cheryl have sensed then—when she planted those four terrible words in her heart—'I love you, Dawn'—that she would be leaving her and the group soon? At least for a while? Now those four precious words were like wounds. Yes, it felt like her heart was bleeding. If Cheryl didn't keep her promise and call— well, she would go and find her.

"Stop looking at us with such sadness, Dawn." Jenny's voice was harsh. "We all miss her, you know."

The corsages of pink blossoms suspended above them suddenly seemed unreal to Lucina—almost cartoonish in light of these painful emotions.

Then Hugh joined them: "Three of us can fit under the mask. You'd see six feet, four arms—two hands have to hold the mask. That would be impressive."

"What would that mean?" Dawn questioned.

"Maybe that we're all connected, like you said. At least by grief." Hugh hung his head apologetically. "I don't know."

Jenny smiled encouragingly at him. "That's right—and a black cloth could cover all three of us. You wouldn't know the skin color of anyone. Just a lot of arms and legs—"

"Oh, so now it's a Hindu sculpture," Dawn muttered.

"Or a spider." Lucina forced a laugh.

"Could we all just stop?" Hugh's patience was shot.

"Where's Louis when we need him?" Jenny whined.

"He's talking to the organizers again about our paycheck." Marlene had joined them with cold drinks and chips.

Lucina eyed Marlene warily. "You're so good at keeping tabs on him."

Ignoring Lucina, Marlene addressed the others matter-of-factly, as she passed out refreshments: "He's afraid they'll try to cut our pay by half of what they promised."

"That would be unfair," Lucina responded, staying fixed on Marlene's face. That opaque look, neat bangs, bright blue smiling eyes, made her almost impossible to read.

But when Marlene turned to meet her gaze directly, stating, "It's unacceptable!" Lucina closed her eyes. "Don't worry, dear Lucina," Marlene offered kindly, handing her a can of soda. "If anyone can set it right, it's Louis. You know that."

Lucina took a swig of ginger ale and lay back on the grass. *I have to accept Marlene's support for him. He isn't just my guy. We're all comrades and members of Fire Dragon.* If only she could mellow out with the pink wonder around her before it was time to go.

Now Al, carrying the red drum and clutching a can of linseed oil, joined the group with Marin directly behind him. Hugh and Jenny quickly filled them in on their ideas for a Triple Goddess without Cheryl.

Al was enthusiastic. "Makes sense. Three can play that goddess." He poured a small pool of oil on the top skin of the drum and began rubbing at it vigorously. "It'll be great. They'll wear black leotards and hoods. Nobody will know from red, black, yellow, white—whatever."

"Okay, okay. Just let's not try to be Black Panthers or something we're not," Dawn muttered, suddenly standing and stretching her stiff arms and shoulders.

Al stopped massaging the drum skin to check his watch. "So—what else are we going to perform?" Marin cast adoring eyes at him; she loved his taking charge like that. Why did he only do it when Louis wasn't around?

Courtney, trying his best not to bring the others down, burst out, "Lucina's going to introduce us with a pep talk about our work. That'll take up time."

Al eyed Lucina. *Shouldn't they all know what she was going to say about them?* But with Marin's warm look filling him, he let it go. "Okay, okay, that'll be good," he acquiesced.

"Won't *Catching the Dreamer* be perfect to perform this afternoon, Al?" Marin smiled broadly, hoping they would notice how Al was being strong for them. "That always makes us feel better."

His question, "Well, who decided that?" went unnoticed.

Lucina sat up and leaned toward Marin. "That's a winner with every audience."

"Decided!" Al was beside Marin, hoisting the drum onto his shoulder. Neither of them liked endless discussions. "So that's it. We're just doing *Eco-Drama* and *Catching the Dreamer*."

"*Ghost Dance Tribute* just doesn't feel appropriate for such a small space," Lucina spoke out. "We'll be in the student lounge. It'll be too hard to set up clear projections of our Sioux and Paiute faces and not enough room for a dramatic entrance of the militiamen. Besides, we're all too down to do the intense spirit work *Ghost Dance* takes. Don't you agree, Al?"

Al rubbed his hands nervously. "When you're right, your right, Lucina. Let's get going—what's our choice? Follow me!" Someone sniggered. The word "choice," once a harbinger of hope, now grated on their ears.

Lucina jumped up. "I'm glad you're taking charge, Al." The aroma of the cherry blossoms suddenly oppressed her. "I need some fresh air—it's too sweet around here."

Al turned to Marin. "See, I'm not such a slacker after all, honey." She patted his arm tenderly.

Marlene, hopping on one foot and then another as she put tennis shoes and socks back on, pointed at the empty soda cans scattered about. "Please pick up your own garbage, guys. Remember Jim's advice to us. 'Save our planet. Don't pollute.'"

"Oh, Marlene," someone called out. "You're like the school monitor." Another voice offered, "Well, someone has to be." Then another, "Okay, whose turn to do props?"

"Mine," Jenny answered. "I'll put the ritual props in a circle around the performance area. We're playing in a lounge, right? The audience can sit around us. Now I have to rework the Triple Goddess masks."

"Good, Jenny." Marlene gave an approving eye to the grass, now free of discarded bottles and papers. "We all deserve gold medals for rallying like this. I mean, we have to stop acting like one of us died, and be nice to each other."

"Well, I don't see how you all can be so, so…" Dawn, sinking to the ground, broke into whimpers. As Lucina comforted her, Marin called out, "Everybody cooperate. We have one hour to pack and talk through our changes in *Eco-Drama*." *They just better listen to Al. Things are going to be different now, with Cheryl gone. Something could even happen to Louis, or Lucina. You never know.*

The group slowly padded away from their pink and green carpet and headed toward their dorm rooms.

26
Awakenings and Dreams

Lucina, in loose-fitting cotton pants and madras shirt, stood before the Lighthouse students seated comfortably on cushions. Her nervousness contrasted to their relaxed, confident manner. Their accustomed expectancy of a good time, being entertained by the New York City street theater group, forced her to read her audience quickly and relate to them accurately: if she wanted to have any meaningful communication with them, some of her considered comments had to undergo immediate revision.

She would make a few points about the roots of their theater work and have the students ask her questions, instead of questioning them. If one of them questioned how the group dealt with each other's various personal and political needs? No way was she going to admit, "A member of our group left us because we failed to see that her needs were our needs." It was too complex and private an issue to disclose in this situation. Besides, it would dispel the image they hoped to project: that of a close-knit, politically aware street theater troupe dedicated to making a more just, more humane world. Could she simply say they were working very hard to be tuned into each other's particular needs?

*****

Lucina felt that the Lighthouse students were intrigued by her short, clear explanation of the street theater art form and amused by stories about the troupe.

"You sure have to be ready for the unexpected," she enthused, describing their performance at Middletown College. "Those students are becoming energized by rejecting ROTC training as a course for credit. They see it as a way to protest the war in Vietnam. They inspired an impromptu, ecstatic audience join-in of dancing-chanting-ranting and removal of clothes, with most of the participants crowding onstage with us." Her lively account was met with appreciative laughter and cheers.

When she pointed out that street theater work needed flexibility and versatility, "the ability to adapt both body and mind to many different situations," their faces took on questioning looks. "Since we perform outside a lot, we have to be ready to close up shop fast and protect our props, instruments and us from rain, hostile missiles, and mean cops. That's being flexible.

"As for versatility: since we see ourselves as a living newspaper, spreading the word, we have to change the facts we're sharing for each performance. Examples: In Vietnam, where are bombs being dropped today? In our country, what corporation dumped their waste into what river yesterday? How do we handle hecklers, who are preventing our audience from hearing our speeches? We might have to immediately mime an action, or hold up a poster with words on it. In other words, stiff, wooden, unbending bodies and minds won't make it in street theater."

When she invited questions, one student responded immediately, "We don't know that much about you. We know about traditional theater, that has one director who bosses everyone around and the theater people I know are just actors, or prop makers or musicians, just one thing. And what if you only have one skill? So why are you saying we have to be multiple people? At Lighthouse we have to choose one area to major in. And if we're going to get jobs, we have to be really good in that one thing!"

Dawn stepped up to the plate to respond. "You better use this time to explore all your possibilities, you know? The job situation is always changing. Who are you answering to, Mom and Dad or yourself? I'm not much older than you, and I say to you: be open to all your possibilities."

When Lucina talked about the importance of being sensitive to each other and building common ground and then asked for more questions, another student walked directly up to her and demanded: "What does 'build common ground' mean, anyway? That sounds like a Sunday school teacher talking. It's just abstract. Everybody knows that each of our egos has to be stroked! And how can you be versatile about subject matter if there's an issue that has to be dealt with immediately?"

Al took this question. "Common ground means that we embrace the fact that we all want to feel seen, to have value, to be stroked. So our plays have to embrace this, speak to the needs of all the people, as best we can. When we chant, 'Our Earth needs our help,' we're saying, 'The Earth is everyone's responsibility to make her a safe and healthy place. And you're right, if there's an issue that has to be dealt with immediately, that's the subject you work on. We find there are many issues that have to be dealt with immediately."

Lucina's comments about hecklers and cops weren't topics these students had faced yet. One women student raised her hand timidly to say, "How do you learn to not be afraid of hecklers and the police? Everybody knows about bullies, but I thought policemen were there to protect me, not attack me. I wouldn't want to put myself in danger, let alone be hit over the head with a club. Are you people into starting riots or what?"

Louis was ready for an answer. "Listen, I know where you're coming from. I'm Jewish and I was bullied as a kid for having a Yiddish accent. We're all afraid of bullies and hecklers. What we're saying is: Listen to your friends, not bullies or hecklers. But this world is filled with mean people and we all have to grow thicker skins to avoid them. Just keep yourself, your own center. As far as the cops go, I'm sorry, sister, but we're going to see more and more of them as we speak out for what we, as human beings, caring people, people who are simpatico with our brothers and sisters, need. We're not saying put yourself in danger. We're saying speak out for what is just and true. You will gradually learn techniques for protecting yourselves from the cops—we call them Guardians of the Oppressors. We're not aggressors. We're people speaking out for our rights."

An agitated, urgent voice called out to the troupe, "What you're doing sounds impossible. Doesn't anyone just say sometimes, "I'm not getting what me, myself, and I need here? Jesus! How can you have the time to listen to everybody's thoughts? You must be meeting all the time."

Lucina responded, "You students are really right on. It's great that you can speak up and say what you feel. I'm so glad we came here. All I'm saying is, you have to be able to incorporate different approaches and deal with misconceptions to find useful solutions. Listen to each other and allow differences of opinions. If an individual's needs aren't met…" She stopped, her shoulders collapsed. Was this the time to come clean with these earnest questioners? How could she go on and on any longer about what was needed to be a street actor? She forced a smile, adding, "To be continued, you all. The show must go on and we have some dramas ready for you." No way could she tell them the truth about what they were going through.

*****

Unfortunately, the student lounge had drawbacks as a performance space. Since they were playing in the round, the slide images for *Eco-Drama* had to be projected on the ceiling, forcing strained necks. Even with drawn curtains, it was impossible to ward off distracting light coming through the large windows. Without stage lighting, their Triple Goddess seemed an awkward invention of youngsters, deflecting its intended meaning. Yet the students were patient and attentive.

After a short intermission, Marin explained how *Catching the Dreamer* worked. Audience members were asked to share an important dream. While speaking into a mike, they were rocked in the dream hammock, which would cradle the Dreamer and rock them through the dream and back to reality when the dream ended. As the Dreamer spoke, actors would interpret the dream.

The audience was more than ready to share dreams. It took some time for each new Dreamer to relate to the mike and the hammock. But the students enjoyed watching their classmates in action and called out supportively to help release tension.

Their dream accounts of punitive professors, unrequited love, attempted suicide, and abusive relationships woke Lucina up. Why had they all assumed the Lighthouse students were rich, pampered kids? She'd better wise up to the wrenching realities forcing so many present day students to grow up fast. They were more than ready for true facts! Look at the no-nonsense questions they asked after her talk.

Jolted by the amount of pain wrung out by the Dreamers, the actors were challenged and inspired in their improvisations. Even Hans had to admit he had short-changed these students. They weren't just entitled, white kids; they were serious young people bruised and struggling. Wrestling with all kinds of contradictions, they needed guidance from their instructors and from change agents like themselves.

The last dream-teller, Elaine, a shy but serious young woman, relayed her dream in a strange monotone as if she were still haunted by it. Lucina rose to act this Dreamer's journey, a kind of primal struggle to find and know oneself. In Elaine's dream telling, she described herself being pulled by some unexplainable force to walk into unfamiliar woods, along a narrow rocky path that led to a small cabin with a locked door. Some force deep inside told her she had to get that door opened; her life depended on it. After an interminably long time of knocking and calling out and hearing shuffling sounds from inside, the door suddenly burst open just as the sunlight broke through the gray cloudy day. There standing in front of her was herself, smiling and eager for an embrace.

As Lucina portrayed Elaine's experience, she revisited a scene from *Markings*, where she was at the locked door of her mother's bedroom. Denied entrance, she now imagined herself, along with Elaine, lighting up with self-love and acceptance. Elaine's epiphanic moment was hers as well: she would embrace herself, not beg for her mother's acceptance.

Elaine's dream had ended but she was still being rocked in the hammock, as several actors hummed a simple improvised lullaby. Jack explained to the audience that they were insuring an easeful reentry back to reality for Elaine. As Elaine stood to return to her seat, seemingly pleased with the experience, the actors all felt some relief. They'd made it through the Lighthouse performance without their Cheryl!

Their relief was momentary. Elaine, emboldened by her dream enactment, addressed the actors abruptly. "What about the women's play? We were hoping you were bringing that too! We've heard good things about it."

As if on cue, another student in horn-rimmed glasses shouted out, "Didn't you know that this is our Women's Lives Week? Last night several of our more famous alumni talked.

We assumed your women's play was scheduled by the Drama Department to tie into the celebration."

The Fire Dragon women seemed to gasp simultaneously. Marlene tried to explain. "I guess there's been a serious disconnect in communications. Your Drama Department did not request specific plays. Simply, 'Perform your street plays for two hours.'" She did not add, "With Cheryl gone, our choices were limited."

As Elaine, now joined by several other questioning young women, approached the women actors, Lucina remembered: the person from the Angry Arts Coalition who had contacted them months before about considering a gig at Lighthouse College mentioned the growing coalition of women students seeking courses and culture that tied into the country's blossoming women's movement. Somehow that focus had been ignored in their later communications with the college. Another fuckup! "My god!" Lucina spoke out awkwardly. "We're so sorry for the miscommunication. The request wasn't made clear by your theater department. Or we misread it." She wouldn't name anyone. After all, it was their own mistake as much as the college's. *Maybe the Goddess was looking out for us,* she thought. *If they'd contracted to perform the women's play, they would have had to break their contract. Another disaster like Weymouth. No way could they have performed any of the scenes without Cheryl.*

Then Marin was speaking out: "We'll have to come back to perform next year. It's our gold-star, gem-in-the-rough drama making big waves."

Horn-rimmed glasses now in hand, the same questioning woman surged forward chanting with fist raised. "We want to see the Fire Dragon women! We want to see the Fire Dragon women perform!"

Marlene took over. "We'll be happy to return to your campus to perform our women's play and give a workshop. You can prepare for our return by telling each other the moments of pain, moments of gain that changed your lives." A row of women in the back of the room stood to clap. The Fire Dragon women clapped with them. Good energy had taken over the lounge.

As students began gathering book bags and jackets, readying for departure, a handful of female students approached the actors. "The Dream Play is amazing," one offered. "You seem so together as a troupe." Another broke in, "I'm majoring in ecology and conflict resolution so I can help communities work together on caretaking our Earth home. I hope your group is also available for performances of *Eco-Drama* to environmental protection organizations."

A tall, thin woman, older than the students so perhaps a professor, the only woman of color present, stood alone by the main exit. She watched the students talking eagerly with the actors for several minutes before she slipped out of the lounge, unnoticed.

*****

Lucina's Journal Entry. Tour: Thursday, April 20, 1967. Thank heavens we have some closure about our interrupted performance of **Choice** *at Weymouth. When Louis went back to the administration office they had our paycheck ready. It was for the full amount we'd expected despite no* **Eco-Drama.** *A guy named Don Blakely had reported to the dean's office that members of the Black activist group, Increase Awareness of Racism at Colleges had criticized our performance of* **Choice** *to help students there get the Black Studies curriculum they wanted. They were using our play as a kind of teaching action to speak to both white and Black students in the audience. So, the administration decided the disruption of* **Choice** *had been a positive action for the college. Louis was thanked for this* *work, given the paycheck and told, "Go on with your tour and carry the message you learned here forward."*

A hand poll right after my little talk yesterday proved I was right—most of the students had not seen street theater before. They were very familiar with the Broadway plays done on grand stages and the avant-garde, experimental plays by Pinter, Beckett, etc., performed in smaller but well-equipped theaters. But performances where the script, dance, music, masks are made by the same people who then act in the plays— this was new! One student told me it took half the program for it to sink in that we hadn't memorized somebody else's lines. That we were expressing our own passionate beliefs. But what really blew her mind, she said, is that we only sometimes live together, but we always share our struggle for justice. I loved it when Hans called out, "We share crabs and lice, too." He hardly ever jokes about anything, and to be able to joke at all with Cheryl gone was big.

I was so happy that most of the students appreciated the work we did show them—despite the fuckup about their Women's Lives Week. I can't believe how disjointed things are at times, and how in sync at others. We promised the women we would come back and perform **Moments of Pain/Moments of Gain.**

I guess our characters in **Eco-Drama** *didn't strike them as too simple. I mean, we're not doing* **A Street Car Named Desire.** *And they didn't need to be coaxed to take part in* **Catching the Dreamer.** *There wasn't enough time to act out all the dreams. One student asked me how we came up with the hammock idea. I told him a spider web inspired it. How Louis wished he could rest in a spider web and that gave us the idea. Actually, it was Al and Marin's idea, unless Louis told them about the spider. Even though the women's plays are the most important to me personally,* **Catching the Dreamer** *is the most* *fun to perform. Isn't it everybody's dream to be rocked? We're all in on the action, audience and us. It gives us a chance to show off our improvisational skills, which somehow amaze people. I guess it's amusing and surreal for people to become objects, moods, even time. When we build on each other's gestures, all kinds of subtleties can develop.*

I like it when someone interprets an entire dream with just his or her face—very hard to do. Or when a dream's characters, objects, moods are acted by just one person. Reminds me of when I worked alone as a sculptor, a reminder of how creative just one person can be. Dylan says, "I'll be in your dream, if you'll be in mine." It's also fascinating when a few of us act out the multiple dimensions of one Dreamer. Some complex dreams need all of us. I can feel when the audience is wrapped up in our dream interpretation, or when they're going ho-hum and falling asleep. If the dream has been a particularly painful one, rocking the Dreamer in the dream nest is really important, that is if it successfully gentles the person back to "reality." Well, for sure Elaine, our last Dreamer, was rocked back to reality so she could challenge us about the women's play.

To see your dream in front of you is almost to dream it again, consciously. If we can touch the nerve of the dream, there is magic. I think it was Black Elk who said a vision must be acted upon or it is not truly a vision. Well, Elaine's dream sure woke me up to myself!

Now I see what I'm doing. I'm writing on and on about our **Dream Play** *to forget our loss. Because to remember what happened with Cheryl is too painful right now.*

27

Tensions

They were packed up, finishing goodbyes to the handful of Lighthouse students that hovered around them. The three troupe members, who would be driving to their next destination, were pouring over roadmaps when Marin sidled up to them. "Can we take a slower, scenic route today—9W south along the Hudson River, then 189 into New Jersey and the Poconos?" The tightness in her voice made it sound like a plea.

"That's a longer route to Michigan, Marin." Louis called out behind her.

"Why does that matter, Louis?" Marin snapped. "You're not driving. The drivers should decide."

"Marin's right." Al turned to face Louis. "We're trying to tune in better to each one's needs, not run over them. Remember, man? I vote for Marin's way."

Jim and Jenny, the other drivers, nodded in agreement with Al.

Marin felt uneasy. Al had just defied his beloved friend. Louis, who could speak out so fiercely, had always intimidated her Al—a silent sufferer, just like she was, probably because he'd always been squelched by his Dad. But today, for the first time, Al had said no to Louis and supported her.

201

Lucina, watching the interaction, was agitated. "We should have switched riding groups after the first gig," she grumbled. "Wasn't that Marlene's plan, to rotate us? Maybe I'll ride in the Dart."

"So do what you want," Al snapped at Lucina and headed to Isadora. "We're going the way Marin wants today and I'm driving."

"You people are idiots," Louis huffed. "Why I didn't get a driver's license—" He watched Lucina open the back door of the Dart.

Marin held onto Al's arm as they headed for Isadora: "I just asked Jack and Hans to ride with us today. They'll be fun. You want to get closer to them, right, honey?" She sure didn't want Louis' funk suffocating her. "Thanks for sticking up for me," she added, trying to shake tension out of her shoulders. "I don't know what's going on. I guess we're all rattled about Cheryl's exit. Jenny doesn't seem to care who Hans rides with. What's with them, do you think?"

Al pulled away from her. He hated gossiping. Anxious feelings ran through him; if it hadn't been for Marin needing the river route, he would have chosen the thruways, too. He hated having to defy Louis for her sake. Made him feel like a kid again—pulled apart by Marin and Louis, like with his mom and dad.

He checked the gas gauge—enough for a while—and adjusted the rearview mirror. Now where did he put the map? "That pair is some boil about to pop!" came out of him suddenly.

Marin shuddered: Was he talking about Hans and Jenny? Or Louis and Lucina? Weird things came out of his mouth, sometimes. She just wanted to relax, be thankful. She was going to see her river again.

Al could see Marin smiling to herself as she twisted around looking for someone. Did she really want Jack and Hans to ride with them? He half-wished she'd decide to ride some-where else sometimes. But Marin had settled in beside him, like he was home. When she turned to him and smiled, ignoring his glum mood, there it was again; they fit together snuggly, like natural. *Geez, poor Hans and Jenny. They don't know about solid love, not like me and Marin.*

*****

As they stood by the Dart, Lucina was trying to tell Louis how uneasy Al could make her feel. "When he sees me hugging Marin, he looks at me in a weird way." But Louis had closed up, as if he could only bear his own thoughts.

"Let's you and I split up today, Luci," he offered almost apologetically. "Marlene's right! Couples can be a drag and we don't want to be like that. Okay? Do you mind if I join Marlene, Courtney, and Jenny in the Dart? They're cool with me."

"Sure, Louis." She gave him a quick hug, then mumbled to herself, *Fuck Al, Marin, and Louis, anyway* and beelined it for Jim and Donna's station wagon. *Good! They seem calm and Dawn and Hugh will be good company in the back seat.*

The back seat was empty, so she hopped in.

*****

Looking out the window of the station wagon, Lucina watched Marlene, clipboard and pen in hand, in deep concen-tration. *Was she going to shuffle them around now or check that no props were left behind? Who cares? We've already left our precious Cheryl behind.* Lucina hugged herself tighter and stayed fussing, *So let Marlene keep track of Louis all she wants. He likes that. Maybe she'll cool him down.* Jim and Donna were getting into the front seat. "Hey guys, okay if I ride with you today?"

203

"Oh good, Lucina." Donna's friendly reply eased tension immediately. "I wanted you to ride with Jim and me so we can talk."

Dawn crawled into the back seat as well, shoving a bunch of daffodils toward her. "Elaine and three of her friends made me promise that we'd return with the women's play and then gave these to me. Marlene wants to give them to her mom, if they don't wilt."

"I guess they forgave us for not coming through for them," Lucina commented, drawing in the sweet odor. "I think they'll definitely arrange for us to come back and perform here." She already felt better; the yellow flowers seemed to be trumpeting a happy spring song.

*****

Lucina didn't see Marlene's eyes light up when Louis crawled into the Dart next to her. "Louis! To what do I owe the pleasure? I just saw your other half with Jim and Donna." Nor did she hear Louis respond, "Yeah, well, it's good to mix things up a bit."

*****

When all three engines were purring smoothly, sounding like an atonal trio, the drivers signaled to one another, planning to stay in a close convoy, and Lucina called out to no one in particular, "Let's go. My homeland, the Midwest, awaits. Hopefully she'll be kind to us."

28
Marin's Way

The grand white houses, edged by emerald green lawns and flowering trees, each one grander than the one before, were not extolled by the band of travelers as they wove slowly out of the placid college town. These travelers inhabited a different land, a grassroots subculture that bemoaned the injustices too often cultivated by the inhabitants of these gorgeous homes. And most certainly they did not believe in "My country right or wrong!" Given the opportunity, like Robin Hood, each one of them just might rob from the haves and give to the have-nots. With the awareness that the land of milk and honey was a snake pit of inequity, there was no turning back and there was no looking out of car windows and longing for those extravagant homes and gardens.

Lucina eyed the daffodil trumpets (she often saw flowers as mouths or instruments singing out to the sun) that Dawn now held against her chest, and sighed. It was hard to believe: that night they would be snuggled into the modest dwelling of Marlene's parents in Hamtramck, a working-class suburb of Detroit. Marin and Louis' outbursts still jockeyed in her head. They each had a point: Louis, having studied the Triple A maps, knew there could be road construction on the very routes Marin wanted to take, which could mean big delays. He didn't want them to arrive after the Wolskis' bedtime. Yet Marin's request for a more leisurely route was reasonable enough; since she wasn't one to demand favors, it had to be really important to her. If this group couldn't fulfill the needs of each individual involved, why the group? *We're going to follow Marin's way. It will be a more meditative day,* she chanted to herself. Cheryl's actions had already blared out a painful truth: they had failed her needs miserably and they were all suffering growing pains because of it.

The majority wanted to follow the river into New Jersey before heading as a convoy into Pennsylvania. They would all go Marin's way. So why did she feel like crying? Because of Cheryl? Yes! But also she felt sad because Al had backed up Marin, but she, Lucina, had not backed Louis. She had shouted out to him as he ran off in a fit, "Why do we all have to go the same way?" And Louis blasted back at her so that the others could hear him, "Our three vehicles should stick together in case something goes wrong, damn it!" She had not even tried to make solid peace between them, like she usually did. *So, he wanted to go in the Dart with Marlene, that was clear. But do I have to like it?*

Let it go, she reprimanded herself. *We can call the Wolskis from the road and apologize if we're going to be late.* Through the birch groves on the left of the road she saw patches of shining water. "That must be the Hudson River!" she exclaimed, realizing at once how much she missed seeing moving water.

*****

Marin, now twenty-six years old, also focused on the river through the front window of Isadora, glad again to be with the great force that could gentle her sadness. Once again she vowed: *I will be good to that young girl who found healing in the river.*

The Hudson River was a powerful force in Marin's childhood, like some kind of miracle energy, making its way from the Adirondack Mountains through the Hudson Valley to the Atlantic. When she read of mythical beings loving sun gods and sky deities, she evoked that same ancient imagination and personified her river. Like a nurturing and demanding maternal being, the River guided her life.

The young girl sat by her River (her mother's house was in Nyack) dreaming of another mother, one not dying of cancer. A mother who stayed and played with her forever. Even as her mother weakened, the River heard her prayers and stayed strong to comfort her.

Each season, the River had a new face. Winter's face took her breath away. Ice floes, like strange temples in a dreamscape, moved in zigzag patterns as estuary tides changed directions every few hours. Bitter winds etched scary longings into her bones, but made her feel alive. In spring, smells of earth and salt spiced the air. As flowers and grass sprang up along its banks, giddy lightness filled her. In summer, sailboats darting like gulls on its surface lifted her sadness briefly. If only she were a bird. When trees wept colored leaves in the fall, she saw her River's sad face again; the leaves floating past told her time was passing, her mother was passing; her mother was leaving her. But the River would always be there for her to see, to touch. Always.

That first death wrapped around the seven-year-old and held her through the second, her brother's suicide two years later. Though she had no way to explain it, that force of flowing water helped her stay on, in her life, in her own body, without a mother and then without a brother. With that River force beside her, she was not alone; she and the River would survive. Her father had left her mother long before and stayed only as a faint shadow in her mind.

During adolescence, living with her uncle and aunt in the city, her grief deepened and gelled into a part of who she was. Her body was taut, her psyche dark, an onyx stone. Yet within her veins, the River flowed. And sometimes she could step past this grief, like when she found a friend in Lucina whom she could admire and love. And then Al, who understood her; his stoic, silent suffering mirrored her own. Her college years—the focus on movement, expression, dance brought healing. When she danced and acted, she could rise out of her sorrow, lift up; then she flowed as a river flowed, with ease.

And there was something to be grateful for: her mother, so terrified with her own dying, would not live to suffer the grief of her son's death.

As the three cars wove their way along the great river toward New Jersey, Marin remembered again the enormous ice floes drifting sometimes down and sometimes up the river. She remembered again watching her mother drift into another world she could not imagine. She remembered lying next to the river and crying out for comfort. Her River, a moving boundary between life and death, was of the spirit world.

Sometimes, when the actors circled the tree of life in the Ghost Dance, their hands interlaced, shuffling and chanting, *wearing the long-wing feathers as we fly*, Marin felt that same sense of being in a timeless realm; clocks didn't tick here, hunger didn't gnaw at you. And as they circle-danced, she imagined her mother and brother somehow present and watching them. They were her ancestral spirits. In this elusive dream space, her spirit mingled with theirs, hugging and finding peace together. This is why the Ghost Dance Tribute meant so much to her. Why carrying and planting the Sacred Tree had to be done with great respect. Why Courtney's and Hugh's sometimes nonchalant style with their tree upset her so. Within their ritual tribute, the sadness she wore like a nun's habit could lighten and flutter away; in that sacred time she felt freed and more whole.

The demands Louis put upon her, on everyone, rubbed at her sadness. Who could come through for him? With Lucina it was easier. There was a lighter feeling between them, like light playing on water. She could even put her head on Lucina's shoulder sometimes and relax. But Louis? If you defied him, he looked through you as if you'd betrayed some essential truth that his life depended upon. Even his praise felt like a weight, like expectation with no boundary.

In her troubled feelings for Louis, she felt love mixed with anger. That's what made it so hard. He did appreciate what she could do; but was it ever enough? When she realized that many of the others didn't feel this pressure from him, she was puzzled. Did he want something special from her? And why couldn't he just have accepted her need for the river route?

*****

By the time the trio of cars left the river and moved through the industrial areas of New Jersey, it was almost noon. Al was locked into driving and Hans and Jack were sleeping in back. No one talked. Marin looked out the window of Isadora and saw that the gray station wagon with the Dream Catcher roped to its top was passing them. Then Jenny's red Dodge Dart sedan moved past them as well. A little later they passed both vehicles; everyone was waving and making silly faces. They were just like children playing tag, she thought, turning to Al for some kind of grounding. They hadn't spoken for almost an hour.

"I don't know why Louis made such a fuss about the river route," she fretted. "The roads were fine, don't you think, Al?" Al shrugged in a way that said, "Let's not talk about that." She tried another topic. "I think our Triple Goddess worked beautifully at Lighthouse College—even with all the arms moving in different directions, it was like signers or something. I also think the faces work now." Marin spoke softly, not wanting to scare away the peaceful River energy inside her. She also did not want to awaken Jack and Hans.

"Were you asleep for a while, sweetie?" Al asked. "You seemed so far away, but I didn't want to disturb you. I could turn up the heat if you're chilly."

So, he had thought of her, during her long silence. Maybe he even understood how upset Louis had made her. She touched his arm gently. "Did you hear what I said, Al, about the masks?"

"Hot and suffocating under that damn mask," came from the back seat. Jack was awake. "I couldn't breathe and someone kept tickling me."

By now Hans was awake as well.

"Oh, shit! I think I was dreaming that Dawn was tickling me," Jack mumbled again. "Sorry," he eyed Hans carefully. "You've got a thing for her, don't you?"

"What are you talking about, Jack?" Hans was clearly irritated. "What's it to me if she tickles you?"

"Don't you remember?" Jack sat upright to talk. "Last night we were smoking some wild stuff at Elaine's house after the show. That truth-telling game? And Dawn was teasing me about something. That's probably why I dreamt—whoops! I forgot about the law laid down by the Board of Four, or whatever you're called."

"Are you referring to Louis, Lucina, me, and Al?" Marin groaned. "That's not like you. We didn't dish out any rules about grass, except for drivers and during rehearsals and performances. I thought you knew we could do what we wanted on our own time."

"The four of you started the group, didn't you?" Jack returned. "I respect that. It does give you some management rights."

"Jenny and I were there, too—in Vermont!" Hans, fully awake now, burst in. "How come nobody remembers that?"

"You don't talk much about that time, brother, and they do."

"I'm not laying anything on anybody," Marin repeated. "Maybe Louis is."

"Aw, c'mon, Marin!" Al snapped. "You guys have to stop hitting on Louis. He keeps track of what's coming down. I sure don't. I trust him."

"It's okay that you didn't support him this morning. Big deal—friends can differ." She turned to the back seat, as if expecting some immediate reaction from Hans or Jack.

"No more, Marin." Al uttered calmly.

She saw his hands tensing on the wheel, his knuckles turning white. "Okay, you like me better quiet," she said. They were back to square one around the Louis issue.

"I listen to God," Jack muttered quickly to Hans, "and good dope."

"But what were you saying about Dawn and me, guy?" Hans fiddled in his shirt pocket a few seconds and retrieved a half-smoked Gauloise. "Dawn's her own person, you know that. And so is Jenny. She needs a break from me—wants to hang out with some of the others for a change." He looked out the window as he lit up. *When would they stop for a coffee and a piss break*, he wondered.

29
Hugh Pulls a Fast One

While Dawn stayed hunched motionless against the back seat window of the station wagon with her flowers, Hugh, next to her, shifted positions restlessly, unnerving Lucina on the other side of him. One moment he was pressed against the back of the seat, the next pushing hard on the front seat as if wanting to get out.

Jim finally jerked around to face him. "What's up, man? You're rocking the seat."

"I was wondering how you guys felt under the fertility mask yesterday," Hugh returned.

"You mean the Triple Goddess." Jim softened, glad Hugh just needed to talk. "Like a steam bath. Only Jack could see. Dawn and I were holding on to him."

Hugh laughed. "You guys looked smashing, or should I say smashed when you came out of there. Like drunk voodoo gods."

"The only way I can do a mask trip is by being a little high," Jim said. "A beer did it."

"Understood," Hugh nodded.

"You could have really tripped," Lucina punned with concern. "I don't know about you, my perceptions change on alcohol, but more on grass."

"I get really paranoid on weed and Jimmy gets silly and talky. Don't you, honey?" Donna offered, then realized she should keep her focus on the highway: it was getting hilly in the Poconos with lots of turns.

"Maybe," Jim muttered quickly. He didn't want her to be distracted. "Let's not talk about it—we're not supposed to perform high."

Donna hadn't thought about the weird wink episode for some time; Cheryl's departure had shocked all quirky thoughts out of her. But there she was again obsessing on the two guys. *Did they like holding onto each other in the dark*, she wondered. *Here we're labelled as counterculture, morally permissive, and yet we're all uptight about homosexuality, including me.* Then the memory of Cheryl, expressing self-love so naturally at the first rehearsal of her scene, filled her. *She wasn't afraid—even with the guys staring at her. Could she be a lesbian?*

Lucina needed to tune out. Dawn said it once: Sometimes you have to get away from all the drama. She would like to rest against Hugh, but Hugh wasn't someone you touched casually, or maybe even formally. He was fun to banter with, but not particularly affectionate. Today in particular he seemed wound up.

A sudden recall of the open, enthusiastic kid she'd met almost two years before at Tamborcini's group show just didn't mesh with the Hugh beside her now. If she'd known then how hidden his feelings were, would she have been so enthusiastic about his joining the troupe? Sure, of course. He was a genius with music. He talked through his playing. She too had to communicate in other ways besides words. That was why she had a special place in her heart for him. And onstage he was intense, unapproachable, an ecstatic being.

It was beautiful to watch the way he dove right into whatever part he played. Perfect as a shaman trance-maker! As he says, he's not trying to be Wovoka, but to identify with him. When he put the feathered headdress on he seemed a warrior-saint who could give hope to many. As he swung them into that holy dance, their Hugh emanated a palpable magnetism, leading them all into a trance state. *He hears his own drummer but he has trouble being regular, hanging out. Maybe he needs to know a person well to feel comfortable with them, that's it. He and Courtney are longtime pals; and they jive together. I wonder what's with his girlfriend...*

Lucina tried for her kind voice again. "How's it going, Hugh?" Young men could be so moody. Had to be handled with kid gloves. Usually it was Courtney who threw his moods around carelessly like dirty socks. Hugh often stayed separate, aloof. What could be bugging him today? "I love the vision song you've worked out for the trance," she enthused. "'All will be as I now reveal it'—it's just perfect." But why was he edging as far away from her as possible?

"If only I could reveal it," Hugh laughed nervously. "I'm right near the rim, but I can't cross over it."

She didn't know how to react to his comment. Was it a metaphor—or was he high?

She turned to the window, scanning the nearby hills to distance from Hugh's odd mood. A voice broke into the silence; her Mother's voice from another time was saying, "Look at the panorama, guys." *Mother, mother, always wringing her heart.*

"If I'd passed over the rim—" Hugh wasn't sounding like himself. "I would have foreseen Cheryl's need better. Wovoka would have guided us."

"What does that mean, Hugh?" Lucina's voice strained.

"I would've had a vision about *Choice* and staved off her disappearance."

"Listen, it's no one person's fault what happened," Lucina assured him. "When we're all calmer, we'll have a meeting to reflect how we as a group failed her." *They were all upset for*

Cheryl. What she's going through around her cousin. He might be in prison—or dead? She needs to find out. Maybe that's why Louis jumped on Marin in the morning! Misplaced anxiety. If only she could go to sleep, find some peace.

"We need to be more playful," Hugh broke out suddenly. "This is all too serious. All those damn meetings aren't going to help!"

"Some of us need to communicate in regular ways, Hugh." Lucina clenched her teeth so as to not say something she would regret.

"Hey, how about riffing on a song?" Jim offered. He knew Donna couldn't take tension when she was at the wheel and he sure didn't want to drive today.

"That's a fun idea," Donna chirped up. "What could be the theme?"

"'The Actors That Got Away,'" Jim quipped. "Hugh's right. We need to loosen up about this. None of us signed a contract to stay welded together. Sometimes a change is necessary." Hadn't he and Donna started to remind each other how they'd needed a change even though it was much simpler when just the two of them were doing puppet shows? *We needed to reach out to the Fire Dragon troupe. Working with the women sure makes her happy and I wouldn't have Courtney and Hugh to riff with. Yeah, it's good we opened up.*

"How about 'The Actors That Lost Their Cool'?" Lucina quipped. She sure needed to loosen up.

"I'll be next to go," Hugh mumbled. "Or kicked out because I said something I really meant." He tried to stretch out, but his legs were too long. *I wish I could tell them about my Dad. Not now—everyone's too messed up with Cheryl gone. She said she'd come back to us—but now everyone's paranoid. I wonder what it's going to be like for her in Chicago, meeting up with some Vietnam vets, or something. I wish I'd asked her more about her cousin, Nelson. Jesus! What if he started doing anti-war stuff over there! No wonder she's worried about him.*

Lucina sent him a "let's make peace" smile, which was ignored. How could she get him off his "I don't belong" hang-up? Maybe he was acting out because he resented all the attention going to Cheryl?

"I love the way we forget our lines sometimes and someone else picks it up," Donna called out cheerfully to the back seat.

Jim quipped, "Then how come you hate it when I finish—"

"—my story," Donna quipped back, laughing. She loved how the two of them could joke about themselves with their new friends.

"You two are so droll," Hugh sighed. He jerked forward in his seat suddenly. "Donna, could you pull into the next gas station? I have to pee."

"Okay—seventh-inning stretch." Donna wanted to wink at him in the rearview mirror, but no, she didn't do that anymore! "Look for the rest stop. I have to pee too."

"I have to do number one," Lucina announced, glad for the chance to be silly, remembering how the words "pee" and "shit" weren't to be used when she was a kid.

Car windows opened and hands signaled from car to car. The three jalopies seemed to dip and bow as their inhabitants agreed to pull into the next gas station.

*****

A couple of the women stood at the door marked "Ladies" as Donna raced to retrieve the key. Hugh and Courtney got their key and headed for the men's room, near the air pump. This would just be a restroom break; gas would be cheaper further away from the city.

217

Those not in a hurry to use the restrooms moved to a grassy spot beside a scarred picnic table. Some stretched in the warm noonday sun, others smoked, waiting their turns. "I'm excited and nervous about being in the Midwest tonight," Lucina admitted. Dawn, Hans, and Jack had never visited Michigan before. Lucina told them about vacationing on the Great Lakes and how they were different from oceans. When she talked about flying down the sand dunes at Sleeping Bear, Michigan, butterflies started up in her stomach. Those joyful memories seemed like an invented dream. Here she was, returning to her homeland, yet her parents, living in Illinois, didn't even know she was making this tour. She would not be contacting them. Lying was not her thing and distance was preferable to the cranky, accusative tone they would use with her. She watched herself trying so hard to be upbeat as she described a family trip to Holland, Michigan, for the annual tulip festival, the time she first learned how to water ski. But all the while tears welled up inside her. Cheryl's face retreated; it was Mom and Dad's accusing looks penetrating her psyche now. The others were so intrigued with her stories that no one focused on the time.

*****

Courtney was still standing at the locked men's room door, begging Hugh to come out; he had to go really badly. Once more he pounded and shouted, "Hugh! Hurry up, will you? I'm leaking." *It's really weird what's happening,* he thought. *Like it's all happened before. Me standing in front of a locked door hollering for Hugh.*

Courtney tried several more knocks with no response. He was desperate. Then Lucina and Al were beside him. "Courtney, what's going on? We're waiting for you. Where's Hugh?"

"He's in there for fifteen minutes and he's not answering me!"

218

"Well, something's wrong, for god's sake," Lucina said. "Go use the women's room—everyone else is ready to leave."

Now Al was at the men's room door, kicking it and shouting, "Hey, Hugh! What's going on, man?" His shouts soon brought the whole gang; they took turns pleading with the invisible Hugh: "Open up!"

Courtney, having used the women's room, went to find the station attendant. He would get another key and open the goddamn men's door!

The attendant, a pale kid with massive hands, apologized. "I don't have no second key, sorry. My dad's got one on his key chain, I think, but he's down the road, getting us burgers. He'll be back before long."

Courtney's report back to the group set Louis off. "How long do we have to wait, Courtney? We've got hundreds of miles to go. Where the hell is Hugh?"

The actors, staring at the locked door, chattered anxiously.

"Is there heart trouble in his family?"

"This isn't normal behavior, something's wrong."

"He flushed himself down the toilet."

"This isn't the time for jokes. Let's break the door down."

Donna had done a search behind the men's room, skirting piles of old tires and rusted fenders stacked against a back wall. She reported her findings. "I think the two bathrooms might have windows that face each other. I went into the women's room again to check. There's one locked window, with pebbly, translucent glass; couldn't see through it. Maybe we should check if—" She had no time to finish her thought before she joined Lucina, Al, Louis, and Jim, already headed to the women's bathroom to investigate further.

While Al used his fists and the screwdriver from his Swiss army knife to try prying the window open, Louis shouted at the top of his lungs, "Where are you, Hugh? Goddamnit!" all the while imagining Hugh slumped over the urinal, passed out or dead. They would have to break open the window; but did it face the men's room, or not?

*****

Back at the men's room, an older man in dirty work clothes, with "Joe-Manager" sewn on a shirt pocket and the same large hands and thin frame as his attendant-son, had his palms up in apology. "No luck, fellas? I don't have another key. The one on the wooden holder is it. What's going on here?"

"Maybe he hurt himself," Jenny shrieked out suddenly, causing Dawn to sputter, "Don't go nuts on us, girl." Jack, usually the calmest when the others heated up, spat on his hands, Al-fashion, and started doing calisthenics.

"Maybe he's gone to be with Cheryl or the Sioux ancestors," Dawn clipped obliquely to Jenny, who responded, "Oh, god. This isn't a time to joke."

"We have to break the damn door down," Marin ordered just as the manager, inserting a plastic card between the lock and the door frame, jiggled it until the door jerked open.

"Why didn't I think of that?" Hans groaned, kicking at the ground.

Joe moved slowly, peering cautiously into the room as if he too were afraid to see a body slumped on the cement floor. Then turning abruptly, he jutted his finger at the anxious faces pressing in on him. "Okay, some kind of joke?"

"No joke," Jim uttered, pushing forward to look through the open door.

"Let's look in there," Louis cried out.

The manager was fed up. "Nothing to see! There's no one in here."

"He's right. And the window is closed."

Jim's report sent Marlene off like a shot. *I'll find him. Of course he crawled out the window like a snake and is hiding in all the junk Donna just described to us. The two bathrooms probably aren't that close. Hugh is outside somewhere sneaking around like a rat. Why? Because he can't deal. He has to one-up Cheryl—act out because he can't do feelings. He's hardly said anything about her. Probably cringing behind that stack of tires—maybe he crawled under that rusting Volkswagen bug. Careful—don't step on the bits of glass—creep up on the prick.*

Marlene heard shouts in the distance—Al? Maybe Louis? *Why were they still standing around like stool pigeons, waiting for Godot? Well, she'd rout him out! He wasn't going to ruin her trip home—make her parents wait up all night for them. Egomaniac!*

*****

Those squeezed into the men's room held their noses and gasped. The smell of old urine seemed to permeate the walls, the washstand, the one grayed urinal and stall. Bits of toilet paper clung to wet puddles covering the old cement flooring. The manager probably hadn't cleaned here for months. No wonder he was in a fit. He'd been found out.

"Like I said, he flushed himself down the toilet," Dawn spoke in a ghostly, deadpan voice, all color drained from her face.

"He's dancing on our heads, for sure," Louis snarled.

"Bastard," Al cussed. "Doesn't deserve to lead the Ghost Dance."

"This is no yoke," Hans added.

"Can't that window be opened?" Lucina whined. She should have made Hugh talk to her in the car. He was off his rocker...having a psychotic episode.

"Pretty good guerrilla stunt, hey, Hans?" Al, struggling with the window, its frame caked with years of sloppy paint jobs, sent a pained look over to Hans.

Seeing veins pop out in Al's neck, Marin felt faint. She'd never been in a men's room before and this one stunk. "We should stick Hugh in a barrel of peanut butter," she growled. "Aren't you guys mad at him? Marlene's parents are expecting us at a decent hour tonight."

"I can't move this sucker," Al groaned. "How the hell did the guy go through this window?" He looked imploringly at Joe, stubbornly blocking the doorway to keep the rest of the actors from pushing their way into the already packed room. Then Joe inched back into the stinking room to Al's side, past Marin and Lucina.

"You got a Houdini wit' ya?" he quipped, trying to quell his impatience. He was running a gas station, not a halfway house for nuts or crazy hippies or a street gang, whatever these kids were. At least there was no bloody body clumped on the floor. He grabbed a hefty screwdriver from the leather holder on his belt and in seconds wedged the window open. His head out the window, he shouted, "I knew this window could open. Your guy wedged it shut from the outside with that piece of wood, see?"

"So, where could he have gone?" Lucina was next to Joe, welcoming some fresh air.

"He's probably hiding behind those tailpipes and car radiators." The man pointed to a pile of car parts that to Lucina looked like a fantastic sculpture. "Houdini is going to need a shower." Pungent fumes of gas and oil flooded the bathroom as voices shouted from outside.

Suddenly a familiar male voice bellowed louder than the others, "Don't move, you hippie freaks. I've got you covered!" Hugh stood expressionless and filthy among the car parts, streaks of oil and dirt making him look like some kind of Halloween ghoul.

"You should be shot, asshole," came from Al, followed by a barrage of harsh remarks from the others.

*****

As Lucina shoved herself through the bodies crowding in on Hugh, she shouted at the top of her lungs, "We thought you were dead, for god's sake!" Gulping in fresh air, she calmed herself.

There was Dawn, lighting the men's cigarettes as the women still hovered around Hugh, shaking their heads in disgust.

Then Courtney shot out, "Man, you're off your fuckin' rocker! Hell, I'm peeing in my pants again."

"Didn't you use the women's room, Courtney?" Donna scolded, holding on to Jim's arm.

"I wasn't comfortable with that, okay? Now I'm going to take a long piss in the men's room, damn it!"

"What some people will do for attention!" Dawn hissed through a stream of exhaled smoke as she headed toward Jenny's car.

Marin grabbed at Al's arm. "I feel sick!" she gasped, just as Marlene limped up to them, blood running down her left leg.

"I couldn't find—" Marlene started, then froze ash-en-faced, as her gaze locked on Hugh, still standing awkwardly among them, dazed, silent, and filthy. "I don't believe it! Hugh? Where were you?" She raised a pointed finger at him. "I could kill you."

Averting Marlene's icy gaze, Hugh began wiping dirt off his face, arms, and hands with wet paper towels someone handed him.

Marin, now kneeling in front of Marlene, was crying. "She's hurt herself badly. You should have a tetanus shot, honey." Then glaring at Hugh, "Look what you've done! For what? You go to the office and get some bandages and peroxide right now.

You're taking Marlene to the emergency room tonight, just as soon as we get to Hamtramck."

Louis, back from running after the manager to give him a ten-dollar bill for his trouble ("I think you're the one with trouble, fella," Joe had responded) urged everyone to get back into their respective vehicles. "Come on! We've got to get to Hamtramck before—" he started, then froze at the sight of Marlene's injured leg. "Christ, what did you do to Marlene's leg, Hugh? Fool!"

"He's going to take care of Marlene right now," Marin declared, edging up to Hugh, who immediately reached for the limping Marlene, supporting her as they headed to the gas station office.

*****

"You got to admit, it was a neat trick, "Jack mumbled on his way back to his seat in Isadora.

"But, he hasn't said he's sorry." Jenny, completely done in, spoke up for the first time. "He hasn't said anything!"

Lucina would not return to the station wagon. She would drive Jenny's car, because Jenny was too upset. Courtney should hang with his asshole pal and with Jim and Donna. And she definitely needed to be with Louis: "Hugh's prank has used up precious time and energy. He owes us all an apology."

"And a full explanation," Jenny whimpered.

30
Love on the Highway

While Donna and Jim stayed focused on each other in the front seat, Courtney found it impossible to keep silent any longer with his friend. *Hugh's guerrilla prank was too fucking disturbing!* He retrieved the wads of paper towel he'd jammed into his jeans' pockets and thrust them at Hugh, who still had grease on his face and arms.

"Clean up. You're filthy, bro."

"Let's talk quietly, Court. This is just for you. I just had to get over the rim, for once. I had to get into a trance place with Wovoka. Like anywhere but reality."

"Are you for real, guy? You're losing it. Reminds me of all the people who think they're Jesus Christ—you know, what I mean! And they're blind to the people nearest to them. You really fucked us over, man. We're worried sick and you're in a pile of metal, grease, and rubber communing with who knows? You're too identified with that role. Just be you, for god's sake!" Courtney didn't know whether to hug or shake his friend.

"I came back again, didn't I?" Hugh returned meekly. "At least everybody forgot about Cheryl for a few minutes." He continued swabbing at his greasy face and arms. "And Marlene's going to be all right. I got her peroxide and a bandage. She had a small cut, just a lot of blood. If she needs a tetanus shot, I'll take her to emergency."

Hugh definitely needed Courtney's support! He felt spacey, confused. *Why was everyone so mad at him? He hadn't meant harm, just diversion. Probably he was trying to escape from himself.* "Court, can we make music to get through Ohio? I'm feeling down."

"Sure, Hugh—let's have a hit first. We've got to ease up a bit."

Courtney was already done in from arguing with Louis all morning about *Choice. Louis wanted to start reworking it before Cheryl came back, in case she didn't. It felt real good to speak up: "For god's sake, Louis, let's not fuck up again—She's coming back! The Black brother we need to support is Cheryl's cousin, Nelson!"* He had a joint already rolled. "Donna? Jim? A toke?"

Donna hollered out, "You know our rules, Courtney. Drivers can't imbibe. Remember? We all agreed on that. Go ahead, Jim, if you want to."

"Are you kidding? And leave you alone with the driving?" Jim pulled a map out of the glove compartment to study.

Courtney was riffing on Hugh's disappearing act. "When Hugh doo-dooed at the gas station loo, he sure did cause a hell-u-va pew." They often slipped into playful twin babble on grass.

But Hugh wasn't playing along. "It wasn't a prank, guy. I really needed to get away. I'm worried about my dad. That's what's happening. I was remembering him—when I was a kid. He used to say I should find a passion in my life—he meant work passion."

"You've got to explain yourself, man, to the whole group! That was really off-the-wall shit, what you did. So, what's with your dad?"

"He's got colon cancer. His girlfriend is really worried, too."

"I'm sorry, Hugh, but how does that relate to you scaring us shitless?"

"I'm afraid he's going to die—I goofed. I upset the whole group. I'm just not myself."

"You've got to tell this to everybody. They might forgive you." With a second toke, Courtney's eyes widened. "It'd make a great scene! Say, one by one we disappear, I dunno, maybe in the middle of a play. The audience suddenly sees an empty stage, then whammo! We all enter from the back chanting: 'Off the stage, into the streets. This is the war we're gonna beat.' You get my drift, man?" He fell into a hacking fit, half laughing, half whimpering as his buddy stared out the window, still thinking about his dad.

"You're not feeling me, Court."

"Here, Hugh—I was hogging the joint. I'm sorry. That's tough about your dad…"

"Forget it for now." Shaking his head no at Courtney's offering, Hugh wedged his guitar firmly between his legs and started working his left hand up and down the neck, his right hand finger-picking softly at the strings.

Donna tried to find some local news on the radio. She hated how grass made people think every little idea was brilliant. *What are those two potheads whispering about? Did I hear "colon cancer"? That's not riffing. And actors disappearing? Her thoughts were swept along by guitar sounds.*

Hugh's fingers danced up and down the strings. When he broke out with an improvisation on "Sergeant Pepper's Lonely Hearts Club Band," Courtney sashayed in with his harmonica, bending notes around the guitar chords. Jim joined in, rapping rhythms on the dashboard. And soon Donna was humming along.

At a break in the music, Donna put her hand on Jim's knee: "Honey, have you noticed how many cars are in pairs? I swear, even trucks have mates. Maybe I got a contact high. Or else I'm crazy as a daisy, but I must have counted ten pairs of matched vehicles." *Probably Hugh's disappearing act flipped me out.* "Do you see those two snappy yellow Volkswagens? I saw two U-Haul trailers tailing each other this morning. I'm not kidding."

Hugh and Courtney stopped their riffing to search for twin vehicles. When two enormous Mayflower vans came hurtling side by side down the highway to their left, all four of them fell into laughter.

"*Birds do it,*" Donna started singing. "*Bees do it. Even Super 88 Olds-mo-biles do it…*"

"*Let's do it,*" Courtney crooned. "*Let's fall in love.*"

Jim turned abruptly to Donna. "How can that guy go so long without seeing Joan?"

"What guy, Jim?"

"Jack. Maybe Oms and headstands are enough for her, but how can a guy go so long without getting laid?"

Donna groaned. "I hate that expression. He's not a carpet!"

"Okay, getting fucked then!" Soon Jim was on a talking jag about Louis and Lucina; he'd been thinking about them. He edged closer to Donna, glad that Hugh and Courtney were at it again were their guitars. "What's with those two? Kinda gutsy to argue in front of us," he whispered. "You know, get it out right away? Must be their shit is getting to her."

"Who's 'her'?"

"Dawn. And that's why she doesn't want to live with them any more in the loft. How easy could that be for anyone? What a moody kid! I sure couldn't take her."

"That's new. I thought you were into her—"

"Besides, I don't think she likes guys."

That was one topic she wouldn't touch! "I've been reminded by my sister actors—we don't talk *about* each other— we talk *to* each other." Donna fell silent. *It wasn't right to talk about Dawn. They all needed to be more sensitive.*

Courtney was tired of trying to catch any of the conversation in the front seat. At least playing music made Hugh look better. He slapped his friend's shoulder. "Something cool now, guy. How about 'Hugh's Loo's Blues'?"

Hugh felt his body relax. The music was helping. *Court's right. Got to admit to all of them—pulling that crazy stunt was psychotic. Oh, god! Maybe I need a shrink. Maybe Dad isn't going to die! Just be sick for a long time.*

31
Private Thoughts

As the Poconos rolled by, Lucina drove the Dart and discussed Hamtramck arrangements with Louis, seated beside her. Soon they'd be on the outskirts of Pittsburgh. Marlene, Jenny, and Dawn munched dreamily on sandwiches in the back seat. Actually, Dawn was in a deep reverie.

How had L and L taken over her life? Were they substitute parents, or what? Their excitement and intensity were contagious. Like things really mattered to them. But this was what bugged her as well. They didn't let anything go. You had to continually deal, confront. That or pretend you were asleep. But she couldn't fool Cheryl that way: "Your wheels are always turning..." And she said she loves me. Heat filled her body. *We love each other! And I don't really know where she is—sure, Chicago somewhere. If she had to leave us to be with her close people, she'll find someone more like her. But wait—it's about Nelson. Why didn't I ask her more? There wasn't time. This is torture—I don't know how to do this...*

No! She wouldn't go back to nights blitzed out on beer, waking up mornings beside a stranger, usually someone she barely liked. L and L had changed that. They made her feel good about herself. Louis liked her poetry, that was it. He always had something good to say, along with the advice. That was okay. Sometimes she even felt happy. *But not now. Even riding along the highway eating chicken salad sandwiches makes me sad. There's no Cheryl to keep me okay.* She felt nauseous; the sharp onion taste in her mouth made her gag. Could she tell Lucina to stop the car? *Get out and throw up!*

Louis, so fierce and smart. He made her feel, well, maybe not happy, but alive. Push, push, making her think. He and Lucina didn't talk about happy; they just got excited. That or mad. They made waves. Professors at her college analyzed but didn't get excited. Just stayed in their heads. You wrote papers. They didn't say, "Now do something about it." Like that. She wasn't the only one who fell asleep in class. But L and L? You must act. Funny, that's what they did, act! Onstage, offstage. They were always acting. *But wait! What I did in that cafeteria—lighting the napkins, crying out for the burnt children. That was real stuff. Cheryl understands me! That was horror and outrage! Is that why Cheryl loves me? No! Cheryl loved me before that. But what does it mean now?*

That first time she saw *Ghost Dance*? Like wow! A wake-up call. The way Hugh looked like a shaman. It was scary. And how Hans was a turn-on with his long blond hair and funny accent. That was before she knew about his guerrilla thing. So serious. Had anyone noticed how he snuggled to her when Jenny wasn't there? It wasn't right, she would talk to Hans and change that. She liked Jenny as much as Hans and that was the truth. *If Cheryl were here…*

Back then, at the Ghost Dance, Louis was playing the red drum. She didn't know how good he could talk, at first. He was so into playing that drum. Right away, she was hanging around after the shows, wanting to be near them, look at their faces up close, their hands. Couldn't talk; it would come out dumb. That was so neat—Louis said she should go with them to the

Cedar Tavern. He liked women; she could feel that. But he loved Lucina. She felt like a big-eyed little kid with them. But they talked to her like she was a real person. Words like passion, fire, duende, that's what they were about. They said you had to talk out, tell your truth. *Okay, I'll have to tell them. After the tour, after I've moved out of the loft, then I'll tell them what I did at Wellingfield.*

The sharp taste was in her mouth again. Her eyes clinched back tears. *There's no Cheryl here to help me figure it out!*

*****

Lucina too was reflecting, glad for the quiet after Hugh's bizarre actions. *Something is off with him. His judgment. Didn't he realize how upset we'd be? Ever since he started leading the Ghost Dance, he's not the same Hugh I first met..* She felt a rush in her head. *My god, that's it. Hugh is obsessed. He doesn't stop identifying with Wovoka. He's struggling with something. Tries to escape to another reality. Have to talk to him—maybe have someone else lead the dance. Courtney's too clumsy. Hans, too arrogant. Jim? Oh, god! His claim to some Lakota blood—and we think Hugh's messed up about that role! So Jack? Yes, Jack. Talk to Louis—later.* Drive and think her own thoughts now. Be with herself for a change.

*****

Dawn opened her window a crack. The nausea went away. She remembered how she'd found a new home. *After that benefit performance for the Newark ERAP project at Washington Square Church, I followed them to the Cedar Tavern with some political science majors. They talked about revolution and evolution. Words I never really understood before. Louis said revolution usually meant a forced overthrow of one system for another. But incorporating revolving into its meaning "brings us closer to evolution," he said. "A slow evolving process of growth," something like that. Then everyone said the word "change" over and over. "Make change." They chanted it and other people in the bar joined them. Then Lucina talked about Happenings and we all tried to remember who started that movement anyway. Kaprow or Cage, or was it Oldenburg or Grooms? They all contributed, she explained. It was an evolution. Lucina talks less than Louis. But when she does, it's so clear.*

As if she'd heard Dawn's thoughts, Lucina started thinking about Happenings and how they influenced her work. Such a common word was used to make a revolution in the art world. Art pieces, paintings and sculptures, could no longer be static objects on walls or bases. Something had to happen with or to them to bring them into *Now*. The things created had to interact with people, both the creator and the audience. They had to come alive, make meaning through movement and change people's perceptions. She should have included these ideas in her talk to the Lighthouse students. How Happenings are part of the evolution of political street theater, an art form inspiring action and movement.

Happenings had inspired her performances: *A Sculptor's Theater*. She couldn't conceive of her works as static objects to be sold. They were almost actors in scenes. *And I made the audience move to different spaces to see each scene. When I hear about "the Movement," I always think of making people move.*

I remember when we first got to know Dawn, at the Cedar Tavern. Louis and I were doing a lot of talking. Dawn came up to me as we were leaving. "You're the smartest people I know," she said. She'd been a student in a college in California, but she wasn't learning what she needed to know. She asked so many questions about who we wanted to reach the most in our theater work. I explained to her that we hoped to communicate with all kinds of people, but certainly students and other young people like herself who cared about what was happening in the country and who wanted to make it better for Black people, for women, for gay and lesbian people, for all people seeking their true identity and destiny. That we were rising up, fighting oppression. And that we were creating our own way on how to do that, but also connecting to others with the same goals. Louis told her how we supported a global humanist community, not an imperialist U.S. When Louis told her about SDS and how students were rising up and organizing for a truly democratic society, something that hadn't happened a lot since the 1930s, she got so excited. She said she didn't love being a college student; she wanted to be a student of the world. Maybe we sounded more like preachers than artists, but she came the very next week to our loft on Spring Street. I found her huddling on the stoop. We were having an open workshop that same afternoon. No coincidence that she was there.

Lucina looked into the rearview mirror. There she was, their Dawn, in the backseat, the youngest member of their little family. If they'd been more careful would they have taken her in? A college dropout with disgruntled parents. No telling what the parents might accuse them of doing with their daughter! Abductors! Traffickers of minors! What was she—nineteen? Twenty? Maybe it wasn't a good idea, letting her stay in the loft. She should talk to Louis about this. What if the police came to their door looking for her? What would they say? *The poor baby is missing Cheryl so much. Like I was missing Sally. Missing intimacy with another woman.*

*****

Jenny was still hungry. Sure, Louis had more sandwiches, grapes and cookies, too.

"Such a good Mommy and Daddy," Jenny said with an edge. "Do you guys ever think of us sometimes as your kids?

235

You know, like a new kind of family that doesn't make you crazy? At least not crazy in the same way as—"

"I was just thinking about that, Jenny." Lucina felt a smile spread over her face. "How we are a kind of little family, not a nuclear family, but a new, clear family."

"You're all my little sweethearts." Louis, emoting, turned to the back seat, eagerly handing Dawn and Marlene packets of food.

Marlene giggled: "We're not so little, Louis." She had more than once thought about the fact that she was almost as tall as Louis. Could he ever really be into a tall woman, she'd wondered.

"All too incestuous," Jenny clipped, eyeing Dawn carefully.

"Maybe we're all brothers and sisters from a past life." Dawn stared through Jenny. She was hearing Cheryl again, like she was right in her ear: *"I know what's going on, sister. The wheels are churning..."* Every time she thought of Cheryl now, she felt the chill of loneliness. Something like that.

"Nobody looks anything like anyone else," Marlene giggled. Warm feelings ran through her from Louis' grin. Then Cheryl pushed into her thoughts. *Cheryl, so there, so real. How could Cheryl have stayed with us as long as she did? Every one of us enamored with her and yet not listening to her. That's fucked up racism!* She looked fiercely into Dawn and Jenny's faces and felt like sobbing.

*****

As she relished the wet sweetness of the grapes, Dawn stayed with her thoughts. *Maybe that fall she would move out of L and L's loft, get her own apartment. Work more on poetry. Have something of her own—like Louis and Lucina had. The theater was more their vision and Marin's and Al's, not hers.*

Maybe with the women's play it would be different. Maybe it would be all their thing. The women's thing. But wait! When she lit the napkins in that place, Wellingfield, that was her doing something. Something amazing. She did that. Hans and Jenny knew. Now Cheryl did too. If Cheryl really loves me, won't she have to see me again? Cheryl doesn't play with people. She will call me—she will—she will.

*****

"You okay, Dawn?" Louis called out from the front seat. Dawn was choking; she had swallowed a grape whole. "Here, take some water." He handed her his half empty bottle of spring water.

She took a drink, then closed her eyes, trying to calm herself. She imagined the grape sliding down her throat into her stomach into a pool of water. Breathe deeply into that pool, she told herself. When she opened her eyes, Louis was still looking at her with concern. She gave him a grateful smile, knowing right then what she had to do: she had to find Cheryl, no matter what happened.

She did love Louis; he was kind, a kind teacher. Lucina was harder to know; she would like to know her better. L and L had love. They stood together and were not afraid to disagree. She couldn't believe it: Louis and Lucina were actually married! Lucina told them, all the women, after one of the rehearsals on her scene. She had tears and then was laughing. How her mother sent them twin bed sheets when she told them they got married at the Justice of the Peace. Some Justice of the Peace, she said. He was drunk and bumbling about. Lucina was spilling the beans about a lot of things: told them she might decide not to be monogamous someday. Things were always changing like that.

Yes, she really better get her own apartment. Maybe Cheryl and Sadie and Marcel could visit her then. But first, she had to find Cheryl. If she had to split from the group soon, she would. A need was growing, like an everywhere ache. There was no one she could talk to—no one she trusted enough, except Cheryl. *Had Cheryl really said those words! She must go over how it happened: The first thing she said was, "I feel the need to say something very private"—and did she say, "potentially dangerous"? Why would loving someone be dangerous?*

32
Storytelling

Marlene's secret was making her really sick: she and Louis had slept together one night in February. Ever since then, whenever she was with Lucina she had a sinking feeling, like she was a phony. Maybe that was why Lucina was edgy with her; Louis had told her, though he'd said he wouldn't. *So why in hell did she jump into Lucina's scene and offer to play her? Like she was trying to be Lucina, the woman Louis was really with. How cuckoo was that?*

Lucina was in Philadelphia visiting an old friend when it happened. Marlene, almost jokingly, had challenged Louis to sleep with her. He took the challenge. She wanted to remember it as a night of easy lovemaking, something casual and no big deal, a one-time only, just as Louis had wanted. But she couldn't do that; it had been just too wonderful!

Then afterwards, the gnawing feeling stayed in her gut. A day hadn't gone by that she didn't ask herself: was it worth the agony? She could still feel him inside her, filling her with plea-sure, sensations she'd never known. How he stayed with her, his penis stroking, probing, and determined to find her deepest places, until she came, twice. His pungent odor, his hot skin, his joy driving her to laughter. Well, she was a fool; if she hadn't liked him, okay, forget it. But she did. She loved him!

Marlene focused on her apple and tried to ignore the loving looks Lucina was giving Louis. Trusting, adoring looks. It was a mistake to ride with them; she would not do that again! Spring was not a happy time. Flowers, birds, bees? Forget it. Spring was torture.

Lucina was telling a funny story about sticking a pea up her nose. *She sure likes to talk and drive.* "By the time I got it out, it had sprouted." *Everybody's laughing.*

"I'm feeling a little nauseous," she offered timidly when Louis turned to smile at the back seat riders. "Oh, no," she added. "It has nothing to do with Lucina's story."

"Now tell them about the bug that went in your ear." Louis looked at Lucina with pride.

Marlene hunched down in her seat wanting to disappear. "Went in where?" she mumbled at the front seat.

"Shush, Louis. I don't want to tell that." Lucina caught Dawn's eye in the rearview mirror and smiled. "Now Louis is going to tell you all a wonderful story. "

"Oh, yes." Jenny leaned forward, touching Louis' arm that rested on the back of the front seat. "I love your stories, Louis."

"Tell them about your teacher, Miss Teitelbaum, and how she made you sit close to her, bubala," Lucina urged.

Marlene cracked her window open. The fresh air would make her feel better.

"Were you always into women, Louis?" Jenny tapped on his arm awkwardly. Touching Louis just then brought a phrase to her mind: 'Remember the yurt.' She hadn't forgotten their closeness in the yurt at the Yellow Farm. But since they'd decided together not to make love, it felt okay to pat him affectionately once in a while.

"He's into me now," Lucina said so softly, the three women in the back seat didn't hear her.

"I was not into Miss Teitelbaum," Louis protested. "She was into me. Do you really want to hear my story?"

"Louis likes to be begged," Jenny teased.

"Yes, Louis. We do want to hear." Marlene put on her teacherly tone and flicked her apple core out the window.

"Okay." Louis cleared his throat; he wanted to tell his story well. "So, I'm this skinny little kid, like nine years old, who speaks broken English at school. We spoke Yiddish at home. Two big boys, Italians, were always starting up with me. I guess Miss Teitelbaum really wanted to protect me."

"That's so sweet, Louis." Dawn tried to imagine him as a skinny weakling.

"It wasn't sweet. It was painful. I was always teased about my Yiddish accent."

"Didn't they teach you to speak English?" Marlene sat up straight, as if suddenly pulled by a magnet.

"Yes, and I was trying to do it right."

"We're all from the -*ish* family," Dawn piped up.

"What do you mean?" Jenny asked.

"Jew-*ish*, Ir-*ish*, Scott-*ish*…" Dawn listed.

"I'm Pol-*ish* if anyone cares," Marlene offered, feeling nauseous again.

"Could I fin-*ish* my story?" Louis called out good-naturedly.

"Miss Teitelbaum was out to seduce Louis—"

"Lucina! It's my story," Louis snapped. "So, one day I couldn't answer the question, what's the capital of New York State? I said Monticello and all the kids are laughing at me. My family went to what they called the Jewish Catskills for the summer, near Monticello. So that's what the dumb Jew-boy thinks is the capital. And Miss Teitelbaum says, 'Louis, come up to my desk.' She either thought I was purposely making fun of her question or she wanted to protect me from the bullies. And she has me sit right next to her."

"That's really weird," Lucina puzzled, as if seeing the story in a whole new light. "Was she protecting you or punishing you, Louis?"

"It doesn't matter," Louis said. "She had this thing for me."

"That thing is called being a pedophile," Marlene quipped.

"Anyway—she's sitting there and I put my leg next to hers and she didn't stop me."

"Isn't that amazing," Lucina said.

"Louis! So, you had a thing for her, too." Jenny tapped on Louis' head. "You've always been a flirt."

"And then her smell got to me. I was choking and coughing."

"Her perfume?" Dawn asked.

"No," Louis said. "Her body smell—it was overpowering."

"Oh stop, Louis." Marlene was the first to start laughing. A nervous, breathy laugh. Soon the back seat was rocking with laughter.

"You're making this up," Jenny managed through her chortling.

"I swear, I'm not. So she got embarrassed and ordered me to the Principal's office with a note she'd written: 'Louis insists on disturbing my class.'"

"What a two-faced!" Dawn interjected.

"I bet she told the principal you were disrespectful to her," Jenny gibed.

"What teacher would admit she made a nine-year-old boy sit that close to her, anyway?" Marlene piped up.

Jenny held onto her theory: "She would have to make up a story. You know, like Louis touched her inappropriately…"

"Do you want to know what happened or make up your own stories?" Louis turned and addressed the back seat: "The principal, Mr. Espolito, sent my mother a note saying that I should take English lessons outside of class, because it seemed my Yiddish accent was disturbing to the students."

Lucina scowled. "Such a disturbing story."

"Miss Teitelbaum didn't know how to protect Louis," Jenny stated. "That's what I get out of the story."

"And Miss Teitelbaum was into me," Louis added. "But nobody would have believed me. The kids laughed at whatever I said, right or wrong, because of my accent."

Jenny, suddenly impatient for her turn, snapped, "Okay, Louis. Is that all?"

"For now," Louis said. *Why hadn't his story come off so well this time? Too much analysis!* He opened the glove compartment and retrieved a Triple A map.

*****

Jenny talked about the time she tried to convince her parents there was a ghost in the house. She was in bed when she heard noises. Doors opened and closed and there were scraping sounds. When she looked out her bedroom window, she saw a dark cloak floating over the hedge. She was so scared she jumped back into bed and hid under her pillow, counting sheep as fast as she could.

Trying to tell her parents the next day what she heard was a waste of time. "You read too many comic books," they scolded. She was forbidden to buy a comic book for weeks.

A few days later, the family cat, Lulu, suddenly became sick with a mysterious disease. She vomited briefly, went into convulsions, and died. The vet said it looked like poison. Had the cat gotten into some of the weed killer her father kept in the basement? Not likely, since that was always kept in a closed bin.

Jenny searched the basement and found some strange grayish powder. She took it to the school chemistry lab and found out it was arsenic. Someone must have gotten into the basement and put it there. Though usually locked, the basement could be entered from an outside stairwell if someone forgot to lock the cellar door.

Jenny believed there was a person in the neighborhood who had a motive for killing her cat. The old reclusive man who lived on the block loved birds. And once her cat had brought home a dead robin. Maybe the old man had seen Lulu catch that bird. If only her parents had believed her when she told them she'd heard strange noises in the backyard and seen a figure fly over the hedge. Maybe they would have searched the basement. Maybe they would have found the poison before Lulu did. Then maybe her cat wouldn't have died. The reason it was so hard to talk to her parents about it was that she, Jenny, had forgotten to lock the cellar door that very same night when she heard the strange noises. It was her own fault that her pet had been killed.

"Those are both very sad stories," Marlene summed up as they all fell into silence and their own thoughts.

*****

Later, as the Dart sped through Ohio, Lucina talked about tornadoes: how one could pick up your car from one lane and slap it down haphazardly in another. This had happened to her once. When she realized her car had almost rear-ended the one in front of her, she saw three little kids staring at her from the back window of a station wagon, their faces pressed against the glass in horror. None of the others had ever had an experience with a tornado, not even Marlene, who'd grown up twenty miles from a tornado belt in Michigan.

*****

In the van, Al was also talking about growing up in the Midwest. He missed the vast landscapes and not being able to see for miles. On his parents' farm in Indiana he could see telephone poles so far away they looked like cat whiskers. The city cramped his style, he complained. Kept him from dreaming.

Hans talked about reading cowboy-and-Indian comic books as a kid in his small hometown in Denmark. His uncle was part of a farm cooperative where many farmers shared equipment and markets—that's why he wanted to major in ecology and why he became political. He always thought the U.S. would be like his country, only bigger. He devoured Wild West legends about the good guys and the bad guys, imagining the big ranches where shoot-outs and cattle branding happened every day. But it was the massacre at Wounded Knee in South Dakota, which he read about in college, that woke him up to how Native peoples had been massacred by the white invaders throughout the United States. The conquerors assumed their right to pillage and take over the land and make it their own.

When Al remarked that some types of soybeans grown in the Midwest were used to make a special car lacquer, Hans was incredulous. "Good god!" he spat out. "You people can turn anything into money-making stuff."

"Even coal into perfume," Al added. "And oil into plastics."

They did not reach Marlene's parents' house in Hamtramck until nine o'clock.

<h1 style="text-align:center">33
The Sacred Tree</h1>

When they reached the Wolskis' green shingled house on Trowbridge Street, Mrs. Wolski had kasha varnishkes and pierogi stuffed with potato and cheese waiting for them. A lamb stew was simmering on the back burner. Since she was Irish and her husband Polish, they'd made it a practice to alternate each other's comfort foods, and assumed the New York City actors would appreciate the diversity.

Though it was after ten p.m. the group was famished for home cooked food. They could unload the cars later; no one would be interested in their props, Mr. Wolski concluded after a careful check of their belongings. Any thieves in his neighborhood wanted TVs and record players, not metal boxes jammed with masks and costumes. (Lucina made a mental note: her father would have labeled it all "junk.") Just to be on the safe side, they brought in their personal belongings, musical instruments, the Fire Dragon and the Triple Goddess masks, and the Dream Catcher from the top of the station wagon. Hugh, on his best behavior now, offered to unload the rest of the stuff after supper, giving time for Mrs. Wolski to clear a place for it in the basement.

"Hurry and wash up, guys," Marlene urged. "Mom and Dad have been waiting three hours for us." Louis noticed how her face had softened; in fact her whole body moved with an ease he hadn't seen before. The easy affection between Marlene and her folks, especially with her dad, was so different from the silent reproaches that came from his parents when he visited.

*****

The next morning, when Hugh broke out in sobs at the breakfast table, everyone assumed he'd finally understood how his disappearance act had been very disturbing to them. It took some time before his stammering made any sense: "Who would want them—it's not like there's a pawnshop for hot props. Who would know what they were through dirty windows? I'm sorry. So sorry."

"Hugh, what are you talking about?" Jim was the first to realize this was no overdue apology; something was amiss with their theater paraphernalia.

"I know exactly what they took," Hugh went into defensive mode. "I take complete responsibility. I know what happened."

"Start from square one, man. What did happen?" Jim strode up to Hugh as if to block him, in case he decided to run off again.

"Jesus! Our Sacred Tree, our masks—Gangster, Politician with Fat Cigar, Stool Pigeon, not the puppets," Hugh rattled on in a tense voice. "Somebody stole them from the station wagon." By now he was surrounded by confused faces.

"I don't believe this," came from Marlene. "Our precious props!"

Hugh fell again into remorseful weeping as several members hovered around the station wagon parked in front of the small wooden house. Others headed down to the basement to check their stuff there.

It took some time for the pieces of his story to jell: He and Courtney had gone out soon after midnight to get their stuff. Everyone else had gone to bed. The moon was bright— shadows everywhere. They smoked a joint, "a small one." Then a sweet smell hit them from the bushes along the side- walk. Hauling the stuff inside could wait; they would take a walk in the neighborhood.

"You're talking about lilac bushes?" Marlene puzzled as they all clustered around Hugh. She felt a twinge in her injured leg. *Should she get a tetanus shot?*

Courtney pulled his chair beside Hugh's and took up the story. "It was the weirdest thing. This eerie blue light was com- ing out the front windows of lots of houses—surreal—people still watching their boob tubes so late. Then this naked woman, I swear, down the block, on a porch doing a sexy dance—like she knew we were watching her."

"I don't want to hear these weird pot trips," Lucina snapped. "What happened to our ritual objects?" She hit her fist on the breakfast table so hard her glass tipped over, splashing orange juice on the white linoleum floor.

"I'm sorry, I'm sorry, Lucina," Hugh whimpered.

"Well, I'm really mad, too!" Jenny, who usually emot- ed only about Hans, was still in pajamas. Long hair hung in strands in front of her face. "Do you realize it took hours fixing up the Triple Goddess and Gangster masks? I gave our bad guys bushy eyebrows and fat lips and covered them with clear ep- oxy, so goons like you wouldn't leave fingerprints on them that couldn't be washed off. I want my Gangsters back again, Hugh and Courtney!"

After this pronouncement, Jenny stomped out of the room, while Jack reported, "They jimmied the back windows open."

Courtney burst out, "We know that! Somebody jimmied the back windows open and unlocked the trunk door from the inside. We could see that they rummaged around and took just a few things, not all the masks. So we went through the props and made a list. The Sacred Tree, you know how we had its sections taped securely to the inside along the side doors—they just yanked off the tape and took it and all the bad guy masks."

Jack groaned. "Why would anyone want our skinny tree pole, anyway? Somebody up there doesn't like us: first Cheryl disappears on us, then we think Hugh is dead, now this. It's time to throw the I Ching."

Louis couldn't contain his anger any longer. "It's time to stop the dope, that's what it's time for. Next thing we'll hear— car keys got lost!"

Mr. Wolski spoke up. "I take some of the blame here," he offered, approaching Lucina's chair to wipe up the orange juice splattered on his wife's recently polished floor. "I sure didn't think anyone would go after your stuff or I would have said right away to bring it all in. But there's some new kind of element in the area. It used to be all Polish and Irish and—"

"Maybe it was that naked lady down the block," Marlene interrupted. Her attempt at humor fell on deaf ears. "Anyway, Dad, let's not report it to the police yet. Probably some kids messing around." She'd heard that the police were coming down heavy on vandalism, especially if they could pin it on Black kids. "In the meantime, how do we replace our props?"

Courtney hooked on to Mr. Wolski's support. "Look, we didn't mean to do anything wrong. It's just some fucking props."

Marin had had enough. "They're not 'fucking props,' Courtney. They're our ritual objects. You have no idea of the work and skill it takes to make masks, because you haven't made any. As for the *Ghost Dance* tree, I'm not going to waste my time telling you what that loss means, if you don't know."

She edged past Courtney, avoiding his apologetic glance, thinking that she'd better do some exercising quick or she might just strangle someone.

"You both better apologize," Louis ordered, and with a grimace muttered, "Mindless fools."

"Listen." Marlene had her energy back. "There's a party store at the shopping center and they have all kinds of masks. You know, creepy kinds, like Halloween faces. And Dad knows all the dumps and junkyards in the area—we'll find some kind of long pole we can turn into a tree."

"Our Sacred Tree did not come from a junkyard! Marin can tell you that." Lucina sought Louis' grounding gaze. But, he too had fled the room, following Marin. She composed herself: "Don't you have to get a tetanus shot for that cut, Marlene? Hugh, you're supposed to take her to the doctor!"

"Dad said I don't really need a tetanus shot. I was cut by broken glass, not rusty metal. Lucky for you, Hugh!" Marlene felt like crying. How often she'd imagined them all having a quiet, homey breakfast in this sweet nook.

Lucina watched Marlene examine her cut leg, then went to find Louis. They had to make contact with the SDS students who had scouted out a performance and rehearsal space for them. Where could he have gone? She needed to calm him and herself. He was her self-medicating pill.

There it was again, trouble. Trouble was always lurking nearby, ready to pounce and shatter happiness. Even thoughts of *Rune—poor wrapped-up thing, all alone in a cold loft—* didn't help. *Find Marin—they could comfort each other.*

*****

Marin had spotted their tree first. That wonderful Sunday afternoon, when the four of them, she and Louis, Marin and

Al, had escaped the others and driven to a park off the Sawmill Parkway.

"Look! There's a wounded tree," Marin had cried out to them. Ahead of them was a young sapling, its buds still alive, leaning at an angle and nearly uprooted, probably by a sudden storm. An older tree nearby, an oak, had been partially uprooted as well. The wooded area hadn't been cleared of leaves and brush for some time; the young tree would just die there. If they used it in the Ghost Dance ritual, it would have a purpose and give their sacred Tribute the respect it needed.

*****

She found Marin in the backyard meditating under a weeping willow, its new, long leaves a fresh light green. She would not bother her; just find her own spot nearby on the grass. Let the earth hold her, take away some of the trembling.

Marin's soulful eyes pulled at her. "Aren't you going to talk to me, Lucina?"

"Didn't want to bother you."

"I can't take all the Sturm und Drang. Every day, a new trauma. You're upset about our tree, Lu. Just like me."

"What it meant to us, the four of us. It was a good luck charm to protect our connections, all of our connections. You know what I mean?"

"You have a thing about sacred objects, Lucina. I think I understand. We make them sacred with our energy and love. But my focus is more on nature. Like when I think of my Hudson River. When I need something bigger than me to get through this impossible life I picture my river. It's my inspiration, my life force. Like *Rune* is for you. You must miss your studio, being alone, no one to hassle you. Sculpting wood into living objects."

"More than I can say. I try to remember the sculptor I once was—to give me some kind of sanity. So I think a lot about my last work, *Rune*. You saw her, right after I finished making her, remember? I've made her my sacred object, like the crucifixion is for Christians. It's like through *Rune* I escape to my secret haven where I can just be me and think my thoughts."

"Someday you'll do that again, Lucina. And I'll come to one of your shows."

Her friend's comforting words were suddenly snagged by an inside voice: *Sally, talking about her welded pieces. The memory of their first meeting in the Spring Street Bar, when Sally had been eager to talk to her about her work. How quickly things between them had changed. So ugly, so sad. Trouble was always lurking in the shadows. Happy to see each other one moment; angry the next. But that had come from Sally, not her. Was it really possible that Sally and Karen might be staying in Shauna's loft where her* Rune *was stored? Too bizarre. For sure, she had heard Sally's voice on the phone recorder! Didn't Marin say she'd met Shauna once…?*

"Did you hear me, Lu? I'll come to one of your shows, if you ever decide to go back to making sculptures again. Sure, I remember when we toasted *Rune*—and I said, 'Maybe now I can have my friend back?' I was missing you so much."

"Oh, Marin…yes. I do remember. Let me ask you something. You met Sally and Karen, didn't you? Once at the loft? Sally is thin, angular. Karen has reddish brown hair, outgoing? They dropped off some magazines during a rehearsal."

"Oh, sure, I remember them. Really talky women. That's probably the thing I notice first about someone—how much they use words to—"

"That's why you and I can rest with each other, Marin. We have other languages besides words. Sally does, too. She's a welder. Makes very interesting pieces. They were shown at the Spring Street Bar."

"I saw them. Gutsy stuff. Do you have something specific on your mind, Lu? You have that distracted look. I can feel when someone's mind is churning. Need an ear?"

"You're a mind reader, Marin. It's scary."

"I just use my eyes."

"It's something I've never told anyone. Not even Louis."

"I promise. I'll keep quiet."

"Sally and I…"

Marin's mind was churning. What could be so heavy between Sally and Lucina?

"Sally kissed me and I kissed back."

Marin burst into laughter. "That's what's eating at you?"

"Marin! I'm not talking about cheeks. I'm talking lips, tongues, a deep long kiss."

Marin's laugh stopped dead. She looked straight into Lucina's eyes. "Oh, my god, Lucina! Does that mean you're—"

"Queer? I don't know. I love being with Louis, so I don't know. I just don't know. I guess I just love who I love."

"I need to go back to my meditation, Lucina. Just be careful who you give your heart to." She closed her eyes to the memory of her brother—bullied mercilessly because he was gay—bullied to death! Why else would he tie a rope around his neck and jump into oblivion? If only he'd fought back—defended himself—found the help he needed. No one in the family, she, Marin, certainly hadn't helped him. She bowed her head and started chanting Om as Lucina slipped slowly away from her dear Marin.

34

In the Den

Marlene found Louis alone in the den, pacing the floor
and smoking a cigarette, something he rarely did.

"It really is upsetting, Louis. So careless of them. When
they hang out together, they get really silly."

He stood near her.

"The word is *stupid*, Marlene. Stupid jerks. They
should have brought the props in right after we ate. Fuck, I
should quit this."

"Quit smoking?"

"I mean quit Fire Dragon."

"Please don't be so upset, Louis. We'll make new masks.
My dad wants to take us to the dump to find a pole to use for
our tree. We aren't going to find a dead tree in the city. Do you
know—my parents really like you. They can't help smiling when
you talk. They see you as the captain of the crew."

"I'm hardly that. But I'm too upset to go looking in junkyards right now. Lucina is really upset. The masks, *Ghost Dance
Tribute* tree, they're really important to her. She's had to deal
with a lot of changes, Marlene. You know, she was an incredible
sculptor. You saw them—the things hidden under the sheets?"

255

"Well, kind of." A concerned look took over Marlene's face.

Louis stamped his cigarette out on the bottom of his shoe and cupped the butt in his hand. Marlene's closeness both disturbed and excited him.

"She never actually showed them to me, Louis." Her lips quivered. "I wanted to—see her work, so I just peeked once."

Marlene sat down at one end of the plaid couch. "My leg's okay—Dad checked it. Just a small cut, if you're interested." Louis, now sitting at the other end, bent toward her to see the injury. Shaking his head in dismay, he muttered, "I'm glad it's not too bad, Marlene." Then he closed his eyes as if he couldn't take anymore. Even though silence overtook them, their bodies seemed engaged in some kind of conversation: his body heard hers. When she circled her shoulders to release tension, he did, too; when her hands clasped together, his hands followed the same gesture.

When Marlene felt a sudden pressure in her chest—as if someone had clamped a hand on it—she inched herself toward him. "Louis," she started. "I need to talk. Not about Lucina, but about us. About our feelings. I've missed you."

Louis pressed his lips together, but his eyes opened wide, vulnerable. "Damn it! You're a good person, Marlene. A really good person. I'm sorry."

She was next to him, rubbing his back. He relaxed; his shoulders fell as he turned to her. "You're actually a caring person." He began stroking her head gently.

"Actually?" Marlene laughed nervously, pulling her hand from his back. "What does that mean?"

"I like you, Marlene."

They sought each other's eyes and hands. Louis wrapped her in a hug, then impulsively began kissing her strongly on the mouth.

"No, Louis. We can't do this! Did you ever tell Lucina about us?"

"I said I wouldn't, didn't I? No, Marlene, I don't want to hurt her, ever!"

She pushed him away. "It's been so painful, Louis. I can't take it. I've wanted to be with you, but I feel like a slut."

"No, Marlene. You could never be a slut. Never, ever."

"Louis! You have Lucina. I don't have anyone. Don't you get it?"

"I do. I do. I've seen how hard it is for you, Marlene. Don't you like me, anymore? Just a little bit?"

"You don't get it!" Marlene tried to stand, twisting her body as she wrenched away from him. She stumbled to the door, letting out short, breathless whimpers. "I don't want to hurt Lucina either, you stupid jerk. But I'm hurting!" The pine-paneled den, usually a place to find solace, now felt treacherous, suffocating.

"I can handle you both if…"

"Sure, you can do everything, can't you, Louis? Everything but stop the pain. My pain." The harshness of her voice startled her; it was her mother crying out.

"It's just more love." Louis stood abruptly and reached out for her. "More love makes more love. Should I ask Lucina if she wants the three of us to…?"

The door banged shut. Louis fell back into the couch; his arms ached from stretching toward the fleeing Marlene. What an asshole idea. He really sounded like an asshole. He covered his smarting eyes with his hands as his body heaved with silent sobs.

35
Massage á Trois

Lucina's Journal Entry. Tour: Friday, April 21, 1967. Now we have to buy masks. There's no time to make them. Well, bad guys don't deserve artful masks; I'll try to think of it like that. Peter Schumann would never go to the Party Store. But the tree—our holy tree? That's a blow. We carved it, made it special. Whoever took it is doomed, that's all I can say. Cheryl, since you left us it's been one jarring trouble after another. Look what's happening to us.

Louis is so upset about the masks and the tree. He was already unhappy about the Ghost Dance. I thought he was still worried that Hugh's emulation of a Wovoka-like shaman would disturb Native people if they saw us perform. But no. Projecting the incredible faces of Sioux and Paiute men, women, young people to introduce and end our Tribute has put everyone at ease. It's given our Tribute its correct purpose. We're identifying with Native peoples terrible, terrible, treatment and too often inhumane slaughter. I just don't know what words to use. But about Hugh. Louis thinks we have to portray the Shaman force in another way. It's gotten to Hugh; he's off, disturbed, doesn't seem to know what he's doing. And Hugh is saying he wants out of the role. That still doesn't excuse his

259

crazy disappearance at that gas station–he wanted to frighten us for some reason. After we've dealt with the loss of our precious props we have to demand an explanation from him. Louis has some idea about a Double Wovoka! That a spiritual leader shouldn't just be male. The women's work must be influencing him. I think he's been talking to Jack and Marin about some new concept.

And Cheryl's absence? We're all scared, even with her assurance through Dawn that she'll be back. Louis can't stop blaming himself because he insisted she talk at the end of **Choice***. I wonder, would it really have stopped the attack on the play if she'd explained? That's water over the dam as my mother would say. And Louis? He's really uncomfortable with Donna's story—at least with the L-word. I've never seen him afraid of a word before. I'm so affected by his feelings. And he needs me to tune into his unhappiness. If I ignore him, he gets even more upset. We're just part of each other, that's all.*

If Louis and I had gotten married in a church or a temple, would everything be different? At least Mom would not have dared send us twin bed sheets and cleaning goods. If she knew the whole truth we wouldn't have even gotten sheets. How the judge's wife had tears in her eyes because I didn't have any family there with me. But if that woman were that concerned with my welfare, why would she leave Lyndon Johnson scowling at us from the TV during the entire ceremony? I guess she needed his company. I can see why. The judge stumbled down the stairs a half hour late, with an enormous red nose and liquor so strong on his breath that I started coughing and couldn't stop. Then when he said, "We are here today to wed Lucina Altman and Louis Holzer," mixing us up, I could have died. We corrected him, but it was still wrong on the paper license. I call it a Movement marriage. Did we need that fias-

co to feel married? Louis and I are wedded in our souls and hearts by our passion to stop war, that's for sure.

It's strange to watch Marlene's parents. Mr. Wolski is always trying to be aware and helpful. And his wife disappears. It's not hard to believe that this pleasant lady never showed Marlene much affection. She stays distant. I notice mother and daughter never touch each other, no hugs even. They're so formal. And talk about wrinkled. It's a good thing I didn't draw her! I guess we must be pretty strange creatures to her, too. I can tell they like Louis. If only my parents could see his goodness, instead of his Jewishness. Why couldn't they at least be happy for me, for Jesus' sake! That's a good one. I should say that to them.

Why can't I remember what we talked about when we sat down to eat together, me, my brother and mom and dad? My parents are getting old before my eyes and I sure can't talk with them now. Oh God! At least let me remember this moment, the feel of the pen right now as I'm writing about them.

I don't know where Louis is right now. Maybe he went for a walk by himself. I think Marlene and her father and Donna and Jim went off to look for some kind of pole—to be what? Just a pole. Nothing will replace our tree.

****

Lucina found a group in the kitchen mourning the lost masks. Al was trying to convince whoever was going to the novelty store to just buy a bunch of big cigars. "I'm not going to wear some piece of plastic shit. I was really fond of my Ugly Capitalist mask, reminded me of my rich-bastard uncle. But, I mean it—we can turn our faces into masks."

"Like this, Al?" Jack pinched up his face to look mean.

"No, pretty boy. You look like you need to shit. Marin's really clever with makeup. She can change us into really greedy-looking bosses."

"As long as we all look different," Lucina joined in, glad they were throwing some good ideas around. "It would be a mistake to make all the bad guys look alike. You can't always spot the sinister ones."

Mr. Wolski had dropped off coffee and jelly donuts (he called them "paczki") before heading for the dump yard with Jim and Donna; Marlene had to do some business with her mother that morning. While the others downed the breakfast, Marin got into telling her version of finding their Sacred Tree, mainly for the benefit of Dawn, who wasn't in the group then.

"We needed an image or object to hold *Ghost Dance Tribute* together both visually and spiritually. Since a growing tree is central to Indigenous philosophy, not a dead one like the Christian cross, we thought it could be the focal point of our drama. When I saw the young tree, just like Lucina said, I shouted out, 'That's our tree.' It had a tragic grace. At that moment it seemed as powerful as the image of a crucified young man—a Jesus—or a murdered revolutionary. I thought of the children slaughtered at Wounded Knee. I also thought of my brother— " Marin stopped short, closing her eyes tightly to ward off tears. Lucina closed her eyes as well, nodding and waiting for Marin to continue. "Someday I'll be able to talk about Michael without... I'm sorry, what was I saying. Oh, yes—And then Lucina told us something incredible. Right, Lucina? The dream you had the night before we found our tree? She dreamt she'd become a tree.

"And then that night after we found it, Al dreamt he was carving symbols into it. We did some research into symbols used by Native peoples and settled on the pictograph images of the Hopi humpbacked flute player, Kókopilau. We would carve them into the tree, like in Al's dream. Lucina and Al did the work. I assume you guys all noticed the little flute players?"

"Lucina made sure we did," Dawn offered ingenuously.

"Lucina always feels the preciousness of sacred things!" Louis had come into the room. His encounter with Marlene had made him unusually quiet, but the mention of the flute player carvings aroused him. "It's not that Al and Lucina carved just any figures into the tree. It's that they carved special figures that gave expression to our commitment to tell others about the wrongs done to the Native peoples of our country."

As he went on to talk about Lucina's sculptures—about helping her carry them all over the city, and how carting them around meant his fingerprints were on all of them—Lucina became uncomfortable. He was going on too long. The others had stopped listening. She called out to him, "Louis, Al and Jack have some great ideas about using makeup instead of buying new bad guy masks."

He understood. *She was right, he'd been digressing too much. Rambling. He was anxious, that was it.* "Great. Sounds like a good idea," he offered.

*****

Marlene stood in the archway of the breakfast nook, watching Louis and Lucina handle each other in a supportive way. She caught her breath, then relaxed. It was clear to her now: they were both dear to her, very dear. She sidled up to Lucina. "I just had a crazy thought. Could it be possible that we lost our old Sacred Tree because it's time to find a new Sacred Tree for this new group? People lose their wedding bands when they're breaking up."

"We're not a new group and we're not breaking up," Lucina interjected quickly, confused by Marlene's comment.

263

"That didn't come out the way I meant," Marlene countered. "I just don't want us to cry over spilt milk. It's a terrible loss, but we're strong. We can go on. Somehow aren't we always changing inside ourselves? So we're always a new—" She stopped suddenly, almost blushing; maybe she was simply talking about how she had changed. About her new awakenings.

"It's a hell of a lot worse to lose Cheryl than a tree," Al spoke up, patting Marlene's arm. "Besides, your dad is going to find us a new tree. I don't know if you all know this," he added, "but he's taking off work from his tool and die shop to scout one out with us."

Then Marlene got them back to the business at hand. They would be staying in her parents' house until Monday morning—rehearsals all day Saturday and performance in the evening at the Unitarian Church; then they had a workshop in the same place on Sunday afternoon. This meant that several more meals had to be prepared in the house. They should buy groceries and help out with the cooking. Her parents had already made food for two days for them. "Why don't Hugh and Courtney go with Al in the van to buy some groceries?" she suggested.

Hugh and Courtney didn't need coaxing. Immediately, they were out the door with a grocery list. After getting groceries at a nearby A&P, Al would get the van checked over. Probably the front tires needed some realignment. Besides looking for a new tree, Jim and Donna were taking the station wagon into Mr. Wolski's repair garage to get the windows and back door lock fixed. Jenny would take her car in too; the speedometer wasn't working. Marlene wondered if all the sudden car energy had anything to do with the fact they were in the auto capital of the U.S.

Hans, Dawn, and Jack went off for a long walk in the neighborhood. Hans had never been in a working-class suburb in the states before. They promised Marlene to not look in any windows for blue lights or naked ladies.

Marlene invited Lucina and Louis to see the small room upstairs which used to be her bedroom. Louis was still out of sorts. So Marlene suggested that she and Lucina give him a massage. "You've done so much work for the group, organizing and making arrangements." She was glad for Lucina's presence. Something major had changed in her, just in the past two hours after her emotional upheaval with Louis. Some need in her had snapped and changed shape. That's the only way she could think of it. No more yearning for Louis.

As the two women worked on his body, a nice feeling grew between the three of them. With tension leaving him, Louis fell asleep and into a dream.

He was in a field of Queen Anne's Lace; white lacy umbrellas towered above him, shading him from the hot sun. A spicy aroma—was it mint? wild onion?—tickled his nose. Energy from the ground vibrated through his body. He relaxed into the earth.

How blue the sky was. How green the grass. How comforting the feel of his body in soft soil. As his breathing deepened, he became aware of a tingling sensation filling his limbs. The hairs on his arms were growing, sprouting into twigs. The twigs became branches, with leaves. His body was becoming a tree.

He heard a voice: "It's Bloom's Day, let's celebrate!" He saw a small bird on one of his tree limbs, hopping about. Again a chirpy voice: "It's Bloom's Day, let's celebrate!" It seemed the bird was speaking to him. Louis woke up to laughter, his own joyous chortling, coming from his belly.

Lucina and Marlene's hands rested on his chest. They were both humming softly.

"I was becoming a tree," Louis said with wonder. "And a wren was chirping, 'It's Bloom's Day, let's celebrate,' over and over."

"Isn't that from *Ulysses*, honey? You love that book." Lucina felt herself lighten, as if she too had experienced the buoyancy of his dream. She was glad for the nice feeling between the three of them. And for the first time since Cheryl's disappearance, she felt some peace.

"What does the dream mean to you, Louis?" As Marlene spoke, she increased pressure ever so lightly on his chest, wanting to soothe him even more. She remembered how his hairiness had awed her, that time, the only time they had been intimate together. Today, feeling more comfortable with their closeness, she looked down on him and was touched by how different a man's chest was from a woman's.

"I think it means I've got to get back to writing," Louis said. "And stop crying over spilt milk and stolen kisses."

"You mean stolen props," Marlene countered quickly, looking out the window.

36
Propelling Forward

The actors' mood swings were out of hand. One would overcome a grumpy spell just as another went sullen and sluggish. They took turns resting on the blow-up mattresses Mrs. Wolski had installed for them in the game room.

Marlene forced herself to take charge. Working with SDS students from Duane University who were organizing blue-collar workers in the area, she, with Louis' help, set up rehearsal, performance, and workshop details. Rehearsals and performance on Saturday, workshop on Sunday—all to take place in the same room at the Unitarian Church.

Inspired by her initiative, the troupe gradually pulled out of their doldrums and got to work. The whole group needed to work on *Ghost Dance* with their new tree, a small, wooden sailboat mast which Jim and Donna found in the nearby junkyard—and a couple scenes from *Eco-Drama*. The women needed to run through *Wink*, *Markings*, and *Birthing*, and to finalize at least one scene from Donna's play. Who would take Cheryl's part, and was it going to be called *Be Real, Be You?*

As Jim and Donna gingerly carried the thin, shellacked mast into the church, Louis looked skeptical. Lucina, with Marlene and Jack's help, had overseen to the replacement of some of the stolen props: comic masks, purchased at a five-and-ten-cent store, would serve as Politician as well as Stool Pigeon faces.

"No Nixon masks yet," Louis quipped. "If he decides to run again, I bet someone's going to capitalize on his spooky punin!"

The actors' own faces, with false eyebrows and enormous cigars, would impersonate Gangsters, period. As props were carefully laid out on the linoleum floor of the performance area for Saturday morning's rehearsal of *Ghost Dance Tribute* and *Eco-Drama*, they took on a new preciousness to the actors.

Jack beamed as Jan and Paul, two of the SDS kids, set up the church basement with chairs, a table for refreshments, and a giant coffee urn. "If you're as good at organizing protests as theater shows, the anti-war movement in the Midwest is in good hands," he offered. They nodded good-naturedly at his praise but stayed at their tasks.

Then Jim called out for everyone to stop what they were doing. "Let's make a toast to our new tree." As the actors gathered around the wooden pole, braced upright in a bright green Christmas tree holder from the Wolski's garage and graced with wire limbs and paper leaves, he uncorked a champagne bottle and filled paper cups with bubbling liquid. Jan and Paul joined the celebration briefly, then excused themselves for an important meeting.

"Where's Louis?" Donna asked. "Isn't he toasting with us?" Lucina, pretending not to hear, threw the champagne down her throat in one swoop. "May our mast now be a Sacred Tree," she toasted. She knew Louis and Marlene were in the church office taking care of business; but she wasn't Louis' keeper.

"To our new sailboat." Courtney lifted his glass to Dawn in jest.

Dawn grumbled back, "Who are you to joke?" She was missing Cheryl terribly, how they always hugged before a rehearsal.

*****

Jim and Donna stood side by side like proud parents. "Listen up! We have this great idea for a ritual to put into *Ghost Dance Tribute*," Donna boasted. Then Jim held forth in a take-charge manner: "An image from a Sun Dance ritual—you know, where the young Lakota males circle the tree with thorns piercing their chests."

"Why would we want to do that?" Lucina wasn't in the mood for their excited ramblings. They had to start their rehearsal! "Now isn't the time for new scenes," she snapped. "We already have work to do incorporating two Wovokas."

But Donna barged on. "Just a two minute image," she insisted. "Almost subliminal. It could be fantastic."

What's with them? Lucina wondered. *Louis better get there quick to handle those two!*

Courtney was miffed. His jaw, slack for the past two days, suddenly jutted out with annoyance. "What does this have to do with our play?" he grumbled.

Good for Courtney, Lucina thought. *Maybe he could keep Donna and Jim roped in for the rehearsal. They had only a short time to work. She almost forgave him for the stolen props. It wasn't really all his or Hugh's fault, anyway. They'd simply been targets for the group's angst.*

Donna called out, "Imagine contrasting the uplifting, uniting Ghost Dance to the painful, rebellious Sun Dance? Thorns penetrate and tear the skin as the men run around…"

Oh, shit! Donna is still flexing her ego, Lucina fumed silently.

Now Dawn piped up. "We have our work cut out. This isn't the time to peddle new ideas, Donna—we're pressured for time as it is. Your scene isn't set yet. We're supposed to rehearse it this afternoon. You do want us to try it out tonight in the women's play don't you?"

Jim shot back, "The young men are testing themselves to see how much pain they can tolerate. They want to emulate the kind of pain women have when they give birth, right, Donna?"

"How disgusting!" Dawn, fully awake now, was getting anxious. Are these two trying to sabotage the rehearsal? "Sado-masochistic bullshit!" she let out. "I want to work on our Double Wovoka. Now!" Spotting Louis and Marlene returning from their meeting, she made her way to them as Courtney addressed Jim and Donna.

"Not now, you two! We have workshops specifically geared to developing whole new scenes."

Lucina felt her shoulders and fists relax. *Courtney and Dawn really came through for us. Why are Jim and Donna pushing their own thing? Is it because they're from Detroit and it's some kind of territorial rights thing? Bizarre!*

Suddenly an authoritative voice: "The Sacred Tree looks great. Now let's get to work." Louis stood proudly by their new tree. "I'm directing the Double Wovoka scene today and Marlene is leading us in warm-ups."

Marlene chirped up, "Yes, let's get started. Take your shoes off and let's do some deep breathing."

For once, Marlene's take-charge manner held no challenge for Lucina. *Massaging Louis together has really helped with that*, she thought.

"Just because Cheryl has gone," Dawn muttered out, "people think they can just move in and change whatever they want to."

"I resent that, Dawn," Donna returned sharply. "You all are okay about Louis' male-female Wovoka thing, which I don't get. But you won't listen to Jim and me." She turned to Jim and murmured something inaudible.

Determined to override these clashing egos, Jack and Marin, slowly mirroring each other's movements, began dancing around the mast-tree. Now they chanted out, "Oh beautiful tree, connecting earth and sky, your leaves and branches grace our lives—our Tree of Life, Our Tree of Life." Their focused enactment slowly dissipated tension in the group. As the actors watched in silence, a spontaneous Double Spirit Shaman took form. Hugh, grateful to be relieved from the role of spiritual leader, breathed deeply as his body relaxed.

Louis spoke out softly. "Damn, that was brilliant, Jack and Marin—our new shamans. Now we can rehearse our Ghost Dance around our Sacred Tree, with our Double Spirit. Right, Jim and Donna?"

As Marlene was stretching her arms upward, ready to lead their warm-up exercises, she commented, "Dad won't be upset if we paint over his Christmas tree stand. Maybe gold or silver?"

*****

When they were finished with the sound-and-motion exercises which forced them to interact with no words and served to lubricate their improvisational and intuitive skills, Hugh stood up and addressed the group: "I gotta talk to you guys. Louis asked me if I was okay about taking a break from communing with Wovoka. I told him and now I'm telling you—it will be a relief! I can now admit, I realized I could never be like him. No way. I felt like an imposter. You've seen how I can fuck up—that jerk-off scene at the gas station, messing everyone up and then Marlene got hurt. I was afraid to show my wimpy true self. You know, guys gotta be strong—so I was trying to be the strong, silent healer. Actually, he wasn't so silent and I'm not going to be any longer. I told Courtney what's really going on with me. My dad, he's got colon cancer bad. He and my mom are divorced a long time. But I relate to his girlfriend. She's worried too. You know, kids don't want their parents to die… I've been feeling like a lost little kid. But I've been trying to see it another way.

The doctors say he has a fifty-fifty chance…" Hugh covered his face with his hands and cried.

Marlene was the first to comfort him, then Donna and Dawn. "I—I'll get through this if you forgive me for being a jackass," he went on, his arms stretched around the three women. "Then me and Courtney being responsible for our sacred objects getting stolen…" He nodded reverentially to Lucina—"I need some serious self-examination, or a shrink. I ain't no bigger-than-life Wovoka…just need to be a more honest Hugh. I love you guys, you're family. I hope I can count on you." He sat down quickly. As the others sent him kind words and gestures of love, he responded humbly, "Jack and Marin will lead the Ghost Dance better than I ever did."

*****

It was decided: they would incorporate the basic movements and timing already worked out with Hugh, but Jack and Marin were free to interpret and improvise in their own styles, sometimes mirroring each other's poses, sometimes countering them, and sometimes moving as if one complex being. When their movements were set, the whole troupe walked through the entire drama deciding who would incorporate the parts Cheryl had played.

37
Dawn Opens Up

During warm-ups and massages at the women's rehearsal that afternoon, Dawn broke out in tears as Lucina worked on her feet. "Too hard, just too hard," Dawn cried out and Lucina backed away confused. People usually cooed when she massaged them.

A few sips of water helped Dawn gain composure and her voice. "It's about Cheryl. I'm worried about her."

Energy ebbed from Lucina's body: *Dawn had expressed what they all felt: What if Cheryl didn't find out more about her cousin? Then she'd have to go somewhere else, find someone else who knew something. It was all so vague.*

"She had to leave; I understand that. But what if she can't come back?" Dawn sought some relief in the circle of faces, mirroring her anguish. "I was thinking last night about Marin's rape scene. Remember how uncomfortable we were when she first brought it up—as the story she needed us to do? It was like we were all thinking: how could we ever act this out without throwing up? And then, Jenny, you said, 'We're dealing with extreme misogyny here. But what if he was a Black guy? That'd be much too complex to handle.' Cheryl stayed completely silent."

"Well, I had to let it go for a while," Marin spoke up. "Did I want to think about it anymore!"

"I felt uncomfortable with some of the things we said that night," Dawn continued. "Someone said, I can't remember who—something about when she's alone and she sees a Black guy down the street, immediately she thinks, 'trouble.'"

Jenny spoke up. "I said that, Dawn. But the whole truth is, I feel the same about any guy I pass by on an isolated street. And I've thought about it more. It's built into our racist headset, to suspect Black people. Just what Hans' guerrilla action in a liquor store is about, remember?" She reached for Dawn's hand, clasping it firmly as she continued. "I know this. There's a huge difference in how Black and white people are treated even in a women's health clinic. When a Black woman needs help because she's been raped and a white woman does intake, there's a bunch of assumptions. Did she egg the guy on? Was she drinking? On drugs?"

Marin broke in. "My friend is starting a shelter for battered women and she's teaching me a lot about rape and racist assumptions. She's given me the courage to share my experience and work with you on creating a scene that can actually heal me and others."

"That's good. I mean, we're all soaked in prejudice." Jenny looked to Dawn for a response. "Dawny, don't we just have to talk and talk and gradually find the truth together?"

Dawns' hands cupped her face. "Well, I can't forget how Cheryl just sat there silent, listening to us expose our various degrees of ignorance, no, actually racism, until Marin finally asked her what she thought. Remember Cheryl's response? 'I'm glad you women are sweating this out together...' And then she said, 'There's only one question: When two men, one white and one Black, ogle the same white woman in the South—which one is lynched? Mull that over and then let's talk some more about it.' Then you, Lucina, said, 'We all have to think how we could work with Marin's scene so that it empowers us and the women in the audience.'"

Dawn paused, letting the memory of Cheryl's words take hold of her again before anguishing aloud: "I personally can't stop thinking about how Black people have it so much worse than we do in so many areas of life! How can they stay so, so dignified?" After another pause, she looked upward and sighed deeply. "Well, I'm going to tell you all something. I love Cheryl. Do you get that? I love her!" Then like a puppy, suddenly whipped, she shot up from her chair and scooted out.

"She's in love with Cheryl," Marlene whispered.

"Well, I'm glad," Jenny piped up, her eyebrows rising expectantly. "All this time I thought she was after my Hans."

"Oh, my god!" Marin shouted out as if the scene before her was just too much. "Humans are so beautiful!" she emoted. She seemed to be caught between wanting to break into peals of laughter or uncontrollable sobs. But she clamped her mouth and eyes shut and started rocking, holding her chest with her arms while the women talked in low tones.

Ten minutes later Dawn returned to them, calm and clear-eyed.

Marlene broke through the awkward silence. "We've got to get to Marin's rape scene soon. But right now we have to work on Donna's scene! Who's going to take Cheryl's part?" She sighed heavily. *So much going on. Working with a new* Ghost Dance *tree; working with Louis, Marin, and Jack on the Double Shaman choreography; now all of Dawn's stuff.*

"I'm going to take Cheryl's part!" Dawn, standing before them, was already miming similar slow, sensuous dance movements that Cheryl had choreographed about a woman standing before a mirror, getting in touch with her own beauty. "I watched Cheryl rehearse this dance over and over, punctuated by the puppet's put-downs. Believe me, I can do it. It won't be exactly Cheryl's interpretation. It'll be mine. Dawn, loving Dawn and channeling Cheryl loving Cheryl."

"You'll be great."

"Holy Cow! I've never seen you move like that!"

"It's just a five minute scene—and you've already got me hooked, Dawn."

"Yes, yes!" Donna enthused. "You're the new *Be Real, Be You,* star. Let's get to our work, sisters."

"Dawn, you've just screwed my head on right. We all need to follow our impulses. I was thinking maybe I shouldn't be playing Lucina."

Lucina responded quickly. "Why, Marlene? I like what you're doing."

"Oh, Lucina, I care about you and I love playing you. It just feels strange sometimes."

Jenny spoke up. "What we're doing is very hard. And very courageous."

"Let's all calm down," Marin called out. "Actresses are supposed to be able to play many different roles, right?' She began flaunting a series of exaggerated poses with matching utterances, enticing the others to follow suit until they were all mirroring each other's ludicrous postures and simultaneously breaking out in hoots and guffaws, coughs and burps. "Get the shit out—get it out," one of them commanded.

*****

Loosened up and refreshed, they were back on track, ready to tackle the work at hand. SDS students Jen and Paul had brought them lemonade and sandwiches left over from one of their afternoon meetings. Yes, they would build on the ideas Cheryl had already set in place for Donna's scene. Dawn's excitement over expressing self-love just as Cheryl had done was palpable.

After rehearsal Lucina, still fretting about Marlene's comments about playing her, approached her cautiously. "Can we talk a little, Marlene, about what you said at rehearsal."

Marlene looked down at Lucina's shoeless feet. *How small they were!* "I don't know what's wrong with me, Lucina," she sniveled. "You and Louis are my closest people. Maybe I can't take close. Close means you have to be really honest. Here I am playing you, someone so desperately needing to break down the ingrained barriers with your mother, and look at me… You see how strained it can be with me and my mom."

*****

On tour: Saturday, April 22, 1967. Emotional roller coasters are exhausting. A full group rehearsal in the morning and a women's rehearsal this afternoon. Creating a "real" Sacred Tree through our imagination by blending awe and sincerity in our voices without overacting, then joining effective movements with the dialogue. It was Marin's idea that we do an exercise to activate our personal connections to the Sacred Tree, a primary power symbol for the Indigenous. Dawn ran up to it and hugged it like a child. "I love my beautiful tree," she said. That simplicity worked. I made up a love song to the tree and caressed it. I was thinking of our old tree, the one Louis loved so much. I was thinking of him and then I started thinking about Marin, too. Everybody added their little bit and finally we had our Sacred Tree back, so we could offer her to our audience in good faith. Then a rehearsal with two new Shamans, a work in progress for sure. As for Jim and Donna's ideas, forget it. That's another play, whether they get it or not. If they still want to do something with the Sun Dance, say in a month, okay, we'll consider doing some workshops on it.

Then the scene with the mayor and his henchmen in **Eco-Drama** *had to be reworked since we didn't have our old masks. We discarded the idea of using scary comic masks, or even tape and makeup to disfigure our faces into Stool Pigeons. We just worked our own faces into dour sourpusses. Finally, we took a break and then the women had to run through parts of* **Wink, Markings, Birth,** *so those are ready to go. As is a scene from* **Be Real, Be You,** *our name for Donna's play. We've started working on Marin's and Dawn's scenes, but they aren't quite ready yet.*

Rehearsals for the women's play always release crazy feelings. We've been bottled up for so long, that's why. When Dawn burst into tears as I was massaging her and couldn't be comforted, I should have expected it. Dawn is not someone who talks about herself easily. She also is not someone who usually cries in front of others. I've seen her shut up like a morning glory does when the sun goes down, if I push her to talk when she doesn't want to. But we finally found out what was upsetting her. It's amazing how building on Cheryl's interpretation of Donna has calmed her down.

I understand Marlene so much better now. She loves Louis—he's been kind to her. I guess I've been jealous and wouldn't admit it—too ready to be critical of her. I now feel she loves me too.

While the women rehearsed, Louis and Al had to check on some procedural matters, like who's going to take tickets? This is going to be a fundraiser for the SDS group here and for us. We women have to learn to do the business stuff around our plays too, for when we perform without the mixed group. Courtney, Hugh, Jack, and Jim went off to practice the music for **Eco-Drama.** *At first I didn't like it that Jim said just the men should do the music for that play, since we women get to do music for the women's play. But then I thought, give it* *to them. Why not? Hans says he has some exercise ideas for our workshop that he wants to develop. Fine, whatever people want to do. It gives me a break from worrying all the time.*

I finally found out what happened at Wellingfield. I knew Dawn had done something, how could I not? She, Jenny and Hans whispering together...But I didn't hear her say anything. Pretty closemouthed. The word "Wellingfield" always came from Hans or Jenny's lips and then all three of them would smile in a funny way.

After Dawn opened up about Cheryl I guess she was freed to talk about Wellingfield, at least to me. She, Jenny, and Hans are planning to talk about it to everyone at the right time. I do think it was gutsy but unsafe to start lighting napkins on fire like that. And paper ones. She claimed they were the extra big, extra strong ones, almost like diaper material because wealthy schools can afford the luxury kind. Dawn was addressing crimes against humanity there; about how we're burning up the Vietnamese with napalm. Frankly, I'm surprised someone didn't call a campus cop and haul her off to the dean's office. Apparently her action did catapult other actions that spilt out to the president's house. Dawn is amazing in so many ways. I'm just beginning to understand that.

Ever since Wellingfield, Hans has been like a different person. How can Jenny take the way he hangs onto Dawn. And Dawn talking to us women about Cheryl. She loves her, she really loves her. It's like I love Sally. I loved Sally. Maybe love between women is jinxed. Our mothers jinxed it for us. But it's weird. Hans isn't in everyone's face anymore. Maybe we can all review his exercise ideas in the morning at breakfast before the workshop.

PART III
CHERYL RESURFACES

38
A Call in the Night

Lucina's Journal Entry. Tour: Saturday, April 22, 1967. We didn't know what to expect at our performance tonight. Could young white politicos and actors really have a dialogue with Black people in the neighborhood? Well, the SDS kids must be doing something right; the reception we got was warm and respectful. They said we were catalysts for their ground-work. Jane, one of the head organizers, asked me if there was any possibility we could stay a couple of weeks and help people in the community put a play together. I told her maybe some other time, we're committed to our tour, but that everyone was invited to our afternoon workshop tomorrow.

I'm too tired to write about our performance. Later. I don't know which are more exhausting, our performances or our rehearsals. I'm hitting the sack, with or without Louis.

*****

Her husband couldn't be roused, so Mrs. Wolski groped for her pink silk robe and went out in the hallway to answer the phone. "I'll see if she's here." Confused, she mumbled and moved slowly down the hall. "Where's my daughter? Someone's calling for Dawn, and why so late at night?" Her voice floated ghostlike in the dark. "And who's this Dawn?" she murmured, shuffling to the partly open door of Marlene's former bedroom.

No, Marlene wasn't in the little room. Two were in the bed. Was that Louis and his wife in Marlene's bed? Such a nice fellow, that Louis, like the father of the group. Always worrying about something. Lucky to have him. Well, her daughter had a fancy for him, she could tell by the way she talked: "Louis wants us at the church by six o'clock for warm ups...Louis loved that tree from New York State." And the woman, his wife, giving so much attention to the young fellows. What kind of a marriage could that be?

She stood at the top of the stairs wondering where to look next. *Like a bunch of kids, all of them. And so concerned about that war. What were they talking about the other night—those new bombs? The smart bombs with the laser beams.*

She would try downstairs next. *So smart they could follow me around the house and into the kitchen, they said. That would be pretty smart, with all my little rooms going this way and that. Not a big, open, modern house at all. No, not a soul in the living room.*

On the narrow wooden steps leading to the basement den and game room, she called out: "Dawn? Is there a Dawn down here?" A voice, wrapped in sleep, came back at her from one of the mats she'd put down on the game room floor. "Not down here. Maybe the living room?"

She bent to the voice. "Get up, fella. There's a phone call for one of you. She wants Dawn. You better find her. Is that the little one, do you suppose?"

Mistaking Mrs. Wolski for Marlene, Hugh cussed and pulled the covers over his head. "I said, the living room."

"Wake up, wake up, now," Mrs. Wolski persisted, shaking him. "It's an emergency! She can take it in the kitchen."

"Oh, Mrs. Wolski! Sorry, sorry, I'll find her."

Hugh located Dawn rolled up in a blanket on the floor in Mr. Wolski's study. "Wake up, Dawn. You have a phone call—long distance."

"Tomorrow, not today," sounded through the thick wool blanket.

"Come on, Dawn. Before we wake up everyone."

Dawn whined, "I don't want to talk to my mother."

"I don't know who it is. It's an emergency. Maybe someone is sick. Or died. I'll go with you."

Hugh and Dawn stumbled toward the night light in the kitchen, showing the shape of a black phone underneath.

Dawn had the phone to her ear. "Hello?"

"Dawn, this is me. I got the Wolskis' number in the phone book."

"Who?"

"You don't know me anymore?"

"I'm not sure—"

"You know who. Don't say my name. I don't want anyone else to know I called."

"Oh my god! It's you."

"What's wrong, Dawn?" Hugh was whispering in her other ear.

Dawn covered the mouthpiece. "My mother, Hugh. My aunt is sick. Thanks—you can go back to sleep. Be careful down those stairs." She held the phone tightly to her ear, waiting until Hugh's shadow had disappeared.

"What's happening, Dawn?"

The phone felt heavy, hot. No—it was her hand, trembling and sweaty.

"Are you still there, Dawn?"

"Yes, in shock—is this real? Where are you?" A sob was rising up; she clamped her mouth to silence it. "Are you okay?"

"Yes, yes. I told you I would call. Don't cry, Dawn. We don't have much time. I'm in a pay phone booth. Just listen."

"Yes—I listen, always—"

"When are you going to be at the University?"

"In Budington, Indiana? Tuesday. We might be in Chicago Monday night, near you. They have to get back to us tomorrow."

"Don't try to find me! I'll see you at Budington U. What's the name of the theater?"

"Just a minute, let me think…It's…Stark Student Theater Building. That's it!

"Good, Dawn. You're my girl."

"Are you saying—you still love me?"

"Those four words—hold them to your heart. And Dawn, I'm getting vital info about Nelson. Uh-oh—no more change. Can't talk any more…"

"Are you in Chicago now? And you'll be there at Budington on—"

"Trust me—I'll be there. Martin Luther King's words are resounding in my head, and the support of my brothers and sisters to work with Fire Dragon to find my beloved cousin. We have to say goodbye now, honey."

"I love you—hello? Hello? Oh, no!" Dawn, dazed, held the disconnected phone for some time in her two hands without moving.

*****

Dear Dawn, What I couldn't say on the phone, I went back to where I'm staying here to write it all down. I still hear your sweet voice in my ears asking me if I'm okay and saying, "I love you." Yes, I heard those words, just when

286

we were cut off because no more quarters. Your caring, a warm, safe blanket, keeps me going.

A week since I left you all and came here with my people to find the truth about Nelson. So painful not to know where he is. Gloria, she was with the activists who came onstage at Weymouth, took me to her sister's apartment with her in Chicago, an area called Bronzeville. Here people look like me and live safely. I don't have much time—she needs my help gathering information for a Black Liberation meeting tomorrow all day. I'll see you soon—all of you— so I need to write down what I've learned and haven't learned about Nelson. Writing to you, my friend, is helping me keep track. I have the words of Martin Luther King resounding in my head, firing me up. As you should know, he has denounced this war in his April 4th speech with the voice of God.

All I can think about is how can this be put in *Choice?* The treatment of someone I know, love—we were like brother and sister and I can tell you now because I've shown you already— I'm one of those women who loves women. You probably sensed it before I told you—I love you, Dawn. Well, my cousin too, my Nelson, is gay and for a Black man that is dangerous to admit. We are brother and sister in spirit.

All so complicated and I'm not outing him, as they say. God knows, you can't say you're gay in the military! No—what I have to do is tell this whole white, racist, homophobic coun- try that my beloved, sensitive cousin-brother is missing under a terrible cover-up! Where is he? What's happened to him? This is what has to go into our play *Choice:* What happened to Nelson Davis? I'll narrate what I know and in some powerful way, the theater group—also I'm going to need students of color from Budington U's drama and dance departments to help us—we all must create a ritual drama that shows what war basically is. The brutal inhumane murder of humans by humans, and in Vietnam it's a racist war. The Black GIs call it the "white man's war" because a white male, colonizing, imperialist United States is bombing, burning, raping the Vietnamese people of color and their land. I have to give personal testimony for Nelson's sake. Honor his courage to not want himself and his brothers to be used as cannon fodder to help a few bastard capitalists get filthy rich. I have to do this for the sake of all of us outraged by this war and all imperialist wars.

I met an honorably discharged, wounded soldier—I'm not going to give out names yet, too dangerous—who knew that Nelson had become a conscientious objector in 'Nam and wanted to organize others to refuse to kill. Do you understand, Dawn? Sam in *Choice* in no way faces the danger that a Black soldier who dares to defy the army and organizes soldiers to refuse to kill has to face? God knows what they've done to him because of that! You have to help me get this understood by white people.

Then I learned from another Viet vet who did paperwork but was wounded by a rocket and hospitalized in the States that he'd actually seen a written document that said Nelson P. Davis—could there be another Nelson Davis with the same middle initial?—was discharged as a wounded soldier, but the hospital where he would be placed wasn't listed. Why??? Where did they send him? He actually knew of another Black soldier that was imprisoned for organizing conscientious objectors. This horrifying information can't all be acted out, but I can tell the audience about this while the repeating image of the endless murder that is War takes place. So, it will be about Nelson within the larger horror, the massacre, genocide of people of color.

I learned more from this last soldier himself at a meeting called "Our Black Brothers and Sons in Vietnam." He came to the meeting to warn others what was happening to those who called it an illegal war and refused to fight. These resistors are falsely reported as having been wounded and hospitalized and discharged, when actually they have been put in prisons either in 'Nam or the States. So you see, the US army could be keeping Nelson in a prison. But where??? And lying about it. All this information made me so sad. So I called Nelson's parents, my aunt Effy and uncle George, and told them where I was—and that I was trying to get real information about him.

There's a lot more I didn't tell you or the group. Being with my Black brothers and sisters is giving me courage. Effy and George made me and my sister Sadie promise not to tell anyone because they feel shame and fear for their son. They got one letter months ago from Nelson that was written weeks before that. He wrote that being in the army wasn't what he thought it would be. When he actually saw Vietnamese people—he felt they looked just like him—he couldn't be forced to kill them. All his excitement about being a soldier had drained out of him. And he was humiliated to write that his job for weeks had been cleaning the officers' latrines. He was shocked that his officers were calling the Vietcong the same racist names that he'd been called back home in this country. You know what I'm saying, Dawn? He said he was going to have to act in a way that the army wasn't going to like. I think he knew more than he wanted to reveal. One thing about Nelson—he couldn't lie to Effy and George, but also he couldn't upset them, so he was caught in the middle. They haven't heard from him since that letter. That's why we are all afraid for Nelson. Complete silence from him.

And then when I told them I took a break from the theater tour to attend some meetings about Black soldiers in 'Nam, there was this long silence. And I said, "What's wrong?" and Effy was crying so hard, Uncle George had to tell me. Yesterday they had government officials come to their apartment—they were so confused about why they were there—these two men in uniform said Nelson had been captured by the North Vietnamese and they were very sorry but they did not know where he was. Can you believe it? Dropping this bomb on my aunt and uncle and then leaving without telling them who they could call to get help to find their son? I couldn't believe it. I started crying too, but I stopped myself.

This all sounds so unreal, doesn't it, Dawn, like a horror movie. Worse—it's not made up! I can sum it all up for you. Effy pleaded with me. "Cheryl, you and your politico actors, you're at those colleges. You can get help. You have to help us find Nelson. We don't know what's happened to our son, our gentle, tender boy."

Dawn, it makes sense to me now—why I should stay with Fire Dragon Street Theater. White politicos are listened to—look at the publicity the protests against Dow Chemical Company are getting for making napalm. Most of them are on college campuses and organized by whites. I need that media coverage for Nelson. And this is what I've learned by coming to Chicago to the Black Liberation Movement Meeting! I have to do this work immediately. Everyone here stresses the importance of publicity, telling the public about this terrible injustice. Gain solidarity with anti-Vietnam War groups of all sorts. Go to Washington and demand the truth about Nelson. I'm saying to you, Dawn, if you all want me to stay and work with you, you have to work with me now. Is Nelson alive, dead, in prison, hiding, AWOL? What has his country done to him? You, the theater troupe, must help me find him.

I'll give this letter to you when we are together, Dawn. It has helped me figure out better how to put this in a drama that students and our audiences can hear. They must be told and then outraged and activated to help me uncover the lies and find Nelson. Because if this can happen to him, it can happen to someone they love as well.

I need you, Dawn. I love you. There is a tender and a fierce me coming to you.

Cheryl

39
Change of Plans

With Cheryl's voice still penetrating her, Dawn awoke to shouting in the distance. She recognized Louis' and Hans' voices. Wait—was it a dream? Had Cheryl really called?

She found Hugh in the kitchen, pouring a cup of coffee.

"Will your aunt be okay?" he called out in a sleepy voice.

"Who? Oh, yes, yes. She'll be okay. Not that sick, after all."

"That's good, sweetie. You were really upset. Listen, something happened in Chicago. They're all in the living room now."

He handed Dawn a cup of coffee and they joined the others; Louis was relating the disturbing news.

*****

Lucina's Journal Entry. Tour: Sunday, April 23, 1967. There are bomb threats for the community center where we were supposed to perform in Chicago tomorrow. A white gang already ransacked the SDS office there last week. No one knows if it's the work of CIA infiltrators or a pro-war gang. Everything is a mess. They don't want us to show up. Maybe the summer of '68 for the Democratic Convention, they said. There is going to be a lot of performance activity then.

And we thought the streets were unsafe! Louis says this is going to be another summer of riots. I'm feeling terribly distraught but I'm going to be strong for the group. That's where Cheryl is, Chicago, with her activist's group. I pray she's safe, getting the information she needs on how to rework* Choice. *The Black Panther Party is rising and so are the Black ghettos in Chicago, Detroit, and Newark. From all the predictions, the shit is going to hit the fan just like in Watts two summers ago. Maybe we should go to the country again. Someplace like Vermont. Nobody riots there. What can we do? The organizers are very sorry. God, it's not their fault we live in a violent country.

*****

The community workshop was in the afternoon. The new plan was to pack up after it and rise with the roosters on Monday and head for Budington U. Should they call their contact and say they'd be a day early because of—no! Don't connect themselves with the bombing news—just say there was a change in schedule, that's all. Play it cool. And before they leave the Wolskis', ask if they could help them out with anything.

Jack was inspired to rally them. "Okay, guys, let's help make the meals today. Give Mrs. Wolski a break. Lucina and Louis are going to buy groceries for a pasta meal, with garlic bread and salad. Tell them who wants beer, soda. That's dinner taken care of. Sign the list on the frig for breakfast and lunch, okay? Also, Marlene says there's a pile of rocks behind the garage from redoing the driveway and a U-Haul trailer beside it. We need the guys to load the rocks into it. That will really help Marlene's parents. The women said they're doing another morning rehearsal in the basement. Workshop is at two o'clock."

Dawn watched Jack with admiration. He was meditation in action for sure! Helping others, dividing up tasks. She would sign up for lunch.

There was Hugh sitting by himself near the low casement windows in the pine-paneled basement. Through the window behind him a forsythia bush blazed yellow. *She felt a burst of joy. Cheryl-joy. But no! She couldn't tell him about Cheryl's call—'cause if she doesn't show at Budington—the troupe would be really shattered again.*

"Hey, Hugh. You planning on doing any more disappearing acts on us?" She spoke softly as she hugged him hard.

40
The Workshop

While they waited for community people to arrive, Jenny and Marlene studied the activity room in the church basement; they'd been too focused on rehearsing and performing to notice details of the large room. Bulletin boards, cluttered with flyers and posters listing past and future events, indiscriminately covered the walls. One caught their attention: "Speak Up for the Voiceless" headlined two photos, one showing a group of Vietnamese women weeping over a napalmed child; the other, a group of Black men, old and young, huddled around a fire from a garbage can. The skyline of downtown Detroit was behind them.

Two huge dark maroon sofas, squatting eyesores with cotton batting oozing from their bottoms, took up one corner of the space. Marlene grimaced. "They look like overstuffed sandwiches with too much mayonnaise. Don't movement people need pretty?" They sat down on one of them to wait for the others.

Jenny worried about the lack of heat in the room. Maybe the wind off of Lake Huron made it so cold—too cold for April. No one would take off their jackets for the exercises! "Can't they afford to heat the place, Marlene? The sanctuary has to be warmer than this, and why wouldn't the women fix it up more?"

She drew her hand across the top of the sofa, displaying a sooty finger to Marlene.

Marlene eyed the walls and ceiling. "Don't the men see how ugly it looks, too? Must be depressing to find chips of plaster in your coffee, or is everybody too busy to notice?"

"I suppose," Jenny nodded. "Well, our mothers care about décor. I can see that your mom enjoys keeping her house in good shape."

Marlene smiled with appreciation. "Do you think so? But, she's not as sociable as dad, though I get along better with her now."

The two women had settled into the smaller sofa, huddling against each other for warmth.

Jenny had a sudden thought. "Do you think movement people are afraid of, you know, pleasure? That they won't make the revolution if they're too comfortable?"

"I don't know anyone as serious as your Hans about revolution," Marlene replied in earnest. "Can he allow himself pleasure?"

"Sure, with me—" she started, then hesitated. *She couldn't remember when they'd last made love.*

Three women moved past them, headed for the bathroom in the back.

"I hope they're here for the workshop," Marlene whispered, standing abruptly. "At least we'll have three participants. Isn't Lucina responsible for setting up?"

"Right," Jenny laughed. "She needs to work off her class privilege a bit. Or is it her class guilt? Her folks sent her to an expensive grad school."

Marlene gave a little laugh and rolled her eyes.

Jenny's tone turned sharp. "I always wonder, Marlene. I guess rich people just want a safe and healthy world for themselves. Well, someone should be paying activists to fix this place up. Don't Unitarians take collections at their services?"

Marlene stretched her arms toward the ceiling. "Liberal democrats like the Kennedys have mucho dinero. But what does it mean? You know, Joe Kennedy supported the Nazis. And FDR kept quiet about the concentration camps—wouldn't let Jewish refugees into our country."

"Really?" Jenny's eyebrows shot up.

"Louis keeps me informed," Marlene said.

"Do you and Louis hang out together a lot, Marlene?" Jenny eyed her carefully as she too stood.

"As if any of us have time to hang out. We barely hang in—right?" Then in a friendlier tone Marlene added, "Sure, Louis and I talk and walk together, sometimes."

An understanding, which the two women could have put into words, passed between them. *People in couples still need their own close friends.*

Marlene checked her watch. "Is Hans going to lead some exercises?"

"I'm not sure. He had a talk with Louis and Al. I think he's decided to wait until we get back to New York to try them out."

*****

By two o'clock, several Black church members from the neighborhood had shown up for the workshop and were chatting comfortably when Lucina called out: "Okay, folks, let's get started. There's enough of us to warm up the place."

Participants were taken through the basic warm-ups, body stretches, then vocalizations. At first, it was hard to get people to chant, but Marlene had a knack at this kind of thing. She told everyone to drop their jaw, think of something that was upsetting them, and say "ah," in almost a groaning sound. Next, an "oh" sound, as if surprised. And then, they were to think of something that tasted good, adding the "um" sound. Soon enough, people were joining all three sounds to voice the Om chant, enjoying the vibrations moving through their bodies.

Next, the participants were led in simple sound-and-motion exercises that further loosened up vocal cords and muscles. Working in pairs, they took turns leading and mimicking each other's repeated noises and movements. Before long, the back room surged with good vibes and body heat. When Dawn asked participants if they would like some storytelling exercises related to how the women actors had created their stories the night before, excitement filled the room. The actors were surprised at the lack of shyness in the group; everyone seemed hungry for these active and playful communications.

When one middle-aged guy, shy at first, volunteered to tell his story, his friends called out, "Tell us, Joe. Real slow." He told about coming north when he was young, filled with expectations, supposedly free to look for a job, but not able to find one. As Joe Moran continued, "I became a janitor, five bucks a week at a Ford factory and gradually, step by step, I worked my way up," Jack mimed the story-line. He showed a young man full of hope, being forced into menial tasks: sweeping, lifting, hauling. "And now," Joe continued, "I work in the same Ford plant, inspecting engines. Managed a high school degree—those college entrance exams were by and for whites. So I don't put the engines together, but I check them out." Jack modeled a man proud of doing his inspection job.

After Joe's account, other participants who wanted to tell their stories asked the actors if the acting out could be eliminated. Telling their stories was enough for them to work on, they said. Maybe people could make short verbal affirmations (like a chorus) to support the storyteller's words, a style more familiar to them.

Bill Hamon, a participant who hadn't removed his woolen cap even during body bends, suggested they stick to a theme. "How about outsmarting the system," he suggested. Everyone liked the idea. Obviously he was a frequent spokesperson for the others. Elderly yet sharp, he said he would start with his "perspective on the situation." His calming, deep voice enthralled the actors; they saw immediately that trying to add action would only distract from his wonderful presence and style.

"Let me talk about this education thing," Bill began. "You can't compare the know-how of different people. You want to compare the so-called IQ of a Black porter and a white civil engineer, for example? I'll tell you what it is. The white guy understands the construction of bridges; the Black man understands the construction of the white man, inside and out." Everyone roared. Each of his points was made with brilliant and biting humor. He ended his talk with, "If you've been denied the library, how're you supposed to read the books!" Lucina saw Bill as deeply wise and shrewd. *Some presences don't require any distracting pantomime,* she realized, flashing on her *Rune,* all alone, wrapped up in a loft corner.

As funny and horrifying stories of the hardship of working class life were shared, Lucina offered quietly, "This country wouldn't have to have welfare if everybody was treated the same. Maybe we need something like socialism, do you think?" Her comments were met with patient smiles but politely sidestepped. And despite Bill's call for stories of outsmarting the system, the accounts that followed his kept repeating the theme of powerlessness and outrage. Outrage at the refusal of those with money and power to take responsibility for the system's inequities.

Mrs. Johnson, an advocate for the elderly, claimed that spokespersons for the system often made the poor, especially people of color, seem responsible for their poverty, thus gagging them from speaking out their truths. "Black people are forced into poorer housing than whites, because of still being enslaved by a capitalist system," she stated, followed by a chorus of "Amen, sister!" "And all the time, the white bosses make us feel it's our own fault. You know, like we don't work hard enough. They want us to be workhorses to make them more money. And they don't care if we live in squalor." More "Amen, sister!" rang out.

Howard Thomas, super for the apartment building across the street, talked about all the money being spent on 'Nam. "One bomber could buy us a new school. That's what keeps us awake at night. More than all those peace ideas you kids toss around. And we don't think no Marx or no Lenin is going to help us out of hell. Only Jesus can do that!" His remarks were followed by a chorus of 'Tell it, brother!'

A woman named Jessie Stall, articulate and angry, had a lot to say as well. "The government spends its resources on those SMART missiles that bomb out our Medicaid benefits. That war is in the rotten plumbing, the crumbling walls all around us," she said, gesturing at the cracked walls of the room. "The rat-infested basements, the leaking roofs, the damp rooms. Just look at this poor excuse for a meeting place! This here is the war."

Marlene and Jenny looked at each other: *Should they say something?* Jenny spoke up first. "I owe you an apology, Jessie. Before the workshop I was saying to Marlene—why can't movement people have pretty offices? Does fighting for our rights have to be done in cold rooms with run-down furniture? But Jessie, you've made me see a deeper truth. Our energy and money have to be used for rent and food and meetings like these to fight the system that's sucking what we need away from us."

"Sisters, right on," Marlene joined in. She nodded at Jessie, who had begun to chant, "Tell it like it is!" gradually joined by others until Jessie called out, "Hey, how much does a bucket of paint cost? We need nice while were fighting the ugly system. Bill, Joe, and Howard, let's you and me cut out on Saturday night's poker game and start brightening up these walls a bit." The four community friends soon cemented a plan to fix up the center with Jen, the SDS organizer who had also participated in the workshop.

*****

Lucina's Journal Entry. Tour: Sunday, April 23, 1967. Our workshop turned into a fabulous story-sharing event. I think "Truth Talks" would be a good name for what happened. Everyone needed to tell what was on their minds.

The workshop was advertised by the SDS group as Community Work and Social. It was also an opportunity for them to give out welfare, unemployment, and health care information. About twenty people showed, including the SDS students, welfare mothers, and neighbors, mainly Black. Later, a couple of Viet Vets Against the War appeared, and some older retired leftists. They said they welcomed every opportunity to analyze Washington's newest strategies with the younger radicals. Dialogue is a way to stay sane, they said. We debated Bobby Kennedy's chances at being elected.

It was probably inevitable that somebody would ask the Big Question. Howard Thomas, the middle-aged Black man who works as a super in a building nearby, was the one to do it. "How come white, middle-class college kids have come into my neighborhood to tell me how to live my life?" By then we were sitting on the humongous couches and folding chairs, drinking coffee. "Why are they telling me what I should be fighting for?" He didn't wait for an answer.

"The best thing you SDS kids can do for us," he said, addressing all of us who put on the event, "is let people know that the white cops are finding all kinds of reasons to arrest

us. They're coming into our bars, rounding us up for illegal drinking and hauling us off to their jails. And they're preventing us Black people from becoming the cops who we hope will really protect us. After you get that taken care of, then work on changing your parents' attitudes. Their damn prejudice kept me out of college and in the tenements."

George Thompson, one of the young organizers, whose father is a dean at the State University, went beet red. He said they would definitely address Howard's points at the next SDS forum in May. Then Viola Knowles, a retired bus driver for the Hamtramck Public Schools, gave a little speech before she left. She said, "You young kids with all your fine ideas, your clever masks and songs and fancy theatrics, had best bring humor and change to all us working folks or all your drama don't amount to a hill of beans." George quickly brought the afternoon's workshop to a close after Viola's speech.

It was obvious the SDS organizers had already begun to question their self-appointed roles as community organizers and educators, even before Howard put it to them so bluntly. I guess they needed him to articulate the weaknesses in their organizing strategy first and then they will rework it. A white girl named Dorothy Bainbridge, bright and talky, who had dropped out of college to join ERAP (Economic and Research Action Project), talked to us after the workshop. She said she was really upset when a single parent in the neighborhood slammed the door on her. She was trying to sign the lady up for an equal opportunity carpentry training spot when the woman laughed at her. "I make more money on welfare, sweetie," she told her. "And the Lord knows the system owes it to me. It owes me for one dead brother in 'Nam, if it don't owe me for nothin' else." Then Dorothy said she was beginning to grasp how she, Dorothy, was coming from a privileged perspective and could barely comprehend the humiliation experienced by the disenfranchised. "How can white folks like me ever really understand how racism has embittered people of color?"

"Live amongst us and experience firsthand how we're treated, sister." Mrs. Johnson, sipping coffee nearby, heard her and responded without a pause. "It isn't hard to understand being treated like shit."

I heard a sad voice: "We have to try...keep trying to understand." Maybe it was coming from inside me.

As we were all leaving, Jessie came up to us and said, "This place is going to be brightened up with a paint job by next Sunday. But you kids already brightened it up for me by coming here. You've given me ideas about making our own little theater group, right here in ol' Hamtramck." Jenny and Marlene gave her hugs and the V sign. The three of them really hit it off.

Mr. and Mrs. Wolski said we were great to be so flexible at the workshop, after we told them the participants really led it. If we try a similar workshop again, I say we should just let people tell their stories and forget about us even trying to act them out. About our performance last night. I'm not sure if our tree came alive in **Ghost Dance Tribute** *or not, I mean for our audience. People did appreciate that we were telling them the truth about Wounded Knee. We did good, solid work. I don't feel like writing more about it right now. I just want to remember how we did the scene from Donna's play,* **Be Real, Be You,** *for the first time. Thank the goddess the puppets weren't stolen; as the Name Callers we need them to squelch all people who put down others with offensive names. Dawn playing Donna describes her early teen years: "I chose to hang with my girlfriends, with no interest in winning affection and praise from the boys. We played sports and did schoolwork." Then she says, "Well this made two of them mad and here's what happened." She then mimes standing in front of a mirror,* *exploring and being with herself, obviously enjoying this as it develops into an engaging solo dance. Simultaneously two of the puppets with masks of white faces (voiced and operated by Jenny and Donna) start their name-calling tirade: "You don't follow the rules— do what real girls do—charm the boys with pretty smiles and girly hair-dos." This is followed by taunting name calling: "You're a 'Bull Dyke,' 'Lezzie,' and a 'Less Being' too." As Dawn's presence grows stronger, the puppets' voices become incoherent and weak. With a strong drum beat on the red drum, Dawn addresses the incoherent, flopping puppets: "You're puppets of Hate and Jealousy. You're not real people, I pity you. All Name Callers need to face the truth: your put-down names only put-down you." Dawn engaged the audience to chant with her: "Puppets of Hate and Jealousy—you're not real people, we pity you. All Name Callers need to face the truth—your put-down names only put-down you!" Strong voices improvised: "Put-down names are for puppet fools."*

Our workshop today has shown me what people really need: a place to hear and speak their truth in their own way.

I didn't even miss our stolen props. For sure, I don't have the desire to find the culprits. Just hope they find a good use for them. Gay gezunterhayt! or however it's spelled. Meaning something like "godspeed," or "go in good health," I think. Louis' mother once said that to us. I never forgot it because she never said it again. After that it was a lot of head-shaking and "oy vey's" when we left her.

<h1 style="text-align:center">41</h1>

<h2 style="text-align:center">We're Famous or Something</h2>

When she saw the exit sign on the thruway, "3 Miles to Budington," Dawn's heart clenched. Her mouth went dry and a voice inside her cried out, "I—love—you—Cheryl. I hope I can come through for you." She pressed her face against the car window and focused her eyes; every street corner, bus stop, café, small park became a potential sighting of her love. She scanned storefronts and sidewalks for the tight jeans and large jacket, holding a confident, alert body. But as she looked for an image to hold onto, the woman in her mind kept changing shape. Easygoing and in charge one moment; anxious and angry the next. Would she ever really know this woman she was loving? *Remember! This complex Cheryl she was drawn to trusted her!* And their private talks like at the thruway restaurant, those were precious moments to hold close. If only they could talk now; there was so much Dawn didn't understand. Did Cheryl know that the activists were going to disrupt *Choice*? And how could she be sure she would find out more about Nelson?

Dawn was perplexed when she heard from Lucina and Louis how Cheryl and two of the militants frightened a roomful of students with their eerie pantomimes. *Cheryl holding a play gun aimed at the students? Cheryl wouldn't do that!* Cheryl was about responsible love—the way she looked into her eyes and said, "I need you, Dawn, to help the others understand."

Once Dawn saw her crossing the street near a post office. But no, the hair was too long, the skin too light. Another time Cheryl stood up from a bench at a crowded bus stop, her hand shading her eyes for she was looking back at her, Dawn. But no—out the back window Dawn watched as two little girls grabbed the woman's hands and the three quickly boarded the bus. Not her Cheryl.

As the van neared campus, she chanted silently, "I need you, too. I need you, too," in rhythm with the van's wheels rapping against the interstices in the pavement.

*****

The troupe decided to park their three vehicles at the edge of campus in a parking garage, "just to be safe," until they knew where they were to be housed by their sponsors. They would head first to the student union for sodas and sandwiches.

The large imposing campus buildings, the giant elms and oaks casting ominous shadows on the immaculate green lawns, seemed to say, 'An Institution for Dedicated Scholars Only,' reminding them of their mission to confront the conservative mindsets that usually guarded such a place.

But when they approached a more modern building, the student union, they were met by an unexpected and thrilling sight. Huge pennants hanging in trees welcomed them: "Fire Dragon—Radical Theater from New York City—Welcome to Bud U." Dragons of all colors and shapes spitted flames around the words, creating a marvelous psychedelic display. One banner proclaimed: "Fire Dragon Street Theater Performing *CHOICE*, A Revolutionary Anti-War Drama, April 26, On Our Campus."

Food could wait! They must go to the Stark Theater Building immediately—speak to the organizers of their event, who knew they were coming a day early, explain the changes to their program, and find out where they would rehearse and sleep.

In front of the theater building, an even grander reception met them: giant photographs from *Choice, Ghost Dance Tribute, Eco-Drama, Moments of Pain/Moments of Gain,* and *Catching the Dreamer* were displayed in glass showcases. Inside, they found posters done by students from the graphic design department displayed on the walls, executed in a variety of styles: impressionism, art deco, cubism. Their name and repertoire had inspired at least one art professor's class at the university.

Lucina could hardly believe how well the promo materials they'd sent this university had been used; it was an outburst of creative marketing. "I think we're famous or something," she joked.

"We had to come all the way to Indiana to find that out," Al grinned, which he almost never did.

After obtaining housing and rehearsal information from the theater department's program director, they headed back to the union's cafeteria. As they scarfed down hamburgers and cokes and shared friendly comments with a handful of students milling around them, they worried. With all the changes in their program, how could they fulfill the obvious expectations shown by the grand display of banners and art work?

"Finally! We're treated right—and seen as being Left!" Hans seemed incredulous. Words he loved—radical, guerrilla, revolutionary—were treated as acceptable, even displayed with artful respect by this powerful university. "Maybe they don't know what these words mean?" he suggested to Jack, who was always reticent to use them because of their challenging nature.

"I guess we don't have to prove a thing to the students here, Hans," Jack offered, mooching a Gauloise from Hans' jacket pocket for Al. "Good to see you happy, guy," he added with a slap on Hans' back. "I just hope they appreciate what we can offer them."

Jack, always suspicious of any overt marketing of counterculture theater, was fretting. *What if someone in the administration suspected them of inciting fires in Watts and helping to spread riots around the country? Why else was the word "fire" in their name? And what if this showy good will from Bud U was actually a snare to entrap agitators—Fire Dragon and the students who came to see them? These billion dollar institutions were clever at co-opting movement rhetoric to prevent change. He always admitted that his own New Age lingo could be confusing. But still—why were they being touted, as if the Barnum & Bailey Circus had come to town?*

"I don't know what to think, Hans," Jack confessed. "Maybe this college is a hotbed of socialism and I'm just a doubting Thomas."

Louis, who'd been raised on suspicion in his wary mixed neighborhood in Brooklyn, was always weighing contradictions. He was well aware that large educational institutions could be powerful manipulators in the community and also dedicated to giving working-class students solid educations. "What they're doing is buying us out with our own words," he concluded to the others. Pulling back from an initial excitement over the generous and beautiful promotion of the Fire Dragon troupe, he became skeptical.

Then the sobering reality hit them: all this grand publicity was misleading. They weren't going to perform *Choice*! And only reworked excerpts of everything else. Cheryl's disappearance, the theft of their props, cancellation of the Chicago gig, and even moving stones for the Wolskis had taken all their attention. They had not notified the Theater Department of changes in their program! They would not be performing what the students expected. Sonya Lighthouse College all over again. Maybe it was a mistake to do college performances at all; Fire Dragon really belonged on the street, where change and improvisation were a daily reality.

They scrambled for a defense: "We are an authentic theater of the streets. Our staging grounds are parks and demonstrations. Like a living newspaper, we bring timely information of confrontations and uprisings to the people. Spontaneity and flexibility are the modus operandi for shape changers. Our motto is 'Perform the play that speaks to the moment.' We decide just minutes before a performance what to perform…"

"Who are we bullshitting!?" Al suddenly burst out. "The Bud U students are going to be fucking mad!" He imagined large jagged words slapped over the posters, banners, and photos on the morning after their counterfeit performance: "IMPOSTERS!!! BETRAYERS!!! PHONY-BALONEY!!!"

Even so, they absolutely could not perform any version of *Choice*. Who could say, maybe rumors had already spread via the student underground: "Confrontation at Weymouth College by Black politicos shakes up bourgeois troupe of so-called radicals."

Ghost Dance, *Eco*, the women's play, and *Catching the Dreamer* were doable. But the word blaring loudest from the trees, walls, and placards on campus was "CHOICE." Everyone here wanted to see *Choice*. Unfortunately, their current *Choice* would not speak to Black students!

*****

Dawn's suffering at Bud U was not like the others. She was in an obsessive state of longing and anxiety. She followed the others' motions and moods just enough not to be noticed. *Why are they all so bent out of shape by posters and photos, fame and drama and intrigue, things that mean nothing to me? If only I could go off by myself. But I need them, my adopted family. Without them I'll go crazy. Meanwhile, I have to watch for her. Somehow Cheryl is going to appear. She promised. She needs us to help her find Nelson.*

311

So, as the others continued to make a nightmare about all the publicity welcoming them, Dawn stayed focused on the angry, assured, intense, determined, bright woman whose glance promised love, Cheryl.

When did she first tell herself, "I am in love"? It was like the feeling just grew, slow and steady. *And this person I am in love with? Can I really be in love with someone I hardly know?*

*****

Lucina's Journal Entry. Tour: Monday afternoon, April 24, 1967. The organizers said it's up to us to announce to the audience any changes in our program. They've done their job, now we have to do ours. They were amazingly reasonable. Not the arm-twisting we expected. "You can bow out of doing **Choice** *by saying that an actor with a major role had to leave the tour suddenly for personal reasons," they said. "Things do happen to performers on tour. Or you can simply admit that the point of view you had expressed in* **Choice** *was limited, and the play is in the process of being reworked."*

We want to live up to the images of us displayed on campus. Maybe we can offer a challenging alternative. Instead of performing **Choice***, we can do improvisations around issues of the war: Are enlistees hired killers, or warriors for their country? We can give students, Black and white, a chance to express all their fears and hesitations about being in the military. We learned from participants in our workshop in Hamtramck, like Viola, Joe, Bill and Howard, how desperately people need to talk about their concerns: Vietnam, race issues, working-class oppression. All of us who want to create a country we can believe in can brainstorm on how we can proceed as one united community. Our group just has to dispel our para-*

noia that the university wants to entrap us. We have to believe in student power. I can only pray that we do the right thing at the performance. Our work, our self-respect, our reputation as a responsible street theater for the people depends on it.

42
Return

One thing in their favor—they were refreshed. Mr. and Mrs. Wolski's hospitality and support had given them new energy. They were determined to come up with a creative solution. Together.

At one o'clock, the troupe sat in a circle on the stage of the college auditorium and began their rehearsal with singing: "Within the beginning is the beat, and the beat is within the beginning is the beat…" Round and around the chant went, helping them get in touch with their heartbeats and breathing and each other. The simplicity of the melody, containing only five different notes, allowed the rich tones and textures of their voices to be explored. While the others sang the basic chant, Courtney and Lucina expelled shorter phrases of "heartbeat, heartbeat," creating syncopated rhythms within the melody line.

Ten minutes into the chant, Dawn knew that she could handle her tumultuous feelings. Cheryl could be trusted to keep her word—she needed their troupe. And she needed her, Dawn, to support her. The deep place of the chant had centered her, shown her connections to her own inner rhythms. How her breathing worked with her vocal cords to make sound; how thoughts worked with her voice to make changing notes; how the inner workings of her body and mind were truly amazing. She, Dawn, had a purpose unto herself; her job was to explore and be open to that purpose, not lose herself in another's body or face or voice. Yes, she could find connection with another who needed her as she was.

When she opened her eyes again, the anxiety driving her had gone. She felt relaxed, peaceful, as if a kind spirit held her. She felt at home. The others were smiling at her and she smiled back at them. She was part of a smiling circle of love.

When her attention was pulled away from the circle of chanters to the stage curtain, made of a soft, velvety, mauve material, she noticed gentle ripples engaging the cloth, as if some force were sending signals to her and her seated companions. *Amazing,* she thought. *The lush velvet curtain with its pulsating rhythms is in sync with the harmony of energies I feel inside. We must be engaging a calm, vibrating force in the space all around us.*

When the waves in the curtain formed a shape moving toward her, Dawn's awareness sharpened. Warmth rose within her chest, her neck; waves of heat and light washed her face. A woman came toward her with a sure step. Footsteps kept time with the singers' chanting. The boots—leather, strong, worn— anchored solid legs snuggling in blue jeans. Then a sudden quickening in her chest; she knew those boots, knew that step!

When Dawn leapt up and ripped out of the circle, the group felt a tearing. All eyes now opened and caught her spiraling away from them.

"Cheryl! Oh my god! Cheryl is here!" Her eerie shouts fractured their peaceful communion as they witnessed her embracing a figure.

Jenny and Marin, yelping like excited dogs, now rushed toward Cheryl. The others, stunned, remained seated. Would they open a space in their circle for this presence, this person that had been part of them? Why was she here now? In shocked uncertainty, they watched her settle in where Dawn had been, Dawn crouching behind her.

Many stayed cautious, as unspoken phrases tumbled in their minds: *What the fuck! Goddamn! Where were you? What the hell have you been doing? Are you okay? Are you back to stay? Dawn told us what you said—what do you want from us now!*

Those unable to reach out stayed numb; they could not look at her.

*****

Later, Lucina remembered her first reaction to this new Cheryl who certainly had some resemblance to the one she thought she had known and mourned. How was this Cheryl different? She flashed on the stone sculptures of slaves by Michelangelo that remained half-embedded in their granite blocks. Unlike those carved figures, this Cheryl emerged fully formed. "I'm clear about what we have to do," this Cheryl affirmed. Her familiar, urgent voice now resounded with a new defiance.

Dawn's voice, the first to become coherent, rose up. "We almost didn't make it, Cheryl, without you. Wow! How you challenge us!" She tried to harness her joy, the smile that made her face ache. She couldn't help it; she wanted to shout out at the top of her lungs: *Cheryl is back like she said. And I love her!*

Then Cheryl was shaking, or was she laughing? *How could she make them feel at ease with her?* "I bet I've really confused you," she blurted out. "Well, I'm Black and I'm back."

In the silence, her face relaxed, becoming vulnerable. *How could she explain herself, it seemed so impossible.* "I wanted to talk to you but I couldn't. Not enough information. Now my head is screwed on right again. I can handle contradictions..." For the first time with them, Cheryl didn't think, *How*

317

do I know what these white people really feel about me? She saw vulnerable creatures, people like herself, questioning, struggling to grow, reaching out. *I'm a woman of color who needs trustworthy help where I can get it to find my cousin. And these thirteen people are people I need to work with me now. I need tenderness and touch to feel grounded. I need Dawn—both of us scared to reach out to each other. I'm scared because she's never been with a woman, Black or white, I'm sure.*

"I can't handle this," was barely audible from Donna, who stood abruptly and jutted off to hide behind the stage curtains.

Jim's lips hardly moved as he tried to speak. "She's returned—but for how long?" his body jerking with each word. "Like a ghost."

"I never felt more alive," Cheryl replied, trying to embrace the group with her eyes, cautiously moving from face to face around the circle as if sniffing out more hurt amongst them.

Dawn, edging into the space Donna had left beside her, reached out to touch Cheryl's knee, her foot, a hand.

"Listen up, my Fire Dragon Street Theater comrades. Your not 'token' Black sister has a truth-telling performance to put together immediately for *Choice*." Cheryl, not waiting for a response, put her arm around Dawn and forged on, her glance focusing pointedly around the circle at each member. "With all that's unknown about where my cousin Nelson is—I see clearly what we can reveal. I know you have a lot of questions for me and I want to answer them, but we've only got a short time—you know. I got educated, motivated with information. There is so much going on in the Black Movement—it's like a volcano has erupted and lava is seeping through the land. I am so grateful my extended family, my brothers and sisters in Chicago had the information I needed, we need. They shared GI antiwar newspapers with me that have testimonies by Black GIs about what has happened to them for refusing to fight. I read them myself. These reports give me clues to what has happened to Nelson. From being beaten to getting locked up in jail. These anti-war GIs are fighting for their 1st Amendment Rights to free speech and to protest an unjust war. Black Liberation Movement put the word out to help me find Nelson. That's the reason I had to leave in the first place…to get more information so I could come back and we could publicize the brutal treatment of GI resisters, like my cousin, in our drama. Just like those newspapers are doing,"

I am watching Cheryl take hold of herself right before my eyes, Lucina thought. She saw again the thoughtful face, weighed by sadness and hurt, that had risen up in her dream the night she'd left them. The face that said, "You didn't understand my need." The night when Cheryl's presence merged inside her with Jack's words, "Keep the faith."

"Okay, let me explain. When I called Dawn Saturday night—you all look surprised—Dawn didn't tell you? Okay, I asked her not to. See? I can trust her. Faith is to trust. And believe it or not, I have some faith."

"Maybe I missed something." Jim spoke woodenly, obliquely. "Does anybody else know what's going on?" Inside, he was remembering all the times he and Donna had reached out to her, hoping…hoping Cheryl would feel comfortable with them.

Marin, her eyes blinking rapidly, chose her words carefully. "Are you saying—that you've come back—to stay with us?" Hurt stained her face.

Cheryl, nodding at them both, offered a look of kind aloofness. Her hand went for Dawn's as she spoke. "If you all will work with me."

Then Lucina had Louis' hand and Marin pressed her arm against Al's leg.

Again Cheryl turned her head slowly, consciously wanting to stroke each of their faces with a tender look. "I called Dawn when I knew what I—we—had to do. And I needed to hear Dawn's voice—someone familiar. You know what I mean?" At her side, Dawn was nodding while forming a plan: *When we're alone, I will show her, hold her, and tell her what I haven't told her before.*

"I couldn't admit how much I'm learning with you. The startling, dramatic ways to drive vital information into people. I was angry sometimes—that you could never understand me. But I saw that I really do belong with you, for now. So, I'm here. Dawn helped me have the guts to do what I did at Weymouth because of her courage—can I tell them, Dawn? No? All right. I'll just say her energy opened me up, too. There's a fire inside each of us that we got to let burn. Dawn helped me with that, okay? Find the thing inside that is you. Not anyone else's. She told me about it. She'll tell you when she wants to."

Dawn wanted to hide, withdraw into her shell. No! That was the old Dawn, not the brave woman Cheryl was describing. No one had ever shown her such genuine gratitude. She eyed Lucina closely. Lucina should know what Cheryl was talking about. *I told her what I did at Wellingfield!*

Lucina, looking from Cheryl to Dawn, saw the feelings flow between them. Their closeness brought up Sally, and she felt tears in her eyes.

Jenny's eyes flashed at Hans. Had he heard what Cheryl said? "Dawn helped me have the guts." *Wow! Cheryl and Dawn have a thing together. Does he get this? Dawn is into Cheryl big time. Now can he admit he's hurt me!*

Hans felt Jenny's pull on him. He looked away from her in embarrassment. Had anyone else noticed? Could he let her in again, the way it was? Maybe he could change too—like Cheryl.

"Cheryl! Cheryl! Cheryl!" Hugh was shouting out her name as if calling out for help, as if he'd fallen into a nightmare and she was his lifeline, pulling him out of swirling waters. "You gutsy woman—who were those politicos you went off with?"

"Fuck it, Cheryl." Courtney jumped up and faced her: she was a force to contend with. "We've been owning how fucked up we are—how color blind we are because our families, our teachers, our politicians—oh, you know, they're so racist it would kill them to admit it. We've been trying to own it—we saw you as our teacher—we knew we had to rework our main play. So how come you didn't stop those guys from demeaning us at Weymouth? Did you know they were going to do that? And that you were going to cut out on us?"

"Why? Cheryl, right now tell us why." Hugh stood beside Courtney as the two of them held out their arms to her, imploring her to speak out, make it better, help them understand.

"Hugh, Courtney, I hear you. Marin and Al, where are you? Can you hear me? Louis, look at me. Jenny, Hans, Jim… Where did Donna go? Oh, Marlene, Jack, Lucina, Dawn—all of you. Let me explain!" Cheryl bent her head down as if in prayer, the others joining her in silence. Then she suddenly broke the silence.

"This is it—my proposal. We've only got this afternoon and part of tomorrow to rework *Choice*. I see they're announcing it all over campus. That is my commitment to Nelson, his family, and you. Trust me, and you'll know why I did what I did."

Jim stared at her, still incredulous with her boldness. She had barged in on a rehearsal and taken over. She was demanding that they follow her. This Cheryl who'd left them in a calculated manner.

Louis, watching silently, had stayed breathing deeply, trying to calm the anxiety in his chest. He soaked up the whole scene, wrote it in his mind, the hurts, the angers, the walls, the wanting to forgive, the awe that rose in him for this woman. Yet, the wound from Cheryl's absence was still raw. He understood, and he did not understand. Yes, obviously Cheryl's time away from them had provoked one challenge after another, as if the emptiness demanded to be filled with angst. And then, whammo! She's bounced back again, wanting to steer them into a new *Choice* in a couple of rehearsals!

"Louis, talk to me."

"Yes, Cheryl, I'm shook up. How do you expect me to change gears so fast! This is you? Talking? Saying what? It's Bloom's Day—let's celebrate?" Cheryl was looking hard at him, perplexed by his remarks. He sought Lucina—did she get his drift? Lucina's eyes blazed with amazement. He swung back to face Cheryl: "I mean, look, Cheryl… I can't quite believe it's you. Dawn gave us your message when you left. But we suffered in your absence, you know. The women had to work without you…Damn it! Explain to us why you left and why you're back. Do we have to rework every damn scene—" his voice broke. This was not the time to fall apart. "This is hard. These sudden changes—mind-blowing. Okay, okay—yes. Let's do it. Let's just fuckin' do it!"

"I hear you Louis. But I had to be responsible to myself and to my cousin." Cheryl blinked back a surge of emotion. "You'll understand, I hope, when you hear about Nelson. I wondered, was I exaggerating about him? The facts? We haven't begun to understand how our Black brothers are treated by the U.S. military. Can you believe? My people sign up, obedient to Uncle Sam and then they're treated like cannon fodder? That's what this is all about, finally. Please, I'm sorry for disrupting the tour, for hurting you." She stopped, relaxed her shoulders and waited for a sign that finally they understood.

As if on some invisible cue, the group also let tension go; she was asking them to let resentment and hurt go…open their hearts again.

"Give me a chance," Cheryl intoned gently. "We've got to do it right this time. It'll be rough, a sketch, okay? But true. Deep true. There'll be a Black brother's story, my cousin's story, and there'll be Sam's story. I know more facts now. In Chicago I learned what could have happened to him. I couldn't tell you before. I didn't know how bad it was. It's not about choice—it's about cover-up. It's about cruelty…If there's time we can invite the audience to tell their stories about the draft. The women can talk about their men friends or about themselves. Women serve too, you know." Again, she took them all in, engaging each one with her eyes. "I left you for what, nine days? so finally we could expose racism in the U.S. military for how long? Years? Decades?"

She had challenged them. Hooked them. Once again she was back as their fearless teacher. What was this terrible story she knew?

Cheryl took them all in with her targeting eyes: "Agreed? We'll work with Nelson's story? I'll tell it to you. I know it'll be rough. But—it'll be the truth. I'll keep the structure simple, doable in two rehearsals." Dawn's hand on her back encouraged her. "I've thought about what to say. You act it out. And we can now tell the audience—this is a current injustice. Please, Jim, go find Donna. Tell her it's a matter of life and death that we all work on this."

"This is the work that has to be done!" Lucina shouted out as if she suddenly comprehended the enormity of their task. "We're actors in the process of becoming activists working to end racism and a racist war. Let's start the rehearsal!"

43
Where is Nelson Davis?

Choice began with Cheryl narrating on stage left.

"Where is Nelson Davis? His loved ones want to know. His Black brothers and sisters want to know. I want to know—don't you? Nelson is my cousin. We went to the same school as children. He was my friend.

"Nelson thought the army would make him feel proud and valued. He thought he would learn skills and be paid decently for his work. He didn't know he'd be treated the same as before he enlisted. Always a dependable worker, yet hesitant to speak up for himself, he was pushed around too often. Like so many young Black boys in his neighborhood, Nelson mopped the floors and scrubbed the pots in small restaurants, mainly owned by white guys. In Vietnam, he was assigned to clean the officers' latrines."

Cheryl continued speaking, while performers dressed in black robes with gray cowls pulled over their heads and faces, circled the stage. This chorus of uncertain race marched mechanically as one of them moved to the center of their circle and mimed raising a gun, readying to shoot at the others. At this point, they all removed their cowls to show faces of many skin colors. The center Shooter was Black. (Cheryl had rallied Asian and Black students from the dance department to take part.) The performers now froze.

"When Nelson looked into the faces of the Vietnamese people, faces of people he was hired to murder, supposedly our enemy, he experienced something very profound. All these people were humble, proud, and definitely not white. They were like him!"

The center dancer (as if personifying Nelson) lowered his mimed gun as the performers circling around him now shouted out: "The racist massacre in Vietnam. The racist massacre in Mississippi, Alabama. The racist massacre in Wounded Knee. They are the same. Think, soldier: How can you be a hired killer for the white superpower, the U.S. government, your enemy as well as ours?" The central figure responds by dropping his mimed gun to the ground and weeping.

The circling figures, faces exposed and bodies relaxed, slowly drew near the now unarmed central figure, embracing him and each other, as Cheryl's narration continued: "Nelson went to his commander and handed him his gun. He wanted out of the horrible, repetitive ritual of genocide. And if that meant prison, at least there he would regain his soul, his humanity, his dignity, and his name. He wrote one letter home to his parents, my aunt and uncle, about his decision to become a conscientious objector while being a soldier. 'How can I kill people who look like me?' he wrote. 'These are Vietnamese peasants who are seeking their rights guaranteed by law, just as Black people in my country are.' He said the army would punish him for that!

"The family has not heard from Nelson again. But terrifying events are making his family sick. Just recently government officials' went to his parents' apartment with the message, 'Nelson is missing in action, and believed to be captured by the Vietcong.' No written report, officially validated, was given to his family. Nelson's family believes it's all a cover-up of the

U.S. military's punishment of him. They still don't know the truth about him. And just last week I learned at the Black Liberation meeting in Chicago that he might have been discharged as a wounded soldier for his refusal to fight. But there is no formal information about what hospital he's in. Where is Nelson? Is he still alive?"

As Cheryl continued to describe Nelson's unknown fate, intimating the ominous, ruthless cover-up that lay behind it, the Black dancer who had represented Nelson moved to the side of the stage to stand alone. Shaking his head side to side he repeated: "I will not kill. I am Nelson Davis." Cheryl stopped talking when two actors in army uniforms approached Nelson, jammed a bag over his head, tied him up and carried him to the other side of the stage on their shoulders, then dropped him and beat him. They exited, dragging his lifeless body off stage.

The other performers, silent witnesses to Nelson's decision to not kill for his country and his possible murder for "insubordination," walked to the exact spot where Nelson had made his last stand, each in turn also declaring, "I will not kill; I am Nelson Davis."

Cheryl took up her narration again. "Our family suffers week after week. We don't know how to approach government officials to help us find Nelson, or at least give us documented truth about his whereabouts. Has he been captured? discharged? thrown in the brig? Is he in hiding somewhere? Is he dead? By whose hand? And why? As of today, the United States government has issued no official documents, no personal belongings, and no proof to his family of his fate. What happened to Nelson Davis? His loved ones want to know. His Black brothers and sisters want to know. I want to know—don't you? Nelson is my cousin. We went to the same school as children. He was my friend."

*****

The next morning the troupe found a review of *Choice* in the student paper being distributed in front of the student union:

New York Street Theater Presents Riveting Drama at Stark Theater Last Night.

Fire Dragon Street Theater issued a profound statement with Cheryl Whitmore's true story in the anti-war drama, *Choice*. This contemporary morality play alerts audiences to the insidious, incomprehensible devastation of war in general and Vietnam in particular, and to the fate of GIs who refuse to fight there. The production at the John Stark Theater at Budington University focused on the currently undocumented disappearance of Black soldier, Nelson Davis, cousin to the author of this play.

The conflicting information of Nelson's "missing in action" story was revealed through Ms. Whitmore's impassioned narration and symbolized through ominous, unrelenting depictions of the faceless, inhumane, machine-like maneuvers that surrounded his vanishing and possible execution. Three Afro-American and two Asian dancers from the university's dance department joined the ensemble, creating solidarity with Fire Dragon and their Bud U audience that was palpable and profound. Saying "No to war," "No to being part of the mass murder machine," is a very courageous act of resistance, serving all who understand the deep, irrefutable truth of human interconnectedness, tragically understood, all too often, only after the killing of one human being by another. That we humans wantonly kill our own species in genocidal numbers is an aberration in nature. The play's premise: We each must choose to not be hired killers, supporters of any kind of an imperialist, colonizing war machine. Fire Dragon's play *Choice*, dramatizing the disappearance of Nelson Davis, was a wake-up

call of profound dimensions for this writer and the students in the audience.

The pressing truth behind this drama is that our government is waging an unjust war in Vietnam. The military is denying and persecuting GIs who exert their First Amendment rights by protesting this war and laying down their guns. GIs see themselves as imperialists' cannon fodder. Theirs is a multifaceted struggle against U.S. imperialism abroad and injustice at home. We need to make the right choice. Let's find the truth behind this man's disappearance! This drama has caused me to research if the casualties of Black GIs are greater than that of whites in Vietnam. And if so, is it because Black soldiers are less trained and are forced to do the grunt work and given the most dangerous assignments?

Thank you, Fire Dragon! And especially Cheryl Whitmore for bringing this urgent matter to our campus!

Charles McCain, Black Journalism Major and Senior, Bud U

44

Reflections on the New *Choice*

Lucina's Journal Entry. Tour: Thursday, April 27, 1967. The auditorium was flooded with students for last night's performance. We invited those who couldn't find seats to sit on the edge of the stage so they wouldn't clog the aisles. I saw a few faces with lines and gray hair.

We began the performance by asking everybody to join us in singing the civil rights songs we've been singing at rehearsals and protests: "Ain't Goin' to Let Nobody Turn Me Around," "We Shall Overcome," "Oh, Freedom." When we sang "Before I'll Be a Slave, I'll Be Buried in My Grave," our voices rose up like flames.

When Cheryl took the mike before we performed our new Choice everybody got real quiet. I had a small tape recorder to record all of her many speeches. We didn't know what she was going to say—there wasn't time at rehearsal. I listened to it all again and transcribed the parts that really moved me. I'm going to try to reflect on some of her comments.

Cheryl speaking: "To end racism in our country, we all have to change. Black people must learn our right of resistance to systemic racism. White people must learn in what ways you are aiding that systemic racism..."

Why is it so hard for me to change! Leave what's comfortable and familiar behind, when I know in my guts I have to grow. And I can't hide from injustice. I have to be more aware of what's going on around me, and I have to believe that I can help myself deal with it. I have to keep reminding myself about the incredible things happening to me now, which never would have happened if I hadn't changed.

Cheryl: "Malcolm taught us it was okay to hate, if we act upon our hate in positive ways. Then he was shot down on February 21, 1965. Maybe when Malcolm saw the way of Martin Luther King, the white man had to kill him, because together they would be impossible to control. Our Malcolm is rising again because his black brothers and sisters are rising up and following his philosophy and that of Martin Luther King. We are acting on our hate and despair in positive ways. Self-determination and resistance to oppression is the right of all people."

So, she's saying that oppressed people have the right to armed resistance. The support Cheryl received in Chicago turned her into one inspired being. She has said that Martin Luther King's way is her way, too. She wants to work through education, through reasoning, through spiritual and cultural groups like Fire Dragon Street Theater to change people's minds. But, she said, she fully supports the right of oppressed people to rise up and fight fire with fire when the oppressors are not willing to be true negotiators at the table.

Cheryl: "Our first version of Choice incorporated primarily the white middle-class man's perception of moral and social responsibility around serving in the military. Tonight, for the first time, we include the Black man's working-class struggle. Remember, all GIs are workers for the military. In our depiction of the Black man's reality in the military we will focus on my cousin, Nelson Davis, who after being sent to Vietnam decided he didn't want to be a weapon of the ruling class, but a worker-force to stop the US invasion and occupation of Vietnam. I have statements from Black GIs like Nelson in anti-war newspapers, who describe how they were treated for their resistance. In the future, we will take up gays' and women's reality in the military."

****

I think back to my talk with Big Chin and Tattoo at the Yellow Farm and how one of them said that gays are really discriminated against in the New Left. I'll have to be more tuned into this, like why aren't we hearing more about gays and lesbians' struggles for their civil rights now. It's like Cheryl said, "It takes time to realize and expose our oppressions." Look how the Fire Dragon women are dealing with the guys' uptightness about lesbians, even just the word. But as far as the military, if you're found out to be gay or lesbian, are you dishonorably discharged?

Cheryl: "It's time now for our dramatic exposé, 'What Happened to Nelson Davis?' As I narrate Nelson's story and it's performed in a stark stylized manner, you, the audience, will have to understand this is a work in progress. Thankfully, several students from the Dance Department have joined us in this performance—but we've had only two rehearsals to pull it together for Nelson and for you, Bud U students. I see you are mostly white and I can assume mostly from the middle class. First off, understand, Black men don't have the same luxury of choice as whites. How many articles have you read about Black draft dodgers, Black draft card burners, Black students arrested at induction centers? The Black man's story has to be told. And I'm here to tell it to you tonight! That young men and women fight and die for this country that treats them like chattel is a kind of patriotism probably only God can understand.

The Black Panther Party Platform and Program, written in October, 1966, states something like, 'Afro-Americans should not be forced to fight in military service to defend a racist government that does not protect them.' The Panther Party leaders are way ahead of many of our people at this time. Right now, Black people need jobs and the military is one place they can find them.

"You will see in the second part of **Choice** *how Sam, a white man, resolves his moral stance. Since he does not want to be a hired killer for the military, he refuses to be drafted. Whereas in part one my cousin, Nelson, enlists with pride. At first, the army uniform had the glamour of a business suit for him. At last he would have a respected job and decent pay. At first, he was blind to the fact he was signing up to be cannon fodder. I remember how proud he was, his parents too. We had a potluck send-off for him at the Baptist church in our neighborhood. When he got to Vietnam, he realized he did not want to murder Vietnamese soldiers, human beings, people of color like himself."*

Cheryl is the first Black woman I've heard talk so boldly. She didn't know we were going to decide right after "Nelson's Story" not to perform "Sam's Story." The audience was overwhelmed by what they learned about Nelson and the unjust Vietnam War; Sam's story wasn't needed then. But we did perform sections from **Ghost Dance Tribute, Eco-Drama** *and our women's play, showing connections between all kinds of oppression and how the Panther women are talking out strong now, too.*

Cheryl: "I'll end my talk by saying I hope you have a better understanding of why the Black Liberation Movement is rising up to organize on campuses now and in the military. They are educating Black brothers and sisters to make choices, and take their freedom. But how many Black men and women go to this college? I bet you can count on your two hands. Connections have to be made. Some of you know that one of your presidents, the two-faced Thomas Jefferson, benefited from labeling Black people as mentally inferior, enslaved them and kept them from an education. The same Jefferson fathered at least six children with Sally Hemings, an enslaved Black woman on his plantation. I don't have the words yet for that. But I can tell you when the victims of tyranny do rise up, their suppressors call them terrorists, perpetrators of destruction. I'm sure the FBI and the CIA will try to wipe out the Panthers for wanting justice for our people!

"It's time to hear Nelson's story so you can understand what I've been saying. You will witness what the Vietnam War is like in general and what Nelson's life as a soldier has been like in particular, ever since he laid down his gun and began to organize other GIs to do the same—refuse to be killers in an unjust war. Alive or dead, my cousin Nelson Davis is a hero in our struggle for dignity and self-determination."

Cheryl received a standing ovation. She is our Martin Luther King, our Malcolm X, our Wovoka.

*****

Lucina's Journal, second entry for Thursday, April 27, 1967. Cheryl's talk and the new Choice was an impossible act to follow. Sam's story, a what-if scenario, had always set off feisty dialogue. But last night, Nelson's story, a real story, touched a raw emotional center. The audience seemed to bow its head, overwhelmed. We decided on the spot that Sam's story did not have to be acted out, at least not last night. Nelson's story was enough.

So much for all the paranoia that we were lured into a CIA backed University out to catch radical SDS fanatics on campus. At least it was dispelled for the evening and bravo for

335

Charles McCain's review of Choice in the student newspaper. He's one of the few Black students here. I hope he'll be at Cheryl's meeting later.

The members of the dance department (one of our sponsors) who participated in the production said they were especially interested in Choice because it was anti-war. Five dancers showed up for the afternoon rehearsal. They were instrumental in creating a symbolic, stark, and minimalist interpretation of Cheryl's disturbing account of Nelson's unknown fate. The case of a particular soldier was described in the context of a symbolic depiction of all war. His tragic disappearance is evidence of the punishment awaiting those renouncing war. Cheryl understood immediately how political theater can be a powerful tool to rally support for war resisters. Her plan to have audience members sign a petition after the performance demanding an immediate investigation into the disappearance of Nelson Davis by a Senate committee means that we are taking action to stop this cover-up and horror. We will be initiating a petition at upcoming performances. The audience wasn't left with the sentiment, 'poor Nelson Davis, what a bad break.' The cover-up around his disappearance puts into question the treatment of all soldiers, and in particular of Black soldiers. We ask: Why is the U.S. involved in Vietnam and, on a global level, why war at all? Nelson's disappearance needs this symbolic yet realistic style to express the enormity of this issue: our soldiers are pawns of the merciless, power-over, profit-driven war machine. The relentless, ruthless intent of our government's empire building must be fought by all the skills caring people in the U.S. can muster.

*After "Nelson' Story," we gave them two new women's scenes—Dawn's scene, **Abortion**, and Marin's scene, **Rape**. So only Marlene won't have a scene performed on our tour. She says she's not ready to be stark naked with us. Without* *the rehearsals last weekend (while the guys filled the Wolski's U-Haul with stones) we couldn't have pulled them off. Then with Cheryl's help we nailed them down at the rehearsal yesterday, late afternoon. For* **Eco-Drama** *and* **Ghost Dance Tribute,** *we kept the versions worked out without her. She was relieved. "Nelson's Story" drained her completely. I never thought we could do it—put new stuff together so quickly. I think how journalists cover breaking news, surgeons perform life-saving operations every day, a teacher works with forty-five kids on a project. Why should I be so surprised at what our group can put together when we have to? We think about our scenes all the time, awake, asleep.*

In retrospect, I think we made a mistake having the abortion scene follow **Choice.** *There was no emotional break from somber stuff; no comic relief. No wonder people laughed by the time we got to* **Rape.**

I don't have much time now to write—we have a work-shop this afternoon—but in case we decide to do the women's play at the Reams' Festival, I'll jot down how we performed two women's scenes last night. We took Dawn's suggestion— dialogue was planned in a general way and we improvised around it.

Abortion, *directed by Donna and acted by me, is an exposé of everything usually left unsaid about the subject. Not only does my character have to suffer the angst and shame of an illegal procedure—it takes place in a doctor's office hidden in the woods— the vacuum aspiration procedure is very pain-ful. Too ashamed to tell her parents and abandoned by her boyfriend, Reneé (my character's name) must suffer this deg-radation alone.*

After the operation, I dance out both the physical and emotional pain Reneé has experienced, so that at least she owns the trauma she's experienced. Donna said I writhed too much but Dawn said she felt herself in me last night. Dawn's perception is what counts for me here. It's her story and she lived it!

As I played this part, I was wondering if I would have to go through this someday. Louis does not want to have another child; how reliable is my diaphragm? I ended the scene with Dawn's own words: "I feel scarred for life. Not only by the painful, illegal procedure, but because I had no caring support. I felt like a criminal for doing what I felt was right and for taking care of myself. Of course, there are countries where women are stoned to death for a lot less. Any kind of challenge of the patriarchal rules on mothering seems to justify all types of brutal torture of women."

Knowing that she went through this excruciating pain has taught me so much about her—about her quiet withdrawal. About her anger, really. And about her love for Cheryl. Cheryl is helping her sister, Sadie, raise a child, Marcel. Maybe Dawn sees one of her possible selves in Cheryl. She doesn't have to have her own child; there are lots of kids that need nurturing and guidance by other caretakers.

Jenny directs **Rape** based on Marin's experience. Marin plays the rapist (she wants to understand what might motivate a person to perform such a depraved act) and Donna plays the woman who is raped. But instead of portraying a victim, Donna stands by the bed, witnessing her own rape as Marin, the rapist, thrusts herself into an empty bed. This was Donna's idea, which we all thought was brilliant. Marin/rapist is alone on the bed doing "his" raping motions, revealing what a brutal and lonely act that is. In our play, the bed symbolizes the woman's body, which is the rapist's object of hate, anger, and revenge.

As the rapist rapes, Donna tells him exactly what she

feels. At one point she says, "I want to murder you just like you are murdering me." We wanted to show that in no way was the raped woman encouraging this devastation of her body.

As the rapist continues plunging into his victim—I should say invisible victim—the rest of us, as Women of the Community, surround "him." In a chorus we say, "Rapists must be confined for rehab and therapy. If society does not prosecute rapists, we'll take justice into our own hands."

The audience did cheer us after this play. They made up for their self-conscious laughter when Marin first started 'his' thrusting motions on the bed.

With the Commitment Not to Kill chorus in "Nelson's Story" and the Women of the Community chorus in Rape, I can see another style emerging in our work: A collective, less individual focus (I'm tending to call it "political or social realism") where individual need, responsibility, etc. is subsumed within a chorus (symbolizing a community of people). It's hard to put into words, but it's about us all developing a common language and being united in struggle. When one person is brutalized, each of us is brutalized. Dawn's abortion experience and Marin's rape experience could have happened to any of us women.

45

A Flying Dream

Choice's dramatic exposé of Nelson's disappearance under Cheryl's guidance quickened Lucina's awareness of the dangerous nature of governments in general, and her own government in particular. Her once-simplistic, caricatured images of politicians' misdeeds, the back room drama with a lot of arm twisting and cash passed under the table by smug, self-serving men who made heartless decisions, paled in the reality of a more calculated, destructive arena: people and organizations who stopped at nothing in the race for power and profit. Perhaps because her conscious mind had trouble conceiving of the extent to which such depraved acts could be behind Nelson's disappearance, her unconscious led her to question more deeply through dreaming.

In one of her dreams, after soaring all night over great expanses of forests, she lands in a small village. One-story houses and shops line the main road. In the early dawn, she summons the men of the village to line up on both sides of the road. As she walks between rows of standing men, she begins an unusual inspection.

The men know what is expected of them. Without a word from her, they unfasten their belts and literally "let it all hang out." She is the Inspector, not of their military prowess, but of their penises.

As she looks at one penis after another, the organs take on other shapes—sometimes vegetables, such as carrots and stalks of broccoli; sometimes unrecognizable shapes that in her viewing become benign, almost friendly, even humorous-looking "things."

She did not want to tell Louis of her night flight until she knew exactly what it could mean. She wondered: *Would there be war if there were no penises, no "weapons of penetration" to rise up against weaker beings? Did she want to disempower all bearers of penises and devalue any privilege they might have? Did Marin's rape scene propel her dream? Or was it Cheryl's testimony and their dramatization of atrocities inherent in the brutal and racist war machine?* All these questions pointed to the one hardest to answer: *What do I really feel about Louis' penis?*

46
Reality Testing

The entire troupe had been distraught by Cheryl's sudden disappearance. Now her conception and direction of Nelson's story for *Choice* had fixed all that. She was truly back. Politically and morally they needed her. Her play chronicled resistance to the Vietnam War from outside and inside the war zone. And Cheryl's renewed commitment to them was fierce: "Our *Choice* has to help me find my cousin and advocate for many others!"

All during the week in Chicago she'd been a neophyte, a student, hungrily taking notes and trying to overcome her fear of asking dumb questions. "But how do you penetrate treacherous power-mongering in Washington to find a missing GI?" she'd asked. "Good question," they had responded. "Their cover-up system doesn't like to be challenged. Confronting the State Department and the Pentagon will take courage and the support of high-powered politicians as well as civil liberties organizations. Use your theater group to help you find your cousin and our other brothers and sisters!"

She set up a strategy meeting for the next day with troupe members, the students who'd invited them to campus and then publicized the event, and the dancers who'd worked with them. Goal for this meeting: evaluate their performance as an organizing tool. Could "Nelson's Story" work both dramatically and politically to move audience members to sign a petition demanding an investigation into his disappearance? Was the plan to gather 10,000 U.S. signatures demanding an investigation a realistic one? Then via Nelson's congressional representative present this demand to Washington and Pentagon officials? What other ideas did they have?

After Wednesday night's performance, several Black students, obviously disturbed, cornered Cheryl. Recently they'd tried to initiate a course, Current Civil Rights Activism for Black Americans, separate from the standard Civil Rights Issues in American Politics after Eisenhower. They'd gotten harsh rejection from the American Studies Department: "Our University is not an organizing instrument for current political movements! We depend upon state and federal funding!"

She had to think fast while they pummeled her with questions: "How can we get courses that speak to us now?" "How do we become a force?" She flashed on an older vet at the BLM, talking excitedly: *"An anti-war newspaper's coming out in June,* The Bond. *The American Servicemen's Union newspaper. GIs will write in their own words what's happened to them for refusing to fight. They won't be alone 'cause they'll connect with many others. Your Nelson might write a letter there… "*

A newspaper could help these students speak out too! She must brainstorm with them.

"Can you come to a meeting tomorrow!?"

Yes! Definitely they would attend her troupe's meeting the next day and then talk with her separately.

"And bring Charles McCain with you," she told them. "He sure can write."

*****

As she sat on her dorm bunk bed the next morning writing down notes on how to talk to the students, she felt anxious. *What about my nephew, Marcel? He and my sister need me. I can't put myself in harm's way! And neither can the Black students here who are asking for my help.*

But she had to do it. Share her own fears about becoming visible. Using theater to publicize the search for Nelson was scary. Soldiers refusing to fight? The military can't allow that! They lock 'em up. Ship 'em off to a secret brig. Build a lie that they were captured by the enemy. What other ways can we protest and not be beaten or locked up for it, she'll ask the students. Think of the secret messages women wove into quilts during the Civil War. They disclosed names of safe places, tactics that the resistance would be using, vital information passed on only to those who could "read" these quilts. She would remind them how the college students in Berkeley created a Free Speech Movement, so students would have the right to take part in political activities on campuses. There are free speech rights and ways to organize smartly without being locked up; never let themselves be demonized or victimized! And if they were locked up, so be it! Like they were in Berkeley. Activists have to toughen up.

But how do you confront a university that rejects a course that speaks directly to your need? They must rally support: reach out to more Black and white students, professors and adjuncts, progressive alumni, civil rights groups and leftist cultural organizations in the city of Budington itself, all working together to create a strong civil rights presence on campus.

What outreach tools could they use? Did they think the "Nelson Story" was an effective organizing tool to move audiences to act by signing a petition? Then use these petitions to build people power. After all, senators and representatives are elected. If they see their votes come from anti-war people, they won't push a pro-war agenda. Get the students to brainstorm on other ways to reach out besides theater. How about a newspaper?

Before focusing on how and who they would reach out to, shouldn't she suggest they do their research? Gather the facts: the huge disproportion of Black students to white students; how lower-income students of color didn't have access to scholarships and loans they needed; the facts on how the few Black students enrolled didn't have the same kind of networking structures as white students to help them build successful careers and families.

Cheryl's head was spinning. Was it possible for her to start the ball rolling in just one meeting with them? She would not be addressing seasoned organizers, but students only beginning to understand what it meant to become skilled activists and political organizers, a path that was rocky and often discouraging and exhausting. She hadn't even thought it out clearly herself: What were the first steps in putting out a small newspaper like *The Bond*?

*****

"Oh, thank god! Here you are!" Marlene and Jenny burst into her room. "You put a firecracker under us, babe," Marlene enthused.

"We all did it…put it together," Cheryl managed, jarred by their sudden appearance.

"*Choice* finally has the right name," Jenny added firmly.

Cheryl gestured them to sit down on her bed. "Okay, comrades. What's really on your minds?"

Jenny sat on the floor, resting against Cheryl's legs. "I just need to be quiet with myself for a while. Sorry."

Marlene began asking Cheryl questions about the political unrest in Chicago. Was it being caused by anti-war demonstrations? Race issues? Or both? She related what she knew about their canceled show there—but the SDS students were reluctant to give out much information about the bombing of an induction center. "I'm sure there are problems in Chicago's Black neighborhoods just like in Detroit. I think my parents' neighborhood is still safe; the Polish and Irish have been getting along for decades. But when I went shopping last week on West Grand Boulevard, the cashier was talking about the cops who raid bars in that area for no reason except to harass Black people and round them up for jail. From what I read in the Detroit Free Press there's a lot of unrest. My dad even suggested some Black kids could have stolen our props. Jenny told you about that, right?"

Cheryl's body stiffened: "Sure, blame the Black kids. The Polish kids in your ghetto are angels!"

"I'm sorry, Cheryl. You're right. My Dad can be racist."

As Cheryl struggled to find a response to Marlene, Jenny at her feet was obsessing on her disturbing meeting with Hans. *No more tears! The guy doesn't deserve them. The amount of caretaking I've given him, while he brings tension into every situation. I'm a fool for defending his flirtations with Dawn. I keep begging him to be close to me again. And what does he do? Slap me with his political crap: "I don't believe in monogamy anymore—it's a control tool for the capitalist regime. I need freedom to find self-determination!"*

Yes, she got back at him. "What are you trying to do, Mr. Macho Politico? Compete with Cheryl? Your Dawn is a queer girl. She's got the hots for Cheryl. She was never into you."

"Dawn does care about me. She's like me, she wants to be part of the Black Liberation Movement—they're the only ones in this country who really understand revolution."

"Well, don't be shocked if you find those two doing revolutionary somersaults in bed together with their clothes off!"

"I can't talk to you, Jenny. You're hurt because I don't want to be with just you anymore. I can't go back. I don't want to hurt you, but I can't go back."

She'd looked into the eyes of her lover for the past four years. But he wasn't there anymore. She saw a hard, determined look coming out of a pale white face, devoid of any passion for her. Or was it the petulant, hurt face of a little boy? She'd left him in the Budington student cafeteria with the words, "Okay, Mr. Big Revolutionary Man, have it your way. I quit you, forever." She was out of there in seconds, but not before she swept her hand across the table, spilling the cup of hot coffee on Mister Big's lap.

*****

Jenny was thankful Marlene and Cheryl were still talking. "All the information you got in Chicago," Marlene was commenting, "it sure energized you, Cheryl. Don't you need to rest today?"

Marlene and I are very different, Cheryl thought. *Would she have left the tour to learn more about a missing relative? She needs to feel safe through it all. And I'm putting myself into constant emotional turmoil.* "Look, Marlene, I know you don't understand me, but don't look at me as if I were some strange creature. I have two vital meetings I'm preparing for."

"I guess—I don't understand. How you're not afraid. I mean, you're challenging our government, all on your own." Marlene spoke in a shaky voice as if putting these thoughts into words for the first time.

"Not on my own! I hope the whole troupe is behind me now. It's our play about Nelson..." She sought Jenny's nod for support, but Jenny had fogged out again.

Marlene grasped Cheryl's arm. "I'm afraid. But you give me courage. I'm beginning to feel that Nelson is my cousin, too. It's scary, but that's what our work is—fighting for justice."

"Yes, and it's about supporting Black soldiers' protest of the killing of Vietnamese and the killing of our people in this goddamn racist country!"

"In Chicago—at all those meetings…Are Black women being listened to? It's not just the men like Seale and Newton who call the shots?"

"It was thrilling, Marlene. The women talked as much as the men. They gave me courage to do what we need to do."

*****

Jenny, out of her reverie now, pulled herself up to a sitting position and, without addressing Cheryl directly, began muttering aloud. "I was just wondering what it's like now—when a Black woman really loves her man, but he can't take her speaking her truth." In the pause that followed this comment, they heard rustling sounds from the hall, then one voice saying, "This is the room," and another, "Hope she's there."

Jenny began her soliloquy again: "And then what if she decided to leave him and be with a woman?"

Three of the dancers stood in the doorway. Cheryl rose from the bed to greet them, whispering to Jenny, "We'll talk more later…"

"Great, we found you," one of the students addressed Cheryl with a big smile. "We're here for the meeting. We can pick up some cold drinks and snacks on the way to the Union, if you want."

Cheryl skillfully juggled her attention to the dancers as well as Jenny and Marlene. "Sure, that'll be a big help. You two are coming, aren't you? I hope the rest of Fire Dragon will be there. We're going to talk together about the performance—what we need to work on, and what we thought worked really well to make it an organizing tool. Then I've got a meeting after that with the Black students who want me to help them organize. I've also invited them to come to our self-critiquing meeting so they can see how we talk to each other."

She fitted her Ché cap snuggly on her head and addressed Jenny quietly. "We'll talk more about that later." Then hugging the three dancers: "I'm so grateful to you for working on the performance of my cousin's story—you all were so great! Okay—it's time for the meeting. Come on, let's get some refreshments on the way."

47
Rising Up

Lucina and Louis walked into the small meeting room in the campus Union; Cheryl was already speaking to members of their troupe, the dancers, and several students, all seated with rapt attention in metal chairs. Six Black students seated in the back were busily taking notes. As she and Louis slipped into empty chairs by the note takers, Lucina's thoughts flew back to the guerrilla action Cheryl and her two "brothers" had carried out at the Weymouth College cafeteria: *She's her own force now.*

"...My sabbatical from the troupe was actually one long meeting with the Black Liberation Movement about our revolution," Cheryl explained. "Black presence, self-determination, jobs, education, housing, and health care for all; shaking off the shackles of racism and the ingrained postures of slavery by becoming activists; speaking out against the insidious, ingrained oppression that's been the backbone of United States history. All discussed in depth. I feel like a nova is going off inside me."

She paused to check her notes before continuing. "The U.S. capitalist system is founded on exploitation, racism, and yes, lynching. So we're warned of retaliation. This means that at times force might be necessary to implement the changes we need. Some groups are focused on building community, like the kids' free breakfast program. Others are focused on armed struggle. Everyone's priority is to survive, thrive, and build. I recognize the need for many directions in our movement, but I'm most comfortable with nonviolence if possible and being a builder. But don't kid ourselves—the more we do, the more there'll be the insidious backlash, the violent confrontations, the street wars with cops, the murders."

Jason, the dancer who'd portrayed Nelson, called out: "How about Newton and Seale? Aren't they pushing for armed resistance in Oakland?"

"Only if our rights are denied do we pick up the gun. And utmost in our demands? Adherence to the Fourteenth Amendment, the right of Black people to be juried by our peers, not buried by our enemies when—" Cheryl stopped abruptly as if taking into account her own words. After a sip of water she continued.

"Okay, enough about the BLM. We're here to critique last night's performance. Will it be effective in getting people to act? Sign petitions to find my cousin? But hold on…Let me interrupt myself again. Several students asked me to talk with them about how to get a relevant curriculum for Black students here at Bud U. And basically how to increase Black presence and power. Could you six students just stand up and shout out your names for us?"

The six stood, at first seeming reluctant, and then with increasing gusto called out their names, repeating them a few times, chant-like.

"Thank you all for coming. They're here to see how our street theater meetings approach issues—maybe get some ideas. After we reflect on last night's performance, I'll be meeting with just you six, to strategize on how to build your voice here. You've tried to add a course to the American Studies Department…Will one of you speak to that?"

After Joella described the rejection of a course on Current Civil Rights Activism, Cheryl began again: "So you see how much work has to be done by all of us? Do you students see that you're facing a similar issue as the Black GIs face? They're protesting that their rights are not being recognized, just like you are. There should be way more Black and Brown students here with a curriculum that addresses all the students' needs and history."

Then she led the discussion back to *Choice* as an organizing tool. "Let's hear thoughts about Fire Dragon's performance last night. For starters, do you think our play is effective in educating audiences about the harsh treatment of Black anti-war GIs, and will it help us find Nelson? You can understand how anxious I am to find my cousin."

The group as a whole felt *Choice* really moved the audience. The six Black students had purposely sat in different places in the auditorium to see close-up how audience members reacted. "Some seemed shocked, some even cried, all kinds of emotions were touched," they said. "But to persuade audience members to then sign a petition to find Nelson?" They weren't sure.

One of the dancers, Ariel, spoke up. "The audience aren't activists, just regular people. I really wanted Jason not only to represent Nelson symbolically, but be him. Make Nelson a real person that needs help now! If Jason had moved from the center of the circle to the front of the stage and spoken out to the audience…You know, have "Nelson" speak for himself about how he changed when he got in the army…instead of you speaking for him all the time, Cheryl. I think people would be more apt to sign a petition."

Listening intently, Cheryl closed her eyes as if to picture this possibility. "That could be very effective, Ariel. Thanks. I'm making a mental note of your idea to take to our next rehearsal."

The Fire Dragon actors present did feel "Nelson's Story" (maybe with the change Ariel suggested) could definitely move people to sign a petition: "If the petition is written in a powerful way."

"So, how would we write a powerful petition?" Cheryl asked.

Malik called out from the back: "Find the best civil rights lawyer in town and be willing to pay him to do it. They're trained, and you want it to sound professional, like it's really going to get the politicians to act."

"Did you hear that, Fire Dragons?" Cheryl asked. "Malik's right. It would take us meeting after meeting to figure out how to write a petition: Who to direct it to? How to describe our purpose, plan of action? I'm exhausted thinking about it. Yes, Malik, we need a lawyer—one who can use language that won't put off white people."

Black dancer, Laila, spoke out. "That's a big issue…not putting off white people. Like I was thinking about how truthful 'Nelson's Story' is. And scary. Probably a more conservative college wouldn't invite you to perform. Colleges supporting white privilege don't want us Black students to speak out for our rights. Nobody's going to sign a petition there!"

"I hear you, Laila," Cheryl nodded. "That's what we're up against! Meeting with my brothers and sisters at the BLM made it clear to me that justice is on our side. But we have to get Nelson's story out where it can be heard, and theater is a better communicator than violent confrontation. I'm hoping that at colleges like Bud U people can speak out, find common ground, you know, discuss real issues, seek justice together and…" As Laila nodded appreciatively at her, Cheryl stopped abruptly and turned to Louis and Lucina, who were also nodding.

"You guys felt I was abandoning you. Now you know how much I'm depending on you!"

Lucina was moved to respond. "I feel safer performing our new *Choice* in colleges like this than on the streets, where the cops, the guardians of capitalism, are itching to beat us down with their clubs. Just for saying, 'No more war! No more racism! Justice for Nelson!' I'd be afraid to push a petition on the street, except at a protest or demonstration."

A student who had been quietly absorbing the meeting, not one of the dancers, held up her hand to speak. Not waiting for an okay from Cheryl, in a nervous voice she confessed that she had filmed the performance of "Where is Nelson Davis?" with her 8-millimeter camera without asking for permission. "You can see what you've done and learn from it! And even use it in future presentations," she offered shyly. Seeing the positive responses from the actors, she went on. "When you aren't able to perform 'Nelson's Story', you can use the film for a mixed media presentation! And you can use it to get congresspeople to act! By the way, I'm Janella, born in Mexico."

Cheryl enthused, "Fabulous, Janella. You see? No one can stop our political and creative work from growing and growing." She shook the student's hand and took the offered film as clapping filled the small room. "Well, I'd say we have enough positive support here to use future performances of 'Nelson's Story' to force an investigation of his disappearance. I feel you all are with me on this. Just keep giving me your ideas on how to do it. By the way…did you know we're demanding that Black men and women should not have to serve in the military of a racist country? Why should we protect our abusers? So who knows? Maybe the CIA will try to pay me to shut me up, that or assassinate me." She stopped. *Wait. Her job is not to frighten the very people she's helping to organize!* "Let's take a break, you all. Talk to each other, okay?"

*****

Marin, fidgeting for some time in her chair near Cheryl, needed to talk privately to this woman she missed so terribly in the women's work. *Without Cheryl the Fire Dragon women were fated to be isolated from women in the Black Left*, she told herself again. Then Cheryl was standing next to her: "You obviously have something on your mind, Marin. Talk to me—I know you Fire Dragon women really missed me." *It was uncanny: Cheryl seemed to have heard her thoughts.*

"Please understand, Marin. When it's necessary, we need to separate from the white Left in order to weed out their issues from ours. We sure don't need them to explain us to ourselves! But as you can see, I need my sisters and brothers right here to help me find my cousin."

Marin responded quickly, "We want to help, Cheryl! We all have to work together, stand united—"

"Thank you, Marin," Cheryl interrupted. "But just so you understand: also there are times it's necessary to separate from others. Just think about our women's work separate from the mixed group. If we didn't go off by ourselves, we'd never come up with our dynamite stories." Her tone had turned gentle, almost imploring.

"You are touching on a sore place, Cheryl," Marin returned. "When you left us because you needed support and information, it was like we were an airplane operating on one engine; we headed for a crash landing. It's a good thing communication got messed up at Lighthouse College, so we didn't try to perform the women's play there, though the students expected us to. A lot of things just got wild without you, that's all."

"I hear you, Marin…I'm feeling a bit overwhelmed now. Not used to being the spokesperson like this. What can I say? If audiences respond to 'Nelson's Story' at our other performances, like here at Bud U, things might get crazy with me! We'll talk more later. Like I said, I'm meeting next with just

356

Black students, the six that are here now—they want to start an activist-awareness group." She signaled to the cluster of students, talking to each other at the back of the room, then called out, "We'll talk soon."

*****

The break also allowed Cheryl to exchange quiet words with Dawn, and give her the letter she'd written to her after her phone call from Chicago. "You've heard me say all this about Nelson at our performance last night. But I want you to know how important you are to me, Dawn. We need private time together to talk and talk."

Dawn, who'd been a silent but eager witness at the meeting, responded by giving Cheryl a quick hug and whispering, "I love you, Cheryl." Then, added, "Later," nodding.

Marin approached Cheryl again: "I'm so glad our new *Choice* can help with your cousin's disappearance. I mean…" Her voice broke.

"Marin, believe me, I know what you're saying." Cheryl grabbed Marin's arm— "You know my anguish—you lost your brother!" Then held her in a strong embrace.

"Cheryl, I need to say one more thing—I respect you so much. I respect what you've done. I just missed you working with us on our stories, that's all."

"Thanks for that, Marin. I need everyone too, for a long time."

When Cheryl went to get a glass of water, Marin's thoughts went to Al. She hoped his absence wouldn't be noticed. In fact, his decision not to come to the meeting had upset her greatly. But she didn't feel like playing the good wife and excusing him. Well, they weren't married.

"Cheryl's speaking again this afternoon?" he'd barked out that morning. "I mean, we did her play. I'm glad—it's great, probably the best thing we've done. But Jesus, I don't have to keep kissing the ground before her, do I?"

Marin had turned away from him, burying a scream. He was always coming up with some absurdity. A repressed midwesterner, she'd concluded once again. When he admitted he was anxious about becoming a political advocate for Nelson, especially with the inevitable rejection of performances of *Choice* at certain colleges, she hugged him, hugging part of herself, she realized. She also was afraid of right-wing backlash. Just as Cheryl was.

Marin had given Al another hug: "It's okay if you don't go today. In fact it's good to have some separate times. I need to hear Cheryl on my own." *Would Louis be easier to live with than Al?* she wondered as she raced toward the Union for the meeting.

*****

Only a few minutes remained before the ad hoc meeting with the Black students would begin. "Any more comments before we break up?" Cheryl asked. She'd noticed Courtney fidgeting and biting at his fingers for some time.

"How can someone like me…" Courtney stood to address the whole group.

"You mean a dynamite harmonica player?" Cheryl returned playfully.

"I mean, a white guy harmonica player—can I join BLM?"

"You can support our party right now, Courtney. You can't be an officer. When we have a Black president, Courtney, maybe then you can be in his cabinet," she added in a tone blending irony and possibility. He sat down, both humbled and awakened by her clarity.

The meeting had woken Jack up to the fact that his recent meditation and yoga retreats had very few people of color in them. He could count them on one hand—one from South Asia, one Argentinean, one Black kid from Harvard (probably on a scholarship), two Puerto Rican women. *Was the mindfulness movement and the practice of insight meditation primarily a pursuit of middle-class whites? he wondered. And what about all the Black people into Jesus? Their civil rights songs that sounded like fired-up church hymns? Obviously all humans needed to be fed spiritually, somehow.*

"Cheryl, I've got a question."

"Sure, Jack, shoot."

"Do you think there can be a Black movement that just focuses on Black power and revolution? What role does the soul and the heart play here?"

"Have you forgotten Martin Luther King, the leader of the civil rights movement, Jack?"

"But he follows Gandhi's example of nonviolent civil disobedience. I mean, all the uprisings happening in California—Oakland and LA—and Chicago and Detroit in the Midwest? This is resistance, not disobedience, and there's violence."

"Thanks for those words," Cheryl broke in. "They are *uprisings*, rising up out of repressive structures. Not 'rioting' as the media loves to splatter all over the headlines. If you buy into the government's take on us…Well, they want to smear us as trigger-happy hoodlums who would rather kill and rob than talk and work. We call it the right to resist and force change."

"So, Cheryl, it's not wanton violence," Jack added.

"It's our bodies and spirits wanting to live! To address your question: By owning our needs, we are owning our souls. We have Christians, Muslims, and Jews for brothers and sisters. Buddhists as well. But those of us who are activists don't think it's enough to sit under a tree all day and seek enlightenment or smell the flowers. We're seeking Freedom, Self-Determination, Education, Jobs, Housing, Leadership Roles in Government and the Arts. All with capital letters. And since these basic needs aren't being given to us, we have to fight for them. It's a lot of work to unlock the chains of enslavement. Sidney Poitier playing handsome Black men in the movies won't bring our revolution, but he sure gives us some dignity, doesn't he? Do you see what I mean, brother Jack? First things first. And leave no parts behind."

Hans put his hand down. His question had been generally answered: *Did Huey Newton require every Black person who worked in the movement to carry a gun?* He could talk to Cheryl some other time about that.

Jim was asking the last question. "Cheryl, would you say you're looking for your roots? By the way, I do forgive you for splitting on us. You probably were told not to talk to us about it beforehand because of the top-secret issues surrounding your cousin. But Donna and I were wondering, is it your African roots you're looking for?"

Cheryl, looking bemused, exhausted, and a tinge put out, dramatically imitated Degas' *Thinker*, her chin resting in a cupped hand. "I must admit to you, Jim, and you too, Donna, I'm looking for the whole enchilada." As the room filled with laughter, Cheryl picked up her cap and notes. "Thank you all so much for coming—we'll talk more. And we'll find a lawyer to help us with a petition. When 'Nelson's Story' is as strong as we can make it, we're going to start getting signatures of support. Okay? Now I've got to meet with my Black students. But let me just say one more thing. We Black people aren't the only ones uprising now. Anti-war protestors, citizens and students, are fiercely protesting a big chemical company that makes the napalm that's being dumped on the Vietnamese. All over this country, mainly on college campuses like this one, uprisers are protesting the Dow Chemical Company for enriching their stockholders' bank accounts with the burnt bodies of the Vietnamese people. You see, protesting for our basic human rights is exposing the rage all compassionate human beings feel." She then joined the six who were anxious to meet with her.

Louis turned to Lucina. "Wow! She's got chutzpah."

"Well, we got a lot of learning today."

"Okay, I've had enough learning for now. You wanna get a beer?"

"I don't want to split too fast, Louis. Someone just might want to discuss the women's performance."

48
What's Going On Now?

The six Black students and Cheryl convened over cokes and sandwiches in the cafeteria. Since it was filled with students crowded into small booths near them, they had to talk loudly.

Joella, anxious to move the conversation past Aretha Franklin's last concert—their time with Cheryl was limited—raised her voice. "Cheryl, you asked us to bring Charles McCain with us, right?"

"Oh, that's right. Did you talk to him?"

"He's so focused on the *Budington Advocate*, I don't think he could hear me. He just kept saying, 'Yeah, that's good stuff,' when I told him we were going to meet with you and get some ideas on how to build Black presence here. When I told him you were impressed and appreciative of his review of 'Nelson's Story,' he said to tell you, 'Thanks, that means a lot to me. Let me know how your meeting goes, okay?' Then he went back to his cubby hole in the journalism office and waved goodbye."

"Okay, Joella. It's good to talk with him. Maybe he can write up something for your college paper about the meeting."

"I got the feeling he just wants to do his own thing." Joella said. "That, or he's afraid to challenge his white journalism professor."

"Be patient, woman," Ada advised. "Charles' review has already challenged Professor Robinson. It'll take time to build the kind of uproar we have in mind. Don't worry, Charles will interview us—you'll see."

Cheryl put her hands together and nodded eagerly. "Listen, comrades. I'm dying to tell you about *The Bond*. I mentioned it earlier. I want to emphasize the power that a four-page newsletter can have in organizing people to work together for common goals. You all can keep your growing community informed as to what you're doing and why. Your process, your research, your needs, your results. Get people eager to read what you have to tell them. Compare Bud U to other colleges where Black history and activism are a part of the curriculum and how that inclusion builds supportive action and spirit."

Imani, seated next to Cheryl, couldn't contain her excitement. "This is for me! I'm a journalism major, wondering what kind of newspaper I would want to work for. I didn't come up with an answer until now, hearing you talk about *The Bond*. And it wouldn't be working 'for' but 'with' others; a collective getting the news out there that needs to be heard. It's absolutely necessary that Black students have their own newsletter. We can have editorials, letters, cartoons." She addressed Calvin, seated across from her. "Here's your chance. You're always showing me your so-called comic strips: white folk boasting about not being prejudiced to Black people and gays and lesbians, while their actions put the lie to their words and show how limited and blind they really are."

"This is great," Cheryl chimed in. "Thinking how you can make something you're proud of together that can educate and inform others."

Malik spoke up for the first time. "Tell us more about this Bond paper. It's not about a bail bond, an investment bond..."

"Right, Malik. This is about connection, a bond between people. A vehicle for communication. It's going to come out in June from the ASU, American Servicemen's Union, and be mailed to GIs. What I'm most into is the letters page where GIs tell each other how they're being abused by their officers because they're standing up for their rights. It will save lives because soldiers will know they aren't alone. Just like your newsletter can reach out to students all over this country, struggling like you to be heard."

Cheryl paused to see if anyone needed to comment. When her listeners were finished writing in their notepads, she continued. "Along with figuring out an outreach strategy, you have to do the research. Then come up with a list of demands and strategize how they can be met. Investigate if any legislation is in place at Bud U requiring affirmative action around Black student enrollment. If not, research how legislation could be put in place, and initiate that process. Incorporate input from supporters from all departments of the university. Another research group could interview professors in all departments as to their feelings about these issues. Somehow, point out that the struggle for Black students' civil rights is no different than the struggle for women's, Latinos, Indigenous, all students' rights."

Joella spoke up. "We're supposed to be thankful that Johnson started affirmative action for job opportunities for minorities? Shit to that!"

"How can you say that?" Calvin questioned, obviously confused.

"Affirmative action has to be mandated in universities, in our University. Or we aren't being educated for the jobs we want! We don't just want jobs as janitors and cafeteria workers, damn it! We want to be doctors, lawyers and professors, don't we?"

"You are so good at speaking out, Joella…"

"That's what we all have to do from now on, Calvin!" Imani stood up and raised her fist as she spoke. "Now we need a name for our newsletter—and a name for us!" She paused, smiling at her companions. "So, how about: 'Black Students Reach Out,' for our paper. For us: 'Black Students Speak Out.'

****

Meanwhile, several booths away, a small group of women students joined Lucina and Marin to ask them about the women's play and their process. At one point, during a discussion of her rape scene, Marin asked them pointedly, "Why do you think it initially set off nervous laughter?"

"The movements were so grotesque, they were hard to take," a student started. "Besides, rape makes everybody uncomfortable," said another, adding, "But you got people involved right away. That was great!" All were eager to respond. "It was nervous laughter, fear laughter, but laughter that made us open up to feel the horror." a third woman remarked. The comments struck Lucina deeply. She must remember that contradiction: *Laughter can mask outrage and open the emotions to express it.*

"It was brilliant how you de-victimized the 'victim' by having her witness her own attack, instead of being subjected to it like we see in too many movies." Cindy, a small, intense woman wearing several political buttons on her blue work shirt, spoke up. "Hollywood's into depicting rape scenes over and over. You know, the scary music, a flaky dame making bad choices walks alone along a dark street. The perfect setup for disaster. But the audience's adrenaline gets going and everyone's on the edge of their seats. People are addicted to these creepy scenarios. Predictable." She began pounding the table. "So we need women to change things! Give us power images where we take charge, use our heads, and change our behaviors. Like you women do in your plays. Thank you so much. I'm going to write about them for the school newspaper. It was great!"

Jim suddenly appeared out of nowhere, edging in on the group huddled around Marin and Lucina. He was looking for Donna. Silence. "Okay, girls. Keep getting your points across!" Lucina and Marin stood up to face him. Jim quickly backtracked. "I mean it, you women really did a brilliant thing." Then with "Uh, sorry—bye!" he sped to the back of the cafeteria, where other Fire Dragon men were hanging.

*****

That night, the producers and publicists of Fire Dragon's campus performance, a mix of students, administrators, and faculty, hosted a buffet in the student lounge in their honor. Many came from the Drama, Dance, and Literature Departments, along with some invited anti-war activists from the community.

Lucina interpreted the restrained behavior of the faculty as some kind of older-people-being-respectful stance, or possibly "older liberals displaying a patient honoring of their younger, more idealistic and energized counterparts." Certainly no one could deny that their own students had glorified the street theater from New York City, as shown by the striking artwork all over campus advertising their arrival.

The actors, plates loaded with food, ingenuously spilled out tales of performing in the parks of New York City to the neatly dressed couples surrounding them. Lucina soon understood that some of the professors had imagined a far more sophisticated Repertory Theater Company coming to their halls of higher learning from a cultural center of the world.

Cheryl, both pleased with this polite honoring and skeptical about its implications, wanted to ask one of the professors from the History Department if "Nelson's Story" could encourage a university course such as The Need for Black Activism.

But that was now work for the Black Students Speak Out group to handle.

When Courtney was approached by the distinguished-looking Dean of Student Affairs with, "Good job, fellow—and I wanted to ask you: Where do you rehearse and do you all live near each other in Manhattan?" Courtney replied, "Yes. We work in a loft in the factory district of Hell's Hundred Acres and we often live together both in the city and the country."

Dean Harrison's curiosity was obvious: "Are there any children in your troupe?"

"Cheryl has a beautiful nephew, Marcel," Courtney beamed.

"So, none of you are parents?" Dean Harrison asked flatly.

"We don't give out family secrets," Courtney emoted slyly.

"Well, good luck for the rest of your tour. I enjoyed your show, and it certainly seemed our students did too!" With a nod and a smile the Dean quickly headed to the table with drinks.

Lucina and Cheryl, having overheard Courtney's conversation with Dean Harrison, looked at each other knowingly: Yes, it was time to leave Budington University and go forward! The Reams College Theater Festival in Iowa was coming up next.

49
The Blue Giraffe

"A blue giraffe! I should have known." Lucina fastened on a small object in the window of the breakfast nook at Professor Joan Donaldson's house, where she, Louis, Dawn, and Cheryl spent the night. Cheryl and Dawn were still in bed on the back porch, but Louis and Lucina had gotten up early to enjoy freshly ground coffee with their host.

"Why should you have known?" Joan set a tray of hot almond croissants in front of them. "I call her Girca. To me she looks more like a camel wanting very much to be a giraffe. A *camelus* trying to be a *camelopard*. They are related."

"It's just that to me a blue giraffe is magical." Lucina spread a buttery croissant with the homemade raspberry jam Joan had retrieved from her pantry. "Suddenly we're having such luck!"

"Well, I'm glad you appreciate my animal. You don't usually see giraffes in Indiana." Joan sat down and poured three cups of steaming coffee in rust-colored mugs, a smile spreading on her face. She really liked these two New Yorkers! "And never a blue one."

Lucina, appreciating their host's playfulness, beamed affectionately at Louis who looked more relaxed than he had in weeks.

"Lucina's enigmatic nature is part of her midwestern upbringing," he said, good-naturedly. "They have a special brand of mysticism in Illinois." He'd already consumed one croissant and was reaching for another.

"A blue giraffe is a symbol of good luck for me—that's all I meant." She tore at her croissant, a little miffed that her spontaneous feelings had been commented on by Louis.

"Why is that?" Joan watched her guests with some amusement. Like all couples, no matter how loving, they had their little tensions.

"I have a friend who repairs antiques." Lucina replied amiably. Not wanting Joan to think she and Louis had problems, she put her hand tenderly on his arm as she talked. "She's the caretaker of an incredible blue porcelain giraffe. It had been her grandmother's, then her mother's. It's not transparent like yours. Been broken several times—but it's still intact, under Alice's care. She claims it has saved her life at least three times already."

"Somehow I thought you were going to tell us an ancient myth about a magical blue giraffe," Joan commented. "But then, I hang around scholarly types too much here at Budington."

"No, it's just about a real-life experience," Lucina returned, adding thoughtfully, "like most of our plays."

"The 'Nelson Davis' story in *Choice*—so profound, real, and unsettling, even as a stylized drama. Let's pray your upcoming petitions to our hawkish government will get the truth out about Cheryl's cousin! She speaks so clearly about the problems involved—I wonder, has she ever considered a degree in political science?" Joan studied her guests' faces; she'd heard how unsettling Cheryl's sudden departure from the troupe's tour had been for them all.

"She's driven to activism, not academia," Lucina responded.

"Okay—she has time," Joan added. "But what wasn't being talked about enough, I thought, was how afraid whites are about the Black community organizing itself. And behind that tremendous fear of Black anger erupting is the guilt for allowing a racist society."

"Cheryl is extremely aware of whites' fears and guilt," Lucina interjected. "How that feeds violence against Black people. I'm sure she talked about it today with a group of Black students who are determined to be heard."

"We're very thankful to have Cheryl with us," Louis added quickly, wanting to ward off possible tension between the two women. "Just think how many people made that production work last night. All the promotion work you encouraged, Joan. I mean, you teach English Lit, but you fired up the Art Department, Theater Department, political science classes to get involved. It's been amazing for us. Did you see the really insightful review in the student paper about our performance of *Choice*?"

Before Joan could answer, Lucina broke in: "A really insightful response! Just wish he'd given the women's plays a thumbs-up. Anyway, another student is going to do that. Cheryl told me her name, Cindy—she wears a lot of political buttons. Do you know her?"

Joan turned to Lucina: "Yes. She's one of mine. Very into women's issues and a good writer. Well, your scenes from *Moments of Loss/Moments of Gain*, powerful. I really enjoyed… that's not the right word for an abortion scene and a rape scene! I was very affected! You women don't fool around, do you?"

"We deal with the hard stuff from our lives." Lucina took a deep breath, her eyes back on the small glass animal, enjoying a window box all to herself. Joan had displayed it well. She breathed in deeply again. *Oh, wouldn't it be great if Louis and I could do something different this afternoon, like a picnic.*

Maybe Joan would like to join us. Oh, forget it! We're heading for Reams in a few hours after we…

"The rape scene…it brought back some unpleasant memories—seeing that on stage. The younger students were laughing at first."

A catch in Joan's voice pulled Louis' attention back to the two women. He'd turned away from them briefly to admire the neat kitchen with all the modern appliances. Joan, about Lucina's age, intrigued him. The way she held her lips somewhat pursed as if frozen in a desire to kiss or be kissed. And her blue eyes, just about the color of her giraffe—fascinating.

"Sorry if it was too much." Now Lucina was talking.

"What's to be sorry for?" Joan interrupted. "One of your aims, I take it, is to say to women in the audience, 'Hey, you're not alone.'"

"Exactly!" Lucina took in a mouthful of croissant as Joan began talking softly.

"I was raped by a guy from the town, the first year I taught on this campus. The university wanted to cover it up— they don't want parents pulling their kids out of school or lose applicants because of the publicity. I was told to not stir up trouble, so I didn't press charges. And I knew who the man was—I'd seen him at a local bar." She hesitated, her eyes closed. "You know, I don't think I can handle this right now. Sorry." Then she was hunched over, blowing her nose into her napkin.

Louis intervened gallantly, pouring them all more coffee from the porcelain pot Joan had carefully placed on a cork tile near one corner of the Maplewood table commenting, "Be careful, this is hot."

"You were telling us something about a *camelopard* versus a *camelus*…"

"That's right, Louis." Joan flashed him an appreciative smile, offering him the remaining croissant.

"How are they related? I know they both have long necks and long faces." He squinted as if to look somewhere in his brain for an answer.

"To reach leaves," Lucina added.

"Exactly. And both are ruminant mammals." Joan delved eagerly into the topic. "Their stomachs are divided into four compartments."

"Cud-chewing." Louis chomped playfully on his croissant.

"You two are great!" Joan exclaimed animatedly. "Actors are so, what do I want to say, curious about things."

"Things and smart women." Louis nodded, gazing warmly at his two women companions.

"Oh, I'm sure." Joan stood abruptly. His way of looking at her, of touching her somehow with his disarming intensity. "That reminds me—oh good! I would have felt terrible if I'd forgotten."

"Forgotten?" Lucina eyed the little animal quickly, wanting to hold its pleasing color in her mind again. Was it cobalt or azure blue? Maybe Joan knew—but she had left the room.

And then she was back holding a letter. "Airmail Express letter for you, Lucina, from New York City. It came last week."

"Oh, sorry, we didn't tell you," Louis apologized. "We gave out our university contacts, sparingly."

"Oh, fine," Joan addressed him, handing the letter to Lucina. "So you're not only fancy free troubadours? You have people back home."

"My family is from a working-class neighborhood in Brooklyn," Louis offered ingenuously.

Lucina stared at the envelope. Was he going to tell her about his parents, his ex-wife and son in upstate New York? Even if Joan had done a dynamite job overseeing their performance, she was a stranger.

"Oh, what part of Brooklyn, Louis?" Like old friends, the two of them were soon describing favorite candy stores and egg creams. "I visited my cousin there when I was a kid."

"It's from Shauna," Lucina spoke softly. *Shauna must have gotten her phone message after all. But wait! She hadn't been able to leave a message! So probably Shauna was reporting that everything was fine, just wanting to know when they'd be coming back to pick up* Rune. *That kind of thing.*

"Oh, great!" Louis turned from Joan momentarily. "Nice of Shauna to write." He stayed silent as Lucina slowly plied the envelope open.

He turned back to Joan. "I'm more poet than actor. Lucina got me into body stuff and helping out in her theater sculpture shows. One thing led to another…"

He watched Lucina pull a handwritten page from the envelope.

"Have you been published?"

"A few places. *Paris Review*, *Antioch Quarterly*, *New in Poetry*. And in my journal, *PAN*."

"A talented guy with many—"

A scream knifed Joan's comment.

Louis lunged toward Lucina. "Lucina, what's the matter? What's in the letter!"

"Someone smashed her—my *Rune*—at a party after we left the city! Shauna doesn't know—h-how it happened. It had gotten pretty wild—but she wasn't there. All she knows is when it was over—my sculpture was smashed to smithereens. That's what she was told. 'Smashed to smithereens.' Oh, my god. My baby! The pieces were removed from the loft—not by her. She wasn't even there!"

"Wait a minute! How does she know this?" Louis grabbed the letter and began reading it silently, mouthing the words. Disbelief, then anger shot across his face. "That piece was sturdy—like a piano. An icon!"

He spoke solemnly. Joan bowed her head and moaned, "How terrible! A terrible assault."

"A criminal assault! It was her last sculpture, a master-piece." Louis stared dumbly at the paper in his hands, adding almost inaudibly, "Lucina's 'woman-whole.'"

Lucina's head sank to the table. "Not anymore," she managed. Joan's hand was on her shoulder. She heard her own breathy sobs, her broken words—"She says friends of h-h-hers—were st-staying at the loft—they told her—no one knows who did it." She wasn't in her body anymore.

Louis stood abruptly, pounding his fists together, ready to smash down on those who had smashed his beloved's work. "Why wasn't Shauna there to stop it!"

"You read what she said—she wasn't there! She was away, vacationing—on the Cape—" Her voice broke as she wailed out, "My baby—my baby—gone!"

Louis's face opened into a roar. "Who *was* there?"

Lucina snapped back into her body again. "I told you. Sally and Karen were staying there! There was some kind of meeting or party…"

"I'm so sorry," Joan whimpered.

"They told Shauna what happened?" Louis, shaking and ashen, sank to his chair. "Someone knows—what happened—and they're going to tell me. Or arms and legs are going to be missing."

"I don't know!" Lucina stood up, shrieking out, "I can't think. My *Rune*, my *Rune* is dead."

"Can I do anything?" Joan managed, feeling quite help-less at the couple's disturbing news. "Please use my phone if you need to call New York."

"*Rune* is gone! My *Rune* is gone!" Lucina repeated over and over.

Louis shook his head in disbelief. Joan's eyes had closed again. "I used to carry that sculpture around to all the shows Lucina was in." He couldn't hold back the tears flooding his eyes. *When was the last time he'd seen* Rune, *not wrapped up in that mummy's sheet, but really seen her in all her beauty?* He turned his whole being to Lucina. She clutched Shauna's letter, her eyes locked on the blue giraffe

50
Joy

The sun coming through the bamboo shades in Joan's sunroom cast linear patterns on the quilt. Dawn snuggled closer to Cheryl, wanting to stay there forever, kiss her neck, her ears, her face, and her lips all over again. But Cheryl was asleep.

Dawn basked in a healing light or some kind of balmy air. Her new self was emerging, a butterfly from a cocoon. Her real self, the self she wanted to be. How did this happen? This amazing thing?

Last night at the gathering with faculty, she'd been talking to a student about the Manhattan Fire Dragon loft, how the long rectangular space at first seemed scary, an endless cave, because there were windows only at the ends. But with so much happening in that space, the groups' rehearsals, living with Louis and Lucina, she was in a constant state of excitement. The walls just disappeared. The young woman was awed by Dawn's stories. Whatever she said brought out more laughter and, "Wow! How could that be?" Dawn laughed with her, swigging down her third glass of wine with abandonment.

Suddenly Cheryl appeared, grabbed her hands. "I need to talk to you, Dawn!" Dawn, confused and apologizing to the student, let herself be pulled away from the party and out an exit door leading to the fire escape. They stopped to catch their breath. Cheryl pulled her close and kissed her hard. "I love you, Dawn!"

Then Dawn was laughing, melting, and flying. Cheryl took her arm and led her down the stairs to the ground. She heard familiar voices. They were climbing into the back of someone's car. Lucina and Louis were in the front seat talking and she and Cheryl kept holding hands and kissing and smiling.

The car stopped at a small house surrounded by white trees.

"You two will have to share the sunporch." Professor Donaldson was looking right at them. *So, it was her house.* Cheryl said, "I think we can handle that." She couldn't remember—why were the four of them not staying at the dorm with the others?

"There are eggs and fruit and, oh yes, there'll be some fresh croissants for breakfast. Help yourself. Mi casa, su casa. Okay?" So cool coming from a professor. That's how it began— the most wonderful night of her life ever: she and Cheryl were alone—not alone, together, holding each other in a room smelling of pine and lemon.

*****

"Dawny, stop shaking the bed. I need to keep sleeping."

Can't she stay resting against that cool, responsive body? This might never happen again. If only she could quiet the thumping in her chest. Her insides tingled, new strange feelings. She was afraid. "Cheryl, I need to talk to you. Please, I've never done this before."

"What, baby? Never been with a woman, a Black woman, a Black woman radical?" Cheryl reached out to pull her back close. "Just so you know, babe. I've never slept with a white woman. This is new for both of us."

"That makes me feel better. But, I still don't understand how you trusted those strangers so completely. Weren't you afraid to just go with them like that?" Despite the warmth spreading between her legs again, Dawn needed some answers: "You left us, me, and went to some stranger's apartment?"

Cheryl pulled herself upright so she could look at Dawn's loving, anxious face. This woman she was caressing all night, her new honey-love. "You don't understand. They knew others who might have some leads on what happened to my cousin. I had to go with them."

"I love how dedicated you are to all your family."

"I stayed with Gloria's sister, Magda, in Bronzeville. Gloria was one of the four activists I went with." Cheryl closed her eyes, her face contorted. Hadn't she given Dawn the letter she wrote after their phone call? It took several moments before she could continue. "Okay, I guess I can trust you. I didn't say this in our performance of Nelson's story. First, I want to build up awareness that he's missing. Can't jeopardize his safety. I can't believe that someone in the government will help me, us! So, yes, BLM had information about a meeting in Detroit this summer. Soldiers who know Nelson are coming back from 'Nam and they'll be meeting us at one of our safe places…" She paused. She couldn't tell anyone where, not even Dawn! She'd almost said too much, endangering everyone. "I'm scared to go to Detroit. I wasn't scared to go to Chicago."

"You mean, there might be a crackdown by the FBI or something?"

"I know there's a lot of unrest in Detroit. The white cops are raiding our bars, claiming it's because there's no license to sell booze. They're arresting us like crazy. Something's going to explode. You've heard the hype about Detroit's Mayor Cavanagh making it a model city for Black and white people to get along. Bull! He's not letting my people in the police force, for one thing. Anyway, I've got to figure out if I'm going there in July or not. When someone goes missing from your family you have to do everything to find them. You know that, Dawn."

They faced each other, heads propped up with pillows. "That's what I felt about you! If you hadn't called me at the Wolski's…I was going crazy. I almost ran to Chicago to find you." *This talk of the violence in Detroit—and she might go there!* She grasped Cheryl's hand. "I have to say this, what I was also afraid of—"

Their hands clasped now, Dawn blurted out: "I was afraid I couldn't kiss good enough for you."

"Do you think I would be attracted to a woman I didn't feel could kiss me with her whole being?" Cheryl tightened her grip on Dawn's hands and closed her eyes. "You do real good, girl. You're a damn good kisser."

*****

Voices came through the open window. Was someone calling out to them? No, it was Lucina crying out, "My ruin, my ruin!" Like a broken car alarm. And something about a baby. Dawn jumped up and shut the window with a bang. "Fuck! Lucina can be so goddamned dramatic!" Nothing should disturb them in this small lovely room, all windows, bamboo, and pine paneling; the sunlight touching them, warming them. Just the two of them, safe here. She and Cheryl together, like a dream.

As soon as she climbed back in bed, her angst resumed; she had to know more. Had Cheryl gone back to sleep? As Dawn snuggled close to the warm incredible woman-on-a-mission, she felt again her lips pressing velvet-soft flesh, her tongue lapping a tangy elixir. How did this happen? She closed her eyes to remember: they'd both had a lot of wine—and then, the first kiss! But how could this person, this wise, tough, grownup woman, this other-mother for her nephew, this articulate, political, fearless woman have chosen to be in bed with her? This amazing woman now breathing softly beside her.

Could a dream come true so quickly? She'd only said it to herself—how many days ago? *I'm in love with Cheryl.* Never, she'd never been in love like this with a woman. But that wasn't it. She'd never been in love with anyone! The theater women had no idea. They only heard, "I love Cheryl." *But, I'm in love with Cheryl like Elizabeth Taylor and Richard Burton are in love. That's what I really need to tell them.* At that moment Cheryl's hands cupped her breasts strongly. *Wait! This isn't movie-star love! We're two real women. Our love isn't in the movies.*

The only movie she could remember about a woman having sexual feelings for another woman was a sinister and sad German film. The school principal caught a teacher and a female student making out in a bathroom. They were punished.

No! Definitely not that. This was laughing and crying and kissing and hugging and caressing and not alone. For the first time ever, she didn't look at someone lying next to her and feel like vomiting, wanting to slam the door on the stranger who had taken over her body, made it feel dirty, not even hers anymore. With Cheryl she had touched, explored, caressed, suckled, and entered wet, deep folds and dark, secreting flesh all night. *I've been opened, caressed, turned into a scintillating, syncopating, symphonizing*—playful words were making her giggle.

Cheryl pulled her close and kissed her a long time, their tongues caressing, their hands exploring, fingers massaging, their bodies fully open to be explored until they both exploded, and she heard herself say, "Cheryl, I think this is what they call 'in love.'"

They sat up, backs against the wall of the small, porch-like room, surveying the comfortable natural furnishings, hand-sewn quilt, rattan chair, painted wooden table, bamboo shades, one picture—the poster of Van Gogh's Sunflowers in a stained wooden frame on the wall in front of them. "It all fits perfectly, doesn't it?" Dawn managed. "Like a joyous feeling."

"Are we lucky!" Cheryl beamed. "How did you know what to do? You sure you haven't been with a woman before?"

"I didn't know." Dawn took her lover's hand and massaged each finger slowly, noting the look, the feel of each one for her personal journal of sensations. "I just listened to your sounds and followed."

"Damn! Well, finally my BLM comrades agreed, I could work with you all. But, they didn't know love was waiting for me in the wings!"

Dawn touched Cheryl's face—first cheeks, the bone under her eyebrows, pressing on the small indentions there, then moving toward her nose, wanting to learn its shapes, her nostrils that flared in defiance when she was angry, softened when she relaxed, lifted in laughter when pleased, and her lips, tender, velvet, mauve, sensual, exquisite—there weren't enough words to express the beauty her fingers were feeling. She would work at it. She would write a whole series of poems: *A Body in Love*, something like that.

"Was it all meetings, Cheryl? Did they have sessions, a blackboard, and diagrams? How did they treat you? I need to know." If only she could stop asking, just be in the moment, like Jack was always talking about.

In Cheryl's silence, Dawn saw a woman being led by four masked figures, maybe like the politicos who came on stage at Weymouth—before Cheryl had come to her and told her what was going on. She'd been frightened, thinking they were going to hurt her.

"What did you think they were going to do with me?" Cheryl started laughing softly, each movement of her body causing her breasts to caress Dawn's arm and make Dawn shiver.

"That could be your internalized race-phobia acting out. These are my brothers and sisters, not aliens."

"This was about caring for my friend's safety, Cheryl! I didn't know they were like your family. I have to ask you—did they support you to do Nelson's story with us—because a white theater group might be listened to, while a Black group would face more resistance? I'm sorry, Cheryl. I sound so dumb. I just can't believe you want to be with me when you can be surrounded by such beautiful women…Don't you see, I'm afraid. I'm afraid you'll go away again and next time never come back." Dawn pulled her arm free to think better. She must not cry. It was one thing for Cheryl to work on her cousin's situation within the theater group…but to go to Detroit? Maybe that's why she was being cautious—couldn't completely confide in her, the white bourgeois enemy.

"Listen to me, sweetheart," Cheryl spoke up. "For your ears only. I don't think the others can hear it or handle it easily. I went to Chicago with my people because I wanted to. I learned more in seven days than I've learned in seventeen years of education, seven years of helping my sister with child rearing and seven weeks of life in the fast lane with Fire Dragon Street Theater. My brothers and sisters were holding a teach-in for their own people and invited guests. I was invited—true not by usual means—but they don't do anything by the expected routes. In fact, they wanted to track down someone from Nelson's family. They knew of several enlisted Black guys who were being abused. It was kind of by chance that these four showed up at Weymouth when we were performing. God was helping us out. I'm trying to tell you, anytime the BLM meets, they know the FBI, even the CIA is sniffing their tracks. So I couldn't tell you all what I was doing, just some of it to you.

"Dawn. Listen. They tried to locate me in New York City, but I wasn't there of course. Maybe someone saw my name on a flyer as a performer in the street theater at our first gig at—what was the name of that university? So, actually the four that took over our performance were on the lookout for me. When they saw me onstage in that incomplete version of *Choice*…it was like, 'We gotta talk to Cheryl!' Maybe it just coincided. They were at the college to help the students organize a Black Studies program and we were performing *Choice* and there I was, in the performance."

Did Cheryl want her to say something about all this? Or just be quiet? They'd just made love. They were like blood sisters now; she must trust Cheryl's judgment and motives; that was all she could do. Couldn't they just hold each other again?

"Everything the BLM people do is on a precious time frame. The government is terrified of the power they're unleashing. As best they can, they're building a power base across this country the likes of which has never existed before. The underground railroad paved the way for what's happening now!"

Dawn's body went limp; she placed her head on Cheryl's shoulder. "I so badly want to understand. Please, just tell me what you can."

"I know it's hard, Dawn. Yes, they wanted to recruit me to work with them at first. 'Why are you hanging out with them!' they asked me. I attended meetings for a week. I have my notes, the histories of our struggle, all in my bag. It's what I'll be studying from now on. But—when they realized I was the cousin of Nelson Davis, that they'd been looking for me, and when I told them how you all could help me find out the truth about what happened to him—they were all supportive. 'Get the information out there with your theater group.' So here I am." She clamped her hands on either side of Dawn's face, looking deeply into her eyes. "Let's trust each other, okay?"

As her hands stroked Dawn's face, she spoke softly: "Listen, I'm just as amazed as you are, sweet cakes, about us." *How would her political comrades, the ones who were separatists, feel about her new lover?* "Whose hand am I holding now, Dawn? Whose smells and tastes and looks and sounds and skin wrap round and round me with such love?" As she eyed the lovely woman beside her, with luscious, soft skin, caressing hands, her voice suddenly sharpened with determination. "Oh, my sister! I love you, Dawn. I love Fire Dragon, the work we're doing. I love performing and shaping people's lives into stories and sharing them with others. I love chanting and exercising and trying to be someone else besides me once in a while. I love being with people who are trying to make things better and safer and saner and who are speaking out the truth. I don't want to carry a gun. I'm like my cousin. I don't want to kill. I will talk and dream and act and teach."

"Did you tell them how you feel about our work?"

"Magda understood. She said to me, 'Then work with them, Cheryl. Tell Nelson's story through them. BLM has cadres working in different ways, sometimes at odds with each other, sometimes with understanding. You can educate white and Black audiences, gain wide support,' she said. 'Our civil rights can't be won without their support. Come back to us when you need strategy, support, and rest. You aren't choosing an easy path—there is so much antagonism between Black and white political groups now—deep mistrust. But follow your instincts—do what you love and need.'"

"I'm glad you found Magda to talk to."

"Listen Dawn, it's going to take your love and human smarts to understand all of me: second mother, lesbian, lover, actress, shape-changer, Black woman activist, you name it. I'll have to juggle many worlds—" She stopped suddenly, bowing her head and putting her hands together as if in prayer. "I'm telling you and God right now: I will follow my instincts."

Dawn reached out to her friend. Her larger-than-life, multi-dimensional woman friend. She was only beginning to grasp the complexities that Cheryl spoke of. But in time, yes, in time.

"Oh, Dawn, I can't believe we found each other. But know this now! I might have to leave you at times. We're building a broad-based movement and we're already being massacred for it. The Black movement needs me and I need them. This goddamn white racist country called Amerika. Oh, Dawn, I wish to god it wasn't so. 'Black and white together, we shall overcome,' Dawny, like we sang on Wednesday night. Yes, together! We aren't there yet, my Dawn. Dawn of a new day—we aren't there yet. But know this too—I will always come back."

As they kissed, their lips pressing together in a pact, Dawn saw two figures together on a cake, a wedding cake. Her tears glazed over the image. "Cheryl! I need to know what happened to Nelson too!"

"This is what we have to find out. Someday it will all be exposed. I'm so afraid. Nelson had a lot of buddies in the army, that's what I'm learning. And they're going to start speaking out on how war resisters like Nelson, were treated in the jungles of 'Nam." As she collapsed into Dawn's arms, she uttered, "Nelson was the only one in my family I could talk to about being gay. Because he was too. I'm not outing him to anyone else. Don't you see how complicated all this is? Nelson was the target of two diseases: racism and homophobia. He didn't have a chance!" Her tears were like a storm, a flood.

Dawn stood abruptly, overwhelmed, needing to find joy again. "Are you hungry, Chérie Cheryl? I make a really great omelet. It'll go great with those croissants. You'll see—I want you to feel better."

51
Anguish

During the trip from Budington, Indiana, to Reams, Iowa, as most of the troupe was enjoying a holiday mood, Lucina and Louis were suffering silently. Marlene chided them, "Why can't we all be happy at the same time, just once?" She turned away from their unexplained depression. *Just when our Budington University performance was such a dramatic and political success, why are they so sad? They should be thrilled! Cheryl and* Choice *are back—at least for the rest of our tour.*

Though Lucina was thankful they'd constructed such a strong statement on Nelson Davis, she was in mourning and filled with guilt. She should have wrapped *Rune* up in thick padding, not a flimsy sheet. A curious person could have easily uncovered her—left her bare, exposed, vulnerable to a vicious attack. So it was partly her fault… And she'd thought *Rune* would be super safe at Shauna's!

Attempts to reach Shauna's loft for more answers were futile. The phone recorder still wasn't working right. Didn't Shauna need it on, to keep in touch with her jewelry business customers? Lucina had to know: Were Karen and Sally there during the brawl—or whatever happened? Maybe only a sick imagination could believe they'd had anything to do with it.

Still, they must know something. She was surer than ever: she'd heard Sally's voice answering, that one time.

No, she would not whip herself with guilt. She'd tried to store *Rune* in the best way she could! And *Rune* wasn't the only piece she'd had to leave behind in someone else's care. To pay for storage of her artwork was out of the question; she and Louis lived month-to-month, scrounging money for rent and food as best they could. "Whoever did this despicable thing should be blamed, Louis! This destruction—it's like murder!"

Louis advised her against talking to anyone else in the group about *Rune*'s loss. Whimpering over a lost sculpture would no doubt confuse them. After all, Fire Dragon Street Theater was out to stop the genocide of a whole country! The others didn't need any more drama. Though he, Louis, could grasp the depth and complexity of her shock—he had loved *Rune*— "I don't think anyone else would interpret the attack on your *Rune* as a kind of murder, Luie."

She'd always been able to talk deeply with Marin. But how could the loss of a sculpture compare in any way with the tragic suicide of a brother? How about Cheryl? Even the wish of some alone time with her seemed impossible; *Cheryl obviously has settled on Dawn as the one woman in the group she can trust with her anguish and her heart. Besides, she might not be sympathetic: 'You can remake a sculpture,' she might say. 'No one can remake my cousin, Nelson.'*

She finally agreed with Louis: just concentrate on the work they had to do for the rest of the tour. That's what she must do. The troupe would take a two-day scenic route to Reams and stay in an inexpensive motel. A mini-vacation. Get her mind on nature, the great healer.

*****

The three vehicles followed each other with ease. If a view caught their attention, they stopped to picnic and marvel. Fields of young wheat, oats, barley, and corn heralded a land of plenty. They could see the horizon extending far beyond them. Ahead, past the tiny toy barns, a spattering of green triangles—"Those are aspen and fir, Lucina." Sometimes they saw an almost ruler-perfect line dividing land and sky. Think of it! They were riding on a giant sphere, which itself was revolving in an infinity of blue.

White and gray clouds became horses, dolphins, and mythical creatures playing out grand dramas above them. They were in another dimension. Time slowed. Each panorama expanded their vision and appreciation. Their land, though a country in anguish, opened its rich fields before them like a promise, a hope. Lucina felt the longing for joy tear at her insides; if only she could rid herself of the oppressive sadness. As she watched fields of wheatgrass bend rhythmically in the wind, Mother Nature seemed to be telling her, "Your country is a place where compassion and justice can wipe away violence." If she weren't suffering so over *Rune*, she would be ecstatic with the sight!

She could mourn in the sanctuary of her black book, her journal and faithful companion. Home for her most private thoughts. Her handwriting, as wavering as the grasses around her, struggled to express the emotions churning inside her. As their caravan sped down the highway, she retraced her words to steady them, deciding at times to print out her thoughts slowly, each letter marking her sadness within the ever-moving present.

*****

Lucina's Journal Entry. Tour: Saturday and Sunday, April 29-30, 1967. On the road to Reams, Iowa. I'm trying to

understand how disjointed I feel. Lost. That my **Rune** *has been destroyed seems a punishment. How dare I make such a large female icon!!! I wonder if I can ever make a sculpture again. If I were planning on having children, or if I had a child, would I feel so devastated by this loss? A sculpture is not a person; my sculpture is not my child. I do have a few photos of her; would I really be able to remake her?*

What is the deepest reason I am so bereft? I know **Rune** *expressed my need—how I need to be seen: strong yet vulnerable; present but not easily understood; playful and still deadly serious; longing to connect though inward-turning; both active and meditative. Do I feel that I, Lucina, have lost these complex qualities because* **Rune**, *who represented them, has been wantonly destroyed? The essence of Jesus wasn't destroyed when he was crucified! His Spirit blossomed and has breathed life into endless human beings for all the centuries since His murder.*

I've got to get ahold of myself; **Rune** *is not me. I am not that murdered being. God, help me. Look at all the real human beings—civil rights and human rights activists murdered just in this country in the last few years! Chaney, Goodman, Schwerner, Evers, Luizzo, Malcolm X. Here I, Lucina, still exist and so many brothers and sisters have been slaughtered. I must keep using my creativity, love, empathy, and desire for justice to help heal our troubled planet as best I can.*

I'm trying to learn from Cheryl what it's like to truly not be treated justly. That's why the awareness of Cheryl's force and purpose fills me as I try to understand all the emotions I have with **Rune**'s *loss. I'm just trying desperately to understand why another human being needed to destroy her. I'm grasping for understanding. That Cheryl is back with us is a miracle. I went away to do good and my sculpture was destroyed. Cheryl was guided away from us by supportive brothers and sisters;*

and she went with them of her own free will. She found herself away from us and she came back! **Rune** *fell into hostile hands and was demolished. My sculpture will never return. I must be writing about Cheryl and* **Rune** *at the same time because they are monumental in my life.*

Like me, Hans has suddenly gone into a depression. He's never been so silent. Smokes one cigarette after another and stares out the car window. I think he misses Dawn, who is all eyes for Cheryl. A real love affair is going on between these two. But he doesn't seem to want to be with Jenny.

Hugh has pulled away from Courtney, who shadows Marlene like a puppy dog. Jim and Donna have stopped being pushy and acting like they want to take over. Even Louis is friendly to them.

So much swirling in my brain—I better stay focused. Calm down, Lucina! You better find out what those circular tanks are that keep taking over Iowa's fields. There's something ominous about them; they're storing something connected to nuclear warfare, I bet.

I have mixed feelings about performing at the Radical Theater Festival in Reams. All those fired-up political actors in one place? One thing I've learned is that movement people can be as competitive as anyone else, if not more. Maybe it seems more, because they aren't supposed to be that way. Remember Rhode Island, for god's sake!

I feel that Hugh is tired of hearing all the praise Jack and Marin are getting for being a double-spirited Shaman. Yet he keeps saying he doesn't want to do the part again. He's really a moody guy.

And Al is more silent than ever. It's a good thing Marin and I aren't lovers. I know I feel attracted to her sometimes (when she's not with Al). If I made a move on her Al would probably kill me. How? Slit my throat while I'm sleeping. Then

I wouldn't have to suffer Rune's death anymore. Every time I think of Sally and Karen I feel nauseous.

If Louis wasn't here with me, I think I would become catatonic. I don't know what that really means, but to me it means I'd stop feeling and thinking and just pretend I was a member of this group. I'm trying to fight it, but I feel like the pain of what happened to my Rune will turn me to stone, especially if I can't talk about it to someone in the troupe beside Louis. Am I embarrassed to own my emotions, such a mix of rage, impotence, and shame?

52
After a Festival, Changes Occur

Street theaters from across the country gathered to participate in the three-day festival at Reams College, with anti-war themes as the primary focus. The Fire Dragon actors were excited that Amerikan Express from Boston, Circus Players from New York, the Storefront Theater from Los Angeles, People's Rites Theater from Oakland, the Guerrilla Band from Putney, Vermont, the Red and Black Collective from Atlanta, and Take-to-the-Streets from Chicago were there. They had seen some of these groups perform and had made some contact with their members, but never had they seen them all perform for one event. The organizers hoped to inspire an ongoing enthusiasm for street theater festivals across the country to match the huge attendance at rock and roll concerts, building a civil and human rights culture with a friendly, accessible style. But street theater, not giving birth to a billion-dollar business with record sales, label contracts, merchandise and stars to market, stayed at the grassroots level, along with demonstrations and protest marches.

On the first night of the festival, the two best-known groups, Theater of Changing Times and San Francisco Masque Troop, gave performances. These two established repertory companies were sometimes nationally funded, while the smaller, self-supporting street theater groups (like Fire Dragon) survived by audience contributions, college tours, and donations from the actors' pockets and an occasional grant from their local arts councils. Even in the radical theater world, a pecking order existed. When the Theater of Changing Times (with a repertoire of long works on international issues and actors from all over the world getting weekly salaries) invited the Fire Dragon actors to perform within the context of one of their plays, a bridge was made between the larger and smaller troupes.

The Fire Dragon actors were both ecstatic and anxious. Though this was an opportunity for *Choice* to get a larger audience to dialogue how best to advocate for the missing Nelson, they couldn't perform Nelson's story without the Black and Brown dancers from Budington. When they'd invited them to join them for this festival, their professors intervened saying it would be too disruptive of their classwork. Performing with Fire Dragon at Budington had already taken them away from their other subjects and end of semester exams were coming up. So, the troupe performed Sam's story, followed by Cheryl giving a powerful interpretation of Nelson's story, including excerpts from her speeches and descriptions of how it had been dramatized at Budington University with Black and Brown dance students joining their production. Dawn accompanied her on the red drum, adding a low, driving beat to heighten the urgency of Cheryl's talk, ending with an explanation that many Black and Brown actors and dancers would be incorporated into their performance of the full *Choice* upon their return to New York City.

A short panel discussion followed that incorporated actors from both troupes. Hans, willing himself out of a funk and fired up by Cheryl's return and forceful drive, volunteered to join her, Dawn, Marlene, and Jack on the panel. Louis and Lucina welcomed their enthusiasm, deciding to stay in the background; they were too beset with news of *Rune* to take part.

Since, they hadn't actually performed Nelson's Story, Cheryl decided it was not the right time to distribute a petition calling for an investigation of his disappearance; besides, this festival was focused on "Stop the War in Vietnam." It pained her not to get at this urgent work—if her BLM family was there, they would have pushed her! But she still needed a leftist lawyer's advice on petition procedures. The real problem? There weren't any radical Black performance groups present! Only one sort-of multiracial group was taking part; even their focus was on "Stop the War in Vietnam," not "Stop the War on Black people in the U.S." or "End Racism in the Military." Not enough connections were being made between injustices. She would, at least, weed out individual participants who might have tactical advice.

During the panel, Hans lauded Changing Times for including audience participation as part of their performances. "It's a revolutionary concept, same as guerrilla theater groups who transform grocery stores and laundromats into centers of spontaneous dialogue, if not fistfights." When he was asked by a Changing Times actor if Fire Dragon did guerrilla actions, he said, "Yes, but I can't talk about them, as I don't want to put anyone at risk."

Dawn, seated between Hans and Cheryl at the panel table, grew tense. *What's wrong with Hans? Doesn't he see that his comment could ignite suspicion about how we might be challenging the state? The festival most probably has government spies nosing around! No wonder Cheryl thinks Hans' need to cloak himself in danger and intrigue could mess up the search for help around Nelson. She isn't paranoid; she's plugged in.*

As Hans continued emoting, "We can't talk about all our actions since we need to get paid by the capitalists..." Dawn felt sick. The jerk was making flip comments to get attention.

Aware of the tension Hans was causing, Marlene, seated beside him, broke in, "Some of us like to romanticize what we're doing. But first and foremost, we're dead serious educators and communicators." With a calm demeanor she continued, "So we take a less aggressive, more conciliatory approach than other grassroots theater groups might."

Karl of Changing Times jumped into the discussion. "Let's talk about audience involvement. Can one of you Fire Dragon panel members say something about how you create a discussion about the war with your audiences?"

Seated in the front row, Lucina was still considering Hans' implication that their troupe did illegal guerrilla actions at times. *I would love to know what this audience really feels about his comments,* she thought. When she finally tuned into the discussion, she saw Hans give Dawn a guilty look. *And how does Jenny feel about her chameleon boyfriend—always slipping into different personas? I'll never forget his bizarre, petulant actions that aided the cops' beating of Louis. Now, once again, he's upsetting me—and Dawn, Jenny, and Cheryl too. Thank heavens Jack is responding to Karl's questions*: "First thing is to have a handle on who your audience is—so you can evaluate how best to communicate with them."

*****

After a performance by People's Rites, actually a work-in-progress demonstrating the rotation of directors and role-switching among actors, Louis, Lucina, Al, and Marin went into a huddle. There might be less tension within their own group if each of them had to direct a scene they'd conceived of.

"I think this would be really important for Hans, Hugh, and Jim," Al said.

Marin reminded them, "We women have already come to this conclusion." When they presented the idea to Donna and Jim, the four were met with shocking news.

396

Jim, Donna, and Hugh had decided to leave the group after the festival. Jim and Donna would probably work with Storefront from Los Angeles. If that didn't work out, they would start their own groups, focusing on women's and working-class issues. "And Native peoples' rituals," Jim added pointedly.

Lucina was bowled over. How could Donna tear herself away like that? She was so attached to the women's play. The need for it within the growing women's movement was enormous. And they'd only developed one scene for her story, *Be Real, Be You.* Didn't it need a second scene? The more Lucina thought about it, the madder she got. She raged to Louis, "Those two have sucked from our group. And just like that, they're out of here. Just watch! Jim and Donna are going to take our Fire Dragon scenes to Storefront and pretend they invented them!"

"Forget it, Lucina. We don't have a copyright on our plays. This festival is about sharing ideas…Anyway, haven't you suffered enough loss? Deep loss! We can't let this devastate us. We were never sure of them. We didn't know they would seduce Hugh, since it seemed Cheryl was the one they were after."

Lucina burst out crying. "I'll miss Hugh. Sure, he's done some jarring things, but he's owned that. He was off, but he really looked for what made him do that crazy disappearing dido. I thought we were a solid group—a family, with Cheryl back and our commitment to her."

As he tried to comfort her, she pulled away, wiped her eyes, and snarled, "Sometimes I'd like to split this scene, too."

Marin was not surprised by the news. "Those three were always impatient," she reflected. "Look how often Hugh disrupted the flow. Ego maniacs, that's what." Al wrung his hands and stayed silent for a few seconds. "Who wants to work with anyone who can turn like that on a dime? Jesus Christ!"

Then with no explanation, Courtney announced that he would need a vacation after the tour, not clarifying if that meant a short break or leaving the group as well.

Marin tried to cheer up a sober Lucina, not aware of the letter from New York. "Hey! Not everyone's leaving, sister. It's only four out of fourteen. We'll carry on—don't you worry." She was eager to direct more of the women's workshops when they got back to New York, and to recruit new members. Al talked about the series of puppets he would make.

Lucina tried to rally enthusiasm for the work to come. After all, Cheryl was back and Louis was talking about writing a script for them. That would make him happy and put his brilliance to work.

Cheryl responded immediately to the news of departing members. "Damn! It's not easy when people leave suddenly, as I did. We go on—and I'm committed to continue with Fire Dragon and bring people of color into the troupe. It's obvious that Nelson's story needs more of us. I'll be giving workshops to Latinas and Black people and gradually, with the troupe's support, we'll recruit some of them. My main focus is on finding my cousin."

Jenny, Marlene, and Marin approached Cheryl anxiously. "You'll still want to work on the women's scenes, we hope? We need you!" Cheryl clarified her position. "Are you kidding? I'm hoping to find another Black lesbian sister to join us. And I'm going to need all the women's support and energy I can get to track down what they did to Nelson! My question to you: Are you going to help me make *Choice* an effective rallying call for a legitimate investigation into this nightmare? I need you, more than ever, to make this happen!"

*****

"We need to talk to each other before anyone splits!" Jack, always adept at helping others find something positive about changes, organized a group meeting and meditation for the next day in the rec room of the Reams college dorm, serving as their quarters during the festival. The comfortable leather chairs and sofas, and the sodas and snacks Jack set out, all helped soothe frayed nerves and weepy emotions. Jack started the meeting simply with, "It's obvious we need to talk to each other, understand better why some members are changing direction. We've been through tough and magnificent times together, like happens in any complex relationship. We have bonded—well, I can't say forever, but for a meaningful time. Those of you who have decided to change direction and not return to New York City with our Fire Dragon troupe, we need to hear from you. You owe us. What's up? What's going on?"

"I need to talk now!" Dawn had leapt from a nearby chair and was facing Jack. "Sorry for breaking into your sane approach to this shit show, Jack. I'm really upset." She spun around to face the others. "How can any of you think of leaving now? Now!? Just when the most necessary work has been made clear to us? I can't believe it—how could you? Jim and Donna, I feel very angry with you. I can't even hear what you have to say! Hugh? I know your Dad's sick, but he's been sick—how could you leave now? Courtney, you have no excuse…We're talking about real pain here, horrible injustice, and we've all just worked so hard together—we've never been so together, such a force, until we performed 'Nelson's Story.' We really came through for her for the first time, for Cheryl! And now you all are breaking us up. It's wrong, it's destructive—it's criminal…" Shaking and stomping her feet, Dawn thrust her fists in the air.

Jack stood next to her, arms folded, his face frozen in angst. A disturbed silence overtook the others, unable to respond. Cheryl, who had rushed to Dawn and was holding her tightly as she began rocking precariously from side to side, took charge. "We all know why Dawn is so upset. All of you have been working with me so intensely, getting 'Nelson's Story' together. We did it and Dawn knows how grateful I am that you came through for me, for Nelson. And now this news…" She faced the calmer Dawn now. "Dawn, no one—no small group will stop me from going forward. We've put it out there. There's eight of us left, and sometimes Courtney, to keep up with the work. And now many, many others—in fact, all the people at our performance in the festival know what we have to do. Find my cousin. Find Nelson!"

Jenny and Han's voices shot out, "Find Nelson!" "Find Nelson" rang out over and over until the whole troupe, including the departing ones, were shouting, "Find Nelson." Jim and Donna were hugging Cheryl, their eyes shut as if praying for her forgiveness.

Then Jim spoke out awkwardly, "Okay! I gotta respond now. We'll find a way to spread the information about Nelson. I swear to you, Cheryl," he offered somberly. "Listen, you guys, I mean, you Fire Dragons. It's not like I knew this was going to happen. It's just—it's just a lot of things came together. I'm not speaking for Donna—it's harder for her because…" He looked for her encouraging nod, but she was back in a folding chair, sitting stiffly, arms folded and looking down at her lap. "Okay— she'll speak for herself," he continued. "How can I say this? When we, I joined up with you—wow, that was a big change. From Detroit to New York City, from a city to a metropolis. I was always getting mixed up about where I was—ending up downtown when I wanted to be uptown, ending up in Queens, instead of Brooklyn. Okay, you don't want to hear about that… Well, the loft, our rehearsal place, the factory buildings, all the artists there, a whole new exciting world for us. Donna and I rehearsed in garages in Detroit, not a huge warehouse space. And there I was, trying to remember everyone's name—it's easy to remember the names of puppets because we named them—

and then follow all the new exercises and scenes. I was the boss of my own puppets, just me and Donna. I got an idea and I could make it happen right away. Snap, bang. So—patience. That's what I had to learn—to not be bullheaded, rambunctious. There's eight, ten, then fourteen of us wild-eyed radicals to relate to, to consider."

He paused. "Okay, cut to the chase. It's time for Donna and me to do another change. Something in me is needing to grow or I'll burst out of my skin like a balloon shot up with too much helium. What am I saying? I need to try out my ideas while they're burning inside me. You all witnessed my lack of patience. I couldn't be helpful to this group at this time. Believe me, I'm sorry! It seems like a betrayal to you, Dawn. But we'll find a way to help the search for Nelson. We love Cheryl.

"It was my idea more than Donna's—wanting to add the Sun Dance ritual, where were we? Hamtramck. Everybody else was rallying when we lost so many props. Excuse me, Lucina, 'ritual objects.' And what was happening to me? Some wild psychic stuff. Yeah! I was having these images in my dreams and no, I wasn't high on grass. I dreamt, over and over, that I was in a Sun Dance ritual. I danced and danced, like flying, around a pole with the other men, until I lost my sense of self. I really merged with the other guys more and more, and then getting pierced, my blood flowing. It was so freeing. I went back into the earth…I'm getting off track.

"Here it is. I need to find myself, my ancestral roots that connect me to the Lakota tribe through my mom. I spoke to her recently and she has definitive information now that she's part Lakota, so that means I am too. But, I'm going to get my own genealogical proof, take a blood test. You see! That professor at New Point College said some of us might be part Indigenous. You never know. I know two of the guys in Storefront. They're part Lakota. They're into the Sun Dance and exploring their

Indigenous roots and I want to do that with them. I can't give my all to Cheryl's search, helping her find Nelson. God, I feel for you, Cheryl! You've taught me to own myself, know what I need to work on. And everybody here, you've helped me grow. I want to keep growing. I want to keep in touch with you, as well. You're part of my new family. You've been a new home. And you all know, we sometimes have to leave family, leave home to find an even newer family and home, to find ourselves, over and over again."

Jim apologizing for repeating himself, said he was exhausted for now, as he slumped back to sit on the soft couch, reaching for his coke and taking a long drink. He was visibly crying, showing a fragile Jim that only Donna had seen. As if on cue, she stood upright and walked measuredly to the place where Jim had stood moments before.

*****

"My comrades," Donna said softly and solemnly. "Jack, you're so good with caretaking a group. How many times have I heard about your moon ritual at the Yellow Farm. It sounds so exotic. But what I gather is, you suggested it and everybody made it happen. That ritual made everyone feel their natural connection to the earth, moon and stars, the universe and to each other. And the whole-group experience of that connection, it helped you all to leave our healing Mother Nature and return to the hard-edged city, with all the tall buildings that block out the stars and moon, to continue your work while still sustaining the knowledge of that interconnectedness we share and which can't be taken from us.

"I'm trying to say—Jack, there you are, caretaking again. I mean, it's sacred, being in a group—revealing ourselves to others in an organic, developing, considered way. Oh, god! It's like being reborn. But you requested, kind of demanded, that

Jim and I—and I guess Hugh and Courtney are considering not going back to New York as well—you asked us to be upfront with you all. Why are we planning on leaving the group now? Well, it's hard to stand up here and own that in some way we're breaking a very important bond we had with you all. A group is as precious as a couple, I really believe that. But everyone needs to grow—as Jim says, we all have to leave home, move on to where we can—what to say, seek our full identities? Fire Dragon Street Theater has been a home for us—a supportive, loving, creative home. A home we chose; not one we were born into. I mean, Jim and I owe so much to all of you. You took us in, you original members, just when we needed it. Needed to expand our theater work and ourselves. And I have really grown with you women. How can I leave you at a time like this—when…"

Sobs broke into Donna's words as Jenny and Marlene approached her, their arms outstretched to comfort her. "Thank you, my sisters—I love you. If this doesn't work out for me, I'll be back. If you'll have me. You've helped me gain a sense of myself separate from Jim. But I'm not ready to leave him. I've wanted to have a child and I'm not getting any younger, in case you haven't noticed." To rid her face of wrinkles, she forced a smile and stretched her cheeks back. "Well, he and I have to work that out. And if I don't find a place with Storefront? Their women aren't as strong, I feel, as my Fire Dragon sisters. I might have to find other women to work with and use everything I've learned here with you to tell our stories. Isn't that what we hope our women's play will do? Inspire women to own themselves, share themselves and defy the patriarchy and all the repressive, demeaning, false assumptions men belittle us with, so they can remain lord and master." Her glaring look at Jim suggested that the two of them would have a lot to work out in their new situation in Los Angeles. "I'll miss you all so much, especially you women. I guess I said that."

Her chest heaved suddenly as if she were finding it hard to breathe. Pulling herself together, she joked, "Hey, maybe I'll convince some women actors struggling to become Hollywood sexpots to work with me and tell the truth about who we really are!

"So that's what I have to say, Jack, for now. I'll be able to tell my Fire Dragon sisters more. I want you all to come to L.A. to perform, okay?" With this invitation, she went to the couch where Jim slouched, sat down next to him and put her head on his shoulder.

*****

Hugh spoke from his seat, which faced most of them. "I don't have anything dramatic or earthshaking to say. My dad's sick and I want to stay with him. He lives in Denver, Colorado, not exactly a stone's throw from New York. You've all helped me be more truthful about myself and get into my body more. Would you believe it, before *Ghost Dance Tribute* I'd hardly ever danced. Too self-conscious.

"It's not like I want to leave Fire Dragon. I hope I don't have a nervous breakdown without you all. You've helped me trim my ego down to human size, so I can live with it. But my dad needs me now and I need him. He split with my mom when I was a kid. I was really angry with him. Now? It seems like we all want to find out what's really going on with ourselves. Why do we have the problems we have? Why do we make up stories to fill the gaps? Well, I want my dad to tell me his story, and maybe I can edit my own, so I feel more in charge of myself and don't feel like I have to disappear to be appreciated. This is me finding myself more truthfully. And believe me, I'll keep in touch with you all, until you're sick of how often I appear in your mailboxes. I love you to pieces."

After an emotional silence, with everyone wondering just how sick was Hugh's dad, Jack called out from his chair nearby, "Okay, so we've heard from the heart. It's not that we're being abandoned by Jim, Donna, and Hugh… They're fulfilling their urgent, personal needs and we have to give them our blessings. You know, those things we often didn't get from our folks when we needed them the most? So, let's let their words sink in—we don't want to leave each other with unnecessary hurt. But before we do a healing meditation—Courtney, I think you want to speak to us too, right?"

Courtney was already standing by Jack's chair, rocking slowly on his feet, as if to temper his nervousness. "Yes, Jack, thanks—I just want to say…I need a break. Yeah, I know… don't we all? It's been intense and rough, and mind-blowing and sweet. What can I say? Here it is! I'm not leaving Fire Dragon. Hugh invited me to stay with him and his dad for short periods, you know, give him support. And I have some college friends who live in Boulder, so I can stay with them, too. And I'll make trips to New York City to help you guys with whatever you need. Promotion, I don't know, writing for grants from New York State Council on the Arts. Marketing work. Get some of the money from the capitalists that Hans was riffing about. And work on getting Cheryl's petition out and backing from our New York senators and reps in Washington. I'll be, like, as helpful as I can. I just need a break from the acting part. I need to reflect and figure out how I can be the most helpful to—well, whoever needs help. Who knows, maybe someday I'll become a therapist or a special ed teacher for kids with special needs."

For the first time, some clapping arose from the group. Courtney had made all the departures seem less devastating. And he would still be there with them, on the sidelines.

"Okay." Jack took over again. "So we've heard from everyone whose thinking of splitting in some way. Sorry, going on with their lives. Let it sink in. I'll say it again: We don't want to leave each other with unnecessary hurts. With that in mind, I've got a kind of meditation…it's actually sitting together in a circle, as we've done a million times before, holding hands and deep-breathing. Reminding ourselves that we're all one, whether some of us are in L.A. or Boulder or on an airplane between here and there. Let's remember all the good work we've done, are doing. The new *Choice* Cheryl has created with us; our continually growing awareness that we live in a troubled world, manipulated by a system putting greed and profit over people; fighting a system that idolizes power over empathy, hate over love. And let's remember— our troupe is not breaking up! We're just changing shape and growing and expanding."

As they sat in a circle, feeling the pressure from each other's fingers while focusing on their breathing, they gradually took on the aspect of one large, breathing, multi-faced organism. The softening of their faces made Jack feel they were all smiling; the tension and pain that had been in the room was slipping away and now they were a large, cohesive, gentle, smiling circle of love. A melody rose up in his mind. He knew it would become a song he could share with them all someday soon.

*****

Jack was inspired by the women's play Rape, with the victim 'fighting back' by analyzing the deranged, brutal, pathetic aspect of the act. He allowed, "You can't meditate some assaults away. You women show us how you have to dissect them with the support of others—and own all your emotions around them. I'm going to incorporate tai chi and karate techniques into our work. Everyone needs to learn how to protect themselves!" He would lead workshops in these disciplines starting as soon as they returned to the Big Apple.

406

Dawn, secretly penning love poems to Cheryl and openly writing homages to Vietnamese women (a project begun after her action at Wellingfield—by now, the least-kept secret in the group), would start a "Sappho Rising" poetry newsletter, along with continuing the theater work. She would move out of L and L's loft and share an apartment with Cheryl in the fall. In reference to their intimacy, the word "lesbians" was carefully avoided by most of the guys, while "girlfriends" was used liberally.

On the last day of the festival, Fire Dragon did an afternoon performance of *Ghost Dance Tribute: Massacre at Wounded Knee*. That night, hundreds of students from across the state joined festival attendees for a Stop the War rally. When by midnight the demonstration became unwieldy (liberal and leftist political groups had also been encouraged to attend) and surged to six hundred participants in the football field, the Fire Dragon group was asked by the festival organizers to use their chants and drums to calm and focus the crowd. By midnight a crowd of 1000 people were chanting, 'We Circle Around,' an Arapaho chant set to music by Lucina. (Years later she was still remarking how this event helped her survive *Rune*'s death.)

Before taking his leave with Jim and Donna, Hugh sought out Lucina and asked to speak to her alone. Dry-eyed but remorseful, he begged for her understanding, talking on and on: "I acted out at that gas station—I was afraid it was all going to collapse after Cheryl left—I mean, I was in my Wovoka period then—just trying to get his truth out—at least what I imagined his truth to be. Well, to be honest, I didn't really think I was being insensitive, wanting to be him since he's dead. But I was wrong. Now that Dad is dying, I'm understanding more. He will live on, inside my memory of him, but I can't be my father. It's impossible to explain. I just know, trying to be shaman-like made me crazy. You can't be another person— you have to find your own strong parts."

"Look, Hugh! We're all struggling to figure ourselves out..."

"... creating a double-Wovoka with Jack and Marin was visionary—really connected our tribute to Wounded Knee to us, activists in the 60s, wrestling with changing patriarchal power figures into two-gender beings, male-female power spirits. I don't know how to say it correctly. Wonder what that student, what was his name? José, at New Point College. What would he think of our double Wovoka? Anyway, Lucina—I'm sorry. I'm just nervous. What I really need from you? Your blessing!"

"You have that. I'll miss you a lot, you know." She wanted to remind him that she had understood his confusions back then. But, wasn't he really trying to tell her something else and he didn't know how? Besides, she was tired of playing peacemaker and nice mommy to this kid, tuned-in one moment and completely self-absorbed the next. "So now you're going to be taking care of your dad. That's so loving, Hugh. We'll miss your wonderful music to help us keep in sync." How many times had she endured his petulance? And joyed in his creative, longing self. Now he was leaving them for a very heart-rending situation. She felt sadness weigh her down suddenly, as the crying feeling that she'd been fighting off took over.

"What's going on with you, my friend," he said softly. "I'll be alright, don't worry. Courtney will be there some of the time."

"All these changes—I'm not good at staying calm and collected."

"You don't have to, Lucina. I respect you so much—I mean, Jesus! You're the heart of this group—you gave up your studio, your sculpture work for our work together. And now people are cutting out on you."

Tears brimmed. "Oh, Hugh. Can I talk real to you? Something's happened that has me so overwhelmed. Louis thinks no one but him can understand, but I've always felt your sensitive caring for others, for me…"

"That's what friends are for, Luie. What's going on—something bad happen to a family member, a friend?"

"I've always thought of my sculptures as my family, sometimes as my babies in a way." She finally sobbed. He found her a chair. "You know my sculpture, actually the last sculpture I made—*Rune*? I called her *Rune*—like an ancient mysterious being."

"I know *Rune*! Don't you remember, you showed her to me when I came to your loft for a theater workshop. That giant figure made out of pieces of furniture, yet she looked so regal, so alive. You knew I liked your work because we met at that show at St. Marks—what was it called, *Breaking Apart*? No, not that—it was *Breaking Out*—meaning going out of your comfort zone, at least that's what I thought it meant. I was bowled over by your two sculptures there. I'd never seen anything like your work—you said they were female figures breaking all the rules…"

"That's right, Hugh. And we had the most wonderful talk about the need for female spiritual guides."

"So, what's going on?"

"*Rune* was destroyed… And I wasn't there to protect her!"

"There was a fire in your loft!?"

"No. *Rune* was at a friend's loft where I left her when we went on tour. Someone smashed her to pieces. I just need to tell someone in the group who can understand my pain. Maybe I can tell you because you're leaving…"

"Who would've done that? That's criminal!" Hugh, now slumped into a chair next to Lucina, reached for her hand. "I want to know everything—can I take you for a beer? You didn't tell anybody else? We have to trust each other more—look what happened to me when I couldn't talk real to anyone about my dad, about what trying to impersonate a spiritual leader like Wovoka was doing to me, about how I felt Cheryl's departure meant the end of the troupe. I tried to make myself disappear at a gas station in the middle of nowhere. When you don't tell your friends what you're going through, you disappear. You're too damn important to disappear, babe. Oh, god! I'm so sorry—rambling on about myself. And you've lost your work! I want to make it back to the Fire Dragon group again. I just don't know what's going to happen when my dad dies. And I don't want to make promises I can't keep anymore! Come on, we'll get a beer and you're going to tell me how some bastard could have done that to *Rune*—done that to you, a genius artist. That's rotten, Lucina!"

*****

Al and Marin decided to drive Marlene back to Detroit in Isadora with all the props before going on to New York. She had to finish some money business with her mother and then she'd fly back to the city. They might even take a side trip to Ohio to visit Al's mother.

Jenny and Hans, somehow a couple once again, were planning to drive the Dodge Dart back through the Southwest. Some kind of magic had happened between them the last night of the festival, it seemed. (Maybe it was the note Dawn and Cheryl gave him, something about "Stop putting your foot in your mouth and go back to Jenny who loves you!") They would visit Hopi reservations and friends in Taos. Jack had already arranged to meet up with Joan in Denver for a yoga conference. Cheryl and Dawn were heading straight back to New York. Marcel's birthday was in three days and Cheryl had promised him tickets to a rock and roll concert at Madison Square Garden. They'd been offered a ride with two members of the Amerikan Express, the multiracial theater from Boston with black, Asian,

410

and white students; they were driving straight back, with only one sleepover stop on the way.

Courtney opened up with more of his marketing plans for the group. He had made pals with the Chicago troupe, Take to the Streets. He'd go to the Windy City with them soon—maybe arrange for Fire Dragon to perform there during the Democratic Convention the next summer. "Believe me," he affirmed. "I absolutely am not quitting the group! You might want me to, but no way. I'm in for the long haul."

Lucina studied Louis' pull toward Marlene, still framed as "respect for her organizational skills." Maybe she could be generous about their friendship another time; but not in Reams, Iowa when Shauna's letter had left a hole in her gut as big as a grave.

When Louis suggested they might enjoy riding back East with Al, Marin, and Marlene, she threw a fit. "For god's sake, Louis, no! I've decided—we're going to take the bus to Chicago and then the train to the city. I need a vacation from everyone but you." When she saw his look of confusion, her tone softened. "It'll be like a honeymoon—the honeymoon we never had. I need someone to hold onto, Louis."

Louis readily agreed. *Lucina is too vulnerable to even contemplate challenging.* Seeing her mood lighten, he imagined romantic dinners in the dining car as the train sped across their land. "Yes," he told her, snuggling against her body and enjoying how his penis yearned to be in her again (they hadn't made love the whole tour). "It'll be just the two of us again. But before we leave—I want to have a talk with you. There's something you should know."

A chill ran through her. She couldn't take one more heartache. But what news could be worse than being told her *Rune,* her woman-whole, had been wiped off the earth? "There's a Howard Johnson's near the campus, Louis. We can talk there."

53

The Truth Can Set Us Free

The Howard Johnson's restaurant in Reams, Iowa, was a repeat of the Howard Johnson's in Kingston, New York, and the one in Northampton, Massachusetts, Lucina mused. The same innocuous booths and tables were here as there. She'd seen the same tired waitresses, the same sad-faced manager in all the restaurants, watching over the altar, the cash register. Though the people eating in these restaurants never looked healthy—there were lots of smokers and people who ate too much fried food—they ate with gusto.

As they were waiting to be served, Lucina fought off a creepy thought: what if she and Louis were nomads, wandering aimlessly from one HoJo's to another? They weren't that! They were political artists shaping a morality for their country. *But honestly,* she reminded herself, *I could get as addicted to HoJo's clam rolls and hot dogs in toasted buns as anyone here.*

They found a booth in the back where it was less crowded and less smoky. Lucina would avoid fried food; her stomach was already churning. "Their clam chowder is always good," Louis suggested. Maybe she'd get that and a chicken salad sandwich. Louis ordered the steak sandwich and a small salad ("That will be good for you, Louis") and a large order of fries ("You can have some of them, Lucina").

As usual, Louis was all concentration on his food. Lucina was too agitated to eat with any pleasure. What was it that Louis must tell her? They couldn't be long—Al, Marin, and Marlene needed the van by eleven-thirty if they were going to set off for Detroit by noon as they'd planned.

Face it, she fretted. *We don't live normal lives. Like drinking wine in an arty restaurant or talking about who's invited for dinner, what museums we'll visit on the weekend, what new furniture we'll buy. I'm swirling from the changes to our troupe: Four members leaving (maybe not Courtney or Hugh?) and Cheryl not even back a week. And the ruin of my Rune! Meanwhile, far away, some people are lying on beaches all day, working on their tans.*

*****

Louis' plate was almost empty. He could talk. "What do you want to tell me? Let's get this over with."

Louis gave her his soft bedroom eyes, then looked through her, as was his custom when he was thinking difficult thoughts.

He shoved the plate holding his last offering toward her, a few lonely fries, then gulped down his coke and settled back in his seat with a belch. "Remember that day in the loft—"

"Which day, Louis? There were so many." She wasn't being sarcastic. A fly buzzed around the fries; HoJo's always had flies.

"You were drawing on the papers taped to your wall. I was listening to KPFA, trying to write. The news about Chaney, Schwerner, and Goodman came over the radio."

"Of course! I was hooking into their energy. A terrible, frightened energy."

"You said you were helping them escape."

"And you said we had to call the civil rights workers our 'brothers'—and I said, 'What about our brothers and sisters, the Vietnamese?' That was the first time I thought about those words in that way."

"That's it, Lucina. That's what I want to talk about. I want to use those words—'brothers and sisters.'"

Relief! Then his pressing topic wasn't about the two of them and some dreadful flaw in their connection. Or some yucky, personal stuff, like about him and Marlene, that she just wouldn't be able to handle. It was something political, manageable. Probably it had to do with the play he was going to write. "I think it's a great idea. You'll feel better writing, Louis. The group should try a script."

"I don't want to talk about that now."

His curtness surprised and silenced her. He stared at her for some moments, emotions contorting his face. Confusion, guilt, even a flicker of coyness was there. She'd rarely seen him at a loss for words.

"Talk, Louis. What is it?"

"About us! What we are to each other. What we aren't. How we must carry on with our beliefs. We're not husband and wife. We're more brother and sister—chosen brother and sister. So our lovemaking isn't incestuous, it's natural. What I'm saying is, words can't define us, because our love has many shapes. Comrades, lovers, friends, brother-sister—"

A ringing sensation deep in her left ear began drowning out his voice. *Listen to what he is saying!*

"…love you so much, Lucina. Don't have to worry. But I don't own you and you don't own me. We support each other; we help each other grow."

Was he preparing her for some terrible news? "Louis, I can't stand this. I don't know what you're trying to tell me."

"That time in the yurt with Jenny…"

"You told me about it. What? You smoked grass together. I have too, with Marlene and Jenny at one of our rehearsals. There's no reason for us to be so holier than thou about getting high once in a while."

"Lucina, stop it. You know about Jenny. How Marlene thought I'd fucked with her. I told you, we just kissed. What I didn't tell you—I wanted to fuck with Jenny."

"Louis, don't I know you? You were trying to protect me." She remembered now: at the time she'd thought he was trying to be truthful, while she hadn't been truthful at all. She'd never told him about the kiss with Sally. The kiss that had haunted her all this time.

She grasped her glass of ice water and stared into it. When would she be able to!

"And there's something else I didn't tell you—Marlene and I did fuck! It just happened once."

She watched as her fingers clutched at her glass. "God, Louis—you tell me this in HoJo's—surrounded by people? How many others are there in your guilt list? She watched herself react in the way one would expect. Like watching a movie of herself acting the part, or a part of herself reacting to Louis' confessions. One feeling was real, shock; the other, a distanced I-knew-it-would-happen feeling. She had lived with this feeling for some time, had already wondered if she could accept it—staying with Louis as he desired other women. He was a man who loved women, not only her. Well, she'd already gone through the torment and come out the other side. He did not belong to her alone. Like he just said: *We're not husband and wife 'til death do us part.* He was too complex for that kind of fencing in. He was a sphere moving in his own orbit, having his own muses and journey. She would have to suffer this largeness, this uneasiness, this drama always intervening with her life. Louis was a healthy, virile, spirited man. Of course he wanted to be with—

"Louis, can I say one more thing and then you can go on, spill all the beans to me, if you must. But couldn't you possibly, just sometimes possibly keep your penis to yourself?"

He absolutely couldn't read her. Was she joking? But there were tears in her eyes. "Lucina—that's not how it is. Listen to me. Sit down again. People are looking at us. It's not like we never talked about it before. Monogamy, non-monogamy. We're always talking around it. We said we don't own each other."

Though he whispered, his words felt like needles prickling her chest. "I just have trouble taking changes, that's all." She folded herself tightly into a corner of the booth and stared past him. "Where did you do it with Marlene? In her bedroom at the Yellow Farm? Or in the loft in our bed?"

"No, it was last winter, at her apartment. That's where. It was just one of those things—"

"Marlene and I gave you a massage at her parents' house. I felt she loves us both."

"She does. It won't happen again."

She believed him, but it still hurt. Her eyes spilled tears. She wanted to make him hurt too. She understood his hunger— but it still hurt that she, Lucina, wasn't enough for him. She pounded her glass on the table; cubes and water jumped up and skipped onto her jeans. The spreading liquid shocked her skin: the insides of her legs were burning. If only he would stop talking, stop trying to calm her. She clinched her eyes—shut him away. Shut him up. Then she stared hard at him, into him for several moments. She relaxed her shoulders, breathed deeply. Damn it! She could take it, whatever he had to tell her. She would have to face it, accept that Louis had lusted for Jenny and restrained his lust; Marlene was a different story. And Karen…?

A large, white shape clouded her mind; two small figures appeared on either side of the white cloud. They pulled at the cloud shape; a sheet fell. The shape was now large, wooden. *Rune* was sandwiched between two women. Sally and Karen had sticks in their hands like policemen's clubs. They were laughing, shrieking, hopping up and down. One of them swung her arm back. The doweled crown took a blow, then flew apart in fragments like splinters of bone.

Her emotions were jagged, just like those splinters.

"God, Lucina. It's not worth crying about. You know how much I love you. I didn't think you would be this upset. I just wanted to clear things up. So we could have a really beautiful ride back to New York. I love our life together. We can make a new start. I love you so much, my baby. Lucina, I love you. I'm not in love with Jenny or Marlene. It's just—You know how guys are…"

"No, Louis. I don't know how guys are at all. Besides, I'm not crying, Louis Altman. See, my eyes are dry."

*****

What do those words mean? *I love you—I want you—I need you.* She'd always known that words lie. Even Louis' words. People always trying to find a way to connect, not be alone. They'll lie not to feel alone. "Are we finished, for the time being? I want to go now. Al and Marin need the van. We'd better figure out how we're going to get back to New York, to *my* studio. We'll talk about our tawdry life another time! Is it really a good idea to take the train?" Her studio? What a joke! She didn't have a studio anymore. *PAN* had taken it over. The theater group had taken it over. Dawn had taken it over. SDS students were staying there now. They had all driven her out! She had to reclaim her space.

"We said we wanted to be closer to other people, Lucina. And still be together—be each other's main person."

Louis just couldn't stop talking. He'd die of loneliness if he stopped making his words.

He wedged himself against her as they staggered from the restaurant, like two wounded soldiers holding each other up. "You're working with the women now. We aren't Mr. and Mrs. Right. We're movement people doing incredibly important work. We're helping Cheryl find Nelson, and expose racism in the military. Movement comrades. Brother and sister. We agreed to that."

Don't listen to Louis' fancy talk.

"We said we needed other people to help us grow. That we couldn't hide behind a piece of paper, a ceremony. But we would never stop loving each other. Have you changed your mind?"

His profile was incredibly clear. His gaze razor sharp. And there it was again, overtaking her without warning. The look of him that filled her. Thrilled her. How striking he was—uniquely, heartbreakingly, frighteningly handsome. If only she could feel passionate about only him—even if he couldn't help what his penis wanted. Orange light from his eyes was spreading into her again. And they were both laughing, laughing hysterically.

It was going to be all right. He wasn't going to leave her. He did—she could feel it in her bones—he loved her. She slipped her arm through his as they walked along the street, the sun warming her face, their steps matching. He'd just confessed that he desired others. He was being honest with her. But she had not been honest with him. Her feelings for Sally…He must have known. It wasn't just because Sally was a sister sculptor that she'd suffered from her loss, just as he'd suffered from the loss of Karen. They both needed soulmates outside of the group to give them perspective. If he'd kissed Karen he would have told her, like he just told her about Jenny. Besides, a kiss wasn't like going all the way. Or was it?

Her head was spinning with confusion; her heart was jumping with anxiety. How much farther did they have to walk? Enough for today. They were getting ready to end their tour. What a journey it had been—the world opening up to them in so many complicated ways—an emotional roller coaster—loss and gain—three steps forward and two steps back. But they'd gotten through it—they understood more than before—all the people they'd met teaching them so many perspectives, different needs, different roads to try—but with a common goal. A more just world would take all of them listening, helping, empathizing with each other in the process, never stopping the struggle.

"Lucina, where have you been the last five minutes? It will be okay—as long as we're honest with each other."

"I know that, Louis. I was just forming a speech in my mind." She would tell him the whole truth about Sally on the train back home.

"For my ear?"

"For anyone who can hear me."

*****

They drove through Main Street in Reams. Lucina could tell by the purr of the motor that Al had taken Isadora in for a checkup. Isadora sounded calm, ready for a long drive. A lot of people were walking about, enjoying spring. New butterfly leaves danced on all the trees lining the sidewalks.

"You're attracted to Marin, aren't you, Lucina?" Louis was beside her, still talking. "Why don't you talk to me about that, babe? We've got to be open. I've decided we can't hide behind secrets anymore. Why would we do that? That's treachery. I wasn't going to talk to you yet—because of *Rune*. But

I want us to have a great train ride. Just the two of us—going across country. You'll love it."

"I do like her—"

"I knew it! I've watched you look at her. Snuggle into her, like a puppy dog. Do you think I can't see? Like a needy little puppy dog."

"That's my business, Louis."

"It's not your business. It's *our* business. That's what I'm trying to tell you."

He had penetrated her like a laser beam, like a smart bomb. He had tracked and found her. She looked for the street sign to turn right—their dorm should be somewhere in the middle of the block.

"Al knows it—and he hates me."

"He doesn't hate you, Lucina."

"I tell you—he hates my guts!"

"Who else are you attracted to? Have you made out with anyone? Have you kissed someone since you've been with me? Come on, Lucina, you can tell me?"

His voice, warm now and chummy, was pouring over her. It was too much. He was too much.

"My god, Louis! I don't believe it."

"What! What, Lucina? "His mouth dropped open. He had made her admit it; she had been with someone!

"We didn't pay our bill at the Howard Johnson's."

"Is that what you meant?" He grinned, retrieving the bill from his jacket pocket. "Fuck it," he said, ripping it ceremoniously into two pieces, putting one on the dashboard for her and stuffing the other back in his pocket.

She parked the van in front of a solid, cement-block building, one in a row of four identical buildings, retrieved the car key, and turned to Louis. "Can we go now?" She bent to him and kissed his cheek tenderly.

Louis shut his eyes, stayed seated, silent, biting at his lips.

Sitting there, looking at the man she loved, she remembered again when the three of them, Louis, Marlene, and she, Lucina, had stayed in Marlene's bedroom and massaged Louis. When he was so upset about the masks and their tree being stolen. And how Louis looked up at them both from the floor where he'd fallen asleep with the blissful look of a child. He'd been dreaming of Bloomsday and a singing bird. His look had moved her, deeply.

"Louis—you weren't going to tell me everything at once, were you?"

"I just told you—"

"Now I know."

Louis stared straight ahead listening.

"One thing," she went on in a soft, puzzled tone. "One thing is true, for certain. Louis and Lucina have one thing in common—"

Louis was holding onto each of her words, as if she were telling him something unbelievable, incredible, something that would change their world irrevocably, as if she were telling him that the war in Vietnam would end soon.

"Louis and Lucina," she spoke slowly, as if she too had suddenly come upon some extraordinary piece of information. "They both seem to love—" her voice paused again, as Louis waited, transfixed—"to kiss other women." She vowed again, she would tell him about Sally on the train—when they were close and on the way to their home. And that when she'd kissed Sally, she'd never felt so sexually turned on by a kiss before, not even by a kiss with Louis. And that now she suspected—maybe that kiss had something to do with the end of her *Rune*.

54
The Train Ride

Lucina's Journal Entry. After the tour: Sunday, May 7, 1967. I'm looking out the loft windows on Spring Street to write this last entry in my Tour Journal. The windows in the lofts across the street are reflecting my building and I can see myself muted, fuzzy, like in a watercolor, staring out the window. The late afternoon sun, with that orange glow I love, like Louis' eyes when he looks at me as if I'm something very special he stumbled upon, is making the buildings soft and glowing. I am glad to be back.

We took Greyhound to Chicago and Amtrak from there to NYC. As we passed bush after bush of lilac and forsythia in Iowa—dabs of yellow and purple paint against white wooden houses—a desire to be living in such a house with Louis overwhelmed me. Even though we won't be a wife and husband, I long for a home with a fireplace where I can heal from all my losses and changes.

We reached Chicago at six p.m. and found a diner near the bus station where we ate mushy franks and beans and day-old slaw. But Louis and I were happy being away from the others, so it didn't bother us. Since the summer in Vermont when the whole thing with Fire Dragon started, we have rarely been alone. *Maybe that's why we don't know how to be a married couple—we're never alone with our two-ness.*

So it makes sense that we want to be close with, and even "know" in the Biblical sense, those we hang with, work with, and wrestle with. All our work seems to hinge on exposing and breaking down repressive structures that control, limit, and prevent human potential.

I'm not trying to come up with a rationale that allows us to be lascivious and irresponsible, as the right wing would like to peg us. I mean closeness, intimacy that is caring, that takes hard work and demands patience. In other words, I think it is natural to want to touch the people you live and work with.

We missed the 8 p.m. train out of Chicago; or rather, we decided not to take it, as it was very crowded. In the train station, Louis found a five-dollar bill in a telephone booth. He put it in his pocket and waited awhile to see if anyone would return to pick it up. No one did, so we had five more dollars to spend until the next train left at eleven-thirty.

We were walking around the train station, trying to decide how to spend our five dollars when Louis said an incredible thing to me: "I'll call your father and tell him I'll give him five dollars to take back the words he said to you."

"What words, Louis?"

"Don't you remember? He told you he'd give you five dollars to throw your eyesores, your sculptures, in the river."

Louis has one of the most incredible memories in the world. He remembered this story I told him two years ago. My father seems always more concerned about my medical insurance situation, than about me.

*You can't believe how good it felt to laugh with Louis about that, though when my father said it, I considered patricide. To laugh gave me some small relief from the terrible sadness I feel about my **Rune** sculpture. And the anxiety I'm* *trying not to feel about Louis being with other women. I've got to laugh more and maybe say to myself, "I am not my work, I am not my work," like movement politicos tell people, "You are not your job, you are not your job." The truth is, politicos see their work as a life and death matter! What is the balance between taking ownership and letting go? I don't know yet.*

We walked outside to explore some city streets and maybe find a movie to go to. The on-and-off neon signs of movie theaters make me dizzy, and Louis and I never want to go to the same movie. It's one area where we always disagree. In other areas where couples usually fall apart, like which restaurant to go to, or what to order in a Chinese restaurant, we do pretty well.

And there it was again. We were arguing about which movie to see, **The Group** *or* **King of Hearts.** *We couldn't eliminate one as being too far to walk to; they were both right in front of us. I wanted to see* **The Group** *which follows the lives of several Vassar women graduates, chronicling their twists and turns in life. I love Candice Bergen. I thought the movie might give me more insight into how we should introduce our women's play, especially if we perform it at women's colleges.*

Louis had already seen **King of Hearts** *twice, but wanted to see it again with me. I admire his ability to see a movie three or four times and enjoy it more each time. Even if a movie is excellent, usually one time is enough for me. I'm sure this has to do with the nauseous feelings I get from the hot oil from the popcorn machines and the perfumed cleaners they use in movie houses. And I find it very surreal, how all those people sit in the dark without moving in small seats, side by side, staring at a big screen. I think the movies drove me to do live theater.*

Louis has a very stubborn part to him. **"The King of Hearts** *is an anti-war film," he said. "You should see it." He* told me we can match the inmates from the mental hospital to members of our group, later, on the train.

"Can't you see something new with me?" I asked him. "I don't want to see something new," he said. "I want to see something good. Besides, **The Group** is too long; you'll throw up before it's over. **Hearts** is only an hour and a half."

Louis won. We swung toward the Embassy instead of the Metro. He didn't hold back his glee. "If you think Jenny is a sexy dancer," he said to me (how is that for projecting!) "Bujold is incredible." "I'm not in the mood to hear Jenny's name," I said. Then when he said, "Genevieve Bujold reminds me of you," I was pleased.

Louis was right though, **King of Hearts** was incredible, maybe because it was more like a play than a movie and that's why I didn't get sick. It was over before I had a chance to think about my stomach. We returned to the train terminal and over several cups of coffee convinced ourselves that it was a good decision we made to go off by ourselves. We even talked about plays the two of us could make together. We also watched a peculiar drama unfold. A white man walked back and forth near us, staring at a Black man and a white woman who were sitting at the table next to us. He seemed both fascinated and impatient with them. Something else distracted us and when we looked again, the Black man was gone and the white man sat with the woman, engaging her attention. It struck us both then that the woman was a hooker. To me she looked like an ordinary woman, lipstick, blouse and skirt and sensible pumps. Nothing outrageous. I had never seen a hooker up close. Louis kept kicking me under the table to stop staring, a bad habit of mine when someone fascinates me.

Finally, we ignored the hooker and focused on each other. We talked about play ideas for two actors: a happy clown cheers up a sad clown, Louis' idea; a soldier murders the same

Vietnamese woman over and over, my idea. When we actually tried to picture just ourselves performing alone in the park, it seemed very hard and not much fun.

Louis' face changed suddenly as if he had bitten his tongue. "What aren't we talking about, Luie?"

I knew immediately what he was thinking. "Cheryl's cousin, Nelson," shot out of my mouth.

"I can't stop thinking about him, suffering someplace. If he isn't dead!"

"Are we wasting time, Louis—just reporting in a play that he's missing? Shouldn't we be reporting this to the New York Times, *trying to get air time on WBAI? I don't know— flying banners in the sky across New York City..."*

"I know a Black social justice lawyer who just might help us strategize. He's connected to Hayward Burns, a great Black civil rights activist lawyer who was really out there in the Mississippi Freedom Summer."

"How do you know these Black lawyers, Louis?"

"I've got connections, babe. I talk to people while you women are rehearsing. I'm no dumb cluck! But what I want to say is—we've got to get help in many directions. Performing **Choice** *is one way. Getting the advice of civil rights lawyers is another...We should contact Tom Hayden, a big shot in SDS, and lawyers he knows like William Kunstler and Staughton Lynd. Lynd and Hayden went to North Vietnam in '65. They could tell us how to go about finding Nelson!"*

"That's the main thing, Louis! We can't stop working with Cheryl to find Nelson! Just imagine if you or I went missing suddenly—what would the other do?"

"Have a heart attack!" Louis uttered sharply.

"No!" I barked. "You would act—you would find help—you wouldn't have time to have a heart attack."

Louis, his fingers inching slowly on his chest as if looking for the source of some pain, suddenly spoke out again: "What about Ghost Dance Tribute? Jim could have been our Indigenous actor! But he's gone. We have to find at least one to be our shaman."

"Two! A man and a woman. Remember, we have a Double Wovoka now. It was your idea. Now we're challenging the Patriarchy's spiritual control all over the place. The Sioux might not appreciate our interpretation of their Shaman."

"That's why we need at least one Indigenous actor to help us keep on track. We have to think this through as a whole group when we get back to the city. But, I need a break from all this now, Lucina. What time did we say our train leaves for New York?"

Many young people had appeared in the station, raising money for the Heart Fund, and a photographer snapped our picture, which we bought for a dollar. Finally it was time for our train.

*****

We sat close together on the train, bending toward each other and holding hands to find comfort. We are trying very hard to keep the specialness of our intimacy intact. We do feed each other. We streamed past depressing sights—lonely drive-in movie theaters, worn-out factory buildings, squalid three-story row houses with people in undershirts (men) and wilted dresses (women) playing cards. I wondered all the time why something about my life, or life in general, saddens me. Even before Cheryl disappeared, or the news of Rune's destruction, before the realization that Louis and I would not be each other's one-and-only, I, Lucina Holzer from a small town in the Midwest, was afflicted by melancholy. But it usually comes over me when I witness some kind of injustice. Like when I see a gray, polluted stream chugging along over rocks covered with yucky stuff. Or, when I see an adult jerking a child along the street. Yet, I am capable of great joy, I really am. I don't know why I felt so depressed by seeing people playing cards on the stoops of their row houses. They were having fun.

I kept thinking about it—until I understood more clearly. I had begun to notice more and more how poor people, struggling to make it from day to day, still know how to have fun with their family and friends. This fact struck something very deep in me—something in me had to grow. When I saw those people on that stoop and how they were being themselves, it seemed to me they weren't hiding or afraid. How could I be more like that, not afraid, not hiding? I knew one thing: I was hiding and had been a long time. I was afraid to tell Louis that Sally and I had kissed each other in a deep and sexual way. And I felt I was betraying my love for him with my need for that kiss. I was betraying my parents and all the things I was supposed to be. I realized right then that I was depressed because I hadn't understood or faced that I want to be who I am, accept who I am, and be able to tell Louis who I am.

I turned to him, sitting beside me, jotting something in his notebook, all caught up with his own thoughts. "Louis, I have to talk to you." He looked at me in a puzzled way, then put his notebook down and took my hand. "I didn't tell you everything about Sally and me, about our closeness, well when we were close, and why I was so hurt by her." His face became somber, his eyes closed. "We kissed each other, Louis, deeply, like you and I do with our tongues deep inside each other's mouths for a long time—it felt very sexual, like a warmth shot through me." His hand tightened in mine—his lips were moving trying to make words, it seemed.

"Thank you, Lucina, for telling me, actually thank you for freeing me to tell you about Karen. What happened

with me and her. I couldn't tell you either because I didn't want you to tell me that you and Sally had kissed. Karen and I didn't kiss, sweetheart. She jerked me off. She aroused me and then she jerked me off and I sat there like a slut and let her do it. So, I could say to you that Karen and I didn't fuck. Fucking would have been healthier than what she and I did. Your kissing Sally was healthy, both of you owning your feelings and acting on them."

"Oh, Louis. I can't believe this. I just told you something I'd determined to never tell you. And all the while it was eating me up, that I couldn't tell you. I'm so grateful I had the guts at last to tell you—I feel so close to you now. I feel you inside my body, my heart, myself as I am, opening up, free. Why were we keeping all this secret stuff, like holding onto charred memories, like dying coals from the fires we felt with those two women, fires we kept burning for so long. We didn't want to hurt each other, that's it. There's a part of us that wants to stay pure and true for each other. We have to learn that loving others, touching others doesn't take away from our love for each other. But our relationship doesn't deserve, doesn't need tawdry secrets. We have to accept that we don't have to keep secrets, we don't have to feel guilty. We aren't trying to be Mr. and Mrs. Pure: 'I only have eyes for you till death do us part'. We are trying to love each other fully and honestly and to help each other and ourselves grow and become our true selves as fully as we can."

"Exactly, Lucina! That's what I've been saying. We feel the same."

"Okay, Louis. I can tell you all now. After that kiss with Sally, I went back to the loft—you were at your desk writing—I said I was tired and needed to lie down for a while. What I needed to do was touch myself, Louis. I was so wet down there, I thought I'd peed in my pants. But no, it was all my juices. I was still so turned on from kissing Sally I needed to caress my clitoris, I needed to come. I needed to make love with Sally, so I made love with myself."

"My sexy Luie. No wonder you've mourned her loss. You're turning me on. Maybe that's kinky, but you, just as you are, turn me on." He kept smiling and shaking his head as if he were in Blissville. "You know what, my sister? We loved those two women, really loved them, and there was nothing wrong with how we opened up to showing them we loved them."

*****

Finally, we fell asleep in each other's arms and didn't wake up until we reached New York City around nine o'clock the next evening. We trudged our suitcases to the Automat to get their baked beans and franks. Delicious. HoJo's can't hold a candle to that place. We were back in our New York City. We saw a younger version of the old man who rode on the train with us—they both had wire spectacles that fell down on their noses. Well, the old guy would leave his seat across from us every half hour, maybe for ten minutes, only to reappear and then repeat the pattern. He must have had diarrhea, or Louis thought maybe a colostomy, a bag he had to empty. The younger version of him in the Automat sat by himself eating a huge plate of macaroni salad. But he didn't leave his seat once.

Then we took the subway to our loft and collapsed into the king-sized bed in my former studio area where I no longer make sculptures. We were too tired to make love then, but knew we would the next day. File cabinets and boxes of old copies of PAN surrounded us. The two SDS kids who stayed here while we were gone left it just like we left it. But Dawn's area (it was Louis' study in the old days, before communal life) was still a mess. Newspapers, pizza boxes, and coke cans by her mattress. Should I ask her to clean the space up before *she leaves for good, or leave her alone to be in Blissville with her new love, Cheryl?*

****

It's late afternoon, and Louis is still sleeping. Here I am again, in my once-upon-a-time studio. Trucks are honking outside my windows. The factory district isn't a quiet neighborhood. I just have to accept it—I will never have a home like my parents. I will never, ever have a living room and a dining room. I will never own big sofas and dining room tables and chairs like Ralph and Marge do. I will never be married like they are. Louis and I will never have children—he will never want to have a child with me. He has a child. And actually, I'm too busy with my life to really want my own kid. Home is going to be wherever I am. Home is me, now with Louis and all the others trying to stop the war—with Cheryl, tracking down Nelson and what they did to him. Home is my journal.

*I couldn't stop crying last night. I prayed for everyone I know, my blood family, my chosen family. I left Louis on the bed alone and sat in the rocking chair I found a few months ago by the dumpster on Wooster Street. Was that the same dumpster where I found **Rune**'s head, the newel post? I'll ask Louis, he'll remember. I cried for my **Rune** who is dead—I cried for that part of me that has disappeared with her.*

*Then it really hit me when I saw my workbench this afternoon—the dust covering it, and the tools still hanging on the wall behind it. What happened to me! I changed my life so drastically. If I hadn't done that, **Rune** would still be with me.*

*I lost one of my best friends. I know that going over to Shauna's place, where **Rune** isn't, will be like going to a false morgue. At least at a real morgue you know that your beloved's body could be there. Not even a slat or a nail from **Rune** will be there or anywhere. My **Rune** is gone. Forever.*

I imagine her in my studio standing silently under a white sheet, waiting until I uncover her again, so I can explain to someone I care for exactly what she means to me—and why I made a xylophone as part of her altar, when she herself can never play it. Her hands pressed together in front of her face—my muse in continual prayer, fingertips pointing to her third eye, connecting her to intuition, to the whole world as she receives messages from the past and the future. I realize again that her xylophone is an invitation to anyone, who approaches her with goodwill, to play with her, tap rhythms on those rosewood keys I've hewn so lovingly.

I look to my work bench, abandoned for three years. There behind it, still bolted to the wall, is the Masonite board with my tools. My empty hands long to grasp my beloved mallet and chisel, and my wood saw. With them I gave birth to **Rune.**

I birthed her myself. A miracle I want to always remember. My imagination, spirit, hunger, loneliness, longing had shaped her. I needed her to be with me. Maybe, as I've thought many times, it's the same kind of driving force a woman who longs to be a mother has, a force that guides her, drives her to make that happen. Humans need to give birth in many different ways, bring forth their visions into this world, showing themselves and others what is meaningful.

My breathing slows and deepens as I explore the space I'm in. A new awareness now. I'm no longer alone. I feel their presence. I hear their voices. I'm with people I love—Louis, Marin, Cheryl, all my theater comrades and my other friends, alive, struggling, caring, complicated, confused human beings just like me. We have reasons to be together. We must meditate, think, intuit how we can make a world of compassion, of sharing, of laying down weapons, our defenses, and reach out with our hearts, open to love one another in the only world we have.

Rune *is gone, but I am here. I will harness my body, mind, and spirit to join with my theater troupe and all others who, like us, want to stop the hatred that makes a war in Vietnam, that punishes a compassionate man like Nelson Davis. I will join with women like Rosa Parks, who challenged the racism this country was built on— the never-ending struggle to stop all forms of genocide.*

I want to stop speechifying. I will pray like **Rune** *would: May I move forward with the courage to embrace my full identity; use myself as a vehicle for growth and love and empathy and understanding and forgiveness; always rise up in the resistance to injustice of all kinds. If* **Rune** *could hear me, she would drop her praying hands, pick up the mallets and play a joyful tune, encouraging me to dance with gratitude, playfulness, and humor, thankful that I have my Fire Dragon comrades with me in struggle.*

I feel percussive rhythms move my body. I begin to gyrate around our rehearsal space, crying out, "I am alive!" My whole being lights up with awareness and thankfulness. "I, we, have a lot of work ahead of us!"

Acknowledgements/Appreciation

Wheelin' Across the Land: Spring 1967 is the second of four novels in my memoir-based *Rune Quartet.* During the forty years of its arduous construction, many people encouraged my writing. Isabel Miller (*Patience and Sarah*) praised my debut historical memoir novel, *Mari,* a cross-cultural lesbian romance (New Victoria Press, 1991): "Admirers of Jeri Hilderley's music will be happy to see that she brings the same creative boldness and energy to this novel...heroic women...passion for justice...." Nancy Willard (*Things Invisible to See, A Visit to William Blake's Inn*) wrote: "Full of imagination ... a unique voice...."

And then I am most grateful for the enthusiastic responses to my many readings at women's cultural centers and from my readers. They gave me courage to chronicle my struggles, find my identity and voice even as I worked to understand and join the larger body of political activists whose inclusive, compassionate awareness fed my own.

I am also grateful for the generous support of fellowships from Cummington Community of the Arts, Virginia Creative Center of the Arts and Blue Mountain Center—where I wrote the early versions. I am appreciative of the tender and incisive critiques at the workshops: Writer's Voice with Marcia Golub (*I'd Rather Be*

Writing); In Our Own Write with Jennifer Levin (*The Sea of Light*); and Memoir Writing with Florence Howe (*A Life in Motion*). I shared writing for many productive years with the PEN Women Writers' Group. Novelists Jerome Badanes (*Final Opus of Leon Solomon*) and Padma Hejmadi (*Room to Fly, The School Master and Other Stories*) gave me vital suggestions over many decades.

Additionally, I am indebted to the members of my writers' group of recent years who have critiqued my current novels: Josephine Diamond, Caroline Thomas, Sue Elizabeth Davis, Janet Mayes, Loretta Goldberg, and Sarah Relyea. I am indebted to Sara Flounders (Director of the International Action Center and co-author of, among others, *Sanctions—A Wrecking Ball in a Global Economy: An Anthology by Social Justice Activists*), and to Sue Harris (Co-editor of Peoples Video Network and director of *Poison DUst: A New Look at U.S. Radioactive Weapons*), who enthusiastically praised *Fire Dragon Street Theater: 1962-1967*, the first novel in *Rune Quartet*, for its dedication to our struggle for a better world. Their support played no small part in propelling me forward as I endeavored to complete this sequel.

Sarah Relyea (*Playground Zero: A Novel*) served as a careful, insightful substantive/content editor, copy editor, and proofreader of the final version. Monica Moorehead (Workers World managing editor and co-author of, among others, *What Road to Socialism?*) was my sensitivity reader, offering vital political perspective and guidance. Their insights about the complex issues arising in this process have been particularly precious.

A natural and necessary part of my relationships with my significant artist partners through the years has been the sharing and critiquing of each other's creative work. Jerome Badanes, Rain Bengis (award-winning photographer) and Janet Mayes (*Beyond the Horse's Eye: A Fantasy out of Time* and co-author, *Interpersonal Psychoanalytic Theory for the 21st Century; Evolving Self*) have been extraordinarily generous and supportive in reading and critiquing my work. Janet and I have been partners for eighteen years now; our writing projects have become as necessary and integral to our relationship as our love.

I am grateful for the supportive exchanges about our creative work over the years with many colleagues, partners, friends, collaborators: Diana Bellessi, Paul Bernstein, Joan E. Biren, Marianne Burke, Lynne Cooper, Verity Dierhauf, Julie Enszer, Vicki Felder, Merry Gangemi, Kay Gardner, Shelley Grabel, Avital Greenberg, Sorrel Hayes, Gail Kinn, Eileen Downey, Eric Lindbloom, James Lindbloom, Bruce Macpherson, Jodi Miller, Helen Pine, Jeffrey Rabkin, Marilyn Ries, Mei Mei Sanford, Jacqui Schnider, Elena Sheehan, Lois Sperakis, Ronnie Tuft, Fleur Weymouth, Nancy Willard. And to friends for their encouragement: Ginny Davies, Susan Elliot, Fran Israel, Linda Ito, Dee Livingston, Nancy Myers, Dianne Oakland, Lynda Radar, Judy Winters. And to all my Facebook friends, too numerous to mention, but whose own creative works and support of my work have nourished me through the years, I send my gratitude.

I extend appreciation to family members who have encouraged me to "get that book published!" as I described my efforts to take the reins and self-publish: Johanna, Clifton, Laura, Clif, Andrea, Gioccomo, Cassy, Parker, Cris, Beth, Lauren, Dylan, with special thanks to Brad Patri whose insightful and passionate review of Fire Dragon Street Theater: 1962-1967 is posted on the Amazon and Barnes & Noble websites.

My therapist Lynne R. Alterman continues to guide and support me through all the insecurities and obsessions we writers suffer.

I would also like to extend appreciation to the many dedicated activists in the International Action Center who have inspired and educated my revolutionary optimism and that of my characters.

And to all other dear supportive friends and colleagues I failed to mention, I offer my apologies.

I am grateful for the patient expertise of Dave Bass, who designed the interior of the book and served as my self-publishing guide/facilitator. To Jodi Miller, my graphic designer friend, who artfully executed the cover for the book and accepted my feisty dragon drawing with enthusiasm, I give thanks.

Finally, how can I possibly list the endless writers who have led and fed me since I first visited my hometown library when I was five? Their impact is embedded in my writing.

Acknowledgement of people and organizations is not meant to imply that they endorse or in any way agree with assumptions put forth in my book. Those are entirely mine.

Bibliography

Abbott, S. & Love, B. (1972). *Sappho was a right on woman: A liberated view of lesbianism.* Stein and Day.

Anzaldúa, G. & Moraga, C. (Eds.). (1981). *This bridge called my back: Writings by radical women of color.* Persephone Press.

Blevins, A. (Ed.). (Spring 2024). *How can a woman who is with a trans man call herself a lesbian? Sinister Wisdom* 132.

Catalinotto, J. (2017). *Turn the guns around: Mutinies, soldier revolts and revolutions.* World View Forum.

Catalinotto, J. (2022). *Cold war: A love story.* The Glocal Workshop/L'Atalier Glocal.

Churchill, W. & Vanderwall, J. (1990). *Agents of repression: The FBI's secret wars against the Black Panther Party and the American Indian Movement.* South End Press (Classics Series Vol. 7).

Goldstein, F. (2012). *Capitalism at a dead end: Job destruction, overproduction and crisis in the high-tech era.* World View Forum.

Hodges, E. (2020*). Indian enough.* Oregon Humanities. oregonhumanities.org.

Nestle, J. (2022). *A sturdy yes of a people: Selected writings.* Sinister Wisdom, Inc.

Stapp, A. (1970). *Up against the brass: The amazing story of the fight to unionize the United States Army.* Simon & Schuster.

Tischler, B. (1990). *Breaking Ranks: GI antiwar newspapers and the culture of protest.* Vietnam Generation, Special Issue, PDF.

About the Author

I have been engaged in the intriguing and complex relationship between artist and activist for seven decades. With a first career as sculptor (after studying art at Smith College, University of California, Berkeley, and obtaining a Master of Arts in Sculpture from the University of Michigan Ann Arbor), I settled in New York City's artists' district in the 60s to construct large wooden female figures in action. The ritual-like sculptures, described in the *New York Herald* as "highly ingenious and mad," didn't fit into sedate New York galleries then, so I invented Sculpture Theater, incorporating dancers and musicians to accompany my work. Like protagonist Lucina Holzer in *Fire Dragon Street Theater: 1962-1967,* I was soon propelled by the anti-war movement to use my artists' skills for political activism, working with collective street theater groups.

In the late 60s and early 70s, I co-founded the women's theater groups, Women of Burning City and Painted Women's Ritual Theater, to showcase our life stories, which played an integral role in building the Women's Movement. In connection with the Women's Music Network of the 70s, I founded the SeawaveRecordings label and recorded my original compositions for voice, marimba and guitar: *A Few Loving Women* and *Jeritree's*

House of Many Colours. Extensive performances throughout the United States allowed me to reach out to and be educated by other artists/activists, feminists, women of color, LGBTQIA+ audiences, and the many community activists concerned with building an inclusive culture of caring in a true democracy.

While teaching autobiographical and essay writing in Women's Studies Departments at SUNY Purchase, Empire State College and CUNY's Seek Program, along with language and music skills to Special Ed students in the New York City public schools for the next 3 decades, I continued to write fiction and articles about the creative process.

After retiring from full-time teaching, I built my own recording studio, producing original songs for *12 Meditations on Love* and *Talking Truth* with the trio, SeaWaves. (Janet Mayes, bass/vocals; Susan Ahlborn, guitar/vocals, composer, and myself.) With partner Janet Mayes, I produced the CD and accompanying booklet: *Time Traveling with Sappho,* a song-cycle of Sappho's poem fragments translated by Pulitzer Prize nominee Konstantinos Lardas, set to my original music. My CDs have enjoyed world-wide distribution.

Although I have moved through different media, I have always found a deep interconnection between the many art forms that fed my need to create collectively with other artists/activists. My sculptures moved me into theater, where I began to compose dramatic, personal and political songs; my writing began with journaling to record the exciting drama of my street theater work. My essay, "Burning City Street Theater: Analysis of a Theater Commune" [*Chicago Review* 23, no 1(Summer 1971): 40-92], inspired much of the flavor of *Fire Dragon Street Theater.*

The sequels continue chronicling my evolution. The second novel in *Rune Quartet, Wheelin' Across the Land: Spring 1967,* follows the Fire Dragon troupe on their life-changing tour. Then the third and fourth novels bring readers into the 70s, 80s, and 90s.

New protagonists unite with the old as they and I discover same-sex love; join anti-racist, anti-misogynist and pro-choice movements; deal with the AIDS crisis and support the Palestinian right to resistance, balancing careers and political activism. Consciousness raising never ends!

Publications (partial list):

"To Be Extra-Ordinary", *Opyrus, Corona Silver Linings Anthology*, 2020.

Mari, Norwich, VT: New Victoria Publishers, 1990.

"The Alphabet Wedding." *Sinister Wisdom: Pleasure* 99 (Winter 2016): 104-108.

Badanes, Jeriann. "Burning City Street Theater: Analysis of a Theater Commune." *Chicago Review* 23, no. 1 (Summer 1971): 40-92.

"A Woman Remembers Her Music." *Heresies*, no. 10 (1980): 16-17. Women and Music. [http://heresiesfilmproject.org/wp-content/uploads/2011/09/heresies10.pdf]

"How to Find the Music in You." *Paid My Dues* III, no.1 (Fall 1978): 6,7, 38. [https://queermusicheritage.com/pmd3-1.html]

"Burning City Street Theater's Ecology Play." In *People's Theater in Amerika*, by Karen Malpede Taylor. 317-320. Drama Book Specialists/Publishers, New York. 1972.

"I Was There and I Am Here." *Sinister Wisdom: In Amerika They Call Us Dykes: Lesbian Lives in the 70s* 82 (Spring 2011): 78-86.

Website:

jerihilderley.blog